Neutral, No Brakes

A Novel

Patrick Howard

GREEN
MILL
PRESS

Portland, Oregon
MMXXII

Copyright © 2022 by Patrick Howard

All rights reserved. No part of this book may be used, reproduced, stored or transmitted in any manner whatsoever without express written permission from the publisher, except in the case of brief quotations embodied in critical articles and reviews. For information, contact Green Mill Press, 1327 SE Tacoma Street, Suite 253, Portland, OR 97202

The characters and events portrayed in this book are fictitious. Any similarity to real persons, living or dead, is coincidental and not intended by the author.

Published by Green Mill Press, Portland, Oregon

www.GreenMillPress.org

Library of Congress Cataloging-in-Publication Data:
Names: Howard, Patrick, author
Title: Neutral, No Brakes / Patrick Howard.
Description: Portland, Oregon : Green Mill Press (2022)
Identifiers: LCCN 2022912444 | ISBN 979-8-9862181-0-6 (e-book)

First US Paperback Edition 2022
ISBN: 979-8-9862181-1-3

Cover design by *the*BookDesigners
Cover art © Shutterstock

For Carrie

CONTENTS

1	Morley	1
2	Nic Departs	6
3	An Afternoon at LaFontaine	11
4	Fair Warning	17
5	Sandwiches on a Bus	22
6	Darla's Plan	33
7	Nic Arrives	42
8	Dumpster	48
9	Celine and Jeremy Hit It Off	53
10	Restless Brooding	63
11	A Falling Out	72
12	Richard and Nic Build a Life	83
13	Konnichiwa	97
14	Celine Dines Alone	110
15	Crime Wave	124
16	Task Force	132
17	Deb Looks for Celine	143
18	Cuts and Color	158
19	Neutral, No Brakes	173
20	Rapprochement	187
21	A Spell Is Cast	194
22	Ugly Truths	202
23	Carnivàle	211
24	The Shoe Drops	224
25	Where Are the Keys?	235
26	Balloons	244
27	A Life Simplified	256
28	Donna Nobis Pacem	276
29	Rex	286
30	Folding, Part I	299
31	Folding, Part II	306
32	Almond Biscotti	311
33	Purpose	326
34	Along Came Betty	336

1. MORLEY

Of all the big and small towns in west Hensen County, none was more disagreeable than Morley. Once full of promise and possibility, for most it had become merely a place to exist and ultimately a place to die.

The hour-long trek from civilization to Morley took travelers from the last offramp on I-14 through a vast, monotonous chaparral of low shrubs and grasses, sporadically in and out of uninspiring agrarian hamlets that had sprung up to support the valley's once-prodigious output (long since wafted away), past the mothballed San Benitez Air Base, skirting the cookie-cutter houses of Antioch Hills, and finally out onto a broad boulevard of discount stores, abandoned franchises, and cheap taverns. Once you arrived, it hardly seemed worth the effort. Once embedded, the odds of leaving were insurmountable.

Morley was one of those hamlets. It had enjoyed a burst of productivity and prosperity in the early and mid-twentieth century, thriving on water diverted from more verdant climes, settling into a comfortable cadence of grow, pick, ship, repeat. But the late-century exodus out of the cities in search of the bucolic life sent the value of buildable land in Morley soaring far beyond any profit to be made by simply growing fruit. Discovery by a generation of retirees with big pension accounts triggered an overheated golden age that was ultimately extinguished with the bursting of the real estate bubble, sending Morley into its current state of degraded obscurity. Once an attractive alternative to the fast-paced city, Morley now bore all the stigmata of urban blight without any of the culture, depth, or diversity of a real city, a decadent taint that neither drenching cloudburst nor blistering sun could cleanse.

The twin scions of the Morley family, Nathan and Elias, had arrived by mule cart in 1908 to negotiate a land deal with the Connahoctuh nation. The tribal members resided there in small hovels arranged on a dusty patch of ground, encircling a community well that produced sparse volumes of cloudy, acrid water in the winter months and nothing in the summer. From afar it resembled a storybook village, but on closer inspection, its tumble-down structures, rutted paths, and washed-out facades lacked any hint of charm. The forces of decay had had their way with the little settlement, a victim of indolence, neglect, torpid heat, and ceaseless wind.

The native inhabitants were thus keen on the Morley boys' promise of better days ahead. Most lived as subsistence farmers, working the sometimes mucky, but typically parched, land. Those without the means or gumption to farm made their way in the world as laborers on the big ranches that spanned the rolling hills far in the distance. Despite their penurious state, the Connahoctuh possessed two things the Morleys wanted: that patch of flat land on which they could build a rail station, and the rights to an adjacent expanse of baked grassland that to the imaginative mind could be transformed into arable soil in response to the country's rising interest in fresh produce from the west. The Morleys had settled on this spot based on a tip from their friend, an Indian Affairs agent who assured them the needy Connahoctuhs' land could be had for very little. That the tribal elders were also corruptible did not hurt their cause; they were willing to make a deal for a little personal pocket money up-front and an ongoing piece of the action on the back end.

And the Morleys had another secret. The Hensen County Aqueduct, thus far under wraps, would soon turn the occasional flow through Connahoctuh Creek into a lush and predictable source of water, providing much needed irrigation to farms within ten miles of the project. Orange, lemon, olive, cherry, peach, apple, walnut, and almond trees could thrive in this climate of hot summers and chilly but mild winters, if only they could take a drink now and then.

Soon the Town of Morley sprang up. The rail station was realized, along with a general store that supplied dry goods and notions to farmers and their families, a livery service, three taverns (each with its own unique cat house on the story above), and other sundry businesses all supporting the acres of fruit trees and their human attendants. Grovers would daily cart their produce to the rail station bound for busy switching yards and bigger towns to the east. The trees brought forth their bounty, the townspeople flourished, and a rhythm was established that seemed it would last forever.

But after decades of extracting what the earth gave up willingly, the inexorable migration out of the cities to the suburbs and exurbs began. Land in Hensen County was worth more as a mooring spot for doublewide mobile homes than as farmland. Luxuriant acres of olive and apricot, orange and cherry were allowed to whither, then ripped from the earth, their sturdy roots unrelenting until the last crackling tug of the bulldozer. Soon one could not find a grove that had not been ravaged. The resulting flat tracks of land were paved over and further improved with chain-link fences and electrical, water, and sewer hookups.

The Morley America Company was formed to develop the area into a master-planned community. The company was headquartered in a glorified shack at the corner of San Sebastian Parkway and Juniper Springs Road, but soon a snappy new building was constructed. Street grids were laid out and paved, sidewalks poured, and homes thrown up. The new developments—some with stick-built houses, but most catering to mobile and manufactured homes—were adorned with rustic names like Olive Bend, Apricot Farms, and Shady Grove, where not an olive, apricot or even shade could be found. Public amenities and businesses were established, and by the end of the second year, a public golf course, medical clinic, and shopping center were up and running. Morley was a boom town once more.

The new subdivisions were promoted like none in California had ever been. The company contracted with a local fleet of crop dusters to pitch the development to adventurous prospective buyers from the air. Celebrities like Crystal Gayle, Buddy Hackett, and Yacov Smirnoff were brought in to do short TV promos or lend their images to brochures touting the benefits of life in the high desert.

An episode of The Fugitive was filmed on a defunct tree farm outside of Morley, bringing the entire production crew to stay at the accommodations in town. Retirees, with their overvalued T-bills, canvassed the region looking for warmth and safety; they flocked to Morley en masse.

But as quickly as it had flourished, the town's second surge of good fortune dried up, parched and withered as its denuded groves. An economy scaffolded solely on retirees with money and the services they required proved too fragile. Despite the natural thriftiness of its new inhabitants, savings dried up or were lost in land speculation or other investment schemes. Second and third mortgages collided with falling property values, leaving most homeowners underwater. Once famous for having the most banks per capita anywhere in the nation, Morley descended into a deep state of financial decay, banks replaced by methadone clinics and drug rehab services. The beautiful groves, a point of nostalgia for the old timers, would never return.

Slothful young people who had grown up in Morley serving the affluent cohort of the Greatest Generation now found themselves with little to do. Lacking ambition, skill, or opportunity, they felt useless and unwanted, and they were right. Biology undaunted, families exhibited the fecundity that the groves once had, churning out new Morleyites as fast as the San Sebastian Birthing Center could accommodate. Section 8 housing flourished, while the school district laid claim to the greatest teacher turnover rate in the state. The notorious Morley Sherriff's Department exercised discretion in the speed with which it answered (or ignored) 9-1-1 calls, based on their deep knowledge of neighborhoods and certain individuals, couples, and families with whom they'd dealt before. Morley's only true local industry was the production of meth, which had long surpassed alcohol as the drug of choice. There was no middle class, and arguably no "better side" of town. To the casual visitor, Morley had become a destination spot for families on the dole, evangelical cults, and gun-sporting crackers. No one could get a break it seemed, and life for many became a hopeless pursuit of distractions to salve the pain of existence. Everyone lived on edge—listless, belligerent, without ambition or solace. Anger and violence simmered just below a thin veneer of forced restraint. Fights would break out with a look, or less. There was just no point to any of it anymore, no lessons from the past or hope for the future, a town of dreams lost or never dreamt.

2. NIC DEPARTS

Nic Troxell gazed out his window into the shapeless black landscape. His reflection stared right back at him. A solitary barn light whizzed by, dimly illuminating the mist and an abandoned thresher below, reminding him he was still in farm country. His stomach growled loudly over the rumble of the Trailways bus, two hours out of Indianapolis en route to Fayetteville, Arkansas, a trip that would last, according to the timetable, exactly fifteen hours and five minutes.

He'd bummed a ride into town from Plainfield with another inmate and his wife who was waiting for him at the main gate. *Nice girl*, he thought. *Great teeth.* Not till they'd dropped him at the station and driven off did he learn the Fayetteville bus would not depart until three fifteen the next morning. To show how pissed he was, Nic raised his voice, waved his arms, and raged menacingly around the station until the middle-aged ticket agent threatened to call security. "I don't make the schedules, sir. And this is Indianapolis, not Chicago . . . Three fifteen."

He backed off, resigning himself to catching some sleep until the bus arrived. But he could not sleep in the orange plastic chairs under the station's piercing fluorescent light, nor later on the cramped droning bus. He sipped lukewarm coffee from a paper cup and pondered his situation, looking forward to the first scheduled stopover in St. Louis, where he could finally get something to eat.

Joan had sounded irritated when he phoned last week to let her know of his release. "You can't stay here, Nic. Just wanna make that clear up-front." He'd anticipated the attitude, but was not deterred. Never deterred. He'd been down this road with her many times and knew he could eventually get her to come around. She'd tolerated her kid brother his whole life—his dark moods and nasty outbursts, his penchant for cruelty and violence, dragging down anyone who tried to help him out of a jam. No, it was Tommy, that goddamn husband of hers, he had to get past. Tom had loathed Nic from the start, thought him careless, lazy, dishonest, underhanded, self-serving—all demons Tom had proudly conquered in his youth and thus refused to suffer in others.

Nic planned to crash on their couch for a few days till he could figure out his next move, try to get something going. It was either that or live on the street. He'd been in and out of the system for years, this time doing twenty-eight months for second-degree manslaughter. Joan had been there for him on every trip through that revolving door. But her growing impatience, her reluctance to accommodate his faults, to simply hug him and welcome her baby brother back into her heart—that was a change. It had to be Tommy.

He dug around in his duffel bag and pulled out a sheaf of tattered envelopes in a rubber band, all from Richard Kornbluth, c/o Mr. Richard's Cuts and Color, Morley, California and addressed to Mr. Nicholas Troxell, Block 4, Indiana State Prison, Plainfield, Indiana. He needed a backup plan, in case Joan had finally had enough of him. He thumbed through the stack, found the newest envelope dated three weeks ago, and unfolded the letter.

My dearest Nic,

Well, that was certainly some wonderful news you laid on me in your last letter! Wow, I just knew you would be set free soon. I could feel it in my bones. I hope they give you some nice clothes and some money to help get you back on your feet. Have you learned a trade or any marketable skills while serving your time? That will be very important to help you stay on the straight path. You could always consider hairdressing! Ha!

    I've said it before, and I'm probably boring you by now, but I truly believe we are all blessed with a capacity to reconstruct our lives from the ashes, no matter how dire our circumstances.

Whatever failings and missteps you may have suffered in the past, dear lad, I know you can do likewise . . . and will! It's never too late to become a good person!

Please consider a visit out to California. You are always welcome in my home. I have a spare bedroom that's ready for you. Perhaps you can find work out here. Morley is just a teeny bit of a town, and you'd probably find it a little quiet . . . OK, it's really dull. But the people are nice . . . OK, some of them are nice, mostly rednecks, just like you and me, real salt of the earth! And if you still long for excitement, we're right down the road from the "bustling metropolis of Rellman." (Can you see my air quotes?)

There was much more, but he could read no further. He closed his eyes. *Man*, he thought, *twelve of these letters over the past year, always the same sickening tone. "Feel good about yourself, Nic. Walk out of the dark and into the light, Nic. Have faith in the future, Nic." For fuck's sake, he knows I killed a guy, right? And I'd kill him again. He had it coming. There's no way I'm gonna shack up with this old daddy. Joanie's place had just better work out. I'll have to work on Tommy, though—do guy things with him, make myself useful, go hunting maybe. I can fix a car, build a deck, hang stuff up. "Good old brother Nic," he'll say. "Straight arrow Nic. Easygoing Nic. Why, he's a changed man, that Nic! He's seen the light. He goes to church, attends Men's Fellowship Thursday nights, talks about salvation, even wears the T-shirt ("WWJD?"). This guy's for real. Solid, like bedrock. You can count on Ol' Nic."*

But his sister's words echoed in his head: "You can't stay here, Nic. Just wanna make that clear." He'd have to work on her too.

Nic was jerked out of a troubled sleep by noisy air brakes as the bus pulled into the St. Louis station. His coffee spilled in his lap. The covered breezeway was filled with diesel exhaust from busses coming and going. The street beyond was dark. A fine drizzle fell outside that every strong gust blew sideways into the otherwise dry depot. Nic disembarked stiffly, stretched, and ambled slowly into the station. He headed for the snack counter across the brightly lit terminal. It was deserted.

"Hey, anyone work here?" he yelled to no one. The ticket agent

NEUTRAL, NO BRAKES

looked up at him from across the room and went immediately back to his computer screen. "Hey!" he yelled louder, his voice reverberating through the station. "I need some breakfast here, and coffee . . . Where is everybody?"

The ticket agent looked up again and casually pointed to the small handwritten cardboard sign propped up against a napkin holder. "Don't open till seven," he said. "Sorry. Got the machines. That's it till seven."

"Jeez! When's the bus to Fayetteville leave?"

"Fayetteville, North Carolina, or Fayetteville, Arkansas?"

"That bus, asshole!" He was suddenly in the agent's face at the ticket window. "The one I just got off."

The ticket agent was unruffled. "Fayetteville, Arkansas. Thirty-minute stop, leaves at six forty—right on time. Snack bar don't open till seven. Got the machines, though."

"Jesus Christ!" He slammed his fist on the countertop and marched over to a row of vending machines. A soft, low-pitched thrum emanated from the refrigeration pumps, and above that the barely audible whine of the fluorescents inside the machine. Several packaged choices confronted him from behind little plexiglass sliding doors.

BREAKFAST BURRITO
TAPIOCA PUDDING
LO-FAT STRAWBERRY YOGURT
APPLE
COTTAGE CHEESE WITH PINEAPPLE BITS
TUNA SALAD SANDWICH

"Fuck," he said loudly enough for the ticket agent to look up again. "I hate tuna fish." But he was starving, mad at the world, and craved something like meat. He pulled a crumpled five-dollar bill from his pocket. The bill was damp; some of the coffee had soaked through his pants. He fed the limp five into the machine. It was sucked in on the third attempt. He slid the door to the left and retrieved his breakfast, a diagonally cut tuna sandwich on whole wheat in a triangular plastic box. *Best by Tuesday*, he read. *Hey, today's Tuesday. My lucky day!* Two one-dollar coins plunked down into the coin trough. He moved to the coffee machine, slid them in, and punched the code for black coffee, extra sugar. He watched as the cup landed in its holder and filled up behind another sliding door. He pulled it out carefully and retrieved his three quarters in change.

Travelers were slowly populating the station. Nic found a spot in the front row of chairs where he could keep an eye on the bus and the clock, unpeeled the plastic box, and ate his sandwich glumly. A rotund black woman sat with a studious little boy in the row behind him, each reading their respective books. A scruffy young couple with blond dreadlocks, backpacks, soiled jeans, and dirty hands walked past, smelling of body odor. A callow teen wearing a college sweatshirt and pulling a roll-around suitcase was dropped off by her parents.

Nic rubbed his eyes and rested his chin in his hands, wondering how the hell he'd landed in downtown St. Louis on a dark Tuesday morning in the rain. *Joanie better come through for me*, he thought. *She's just got to, or I am so screwed. God, I could use a ciggy.* He scanned the breezeway for someone to bum a smoke from, but saw no one. He again pulled out Richard's letter and weighed his options. *A spare bedroom ready for you.* He sighed and shrugged. *Oh well, wouldn't be the first time.*

Nic finished his sandwich and left the empty box on the chair. He grabbed his coffee and duffel bag and walked out to the breezeway where a queue had already formed. The coach was warm and musty. He settled in at the rear of the bus for the long ride to Fayetteville.

3. AN AFTERNOON AT LAFONTAINE

Rusty Purnell scrunched down over his gin and tonic, hidden within the tallest booth at the far end of LaFontaine Bar and Grill. The room was blessedly dark. He'd taken a minute to adjust to it, having come from the unremitting glare of the pounding Rellman sun, grateful for the respite of "Conditioned Air" touted on the vintage neon sign out front. It was indeed "Cool Inside!"

He waited impatiently for Monica to arrive. She had texted him that morning to meet urgently, and of course, he complied. *But God, I wish she wouldn't ping me all the time!* He promptly deleted her text, preferring to keep their meeting on the down low, though it wouldn't be hard to explain. The county's premier real estate broker asking to meet with the mayor of Morley? What's unseemly about that?

Still, he was skittish about being seen with her midday in a dark bar in upscale Rellman. He sat with his back to the door and ducked down each time a patron left or entered. Just four miles up the road, Rellman was out of his jurisdiction and way out of his league, a world away from the dusty, depressed streets of his beloved town of Morley. He sipped his drink and thought of the convenience stores, payday loan outfits, discount houses, and dialysis clinics that dotted the landscape, catering to an entrenched underclass, with muscle cars and methamphetamine eclipsing snowbirding and golf as the populace's primary interests. Not much of his once-affluent town remained. *It may be a piece of shit,* mused the mayor, *but it's my piece of shit.*

Rusty's foot bounced nervously as he glanced at his phone.

Thirty minutes late! He downed his gin and tonic and ordered another, chomping his lime wedge as he examined the booth's cracked tuck-and-roll upholstery. *I hate this place,* he thought, *I should get out of here right now.*

At that moment, as if on cue, the front door swung wide and in strode Monica Sampson-Smith, silhouetted by a glaring sun that added to the mystique of her entrance. Every noontime drinker could not help turning to gaze wistfully as she glided through the bar. She wore a red pencil skirt and flowing white silk blouse, and walked with the confidence and grandeur befitting her celebrity status among the local power crowd. A member of the Ten Million Dollar Club and the Elite Producer League, she was a dominant figure at Rellman City Council and Development Board meetings. Monica could always be counted on to show up wielding persuasive stats, a commanding tone, and a killer wardrobe. Rusty referred to her as "the spiciest forty-year-old in the county," an appellation she secretly savored; she was well on the far side of forty.

"Mr. Mayor," she announced, thrusting her hand out to firmly shake his. "Good of you to meet me on such short notice."

He stood up and greeted her fawningly in a voice all could hear. "Ms. Sampson-Smith. So good to see you. Please sit down. No trouble at all. I'm very interested in hearing what you have to present. What can I get you?"

"Club soda, please." She slid into the booth across from him, and Rusty called out her order to the barmaid. Having established for the room this was a public business meeting, they now spoke in a low, private tone. From her oxblood leather valise, she produced a laptop and a matching leather notebook filled with documents, correspondence, and photos clad in plastic page protectors.

"So what's up, Your Hotness?" he murmured, with a toothy grin and a wink.

Monica smirked but otherwise ignored his attempt at flattering humor. She had long endured Rusty's juvenile wisecracks and tallied them into the cost of doing business. Same went for the clunky intimacy they occasionally shared in his private back office to consummate a new development deal or real estate coup.

"Now, none of that today," she said in a whisper. "I've got something really hot here to show you!"

"I'll say," he said.

"No, really. Be serious." Her irritation was starting to show.

"OK, OK. Serious as a heart attack." He made a mock stern face. "So what's so urgent and amazing?"

She logged onto her computer. As it booted up, the barmaid brought her club soda to the table. Monica waited for her to leave, then opened an image file and turned the screen toward Rusty. It bathed his face in bright green light, casting a spectral glow in the darkened bar. He soon realized he was gazing at a map, but of what? An irregular blue patch, presumably water, nestled among the greens and browns, occupied the greatest portion of the map. It recalled the hand-drawn maps he'd seen as a boy in old fantasy adventure books, depicting strange, faraway lands with outlandish names and unfamiliar boundaries. Puzzled, he studied the map further and now could identify some topographic features, street grids, and thoroughfares, his eye catching one stretch he finally recognized—the very street his own City Hall office sat on.

"Hey, this is Morley!"

"Shhh, quiet!" she said, waving her hands in frustration. "God! Of course it's Morley. But with something extra." She checked around the bar for listeners. "See? Our little water feature here. A very large one, actually. Let's call it Lake Nelson."

"But—but there is no Lake Nelson."

She sometimes wondered how a man like Rusty could get so far in life and be so slow on the uptake.

"Not yet, there isn't," she explained, "but there will be soon."

He was suspicious. "Say, where did you get this map? I haven't heard anything about a reservoir project coming to the valley."

"Let's just say, Mr. Mayor, that I have a few contacts at the state."

"Such as?"

"That's not important right now. But they're very supportive."

"You'll need more than supportive contacts, my friend. This lake of yours will cost a few billion, not counting the usual overruns, which'll add at least another billion."

"Again, not important. Work with me here, Rusty. Try to get the vision. The valley needs water, as everyone is painfully aware. The whole state does."

"OK, but we're talking years away to complete something like this. First the financing, then buying up all those properties, then construction." He rubbed his brow in exasperation just thinking about it. "Then you've got to give the thing time to fill up, you know, naturally. If you hadn't noticed, it hasn't rained here in seven months."

"Exactly why we need a reservoir. Now you're getting it."

"And what do we do in the meantime?"

"We build, baby, build!"

Monica explained first how water from the old Hensen County Aqueduct would be diverted down into Morley Canyon to fill the reservoir. Rerouting would take place as the dam itself was under construction.

"The main dam project would begin here." She pointed with her finger, her immaculate red nail sliding smoothly across the screen. "With a new road leading to it just here." She became more animated. "It'll be quite a tourist attraction, like Hoover Dam. I can see a nice lodge with restaurants and snack bars right there, RV camping over here, a dock with slips and houseboat rentals over there. And fishing—once the lake is stocked, of course—for trout, bass, that sort of thing. Water skiing, jet boating, sailing, windsurfing, paddleboarding . . ." She was out of breath, giddy with excitement.

"And the money?"

"We'll need some big bucks from the Feds, for sure. Aren't you on good terms with Congressman Hattenauer? He's still Chair of Ways and Means?"

"Ranking member."

"For the moment. Plus there's the state grant program. Then we'll need to pass a local tax levy of course, perhaps a bond measure or two. My contacts think we can materialize as much as a couple billion in seed money. Once we're underway, financing will flow like water. I know, it's all very preliminary, but they're confident it'll go through. Besides, we don't actually have to build the dam to make a killing, if you catch my drift. Everyone will be so excited about the new reservoir, the market will get a real kick in the pants."

He was impressed. Of all the calculating, back-channel schemes she had cooked up over the years, this was by far the most ambitious.

"I also know, sir, that there is a fair amount of local interest in this project among our friends." She raised her eyebrows and smiled. He immediately knew the friends she referred to—a band of willing collaborators that over the years, and perhaps forever, had run things in towns like Morley and Rellman and most of the surrounding county, an inner circle of VC investors, financial advisors, realtors, mortgage brokers, insurance agents, go-betweens, ad agents, and construction guys of every stripe, from excavation and concrete to drywall and build-out. Most essential were the handful of friendly employees in the county's Bureau of Zoning and Development, willing to bend a few rules, expedite an application or hold one up, raise a fuss or look the other way—whatever the wheels of progress demanded in the moment.

"Sounds like an awesome opportunity. There's just one small detail." He pointed to the map. "People live in this valley. Actual flesh and blood, living, breathing human types. Trust me, the fine citizens of Morley will not take kindly to being displaced. They're a distrustful bunch for the most part, maybe a little short on smarts and long on tattoos but all of them with a thing for freedom. And guns. Sometimes it's all I can do to keep them from taking up arms against the deep state."

She stared at him blankly, unmoved by his display of what, to her, seemed fake concern. "Two words: eminent domain."

"Right. I suppose you could make the case for it as a public good."

"And the jobs? Just picture it. Pickup trucks lining up every morning. Men, and maybe some girls too, in their Carhartt overalls carrying Coleman coolers. They will love it. Nothing trumps civic concern and outrage like a paycheck."

"OK, OK, I get it. But who's going to carry the water on this project—no pun intended?" He sensed he had just arrived at the very point of their meeting.

"Why, Your Honor. You know the people of Morley look up to you with the greatest admiration and respect. You're a true man of the people!" She gave his thigh a gentle squeeze under the table.

"Pfft! Yeah, that's me. A man for all seasons," he mused dramatically, "'A man of marvelous mirth and sometimes sad gravity.'"

She gaped at him wide-eyed.

"Something I memorized in high school. Anyway, I do feel their joy and their pain, truly I do. Let's hope they don't figure out that up till now I've been responsible for a good portion of the latter."

"In the long run it'll be good for everyone. They'll all be entitled to fair market value for their property, don't forget, in a market where right now you couldn't sell a house in Morley unless your buyer was setting up another meth lab. Plus the jobs, all the positive press. People love that kind of feel-good message. What a shot in the arm a lakefront resort would be for the economy around here, which at the moment, I'm sure you'd agree, is kinda sucky."

Rusty cringed. "Ouch, that hurts a little." He had run twice and won on a platform of bringing more jobs to Morley but had so far failed to deliver. "Hey, we're doing the best we can with what we've got. Unlike your shining city over the hill, Morley isn't lucky enough to have an economic base of well-heeled professionals with money to waste on froufrou wine bars, pottery painting classes, and personal Pilates instructors. And if I see one more healthy-looking septuagenarian bicycling along the River Walk, I'll go fucking ballistic!"

"Hey, all your inbred hillbillies need to do is 'Say yes to Rellman.'" She referred to a recent effort on the part of a few homeowners at the edge of Morley to become annexed to its bigger, richer neighbor to the east. For years, Hensen County had remained largely unincorporated; that's how the residents liked it. But as lifestyle amenities and natural beauty drew new arrivals to Rellman, the two communities bumped up against each other, especially at the city limits, where Rellman had slowly, relentlessly encroached onto surrounding lands in order to accommodate new development. Their beautiful neighbor now loomed like a storm cloud over their modest little town. Everyone in a position to capitalize on Morley's vulnerability had their knives and forks out ready to take a bite.

"How about 'Say yes to Morley'?" he asked. "With all the growth and development you're talking about, we may end up giving you a run for your money."

"I'm not worried. If all goes well, someday there may not even be a Morley."

4. FAIR WARNING

It was a slow day at ReddyCare Urgent Care Clinic. Cloistered in her private office, Dr. Sunita Reddy clicked through her emails, mostly spam—the miracle of acai, a blowout sale at the Mattress Place, discreet access to Viagra. Delete, delete, delete! They disappeared in rapid succession.

Her finger froze as her eyes were drawn to a personalized email. URGENT CALL TO ACTION! read the subject line. It was from monica@rellmanrealty.net. *Oh God, not another one,* she thought. Monica Sampson-Smith had for years sent out a monthly clarion call, usually a hyperbolic warning about rising interest rates or a softening market. At first the doctor had taken the bait, hoping for edification, but soon learned that Monica's prime motive, her only motive, was to sell real estate as expeditiously as possible. She was poised to delete this email too when curiosity won her over. Maybe this time there'd be something of value. It was, as well, a very slow day.

She double-clicked and saw a photo depicting a row of shops she recognized instantly: Pickwick's Paperback Shack in the middle, flanked by the other businesses at Morley Plaza, including her own clinic. Below appeared its dire message in red block letters: Warning! A SMUT PEDDLER IN OUR MIDST!, followed by a detailed narrative on the pornographic books and magazines on display at Pickwick's. The Citizens Action League, an organization led by Monica made up of fellow real estate brokers, associates in the building trades, and a handful of development-friendly nonprofits, wished to express their grave concern over the store's proximity to

Robert T. Whitehead Middle School. A forceful directive followed: circulate the attached petition among local business owners, their customers, and residential neighbors to put an end to this scourge.

Dr. Reddy immediately printed the petition, clicked her screen closed, and hung her stethoscope on the doorknob.

"Lori!" she called, emerging from the back office. "I'm going over to the bookstore. Page me if anything serious walks in."

"Sure, Dr. Reddy. Will you be gone long? This is our busy time, you know."

"Busy? Does it look busy to you?"

"Well, no, but . . ."

"If anyone looks really sick, call 9-1-1 and text me. I'll just be over there." She pointed out the window to Pickwick's that was catty-corner to the clinic. "I'll keep an eye on the front door. Remember, call 9-1-1 *first*. *Then* text me."

"Yes, Doctor."

"Good girl."

"Dr. Reddy? How will I know if they're really sick?"

She turned back from the exit and leaned on the reception counter with a smile. "Good question. Lori, remember that fellow who came in last week, the gentleman who thought he was having indigestion?"

"Uh huh."

"Remember how pale and sweaty he looked? How he was having trouble breathing? Then he vomited?"

"Yes, he did not look good."

"That's when you call 9-1-1. OK?"

"Got it!"

"Good." She walked briskly out into the afternoon sun, across the parking lot, and into the cool darkness of Pickwick's. The smell of joss stick was pleasantly pervasive.

A lively Tex-Mex jam came from the boom box at the far end of the shop:

> "No seas tonta, mujer, no seas tonta,
> que no ves la esperanza perdida . . ."

Elizabeth Donatella Hart groaned as she heaved a large

cardboard box of books onto the desk. Her hips swayed to the bouncy accordion and bajo sexto tune as she examined each title. The books spanned a range of topics: *Art and Industry*, *A Graphic Survey of Physics*, *Langenscheidt's German-English Dictionary*, *The 1957 Platinum*, a yearbook from Morley High School. The books had a musty smell, having sat in the back corner of someone's garage for many years. Some had grown dark specks of mold along the edges. A few were crinkled and swollen from water damage. *Were these left out in the rain? What a shame.* She flipped through the salvageable ones, examined the bindings, inspected for scribbled side notes and graffiti, and assigned prices in pencil on the inside front cover. One dollar for the dictionary, ten dollars for the yearbook, and so on, until the entire box was sorted by category and salability. The damaged books were carefully replaced into the box. *These will still be great for the community reading room.* She lugged the priced books to their respective sections—Art, Science, Reference, Local History—and slid them into place by subject and author.

As Sunita Reddy entered the shop, she triggered the electric eye that chimed a tinny version of the Big Ben theme.

"Hi there, Doctor. Ugh, I've just got to get rid of that door chime. It sounds so goofy."

"I don't know. It reminds me of my London days."

"Anyway, how are you this beautiful afternoon? Shouldn't you be at your clinic saving lives?"

"I think Morley will survive my taking a little break. Anyway, most people who think they are sick are not really sick at all. Everyone with a cold thinks they have pneumonia or, at a minimum, a terrible infection that absolutely needs antibiotics."

"So what do you do then?"

"I try to talk them out of it, of course."

"And if that doesn't work?"

"Then I give them exactly what they want. You see, the less I do *for* them, the more I have to talk *to* them. I've got a business to run, same as you."

"So, did you enjoy the Fitzgerald?"

"I loved it."

"I knew you would."

"But depressing as hell!"

"God, I know. He didn't just write it; he lived it. How sad is that?" She continued to sway to the music. "Can I show you some of his other work?"

"Perhaps another time. I wanted to give you a heads-up and a bit of advice, if I may. Donna, are you selling pornography in your store? I'm not judging, just asking."

She made a funny face of surprise and puzzlement. "What? You mean like child porn? Never! Why would you ask such a question?"

"This came from our dear friend Monica. She's at it again." Donna examined the flyer.

"Oh my, this *is* creepy. Doctor, I swear to you I do not sell pornography." She paused. "Unless you mean my little Adults Only section behind the curtain there."

"You'd better show me."

She motioned for Dr. Reddy to follow her through a bead curtain into the back room. There on display was an entire wall of books, videos, and magazines, whose covers depicted long-haired mustachioed men and overly thin women in various come-hither poses. Titles included *Greek Cabin Boy*, *Frannie Does Fresno*, *Swamp Girl*, *Thirty Seconds Over Tina*, and the golf-themed *A Hole in Juana*, all carefully bagged, sealed, and arranged by genre and title.

"This isn't pornography?" Sunita laughed out loud. "It's more like a porn museum in here!"

"Yes, exactly! This material is of great historical significance, nothing past 1980. They're strictly for the connoisseur. Very collectible."

"Well, my dear, you'd better collect it, box it up, and get it the fuck out of here."

Donna was amused at hearing Dr. Reddy swear in her heavy East Indian accent but reassured her there was nothing to worry about.

"Monica Sampson is a terribly sad and disturbed person. She always has been."

"And she's out to get you, my friend. But why?"

Donna shrugged. "She can't help herself. Don't you worry about me. I can handle her."

"How exactly do you plan on doing that?"

"Come with me." She led Dr. Reddy out of the Adults Only

room to the section on metaphysics, pulled down a thin tattered volume, and handed it to her."

"*The Higher Powers of Mind and Spirit* by Ralph Waldo Trine. Donna, this woman is circulating a petition to shut you down. She means business. How is this going to help you?"

"We'll just see about that. There is power in spirit, more potent than all her silly petitions and nasty lies and finger pointing." She stated this not as some faith-based aspiration but as a concrete matter of fact. "Here, you take this copy. On the house. I've got my own at home."

The doctor shot her a skeptical look, slipped the book into the pocket of her crisp white coat, and extracted her cell phone, which was humming away. "You are really something, miss."

"Yes, well . . . Read that book. You'll thank me."

"Oh, shit." Sunita glanced at her phone. "It's Lori. She's got a live one. I've got to go. Bye!" She dashed out the door.

"Bye, dear." Donna looked at the flyer and sighed. She walked back to her workspace and passed it through the shredder behind her desk. It made a satisfying crunching sound.

5. SANDWICHES ON A BUS

The town of Catton Mills sat on an isolated stretch of frontage road parallel to US Route 71. The highway headed south out of Fayetteville, Arkansas, to join up with Interstate 40 at Fort Smith, one of hundreds of tributaries flowing into that massive arterial from a swath of states stretching from Michigan to Alabama. From there it was a straight shot to Barstow and points west, making it a preferred route through the southern tier for long-haul trucks, regional reps, and vacationing families heading to California.

On this particular evening, Nic Troxell dozed lightly, slumped sideways in his aisle seat. As the Trailways bus pulled into Catton Mills, it slowed to small-town speed in anticipation of the next station stop. Nic's eyes opened a crack. There was no visible human activity on the street, bathed in hot red and orange by a setting sun. Neglected planter strips were sunbaked and untidy. Bits of trash clung to stubby weeds. Many of the town's buildings had long ago been boarded up. One weathered sign, its letters cracked and flaking, boasted "Best Ribs in Town," as they may once have been. Now thick brambles blocked any attempt to enter the premises, for ribs or any other reason. Other low-slung buildings, like Tina's Tiny Treasures and Catton Corner, lay abandoned, their plywood windows and stucco walls blanketed with thick graffiti.

A brown-skinned boy about eight years old pedaled his Stingray into the track of the bus, causing it to suddenly brake and lurch forward. The boy pedaled safely past Nic's window, their eyes meeting briefly. His gaze followed the boy as he rode off.

NEUTRAL, NO BRAKES

A bluish-white glow now emanated from beyond the horizon, growing brighter as the bus approached, challenging the advancing twilight. There soon emerged, in piercing detail, the lights of a massive structure and its contiguous acreage, standing in sharp contrast to the squat, dilapidated profile of Catton Mills.

The Texaco Travel Center appeared to be the one enterprise doing quite well in this town of otherwise impoverished remains, an immense twenty-four-hour oasis bubbling with an air of exotic charm offering a full spectrum of comfort-oriented amenities. Besides cheap diesel and gas, the tired traveler could obtain truck and auto supplies and repair services, while enjoying free internet, showers, lodging, a natural foods marketplace and deli, hair salon and day spa, movie theater, live performance venue and, of course, the Comanche Bar and Grill.

Nic surveyed the collection of vehicles littering the parking lot— sedans, minivans, SUVs, small pickups, diesel dualies, cabover campers, horse trailers, fifth wheelers, mini-Winnies, full size RVs, passenger buses, and big-rig transport trucks. They were queued four and five deep at the cheap fuel pumps or vying for parking. Ballcap-wearing truck drivers with ample guts moseyed from their cabs in slow motion, their motors left running to keep the AC on, into the main lobby made frigid by its own cranked up air conditioning. Grandmas nimbly piloted wheeled walkers up the ramp through the automatic doors leading to the main dining area. School aged kids, unsuccessfully restrained by parents, gleefully bounced up and down wearing little paper crowns displaying the image of a truck barreling down the highway, declaring them King or Queen of the Road. The mood was breezy, optimistic, and convivial.

The bus pulled in diagonally and idled to pick up two new passengers waiting below. Country music echoed loudly on tinny speakers through the breezeway. Nic eyed the couple where they stood—a large, young woman and a slender, pink-cheeked young man, happily chatting in warmhearted whispers, each carrying two shopping bags filled with clothing neatly folded and arranged. The bus tilted as they boarded.

Don't even think about sitting here, thought Nic, glancing sideways at the window seat beside him. He allowed his shoulder and elbow to migrate toward the empty seat and pretended to sleep, his face expressionless, eyes fully closed, jaw slack, hoping a bit of drool would slide out the corner of his mouth, adding a light snore to leave no doubt he was deep in slumber.

"Excuse me, sir," said a woman's cautious voice. He continued to feign a listless snooze but caught the couple speaking in low tones to one another. "Go on, sit," whispered the man's voice. "I'll just be back there." He heard them smack a kiss.

"Pardon me," said the woman's voice. Again he did not answer, but a moment later felt a nudge against his knee. He cracked open one eye. Before him loomed a pair of large hips in bedazzled blue jeans about four inches from his nose. The woman was trying to slide past him toward the open window seat without waking him. With every restrained baby step she made to avoid treading on his feet, her buns gave a little wiggle, and her pink cotton top, damp with sweat, rode up over her hips. She made it past him at last and landed in her seat with a huff, her two paper sacks positioned between her knees.

"Oops," she said, feeling his gaze, her hand over her mouth. "Gosh, did I wake you? I'm so, so sorry." She carefully arranged her bags and purse, cheerfully checking to see that she had all her belongings with her. "I've just got to sit at a window, or else I get terrible car sick."

"Guess I'm up now," he said. Abandoning his ruse, he sat upright and stared at the seatback in front of him.

"Say, are you hungry?" The woman reached into her purse. "I've got plenty," she said, pulling out two foil-wrapped sandwiches and offering him one. "Let's see." She carefully peeled back a corner of the foil. "This here's tuna fish."

"No tuna fish!"

"I've got egg salad too if you'd prefer. I just like to see people eat."

"Nope," he said finally, staring at her long enough to make her feel uneasy, then closing his eyes and slouching down into his seat.

The woman glanced over her shoulder at her husband two rows behind. She gave him a girlish finger wave and drew an air heart. He smiled back at her, gritting his teeth in mimed frustration for having to sit so far apart from her. She giggled.

The driver grinded the bus into reverse and, using his backup cameras, mirrors, and patience and skill, inched the behemoth out of its slot, the bus beeping insistently. He slowly navigated through the crowded parking lot and back onto the highway, quickly gaining speed toward I-40.

The woman glanced at a sleeping Nic, silently wondering what on earth would put him in such a bad mood. She saw on his neck a tattoo of a skull dripping with blood, next to an anatomic rendering of a heart with a dagger run through it. Just under his collar were some angular lines. Was that a swastika? She munched away at her egg salad sandwich.

"Mmm, I was so-o-o-o hungry," she said, chewing audibly. "You sure you don't want half of this tuna salad? I'll be fine. We haven't got far to go." Nic, eyes shut, waved her off. "We're bringing my sister clothes for the new baby." She patted the bags of folded clothes. "I got two at home. My mom's watchin' 'em tonight, but they're outgrowed from these, so . . . She just had a little baby boy. Robert LeRoy Richards. Can you believe it? 'Robert LeRoy.' Sounds so regal, don' it? LeRoy's my, um, *our* daddy's name. Different mommas, same dad, but we're all real close. That's my husband, Trevor, back there." She waved to him. "I'm Grace Eileen. Pleased to meet you."

"Mm-hm."

She took another bite of sandwich and looked away as they flew through open countryside. The sun had fully dipped below the horizon, creating a brilliant deep blue. The interior lights began to flip on as darkness filled the bus. She turned to him with an air of determination and resolve.

"Say, I know it's not my place and all, but you sure seem down about something. I realize it's not for me to ask, but I hope it's nothing too serious. Let me tell you, we've had our ups and downs," she said, tilting her head in Trevor's direction. "But there's nothing, and I mean nothing, the good Lord gives us that we can't endure through his love and salvation. Not one thing!" She leaned toward him and whispered with compassion, "Are you saved, sir? Are you a believer?"

He turned to her slowly, stared blankly and shook his head.

"Well, whatever it is, I'll be praying for you. God answers prayers for folks whether they're saved or not. 'Even if you don't believe in Him, He believes in you.' That's what I always say. Last chance." She smiled and again offered up the sandwich. "Sixty-eight miles to go. My brother-in-law Bobby'll be meeting us at the station. We'll have a quick dinner at the house, see the baby, drop off these here, spend the night, then back on the early bus home. Boy, I'll be dog-tired at work tomorrow."

As the bus droned on, Grace Eileen eventually fell quiet and napped. Nic eyed her surreptitiously with contempt. *Irritating do-gooders!* he thought. *Always asking if you're OK, praying for your salvation. They've all got skin in the game. Wonder what this one's after.*

The Trailways coach raced on into the night, gently rocking its passengers into a tranquil silence. But Nic's thoughts continued to plague him. A few days ago, he was confident he could talk Joanie into at least a couple of weeks on the couch. On the drive home from the Fayetteville bus station, he'd filled her in on recent events: his life in Indiana State Prison, his parole hearing, the parole board (*a bunch of assholes,* he called them, even after they'd granted him early release). She in turn talked about Tom and the kids, their latest financial struggles, the sheer joy and utter chaos of raising three children on their combined but barely sufficient paychecks.

But something had changed. A year his senior, he and Joanie had always palled around, playing jokes on the neighbors, getting in and out of trouble together. She'd always cheerfully engaged in his standard "fuck 'em all" comments. Now his big sister seemed like a stranger to him, all serious, cautious, circumspect, laughing only politely at his off-color jokes.

It had been four years since their last meeting. What happened? Was it money trouble? No, that had always been true. Was she sick, or Tom or one of the kids, and she didn't want to talk about it? Perhaps she had found God, though she never mentioned Him by name, or worse was under the influence of the sanctimonious, unforgiving Tom. Whatever it was, they quickly fell into an uncomfortable silence. He fiddled with the radio but eventually quit that and gazed out the window.

About a block from home she turned in to the King Drive-Thru to buy burgers for the family. At the checkout window, Nic did some quick reckoning and realized she had ordered dinner for him without asking. As he rummaged in his pockets, she waved him off. "My treat."

The evening with Tom and the kids was worse than the drive home. No handshake, no easy chatter on the sofa. The kids regarded him with a cool distance at first, like a strange alien presence, a dangerous one—and wasn't he, after all? He was Uncle Nic from jail. Yes, he'd killed a guy, but he had it coming to him. Wide-eyed Tommy Junior seemed to get a big kick out of that, and Nic made the most of it, despite Tom's and Joanie's disapproving looks. But Cecily, the older girl from Tom's first marriage, seemed bored with it all, declaring she was leaving for spirit team practice right after dinner, then had to work on her term paper with a friend. She was not impressed by Nic's roguish swagger and handsome features. The baby girl, of course, was neutral. Nic had held up his little niece awkwardly for a few seconds, then handed her back to Joanie.

Around burgers, fries, and Cokes, Tom broke the silence. "So, Nic," he queried. "What are your plans now that you're a free man?" His icy tone shouted: *You're not staying under my roof any longer than it takes to get rid of you!* Nic didn't even try to pitch the idea of sticking around. He knew it would be wasted.

"I'll be heading out to California," he said with false confidence, thinking of Richard's letter. "I've got an old friend out there, good friend, says there's lots of work." It wasn't a complete lie but close. "He's willing to put me up for a few weeks, help me get on my feet." *Unlike you, you son of a bitch!*

"Well, we wish you the very best, Nic. I know God will help you find your way on the straight path. We'll be praying for you." *So that's it. Joanie went and found God, courtesy of goddamn Tom!*

Joanie made up Cecily's room for Nic. She would sleep on the floor in her folks' room, which gave her another reason to hate him. Nic spent a troubled night staring up at the pink ceiling. A dozen stuffed animals loomed over him, mutely judging him. He could not meet their eyes.

He was up before sunrise, ahead of anyone in the house. He crept to the bathroom in his stocking feet, quietly scrubbed his face and pits at the sink, changed his socks and underwear, stuffed the dirty ones into his duffel, and tiptoed to the kitchen. He ran the hot water till it was scalding—he didn't want to risk the microwave beeping—and used it to make a cup of instant coffee. He gulped it down and rinsed the cup.

"Headin' out? So early?" Joanie appeared in the doorway behind him.

"Caught me." They exchanged a smile. "I didn't want to, you know, bother—"

"Yeah. I know." She nodded. "Here, let me make you a proper cup. You'll need it." She loaded the coffee maker. "Don't worry about those guys, they could sleep through a nucular bomb."

She brought out a loaf of white bread, bologna and cheese, mayonnaise, and a tomato. He watched in silence as she toasted the bread in her four-slice toaster, sliced the tomato, and efficiently assembled several sandwiches, cutting them diagonally and inserting each into a plastic zip-top bag. She stacked the sandwiches into a large grocery sack, threw in a couple of juice boxes, some navel oranges, and paper napkins.

"What are you, packing me off to school?" They both chuckled. The coffee maker's gurgles slowed and stopped. She served them both a cup and sat down across from him.

"Don't forget, I do this every day. Cheers!" Their cups clinked. "It's been a long road, Nicky. I've missed you." She smiled, staring into her cup. "You were always the smart one in school, remember? Teachers loved you. Everything seemed to come to you so quickly. Unlike me. Man, I had to struggle every year."

"Yeah, but look at you now. You've got it made. Family, career . . ."

"I wouldn't exactly call working the books at the tile warehouse a career."

"But at least you've got a home. What've I got to show for it all? A bag full of sandwiches and not a whole lotta prospects." He thought again of Richard's letter but did not bring it up.

"If you don't want 'em . . ." She grabbed the sack of food.

"No, no," he said, trying to grab them back from her. They tugged back and forth playfully for a moment before she let go. "Sorry. I really appreciate it. You know that, right?"

She sighed and shook her head. "Nicky, what's to become of you?" Tears flowed from her eyes now. "You're not a kid anymore, son. You can't get by forever on your clever talk and devilish good looks." He struck a dramatic profile pose, and she could not help but laugh. "Seriously. When are you going to get real?"

"Real?" he said defensively. "What the hell's real? Is any of this real? 'Gee, wonder if we'll be able to pay for ballet lessons this month. Ooh, got to get ready for the church social. I'll bake my special lemon tarts; the ladies love them so.' You have no fucking idea what's real."

She fell silent, eyes lowered, then blankly pushed the sack of food toward him. "Can you go now, please?" She busied herself tidying up her work area.

He watched without moving. "Sorry, sis." She ignored him. "Hey," he whispered loudly, still aware of the sleeping family beyond the kitchen door. "I'm said I'm sorry. Really."

She finally looked up from her cleaning. "You can be a mean son of a bitch, Nicky. Why must you always be such a prick? What did I do to *you*? Uh, nothing, except pick you up from the bus station, feed you . . ."

"Look, I'm sorry." He rubbed his forehead with both hands. "I'm all fucked up. My whole life is this duffel bag and the clothes on my back. That's it. Plus, now you're throwing me out on the street."

"Hey, no one's throwing you out! Can you not see this zoo I'm running here? Don't you understand? It's hard. I love my husband, and I love my kids, but they're a helluva lot of work, let me tell you." She topped off their coffee cups. "I'd like to be able to help you out, I really would, but you can't just parachute in here and prop your feet up." She took his hand warmly in her own. "You know, I'm supposed to be your big sister, but I always looked up to you, Nic. Now I'm all grown up, and things are different. We're not kids anymore. Now it's your turn to grow up. You've got to get yourself together. Get straight. Get a job. Do something, anything, instead of bouncing around from one scam to the next. And by the way, I know you dodged a bullet with that second-degree manslaughter conviction. You may not be so lucky next time."

He opened his mouth, thought of protesting, but knew she pretty much had him pegged. "Maybe this deal out in California will work out."

"What deal is that? Tell me about it."

"I'll tell you, but you won't believe it. And listen, you can't let Tom or the kids know." He handed her Richard's most recent letter. "I got me a pen pal, see?"

"A what?" She suppressed her laughter. "Some eight-year-old girl fall in love with you?"

"No, it's this guy. This older guy. He got my name off the pen pal website." Joanie was giggling uncontrollably now. "He's offered me a place to stay, even help find me a job if I want. He seems OK, just wants a little companionship, I guess."

Joanie motioned back and forth near her open mouth with her fist. "Yeah, companionship." Nic managed a soft chuckle but did not look amused.

"I have no idea what the guy wants. Look, things are not falling my way right now. I need to catch a break. Whatever it takes, I gotta get something going. Maybe I can get out to Cali, see what's what, and go from there. There's nothing for me here. I know that now."

He stuffed the big sack lunch into his duffel and headed toward the door.

"Let me drive you to the station?"

"Nah, I'll walk. It's only like two miles. I need to do some thinking."

They stood facing each other. "Don't I get a hug?" she asked. Nic bent forward, and they embraced. Joanie began to tear up again. "Love you."

"Love you too. Uh, say . . . there is one thing. I was hoping, maybe if you had a little extra cash sittin' around?"

She disentangled herself and pushed him away. "Ugh, you asshole! No wonder you live such a shitty life." She turned away. "You just take and take and take. Get the fuck outta my house!"

"Uncle Nic! Uncle Nic!" Tommy Junior came trotting into the kitchen, his stockings padding on the floor, and hugged Nic around his knees. "Are you gonna have cereal with us? I'm gonna have cereal. And toast with jelly!"

Joanie picked up Tommy and set him onto the stool at the breakfast bar. "You settle down, little man. Uncle Nic's got to go now. He's going to have breakfast in town."

"Aw, how come? I love Uncle Nic. Uncle Nic, I love you."

Nic stared at the floor in silence. Joanie moved toward the

cupboard, set a box of cereal in front of Tommy, and reached for the flour canister on the top shelf. From it, she fished out some bills and handed them quietly to Nic.

"Best I can do. Now get out of here."

He hesitated for an instant, stuffed the bills into his pocket, and bolted through the door. The air was dark, cool, and moist.

The driver's perfunctory announcement came through the scratchy speakers overhead. "Next stop Eunice, Arkansas, ladies and gentlemen. Eunice will be our next stop." The bus slowed as it entered the residential streets of town.

Over his shoulder, Nic sensed the pink-cheeked Trevor standing over him.

"Hi, sir. My wife talking your ear off?" He grinned broadly. Nic shook his head. "Excuse me." Trevor leaned over and placed a gentle hand on Grace Eileen's shoulder. "Sweetie." He wiggled her shoulder gently. "Gracie."

The woman mumbled in her sleep and shifted her weight. "Mmphh?"

"This is our stop coming up."

With one big yawn, she was awake. "Oh, thanks, honey."

"It'll be a few minutes still. I'll see you outside. Thanks again for keeping her company, sir." He made his way back to his seat as the bus rolled to a stoplight on a busy main street.

"My sister. She—she didn't want me around." Nic stared straight ahead.

"I'm sorry?"

"You asked what was bothering me. My sister. She threw me out."

"Oh, no. Oh, no." She touched his wrist. "That's terrible. Did you have a fight or something?" she said as she gathered up her belongings.

"Nope. Not exactly. We had a little disagreement. When she makes up her mind, it's final. Her husband wasn't any help."

"Well, whatever it is, I know you'll get back together." Assured she had all of her stuff in order, she now turned to Nic. "It's such a shame when families turn against each other. I mean, some little thing gets blown up into a big mess, people say things they don't mean, then don't speak to each other for years. That is truly a tragedy. It's not what God wants for us, that's for sure. Family is a blessing. I'm sure she'll come around, you'll see."

At the intersection, traffic and pedestrians crossed in front of the bus in both directions. A soft rain fell on the bus windows, making lights in the street twinkle and glow.

"Nah, she's right. I am a bad person." He looked directly at her. "I don't deserve to be around them. I don't deserve a family. I *am* a bum."

"No, no. You're *not* a bad person. I can tell. I'm a very good judge of character. You just need someone to understand you, to tell you you're OK once in a while. And maybe push you a little bit in the right direction." She made a little shoving motion. "Ooh, gotta go. Take care, Mr.—Sorry, I didn't catch your name.

"Nic."

She held out her hand, and he took it. "Be good, Nic." She arose and again shimmied past him into the aisle, waving at her husband behind her.

The bus pulled up in front of the Trailways station, where the young couple and a handful of other passengers alighted from the bus. A robust dark-haired man enthusiastically greeted the couple, first embracing Grace Eileen, then shaking Trevor's hand with a broad smile. He took their bags, and they walked together down the street to the parking structure. Grace Eileen did not look back.

Nic reached into his duffel and pulled out his last bologna sandwich. He ate listlessly. The turn signal clicked impatiently until the bus eased its way back onto the street. Once on the highway, Nic soon fell asleep, this time for real, his half-eaten sandwich perched loosely on his chest.

6. DARLA'S PLAN

A chilly breeze kicked up along Copley Drive, sending scraps of paper, cigarette butts, and a fine black grit swirling down the sidewalks of Morley. A thick layer of it accumulated in doorways and windowsills where the wind could not reach. In the distance a car alarm blasted, competing with the banter from a squad of youths loitering down the street. Otherwise the boulevard lay abandoned, blanketed in a pervasive indolence. The town was awake and open for business but, at nearly midday, hung suspended in a permanent siesta.

Rounding the corner from San Sebastian Parkway strode Ms. Darlene Joy Skornik—Darla to her friends—mail carrier for the US Postal Service. She stepped with an air of authority and certitude that left no doubt of her mission: deliver the mail, get it right, and get it done. She valued efficiency, accuracy, and most of all her time, knowing she could knock off as soon as her route was completed. She made no eye contact with passersby on the street nor conversation with the various retail and commercial patrons along her route beyond the absolutely necessary. She threw a brief glance toward the frenetic wilding noises from the adolescents nearby but, unperturbed, paid them no further mind.

Darla's route ended each day at Morley Plaza. As she approached Mr. Richard's Cuts and Color, she sorted out one piece of actual correspondence, a thick envelope addressed to Mr. Richard Kornbluth from the Indiana Department of Corrections, and placed it atop the usual advertisements and credit card offers. From there she continued her rounds, dropping mail at Pickwick's Paperback Shack, ReddyCare Urgent Care Clinic, Burger Basket, and Dogg Life Daycare.

Her pace quickened as she approached her last stop: Videodrome. She burst through the door, bumping it open with the huge mailbag on her hip, her entrance made more pronounced by the debris and cold wind that followed her in.

At the far end of the store, behind racks with signs announcing Horror, Comedy, and New Arrivals, sat Jeremy Kelner. His sandy blond hair, pulled back into a thin ponytail, was set off by two days' patchy growth of beard that blended into his pale complexion, his plaid flannel shirt in need of ironing it would never receive.

Jeremy pounded his head with both fists, flummoxed by the pile of unsorted DVDs from the after-hours bin. He'd just begun logging in the overnight returns when the program crashed. He looked up from his frozen computer screen, startled by Darla's blowy entrance. Her olive skin, high cheekbones, wide eyes, tall nose, and full lips transfixed Jeremy, as they did each day. Her riotous dark brown hair, barely tamed by a scrunchie, was jammed under the USPS pith helmet she wore always, rain or shine.

"Oh, hey!" he said cheerily, shifting his attention to Darla. "How goes it?" He always acted surprised when she appeared, despite knowing her daily schedule and anticipating her arrival at any moment. Her brief cameo visits—and they were ultra brief—elated him for reasons he could not explain. Admittedly she was strikingly beautiful, but it was her confident, no-nonsense demeanor that fascinated him. Darla was the highlight of his day.

"Morning," she replied, looking not at him but at the video screen behind him. There she viewed a tuxedoed black jazz combo playing a lively tune fronted by two middle-aged men, one black, one white, also nattily dressed, happily singing a bouncy duet. She tilted her head, taken in by the rhythm, her expression quizzical.

"*High Society*," Jeremy offered with a smile. "Bing and Satchmo. Great stuff!" Spurred by her mild interest, he explained at length the scene—the strait-laced white society folks of Newport, Rhode Island, ignorant of the vernacular of jazz, were about to get a much-needed lesson in popular culture.

But he sensed his windy exposition failing as her attention

shifted back to the mail clutched in her hand. She searched for but could not find a clear landing spot on the counter to set it down, so she gingerly balanced the mail atop the pile of DVD cases. She was about to turn and bolt from the store as usual, but dawdled as a few cases teetered and slipped onto the floor.

"Nice system you have there," she observed. "Wait . . . Is that a paper log?" She rolled her eyes. "Really?" It was not lost on Jeremy that this was now their longest conversation ever. It made him nervous but strangely exhilarated.

"Yeah, pretty bad, huh? It's really frustrating. I need help!" he yelled, shaking his fists in the air in mock dramatic desperation. He let out a huge sigh, like a deflating tire.

"Buy an app."

"Not so simple—or cheap. I've priced some off-the-shelf systems, but they're, like, over two grand. Obviously,"—his gaze surveyed the store around him—"I don't have that kind of cash."

She ignored his self-deprecating dig, bit her lower lip, then offered, "My friend Cee is pretty good with computer stuff. Maybe she could help."

"Really? Oh man, that would be so awesome. But, uh . . . I really can't pay her a lot, you know. I mean, some maybe. But not, like, hundreds of dollars or anything."

"Yeah, um, I don't think that'll be a problem," she said. "Cee doesn't seem to worry much about money." She turned and was out the door, the cold and dirty wind again gusting in.

"Bye-bye" he said, but she was already on the sidewalk. "Thanks."

Behind him, the band was in a buoyant groove. Bing bounced in time, as a wide-eyed Satchmo scatted and mugged, "Arrivadoochee!"

Celine finessed her silver Camry into the tight carport and climbed the stairs leading to the townhouse that she and Darla shared. Darla's bike was not in its usual spot, but Celine expected her home soon from the post office. She knew Darla would probably only stay a few moments before leaving for her night job, tending bar at LaFontaine.

She trudged heavily up the stairs, threw her messenger bag onto the dining room table and herself onto the couch. She gazed out over the nightscape of downtown Rellman, a hilltop view that she felt justified the inflated price she'd paid for the property. *It was definitely worth it,* she assured herself nightly.

Celine went to the bedroom and slowly changed out of her work clothes, hanging up her gabardine slacks meticulously, mindful of the crease. She casually sniffed the armpits of her oxford shirt and hung it up too. *I can get one more day out of this,* she thought. She slipped into her shorts and tank top, and slowly picked up clothes from the floor that Darla had hastily strewn about after arriving home from the bar early this morning, before she'd collapsed into bed. She carefully turned Darla's discarded T-shirt right-side-out, pitched her underwear and tights into the clothes hamper, hung up a fleece jacket, and considered whether a rayon blouse really deserved to go into the dry-cleaning bag. *Yes, absolutely.*

Darla was always hungry after a day of lugging the mail. *I should try to whip up a little food before she gets home,* thought Celine. Having food on the table might also go a long way toward patching things up from their tiff this morning.

Celine preferred to work alone in the kitchen, remembering the last few painful times she'd tried to share the space with her girlfriend. Once while attempting to make spaghetti squash, she was having trouble cutting the tough gourd in half and quickly resorted to looking up the proper technique on the internet. She was about to dive in, as it were, scoring the squash around its longitudinal axis, then halving it carefully with the big butcher's knife, scraping out the seeds, seasoning the two halves with olive oil and salt and pepper, then placing the squash—cut face down!—onto a baking pan, when Darla walked in. "Here's how you do it," Darla had said, grabbing the knife abruptly from Celine's hand and proceeding to perform all the steps Celine had just proudly learned but didn't have a chance to show off.

Darla did not consciously intend disrespect, but her single-mindedness tended to leave others in its wake. She was unrelenting in her criticism of others, not in the superficial things like looks or fashion or money, but more biting commentary on their intelligence, work ethic, attention to detail, and overall fitness for living. "A waste of oxygen" was her favorite expression to describe both her coworkers and the postal patrons on her route. Her customers at LaFontaine were no less vulnerable to her sneering mockery. Darla keenly observed the behaviors of her regulars from behind the bar, silently poking fun at their attempts to be hip, funny, or desirable. These gibes she regularly shared with Celine, who went along with the joke, sometimes laughing a little too loudly, depending on how much merlot she'd had. Still, the invectives had always made Celine feel uncomfortable, fetching up all the doubts and uncertainties she harbored within herself.

Celine heard the clatter and hum of the garage door below, followed by Darla's thunderous stride as she bounded up the stairs two at a time. She was in a hurry.

"Hey, lady. What's shakin'?" She kissed Celine on the forehead. She was a head taller than Celine.

"Hey, sugar." Celine moved in for a quick hug. "I'm making pasta. Mmm, good."

"Sorry, no time." Darla moved quickly about the townhouse. "Gotta jet down to the bar, special event tonight, have to open, lots of prep. I'll grab something on the way or maybe eat there, huh? Plenty of hors d'oeuvres, I'll bet."

Celine hid her disappointment and her relief. She would once again be dining alone in front of an old movie on TV. "What's the gig?"

"Going away party for some geezer, I think. Hasta la vista, loser!" They both laughed. Darla whisked into the bedroom and peeled out of her postal uniform, which she cast about the room in all different directions. She emerged naked from the bedroom and zipped past Celine heading for the bathroom.

Celine heard the shower running. "Hey, speaking of losers," Darla yelled, "I was in that little throwback of a business in Morley today, the video store, you know the one? The guy looks like he's up to his ass in little plastic boxes with no way to keep things straight. And get this: he's actually using this big ledger to check the rentals in and out. Geesh! He looks like freaking Bob Cratchit! All he needs is a quill." Darla had become fond of making references to Dickens ever since Celine had dragged her to see a production of *A Christmas Carol* last December, a work she'd not previously even heard of. "So anyway, I sort of casually mentioned that my very good friend—meaning you!—is a real computer genius, and perhaps she'd maybe like to help him get organized."

"Whoa, whoa! Now hold on a minute." Celine came into the bathroom and sat on the commode.

"No, now you 'whoa, whoa' a minute!" she yelled over the sound of the running water. "Weren't you just saying how you're kinda bored at the office, how you'd like to turn your creative talents into some extra money, and that among your most marketable talents, besides your absolute and unflinching tolerance for assholes, were your mad computer skills?"

"Uh, I believe that was *your* idea, which I never actually agreed to. And besides, I actually like my job. I also like being away from it for sixteen hours a day. I'm not looking for more things to occupy my time. Besides, who is this guy? And who the hell runs a video store anymore? Is he some funny-smelling old fart who shuffles around in a grimy yellow T-shirt with, like, sweat stains and holes, making *Godfather* quotes all day?"

"The last part, maybe. More of a young fart. But otherwise he seems OK. Not a perv or anything, at least not an obvious perv."

Celine stared at the fluttering shower curtain with resignation. It was pointless to argue. Darla's true motive for pushing this notion remained opaque, but once decided, she knew that if she did not agree to meet with this guy, Darla would be relentless, hound her daily, and bring it up again at every opportunity.

"So what's this place called again?"

Darla stepped out of the shower and wrapped herself in a towel. A headband encircled her explosive hair. "Videosomething?"

"Gee, that's helpful! I'll look it up after din—I mean, while you're at work, and maybe stop by tomorrow on the way home."

"Good! Maybe someday you can liberate yourself from that funky-ass job of yours, escorting old crones into the afterlife."

"Technically, a crone is an old lady. I do guide some old men into the light as well, so give me some credit please. And not everyone on Social Security is old."

"Yeah, some of them are 'disabled.'" She made a twisted face and mock claw hands and shook uncontrollably. Celine shook her head slowly in disgust. She left Darla standing in the steamy bathroom, cackling loudly behind her.

NEUTRAL, NO BRAKES

The good fortune cat grinned down at Celine from the kitchen wall as the pot came to a boil. She swirled an enormous cast iron skillet of garlic bits browning in butter and olive oil, the aroma hanging heavily in the air. Darla had just dashed out to work, hair still wet, her black-and-white server outfit hastily thrown on. Celine had waved to her wistfully as she ran down the stairs. *What a mess. But she looks amazing, as usual!*

The plastic cat's tail swung back and forth, back and forth, the big clockface taking up most of her chubby belly. *Seven thirty sharp. Celine Johnson, once again, dines alone,* she thought, feeling sorry for herself, but finding solace in her two favorite pastimes: cooking and obsessing over Darla.

She sulked silently as she ground a generous heap of black pepper into the skillet, followed by sea salt, parsley, basil, and flaked red peppers. She added her secret ingredient—a handful of pine nuts—and brought it back to a hot sizzle as they turned crispy brown.

Another night of surfing the net, flipping channels, and stuffing her face awaited her. *This feels a lot like living alone again.* She used to love solo life, had done it for years, loved the delicious freedom to do whatever she wanted whenever she wanted, not having to answer to anyone's needs but her own. But this was worse. *Now, I'm here alone, like a captive, joined at the hip to this wild, reckless, thoughtless beast!*

She scooped into the skillet a mound of chopped cherry tomatoes. They sputtered and popped, sending little droplets of hot oil every which way, as she poured the package of fusilli into the now-boiling water. Fusilli always reminded her of Darla's wild head of hair, a jumbled mass of corkscrews jutting in all different directions.

She thought of their fight early this morning. Darla had come home fuming at her boss, convinced that he was a son of a bitch and wanting to talk about it at three in the morning. Celine woke up groggily, knowing she would have to be at the Social Security office by seven forty-five. His egregious transgression was to suggest instituting a "shared tips" policy for the bar employees. He saw this as a fair way to even out the take between early and late shifts, weekends and weekdays, explaining it was unfair to those who couldn't work graveyard to be docked on tips because of kid duties.

But Darla called him a fascist, accusing him of stealing from the hardest working people (like herself) to support the weaker, lazier, and more surly staff members who garnered only measly tips from customers.

"Surly?" She'd chuckled into her pillow, still half-asleep. "*You* think *other* people are surly?" This was not a good idea.

"What do you mean?" she'd asked darkly. "I am very nice to my customers. What exactly would make you think otherwise?" Celine did not answer but stared at the wall, pretending to have fallen back asleep.

Darla was hard on people; she thought them stupid, mean, and pretentious. But at the bar, she was charming and engaging. She fancied herself the perfect host. Celine could attest to this from the few occasions she had come to LaFontaine to visit her friend. "It only makes good sense, financially speaking," Darla would say. Off the clock, she would lay into humanity with teeth bared, having mentally cataloged their many shortcomings, unloading her cool observations onto Celine. But when she wanted to, she could make a person feel smart, amusing, and special, as if they were the only other person in the room. *Did she play that trick on me? Oh yes. Yes, she did.* As proof of her theory, Darla always came home with a thick wad of tip money, which she eagerly counted at the dining room table before slipping between the sheets with Celine.

A hard pang of longing mixed with pure hunger simultaneously hit her in the gut as she stirred the pasta. Her mind strayed to their conversation in the bathroom and her heartless mocking pantomime. If Darla could be so unforgiving of strangers, well-meaning souls who meant her no harm, she wondered what Darla really must think of *her*. Celine was definitely the nerdy one, the bookworm, who'd held the steady job for years while Darla bounced from gig to gig and never seemed to mind, always emerging afresh. Darla's face hovered before her in the steamy mist. *Aren't I clever enough for you? Hip enough? Funny enough? And in bed? Am I pretty enough? Bold enough? Butch enough?*

Celine recalled an expression her dad might have used: Darla had been "around the block." There was no denying it; she had shacked up with countless other dykes around town. Celine was just the latest in Darla's long parade of hookups. *How long can this last?* she wondered. *Funny, they all had steady jobs and nice digs, like me.* Were they destined to eventually endure the "lesbian bed death" their crowd constantly joked about? If that ever happened, she was convinced, it would be *Poof! No more Darla!*

Celine tossed the pasta in the skillet and transferred the mix into a blue ceramic bowl. She lugged the heavy bowl and a bottle of dry Riesling to the dining room table, pouring herself a glass and making room on the table for her laptop. She added a jar of marinated artichoke hearts, drained but still with plenty of liquid from the jar, and finished it off with freshly grated Parmigiano Reggiano.

"Voilà! Let's eat." *Oh shit, now I'm talking to myself. I am so doomed!*

7. NIC ARRIVES

Richard sat in the '99 Impreza, impatiently drumming the wheel. The overhead sun poured into an urban canyon formed by two glass-clad high-rises on either side of the street, concentrating its heat and creating a surreal yellow glow. His dashboard hula girl received enough solar rays to wiggle wildly without pause. A weak breeze moved through the canyon. The dusty street trees trembled listlessly in response, as Richard's thoughts were tossed and blown by the whirlwind in his head. He eagerly anticipated his special delivery from Indiana.

He'd played the scene over and over in his mind for weeks, concentrating on Nic, wishing he could make him appear by sheer force of will. Would he look like his picture on the pen pal site? Younger, older, somewhere in between? Would he be beaten down and drawn from months behind bars, or bright-eyed and healthy? What would he be wearing? *What do they give ex-cons to wear, anyway?*

Richard examined his face in the rearview mirror, saw the years reflected in the leathery countenance staring back at him. He gave a tug here and pull there, but gravity and attrition would not have any of it as he sagged back to his old self. He fumbled in the pocket of his silk aloha shirt for a Pall Mall and lit it, dangling the smoke out the window. He thought of Nic's photo and letters, and in the midst of his apprehension he suddenly felt sanguine. He just knew there was something special about Nic, felt it immediately when he first read his bio on the Get to Know an Inmate site last year:

Looking for a Pen Pal:

Hello, my name is Nic. I'm thirty-eight years old from Fayetteville, Arkansas. I have just a few months left on my sentence for doing something I truly am sorry for. What happened that night, in some crazy bar fight so many years ago, just isn't me now. My stint in jail has given me time to reexamine my life and try to be a better person.
I am loyal, trustworthy, kind, and a whole lotta fun to be with. I like country music (old style, not that modern stuff), a good book, and a good conversation. I'm into new things, but am also a traditionalist at heart. I am close to my family, though they sometimes don't understand me as well as I'd like them to.
I am looking for someone to open up to and really get to know. I'd like to get together after my release date, if that sounds interesting to you.

Thanks, Nic

At first they were both reticent, writing about daily life, family squabbles, or the occasional sporting event if it was big enough. But Richard quickly let his guard down and opened his soul, telling Nic about his youthful mistakes and misgivings, his faults and fears. To his surprise Nic did the same. Neither judged the other for it. Richard developed a loving closeness with Nic. He would click on his photo on the Inmate site while reading his letters aloud, staring at the boyish face with an open smile and deep sensitive eyes that penetrated the bottom of his soul.
 He checked his watch, flicked the cigarette to the street, and spotted Nic's bus, hissing and lurching as it pulled into its designated space in front of the terminal. He held his breath and scanned the crowd. People of all descriptions disembarked, but he had Nic's face and features cold memorized. *Not him, too old. Nope, not him. Oh, definitely not him. Not him either. Too young, too fat, too dumb.* Finally he recognized Nic, warily descending the steps and sauntering onto the sidewalk carrying a blue duffel bag. He was a little older and rougher than Richard remembered from his profile pics. But otherwise it was a near-perfect match. *He looks like one mean*

sonofabitch! But my God, he's frigging beautiful! Tall, square shoulders, narrow waist, deep-set eyes, strong jaw, thick sideburns, denim jacket, tight jeans, workman's boots. All swagger and danger and in your face but distant and unreachable.

He leaped out of the Subaru, waving eagerly.

Nic did not see or hear him but continued to look down the street past the crowd. In one cutting glance, he absorbed the scene, checked the perimeter, calculated the opportunities and traps, and assessed the people, movement, and interplay in this new territory.

"Nic! Nic Troxell. Woo-oo, Nic. Nicky!"

Nic startled at the sound of his name, squinting into the crowd. Richard waved again wildly, a mile-wide grin across his face. "It's so good to finally meet you," he said, running up to Nic and shaking him by both shoulders.

"Uh, hey. Richard, right?"

"None other."

"Great," he said with flat eyes and no enthusiasm.

"Right this way, young man. You're coming with me!" He swept giddily ahead to the waiting car and threw the passenger door wide open with a flourish. "Your limousine awaits," he said, tossing Nic's duffel bag onto the back seat.

As they pulled away, Richard glanced over at Nic. "You must be exhausted, being on that bus for how many days?" Nic stared out the window, slow to answer.

"It was the bomb," he said, starting to loosen up but still deadpan.

"Yeah, I'll bet." He laughed, tuning in to Nic's humorless humor. "So, see anything interesting on the way? Meet any fascinating people?"

He thought of the encounters with his sister's family and the scripture-quoting Grace Eileen that now seemed like an age ago. "Nope. Nothing and nobody."

"Too bad. Let me tell you, you won't see much more in this town. Everyone's got their chins in their chests and their shoulders hunched up around their ears. But they tend to grow on you. They're simple, well-meaning folks with very low expectations. There's no such thing as underdressed in Morley. It's strictly come as you are."

They drove past a Dairy Queen with cars lined up at the drive-through. A group of teens on the sidewalk waved large placards beckoning motorists to have their cars washed in support of the football team. Empty lots with enormous For Sale signs flew by. Tents and tarp structures stood clumped like mushrooms along the side of the road.

They had driven for about twenty minutes when the highway narrowed. A road sign read Thanks for Visiting, Come Again, indicating they'd left the confines of Morley proper, followed by another declaring Rellman 3 Miles. Now mature flowering cherry and big-leaf maple trees created a canopy of cool shade. Tall masonry walls protected homes on the other side from road dust, traffic noise, and unwanted entry into neighborhoods christened Jensen Estates, Aronmore Glen, and Deercreek Villas. Richard pulled off the main road and onto a well-manicured avenue, past an illuminated stone wall tastefully announcing their entrance to Briarcliff Downs. Resplendent tall oaks and elms lined the curved streets on both sides. The homes were substantial but understated, nothing garish. While some had expansive lawns, much of the thirsty, demanding sod had over time been replaced with easily satisfied, drought-resistant foliage. Uplighting cast a cheery glow onto the plantings and structures, providing a sense of security and place without being glaring about it. Richard pulled into a wide driveway just as the garage door was opening, seemingly of its own volition.

"Welcome home." Richard reached for Nic's duffel, but Nic grabbed at it first. "Is that all your gear? Don't worry, we'll get you outfitted tomorrow. I've got one quick cut and set in the morning, then we'll make a day of it. Lunch on me, then a little shopping at Rellman Square. Later I'd love to introduce you around, if you're not exhausted by then. Just throw your bag anywhere, dear. Let me show you my humble home."

Nic followed Richard into the hallway. On every wall were displayed framed photographs of Richard as a younger man. Some showed him laughing and drinking at festive occasions. In others, he wore kitschy theatrical garb acting a scene or in dance costumes in contorted postures reminiscent of Greek statuary.

"This you?" Nic laughed.

"In the flesh! Or at least, it *was* me. Now, *this* is me." He motioned to himself. "And the flesh, alas, is weak." He stopped in front of one portrait in particular, a black-and-white photo that had been hand colored in the manner of an old book illustration. Richard wore green tights and a short green tunic, sporting a pointed Robin Hood hat with a feather. "It was the Golden Age, my boy, the Golden Age. Let me tell you, we worked our asses off!"

"And this?" He pointed to another snapshot with Richard and another man standing abreast, arms around each other's shoulders in obvious camaraderie. He'd noticed the same man in several other photos.

"That's Dale," he said quietly, pausing the tour. "He was a very good friend. He's passed on now." He stood in silent reverie but felt the festive mood slipping away and quickly jumped to another frame. "And that's Allen and Chet. You'll meet them tomorrow. The rest of these queens are mostly dead now, or worse."

"OK, sure."

Richard slipped off his shoes and hinted for Nic to do the same. They silently padded on the soft, pristine white carpet, across the living room, and through a narrow door on the far side leading to a smaller study. Floor-to-ceiling bookcases lined three walls, a picture window taking up most of the fourth. By the window overlooking the skillfully curated yard stood a white Steinway baby grand, and in the crook of the piano was a tall birdcage. Inside was perched a white pigeon.

"Let me introduce you to your other roommate." Richard offered his finger through the already open door and the bird gamely hopped on. "This is Baby Bird. Baby Bird, meet Nic. Nic, Baby Bird." Richard petted the bird gently. "He also answers to B Squared, or Baby. Occasionally Mr. Bird if he's misbehaving, or mostly just Birdy."

Nic immediately noticed the pigeon wore a colorful tie-dyed vest.

"What the f . . . what's that?"

"Oh, that's his flight suit. Don't you love it?" He described at length how Birdy enjoyed wearing the stretchy harness, which doubled as a bird diaper for playing inside the house, with a leash hook in the back for outside. "Hmm, he's been in it for a couple of hours now. He's probably ready to be changed." Nic grimaced, trying to hide his repulsion at the idea of a bird wearing a diaper, let alone changing one, but said nothing.

Richard continued the tour of his home, a comfortable and well-appointed split-level ranch. Despite the white-and-gold theme repeated throughout the house, it was surprisingly tasteful.

"And here's *your* room. Now, as you can see, I've decorated it in the manner that I like, but if there's anything, anything at all, that you want to change or get rid of, just toss it into the hallway. We can look at some things at the Square tomorrow, things more to your taste."

"No, no, this'll be fine." He sat elbows on knees at the edge of the bed. "Say, listen, I just wanted to say, I really appreciate your taking me in like this. I know you're going out on a limb for me, kind of sight unseen. Just so you know, I've been a royal fuckup my whole life. I can be a real asshole sometimes too. Maybe I still am, I don't know. But I'm trying to change. You're giving me a second chance to be a better person. So thanks. That's all I wanted to say."

"Listen, dear boy." Richard sat on the bed next to Nic at a decorous distance. "I'm not exactly a prize package myself, this old bag of bones. We all have a past, including me, and I've done a lot of things I'm not proud of. But this just feels right. Consider it my good deed for the day." He gave Nic a three-fingered Boy Scout salute. "Remember what I said in my letter? How we're all blessed? How it's never too late to become a good person? I really believe that. I do." He touched Nic's arm lightly, then stood up and gathered himself. "So settle in, relax. There's the shower. You'll find towels and soap right through there. Clean up, get comfortable, and we'll grab some dinner. Now, I've got a diaper to change!"

8. DUMPSTER

Geoff shoved open the heavy security door leading to the alley behind Dogg Life. The dusk-to-dawn lights were just snapping on, illuminating a light rain. The last of the daycare dogs had been picked up by their owners. Only the sad boarders remained, fed and settled in for the night but still missing their humans. With two hands, Geoff dragged a large black garbage bag through the door and leaned it against the dumpster. He flipped open the lid and, without looking, pitched the bag in.

"Oowww! Fuuuuck!" he heard as the bag thudded and rolled to the floor of the bin. Geoff peered cautiously over the rim and saw a gray shape thrash and wobble, its moaning protests echoing in the metal container. The shape righted itself, then nestled softly into the mass of cardboard, food cartons, drink cups, and mixed refuse.

"Shit!" Geoff blurted out, recoiling in shock with such force his feet rose clean off the cement pad. "Hey, dude! What the hell are you doing in there?" In the amber light, he saw the gray shape move again and pulled back, fearing it would lunge at him. But the shape did not emerge from the bin and made only rustling sounds.

"You can't be in there. You hear me?" No answer. "Get the fuck outta there. I'm calling the cops, like, right now!" He fumbled for his phone. "Better be gone by the time they show up!"

But he knew this was an empty threat, and the shape knew it too, knew the Morley cops would be poky in their response, if they came at all. Only if you were fleeing from a fiery-eyed, machete-wielding lunatic would they flip on lights and sirens and come running like the cavalry. With this realization, Geoff slowly, deliberately inched back toward the open door, keeping an eye on the bin while feeling inside the jamb and grabbing the cool, rough end of a three-foot galvanized pipe he kept there for occasions such as this—an occasion that, until now, had never happened. He felt the heft of the pipe in his hand, and took a few practice swings in the air to test the strength of his grip. Emboldened, he swung the pipe hard with both hands against the side of the bin, leaving a dent and causing a deafening metallic boom, followed by a feeble moan from within. Hearing no further sound, he delivered several more blows to the corners of the bin, discovering the edges made a much more disturbing clang. The boarding dogs responded with a chorus of barks and howls.

The shape now spoke, his voice echoing inside its steel confines. "All right, all right, man. Chill! I'm just trying to find something to eat."

"That's a lie. You were sleeping in there. Probably shooting up too." He struck the metal container several more times. "Come on! Out!" he yelled, then realized he had not yet called the police as he'd promised. He hit 9-1-1 on speed dial and a mechanical voice responded.

"Please do not hang up. You have reached the City of Morley 9-1-1 Emergency Line. Please state if your emergency requires police, fire, or medical response."

"Police!"

"Please stay on the line."

While he waited for a human dispatcher to come on, for caution's sake he moved farther into the alley, phone in one hand, pipe in the other, eyes locked on his quarry, then, like a retreating prizefighter, trotted briskly in reverse toward the access road. He put a full fifty yards between himself and the shape, stopping once he reached the point where he could intercept the cops when they arrived.

"9-1-1. What is your emergency?"

He gave his name and location, and relayed the chilling events leading to the call.

A homeless guy, he explained, jumped out from behind a dumpster, brandishing some kind of weapon, a knife maybe, demanding he "give me all your money, mothafucka!" The guy took a swing at him, he went on, and it was all he could do to escape. Yes, he was still at the scene. Yes, he was a safe distance. No, he wasn't hurt, just pretty shook up. No, he hadn't gotten a good look at him, but, he could have been a white guy, skinny, average height, wearing a gray hoodie, acting all crazy, like he was on meth, or maybe just a whack job.

"Describe yourself please, so the officers know who's who when they arrive."

"Me? I'm kind of a short stocky guy. I'm wearing tan slacks and a blue polo shirt with a Dogg Life logo on the front."

"Stay on the line, sir. A police unit is on its way. Please stay clear of the individual. Do not try to confront or subdue him. Are you at a safe distance?"

"Yes, I'm OK." He took a breath, relieved that help would be there soon. "Wait, shit, there he goes!"

Geoff watched the gray shape hop out of the trash bin in one agile move, then tear off down the alley. Geoff instinctively pursued at a dead run, hearing but not obeying the voice on the phone imploring him to stay put. He flew past the dumpster, making a wide arc around it should anyone be hiding behind it. But there was no one in any direction up or down the alley. The shape had dematerialized.

Geoff walked back to the access road dejected. The cops showed up with lights flashing in exactly eight minutes according to his phone. By then, there was nothing for them to do or much to talk about. The young female officer took his statement, jotting down in her little notebook the same information he had given the dispatcher. Geoff had been careful to stash his length of pipe back behind the door before their arrival. He stuck to his story about being attacked, even embellishing the attacker's menacing persona and the terror he felt.

"These guys are everywhere now. I saw a whole camp of them down the trail there along the riverbank," he said, pointing into the underbrush. "They're like rats! Can't you guys go down and clear them the hell outta there, maybe break some heads? This is getting ridiculous."

She looked at him silently for a moment. "Sir, we can't go around 'breaking heads,' as you put it. Unless we catch someone in the act of committing a crime, there's not much we *can* do." She perfunctorily handed him a business card with her contact information, in case he thought of anything else or if the guy came back, thanked him coolly, and went back to the cruiser to confer with her partner. *She looks pissed*, he thought, deciding not to bring up the fact that camping along the river was illegal and therefore already a crime. She might think he was telling her how to do her job or, worse, to just *do* her job.

The police cruiser crept slowly down the alley, its searchlight scanning the dark spaces, the officers within jostled violently as tires rolled in and out of cavernous potholes. It stopped briefly, inched forward, scanned the perimeter, stopped once more, then, with tires kicking up gravel, turned out onto the main highway.

Geoff felt spent. He made his way back to the open door. A chill had fallen during the chaotic incident. In his excitement he had not realized his shirt was cold and wet. Tiny raindrops ran down his neck; his hair was dripping. With a shudder, he scurried into the dark, heavy warmth of the Dogg Life storage room, and slammed the door behind him.

At the far end of the alley, a gray shape ducked behind a cinder-block outbuilding and made itself small, merging in the twilight with its colorless surroundings. Hearing the cruiser take off, it glided briskly along the buildings and down a gully, hopped a low-sagging chain-link fence, stepped through a muck-filled puddle, then pushed into the thick underbrush toward the riverbank. Signs of habitation began to appear. In a tiny clearing stood a small pup tent, cinched with twine to the bushes nearby and covered with a brown poly tarp. A large black trash bag sat perched atop a handicap walker, filled to bursting with aluminum cans and plastic bottles. Around the tent was strewn all manner of refuse of unclear utility—a corroded shopping cart with a missing wheel, a kid's yellow roll-around suitcase caked with mud, a rusting bicycle frame, several partly dismantled wooden pallets, an assortment of unmated men's and women's shoes, and the discarded remnants of Happy Meal containers and upturned drink cups with straws jutting out the top.

The shape bent over to pull back the flap of the tent, first looking in, around, and behind it, then listening intently for nearby intruders and, hearing only the eddies at the river's edge and its own heartbeat, ducked inside.

9. CELINE AND JEREMY HIT IT OFF

Celine peered over the computer screen at her stand-up workstation and out into the waiting room. The crowd had thinned considerably since this morning. She clicked the button to advance the red LED numbers on the display above her and shot a quick glance at the wall clock—4:40 p.m. This would be her last appointment.

"Number one sixty-seven. One sixty-seven, please. One. Six. Seven." All eyes in the room looked at their little paper slips. Celine, seeing no response, had already advanced the counter to one sixty-eight when a young man with a thin mustache, white button-down shirt, and gray slacks shot up from his seat.

"One six seven. Here. Here." He waved his hand busily as he escorted two women, stark and imposing in voluminous black garments, to the counter, one moving with the grace and carriage of a younger woman, the other slower, stiffer, more guarded.

"Hello. My name is Celine. How may I help you folks today?"

"I am Hassan. Call me Pete. This my wife and my mother. I am try to get benefits for my mother. She very ill. Has diabetes, heart. Very sick."

Both wife and mother wore full cover, with only narrow slits allowing dark eyes to see into the new world they had recently inhabited. Neither looked at Celine nor asked or answered any question. All comments were directed in Arabic to the well-dressed young man nervously doing his best to fulfill his roles of steadfast son, husband, and interpreter.

Celine listened patiently and attentively as Hassan recounted their story—he spoke adequate English—detailing the family's long journey to the US. The war in Afghanistan, their cooperation with US forces, a hasty escape across the Pakistani border, their dismal life in a refugee camp. To show concern, Celine nodded as he spoke, directly addressing the two women. "Oh my, what a harrowing story." She had a hunch they spoke more English than they appeared to.

"How old are you?" she inquired of the older woman, loudly and slowly to make up for the language difference.

"Not sure," answered the son, jumping in. Repeating the question in Arabic and not hearing an answer, he replied "Maybe sixty, sixty-five."

"Sixty-three," the older woman offered in heavily accented English.

"She refugee," said the son. "Things very bad Afghanistan. She work for US Embassy. She clean Embassy before she sick."

"Perfect! You may indeed be eligible." She explained that immigrants from Iraq or Afghanistan who had been employed by the US government may be eligible for Social Security benefits.

"Oh yes, thank you."

Celine went on to describe the benefits available and the process for applying online, asking if they needed her help to complete the forms there in the office.

"Oh no." He smiled, waving his hand. "I take care of. I understand."

"Very good." The mother would need some proof of immigration status, Celine explained, and would be issued a Social Security number once she was in the system. She handed the young man an FAQ sheet and Quik Guide for accessing the website. He studied the sheets briefly, handing them to his wife.

Believing she had addressed all of their concerns thoroughly and compassionately, Celine smiled at the small family group with an air of finality. She gathered together some additional pamphlets, forms, and how-to sheets and slid them into a light blue glossy folder. Her eyes guided them toward the door.

Pete Hassan got the message. He smiled with a secret pride, having again conquered the arcane labyrinth of government services as he'd so often been called upon to do since his family's immigration. He was especially proud of knowing how to speak to Americans and negotiate with them. He had demonstrated those skills today. Things had worked out well.

Nevertheless, the two women fervently questioned him with puzzled looks, animated movements, and pressured speech. He held up his hands, shushing and reassuring them that he had gathered all the needed information and knew how to proceed next. He steered them to the exit even as they continued to interrogate him and stare back at Celine. He rushed them out by the elbows, nearly pushing them into the closed door, then turned and raised a friendly hand of farewell to Celine, who smiled and waved back.

Celine again glanced up at the clock—4:56 p.m., a time she could justifiably close her window and prepare to leave for the day. She shut down her computer, tightened the cap on her water bottle, and stuck it in her messenger bag, checking that she also had her cell phone, keys, wallet, cash money, lunchtime reading (a paperback copy of *The Help*), coat, sunglasses, and hat.

She was out the rear entrance and halfway through the employee lot when she remembered her promise to Darla to contact her new friend in Morley to help him with his inventory problem. She still couldn't figure why Darla wanted to get involved with this person, though taking it at face value—always safest, since she did not have an ounce of guile—this was just Darla encouraging Celine to develop her computer consulting business, which she appreciated.

To prepare, Celine had visited the store's website the previous night. If the website was any indication—whew boy, was it neglected. It was barely one page, no links, only a few stock images with a cursory description of the store and location.

She plotted the route to Videodrome on her phone, which forced her to turn west out of the driveway toward Morley instead of east. Until tonight she had successfully avoided Morley by taking the freeway around it or sticking to destinations in the opposite direction. She'd definitely never ventured past Florida Avenue.

Now she headed due west along San Sebastian Parkway, staring directly into a low setting sun. Even wearing shades, she had to squint and dodge behind her visor to make out the traffic signals, cars, and pedestrians. As she drove through the intersection of

Florida and San Sebastian, Rellman's vibrant, neatly trimmed trademark prosperity slowly dissipated. Buildings became increasingly sparse and low profile. The high-end pet food stores, pho restaurants, and dress boutiques were soon supplanted by tire stores, used car lots, and resale shops. Gray figures in hoodies wandered the street or lounged about in abandoned lots where once-viable businesses operated.

Having driven only a couple of miles but surely, she felt, into a distant and desolate country, Celine's map showed her closing in on Videodrome. Apprehension crept over her. "The destination is on your left," said the smooth robotic voice from her phone. She looked up from her map and was surprised to see a tidy L-shaped street-level mall nestled into a corner lot at San Sebastian and Copley Drive. It was a true anomaly, an oasis of enterprise and cleanliness amid a desert of indolence and decay. The lot was spic and span, not fancy but neat and orderly. Someone had actually bothered to water the trees, weed the sidewalk strips and planter beds, pick up garbage, repaint the parking lines, and artfully cover over the graffiti so that it was barely detectable. A colorful plastic sign rose overhead, advertising the mall's various businesses: ReddyCare Urgent Care Clinic, Burger Basket, Pickwick's Paperback Shack, Dogg Life Daycare and Boarding, Mr. Richard's Cuts and Color, and, there in the corner anchoring the mall, Videodrome.

Old movie posters lined the windows of the video business: *My Dinner with Andre, Crimes and Misdemeanors, Manon of the Spring, Brazil,* and others. Their crinkled edges and occasional adherent fly corpse suggested they had not been changed for some time. A small neon Open sign shone brightly.

Celine parked her Camry and entered, walking past the rack of free local newspapers, event flyers, and advertisements, winding her way around shelves touting New Arrivals, New Releases, and Staff's Choice.

Celine spotted a tall young man at the counter she assumed was Jeremy, but she decided to browse the shelves first before approaching him. She wandered through the Documentary section, peeking between the shelves to get a better look at him. *Sid and Nancy* played on the big screen just behind him, the box propped up to let people know what they were watching. The store was moderately busy. As he worked the line of customers, Jeremy had to run several times behind the stacks to retrieve videos for them. Celine eyed him cautiously, as was her custom, even planning an escape route if necessity dictated, but she decided to stay. He seemed to her a kind soul—a little harried but earnest, friendly, and quick to laugh.

As she waited for the commotion to die down, out of boredom as much as curiosity she studied the Documentary shelves, her head tilted to the right to read the titles. Most of them she had never heard of. She pulled the box for *49 Up* and read the notes: a British documentary series chronicling the lives of twenty children, their growth and maturation every seven years. *Looks interesting.* Before Jeremy finished with his last customer, her attention was drawn to another provocative title: *Forbidden Love: The Unashamed Stories of Lesbian Lives.* On the cover were two conservatively dressed women circa 1950s in an affectionate caress. She giggled to herself, looking over her shoulder before pulling out the box. *Hah! I have got to get this one for Darla!*

The last customer cleared out. Having concluded Jeremy was all right, she casually moved toward the counter with her movie choices.

"Hey!"

"Hey," he responded with an affable smile. "Find something good?" She handed her DVD cases to him. "Oh, these are great! I think you'll really like these."

Wanting to avoid an uncomfortable conversation about *Forbidden Love*, she quickly commented on the other film. "Interesting concept, following people from childhood into adulthood."

"Yeah, these are great vignettes. *49* is a good one to start with." He read the back of the box. "He does flashbacks from all the previous episodes. Very surprising, poignant at times."

"Sounds good."

"Spoiler alert," he said in mock secrecy, "none of them gets exactly what they expected out of life. In the end, though, everyone seems OK with the lives they've been given, the good with the bad."

"Just like in real life, I suppose."

"Well, technically it is real life, I suppose."

"Yes, I suppose it is."

He disappeared behind the stacks and in a moment emerged

with her DVDs in generic white cases.

"Are you a member? I don't remember seeing you in the store before."

"No, I—I guess I've got to sign up or something?"

"Sure, no worries. Driver's license, please." She handed it to him. "Celine. That's a pretty name. Goddess of the moon." He pulled a fresh five-by-eight-inch card from the small file box on the counter and started writing.

"Different spelling. I hate it, actually. My friends call me CJ or just Cee."

"Nice to meet you, Cee." They shook. "Welcome to Videodrome. I'm Jeremy."

"Um, I know, actually."

"Really?"

"Yeah, my friend told me about your store."

"Oh, yeah? Cool."

"And also about your, um, inventory issues." She pointed delicately to the file card. "Said I should stop by, thought maybe I could help, so I did."

"Sure, sure, now I remember. You must be Skornik's friend. Sorry, I don't know her first name, just Skornik. She's the mail person, uh, lady . . . Sorry, I mean mail carrier."

"Yeah, that's right. Her name's Darla."

"Darla. OK, then! Please thank Darla for me, and thank you. I could really use some help."

He recounted briefly the saga of Poor Old Bob, Videodrome's original owner, and his computer whiz nephew Tyler, how they first tackled the knotty inventory problem, their homegrown victory; followed by halcyon days when everything seemed to be working; then the inexorable corruption of the program—the slowing, the seizing, the crashing, the deaths (Bob's and the program's), the exasperation (Jeremy's), and finally the resignation to using the sad paper cards that lay before him.

She listened intently and waited for him to finish his tale. "Wow. Does this program still exist?"

"Somewhere in there." He waved his hands over the computer screen.

"Better let me see what's going on."

"Are you sure you don't mind?"

"Not at all. That's why I'm here. Can I drop my bag somewhere?"

He invited her around the counter and set her up at the keyboard. She dove in. "Passcode?"

"oldbobsfolly. One word, no caps. I had to change it to something I'd remember." He stood over her shoulder as she accessed the program, delving into white-on-black screens Jeremy had never seen before. As her eyes darted across the screen, she did not use the mouse, only keystrokes and the touch pad.

A customer came through the door with a question about a video, then another. "Go on, you can take care of them." She playfully shooed him away. "Go, go. I'm fine, really."

It was a busy Friday evening. Many patrons came and went, and Celine watched Jeremy dutifully attend to them with the same earnest enthusiasm he had demonstrated earlier.

Sid and Nancy was concluding. Jeremy spoke in a feigned British accent in unison with Sid Vicious. "'One more thing. Where can I get a pizza?'"

"Huh?" Celine said, looking up from her screen.

He popped out the disc. "I said how's it going over there?" She gave him a thumbs-up and went back to work. "You'll love this one." he said. "I do, at least." He slid in *Valley of the Dolls*.

Jeremy waited on customers and otherwise busied himself in between. He stopped paying much attention to Celine, though he could hear her fingers deftly clicking through whatever it was she was doing. She seemed almost invisible now, comfortably working away at the counter as if she had always been there. She'd set up her little work area, with her water bottle and a big bag of malted milk balls she had snagged from the counter rack, and felt quite cozy. She had already rebooted Tyler's old program, opened its guts, peered behind the cobwebs and dust bunnies, blown away the debris, and got it whirring again. Occasionally she would ask him a question about titles or genres, his policy on late fees, or other preferences he might have for running the store.

While she worked, she eavesdropped on Jeremy, clandestinely eyeing him as he offered customers his reviews and recommendations. She was impressed by his broad and deep knowledge of film, which he displayed in an unassuming, even childlike way. He was obviously fascinated by this archive of human experience the species had accumulated for itself and he wanted the world to join him on his adventure through it.

While she worked, Celine's attention was occasionally drawn to the melodramatic scenes in the film playing overhead: Neely's drug-fueled freak out, Tony's dire diagnosis, Jennifer's suicide, and Anne's ultimate disillusionment. She loved the over-the-top performances, the ham-handed moralizing, and the characters' frail but valiant attempts to find meaning and redemption.

It was now five minutes of ten, the film was in credits, and Jeremy started his routine for closing up shop. The Open sign was switched off, storefront lights extinguished, and cash drawer emptied. One last customer scurried in right before ten o'clock to drop off a video and Jeremy welcomed him in. "Just made it," he joked. He bid the patron good-night and locked the front door, then straightened up the free newspapers by the door and spot-checked the shelves for any stray titles.

"Hey, let me show you what I've done here," she called out, finally noticing the store was closed.

"Sure, that would be great. Is this a good time?"

"I've actually been done for a while now, since right around the time Helen's wig came off."

"Hmm?"

She pointed at the movie.

"Oh, right, yeah."

"Great film, by the way."

"Oh God, did you really like it?" he asked, genuinely moved, his hands over his heart. "It's a little quirky."

"In a good way. A little dated, but . . . anyway."

"Anyway, so whatcha got?"

He leaned over Celine's chair as she guided him through the newly buffed program. She first demoed its basic functions: title inventory, current rentals, pending charges, late fees, customer profiles. "I used the original guts, just tweaked a few things. Your young programmer—what's his name, Tyler?—he did a really good job. But your files were hopelessly corrupted. I cleaned them all up," she said cheerily.

To demonstrate other functionalities, she registered her own personal data to create a new customer file, then rented the two DVDs to herself, paid the store the eight-dollar rental fee on her credit card, and generated a receipt listing the titles and due dates, which she slipped into her bag with the two jewel cases.

"Oh my God, that is truly awesome."

"Let's keep our expectations real. It may need a few minor changes. I'll need to see if I can break it."

"Hmm, I think I understand what you just said." They laughed.

"In other words, hang on to your card system for a few days."

"OK. Feel free to come by anytime. So"—he winced—"what do I owe you?"

She thought about it, remembering what Darla had repeatedly told her: *A gig is no gig if you don't get paid.* She dreaded what Darla might say if she ever learned she hadn't charged him for her work.

"I don't know. What's it worth to you?"

"Man, I have no clue, something in the hundreds would be fair. I probably should have asked before you started."

"Well, let's see, five hours give or take, at double minimum wage, 'cause I'm worth it, damn it! Let's call it a hundred bucks between friends."

"It's a deal, friend." They shook hands. "But is that really enough? I don't think so."

"Sure, it was fun, a nice break, plus I enjoyed watching the interplay."

"That's really generous of you. Say, how about a hundred bucks, plus I comp you the two videos, plus we go grab a beer on me."

"No, no, no, I'm happy to patronize your store. Besides, I haven't figured out how to do refunds yet!" They again laughed.

"OK. And about that beer?"

"Boy, I could really use one, trust me, but I've got an early morning. Gotta get home. Rain check, though?"

"Rain check for sure!"

As Jeremy moved toward the door and shut off the last of the store lights, she gathered her things into her messenger bag. The store was now completely dark.

"Oh, sorry. Can you see all right?"

"Sure, I'm fine." Following his voice, she felt her way toward the front of the darkened store but bumped into him anyway, and they became momentarily entangled.

"Aaaaggh. Got me!" he said.

She was startled and pulled away abruptly. "Eek. Sorry."

They reorganized themselves and stepped out onto the sidewalk. Jeremy locked up, and they walked slowly to her car. The night air was cold against her neck. She pulled up her collar to shelter from the chill. "I'll stop by in a couple of days to fiddle with things. Let me know how it goes."

"Will do."

"Here I am," she said, turning toward him. "Thanks again for a very interesting evening."

"My pleasure. I think you just saved my life."

"No problem."

They went to shake hands again but hesitated for a moment and, without thinking, hugged instead. It seemed to both like the right thing to do. Her face was up against his chest. He was much taller than she'd realized.

"Cee, make sure you thank Darla for me too, OK?"

The warmth she was feeling diminished slightly at the mention of Darla's name. "Sure," she promised, "I'll tell her." They broke, and she unlocked her car.

"I'm still going to grab that beer." He pointed to the tavern across the highway. "Sure you won't join me?"

"Next time."

"OK, then. Adios."

"See ya."

As she pulled onto San Sebastian Parkway heading east, she turned on the stereo and blasted it, then in the next moment shut it off. She wanted to think. *That was really fun,* she reflected. She'd loved getting behind the screen, tinkering with code, tracking down a problem and fixing it. She felt as if she had crossed over from a dark place into the light, emerging empowered, accomplished, and renewed. *I can do this!*

But there was another feeling, one she could not easily name, something familiar and warm, a contentment she had not felt for a long time, and certainly had never felt with Darla. She knew it was a feeling she wanted more of. She would be back.

10. RESTLESS BROODING

Geoff awoke from a restless sleep, head throbbing, gut knotted. A light drizzle fell on the roof above, its gentle runoff sounding a persistent *ploink ploink* in the downspout outside his window. In his mind he replayed his encounter with the hooded shape in the dumpster, disconcerted by the cool reception of the Morley cops, certain they had blown him off and pondering how he might have handled things differently.

The bed springs creaked as he rose. Geoff was scheduled to work the three p.m. shift and, as usual, had planned to chill out before facing the mass of yapping canines. But today he dreaded the thought of going in at all. The dangerous entity was still at large and likely to make another appearance. He decided to call in sick, figuring his excuse to Dan would be how awfully shook up he was.

He shuffled over to the microwave with a gummy taste in his mouth and zapped the cup of day-old coffee sitting on the counter. He'd fallen asleep in his work clothes again, something he'd done often lately, and smelled of rancid sweat and wet dog, but he did not have the energy to shower just yet. Instead he slipped out of his uniform and into his knockaround sweats, then settled down in front of his laptop. He scanned the local news feeds for stories about the homeless problem in Morley and, expectantly, about his near brush with disaster the previous night.

"Nothing. Not one word. Does anybody give a shit anymore?"

Unfulfilled, he clicked over to his contract bridge site, but none of his usual partners were awake yet. He'd have to wait till the sun rose in Taiwan for the first new game to start. He casually flipped through the days-old stack of mail that lay in an untidy pile on the table but gave up on this just as quickly.

A few minutes after his caffeine slug, his headache began to subside. His legs fidgeted. *Need some air,* he thought. *Gotta get outta here for a while.* He mustered the strength to wash his face, brush his teeth, and spread on a fresh layer of deodorant.

Geoff descended the creaky wooden staircase leading from his second-floor apartment to the carport below, where the Bomb, a Toyota Tercel from somewhere in the '80s, awaited him. Its paint had long ago oxidized to a flat red, except on the hood and trunk, where brown metal now faintly showed through. The right front fender was a mismatched white. A hundred dings and dents speckled the body. He reached through the open window, unlatched the door from the inside and got in. The seat was wet. He had forgotten to roll the window shut but did so now using the Vise-Grip attached to the crank. A swirl of blue-gray smoke emanated from the rear as he drove slowly onto the highway for the short trip to Morley Plaza.

Geoff combed the margins of the highway for signs of the hooded figure he had confronted the night before. He saw all manner of wheeled vehicles being pushed, pulled, and ridden through the streets, enough to affirm his suspicion that the world was coming to an end: shopping carts filled with bottles and cans; baby strollers with no babies but instead overstuffed trash bags on board; bicycles of every size, color, and design, some the obvious former possessions of delighted little boys and girls, now ridden by grown men, and adult-size ones with makeshift covered trailers in tow to safeguard their jumbled contents against the elements. Zombie RVs, derelict recreational vehicles with all the recreation wrung out of them, sat inertly along the roadside, their roofs and windows protected by tarps, with broken household items, folding tables, hibachis, more plastic bags, and still more bikes and bike parts carefully arranged or randomly strewn in clusters along the curbside as evidence of their human occupancy. One RV, its sundry items lining the shoulder of the road, bore a hand-scrawled cardboard sign: Garage Sale, No Reasonable Offer Refused. A gaunt, leather-skinned woman in attendance weaved slowly among her wares.

But he saw no sign of the hooded shape. He began to distrust his recollection of events, details that might help identify the entity to the police. He felt nervous, defeated and alone. It was, after all, only a shape, shrouded in gray, uncannily resembling all the other moving bodies on the street.

He turned into Morley Plaza and slowly cruised the alleyway, the same route the police had taken the previous night, with the same result. He could see where a clear trailhead had been worn through the tall brush leading down to the river's edge, an easy path to enter and explore the deeper reaches of the thicket. It seemed to beckon him. *Something must be going on in there*, he thought. But he felt ill-prepared for such an adventure today.

He pulled around to the front of Morley Plaza and carelessly drifted past Dogg Life. He saw his boss, Dan, working at the counter inside. *Oh shit!* To avoid being seen, he turned his face away and continued to the farthest corner of the lot, where he parked behind a large box truck. He decided to call Dan to get it over with, explaining what had transpired the night before, adding a few new details about how he had defended the business and the dogs, standing in the doorway with his galvanized pipe, warding off the intruder, giving chase a short distance, but quickly returning, not wanting to leave the premises unguarded lest there be a gang of them lurking.

"Yeah, the cops have already been by this morning," Dan reported. "Painted a slightly different picture, but whatever."

"They've already been here? What'd they say?"

"Nothing new, just wanted to follow up. Tell you one thing. They ain't gonna do shit. Gave me their card, that's it. Anyway, thanks for being here. Must have been rough."

"I'll say. I'm still pretty shook up."

"Yeah, well . . . So, see you at three then."

"Well, actually . . ."

"I've got a bunch of errands this afternoon, then taking Daphne out to dinner and a movie."

Geoff hurriedly explained how his heart had not stopped racing since last night, that he was having one of his panic attacks this very moment, and there was no way he could work today. *No way!*

"Mm-hm. Geoff, you know I can *see* you, right?" He waved at Geoff in the distance, who now realized his cover, the white box truck, had driven off. "I saw your smoke as you drove by. If you're well enough to drive that beater of yours around town, you can just sit your ass down in this chair and watch these mutts till closing time. I'll feed everyone before I go, how's that? I cannot have you MIA today. Daphne's on the warpath and I've got to make things right with her. See you at three. Adios."

Geoff tried again to make his case for a sick day, but Dan had already clicked off. He sat for a long moment, eyes closed with his head against the headrest, then pulled his car over to Pickwick's Paperback Shack.

Geoff was an irregular visitor to the bookstore, dropping in on his lunch breaks to peruse the nonfiction sections: History, Anthropology, Biography, Psychology, and so forth. He was working on a thesis—not in the academic sense but a grand personal one—to explain in his own words the "vast panorama of destructive, self-centered, short-sighted, hurtful, and wholly retarded human behavior" he had observed his entire life. His theory was that these were not aberrancies at all but completely normative human traits, critical to preserving the organism and sustaining the tribe. According to Geoff, it was inextricably woven into our DNA to be total pains in the ass and fuck everybody and everything that got in our way! This unified theory gave him solace and helped explain, if not fully comprehend, the odd beings that surrounded him.

While at the bookstore, he routinely visited the vintage pornography section in the back room. No other business in town or on the web offered the rare titles Pickwick's stocked. His latest acquisitions were the hundred-page-thick annual edition of *Gang Bang*, somewhat worn but still extraordinary, and a pristine copy of *Schulmadchen #6,* unopened in its original wrapper. Geoff's growing collection found little use as originally intended but remained encased in plastic, categorized, and stacked, tucked away in a cardboard box in his closet. He was not particularly interested in the erotic aspects of pornography but appreciated the sheer phenomenon of it, admired the commitment and expertise required to covertly produce these full-color periodicals, a triumph of old-school technology at a time when they were considered degenerate, even criminal, but remained nonetheless pervasive.

Donna had replaced the electronic Big Ben chime with an old-fashioned shopkeeper's bell. It tinkled lightheartedly as Geoff walked in. "Hello there," said Donna in her friendliest greeting voice, dimly recognizing him. "It's Geoff, right? Long time no see." He waved back casually and moved directly to the glass bead curtain and the sign proclaiming Adults Only! No Kids Please. "How's the manifesto going?"

"It's not a manifesto," he called from behind the curtain. "What do I look like, the Unabomber?" She did not answer but continued to dust and arrange the shelves. He skipped the magazines on the low tables, most of which he had seen before, but directed his attention to the new arrivals displayed on a tall wire carousel in the corner. As he spun the rack, his eyes lighted on *Undead Hotties III*, its cover depicting a nude female zombie, gray skin, open sores, bedraggled hair, cradling a severed arm, evidently getting ready to take a bite. He examined it closely front and back, then brought it out to the main floor and set it on the counter in front of Donna.

"O-o-oh yeah. Good one."

"Yup. I've got volume I. Still looking for volume II, though. If it comes in, can you hold it for me?"

"Sure thing."

"Is that your best price?" It was marked twenty dollars.

"I don't know," she deliberated. "I just put this one out. Since you're a repeat customer, though, I can knock a couple dollars off. How's that?" He nodded. "So are you into zombies?" she asked casually as she bagged his purchase, prepared for any answer.

"Nope," he said as he handed her the cash. "But I saw one last night. A real one. Right out back."

"Oh?"

He recounted the events of the evening, as he had done with the officers and with Dan, once again adding flourishes. "He was all in a frenzy, wild and crazy, like a rabid dog. You couldn't tell what he was going to do next. Then something snapped. He got all twitchy and started bobbing and whacking himself in the head"—Geoff demonstrated this for her—"then, bam! He went flying down the alley. I tried to catch him, but he ducked into the bushes and was gone."

Donna stood silently, her mouth slightly open. "Oh, poor man. Poor, poor man. That's terrible."

"Thanks, it was really creepy. I'm OK now, but..."

"Of course, it must have been very hard on you too. But I meant that poor creature. What an awful ordeal, forced to hide in a dumpster, cold and hungry, full of fear. Obviously a tormented soul. To have to live like that... Wow, what must have to happen to a person to drive them so low."

Geoff snatched up his package and stared hard at Donna. "Hey, I'm the victim here," he said pointedly, "not them! We all are. Have you seen what they're doing to this town? Sprawled out on the sidewalk, so you can't even walk without stepping over them. Leaving needles in the park and garbage everywhere. Stealing shit out of cars, appropriating dogs right off their leashes! Somewhere a poor little girl is crying right now because some asshole stole the bicycle she got for Christmas!"

Donna nodded silently and maintained good eye contact. This was her listening mode, something she'd learned over the years dealing with her store clientele. Bookstores were a magnet for a spectrum of souls—the wise, the curious, the creative, the gentle, the opinionated, and sometimes the isolated and intolerant, whose principal interface with humanity was through the written word rather than actual contact with other members of the species. She detected this in Geoff and chided herself for not realizing it sooner. *Who collects zombie porn?*

But despite his fanatical tone and her overwhelming urge to disagree with him, something in his words resonated with her. She'd grown up in Morley—high school honor student, Volunteer of the Year, Marauders Spirit Team captain, Junior Service Club president—always willing to serve the greater good but respecting authority and staying well within the established order of things. The status quo, she readily acknowledged, really worked for her; it provided the guardrails and boundaries she valued. But having left Morley to attend college in Boston, she returned with a master's degree in Library Science and a full palette of subversive attitudes toward power, dominance, and corruption, all infused with a guilty awareness of her own privilege.

"Yes, I suppose that's true," she said serenely, her voice honey sweet. "Still, we're all human, don't you think? I try to look at people not for what they are, but what they could have been or could be again."

"Meaning?"

"Meaning every poor drunk on the street was once someone's innocent child, every criminal just some rowdy kid running through the schoolyard. I look at the old guy pushing his shopping cart and see a twenty-year-old hunk." She flexed her muscles. "Strong and proud, ready to take on the world." She looked at Geoff and thought: *Even you, friend, with your funny smell and bizarre taste in porn, wearing PJs in the middle of the day—you could be something so much greater. I can see it very clearly.*

"That was then," he asserted. "Now they're total degenerates! You know, you don't just wake up one morning and find yourself living in a tent. You have to work hard at it—betray your friends, steal from your family, burn all your bridges till everyone hates you. That's how they end up there. I'm sorry. I have zero sympathy. They should be held accountable, just like the rest of us. I say round them all up!"

Donna hated his misanthropic tone but chose to overlook it, instead trying an evasive maneuver to score the next point. "You're obviously very passionate about this," she said. "I get it. We should all be accountable to one another and adhere to higher principles. But look, we're no different from those people out there. You can't lay all the blame at their feet. It's not 'them versus us.' They *are* us. We're *all* victims of this crazy culture. It's a totally corrupt economic system that promotes classism and maldistribution of wealth, yet we seem to buy into it willingly. At the same time, it makes prisoners of us all."

"Hey, hold on there," he said. "No disrespect, but I'm no prisoner. And if we're all victims, then why do some of us lead happy, productive lives while others end up doing drugs or sleeping under a tarp? It's not like we're wandering around at a loss for what to do next. There are guideposts right in front of us. Everyone knows right from wrong. We just choose to disregard what we know to be right and true. That is so weak. It's unforgiveable."

"Now, see here, mister," she said with mock indignation, in full debate mode about to correct him as an older couple walked into the bookshop.

"Hi, folks, welcome in," she called out. "I'll be right with you." Donna turned back to Geoff. She did not want their conversation to end. Her initial wariness had been replaced by delight. It had been some time since she'd engaged in an ethical debate and she was really enjoying herself. She found Geoff intelligent and thoughtful, though admittedly a little unpolished. But she loved having her assumptions challenged and wanted to press on, ply her case, convince him of her point of view, confess that she frequently welcomed into her store the very vagabonds he so derided, where they'd hang out among the stacks, sometimes for hours, ostensibly looking for a book and occasionally even buying one from the fifty-cent rack or, often as not, shoplifting one. She remained nonjudgmental about their petty crimes, believing that if they could derive some value from the books they stole, all the better, because who knew, it might change a life.

Ignoring her new customers, Donna beckoned Geoff to follow her to the Fiction section. "Here, you may find these interesting." She pulled out copies of *The Grapes of Wrath* and *Tortilla Flat*, then headed for the Philosophy section, with Geoff obediently in tow.

"Also this one."

"*The Philosophy of Moral Development: Moral Stages and the Idea of Justice*," he read aloud.

"Kohlberg. Really interesting, vis-à-vis our really interesting talk today." She smiled broadly.

"Listen, I only brought enough . . ."

"Forget it. Have a look, and if you like them, pay me later. Otherwise, bring them back for a full refund." She laughed at her own joke. "Listen, gotta go." She waved across the store at the older couple, who were growing impatient, one looking in her direction, the other bent over the art books. "Working at the doggy place today?"

"Yup."

"Well, stop by sometime, tell me what you think of these. I mean, when you can."

"Will do. Um, thanks."

Geoff watched her for a moment, as she bounced away toward the Art section, then exited the store, the silver doorbell merrily sounding his passage back into the world.

11. A FALLING OUT

The cool nights and damp mornings in Morley Valley inexorably drifted into summer, and Celine had begun to warm as well. Without taking much notice of it, she found herself hanging out at Jeremy's place.

Returning to Videodrome on a Sunday a few days after she'd fixed his dysfunctional inventory system, she reported to Jeremy her satisfaction with the app's performance but still wanted to do some tweaking. Morley was well outside her usual route home, he casually noted, the opposite direction actually, but she was committed. "A promise is a promise," she'd said, so a couple of days later she stopped in again, coming directly from work. Her impromptu visits gradually became more frequent, lasting a bit longer each time. She felt quite comfortable bouncing into the shop, dropping her bag under the counter, and setting out her snacks and Coke Zero to work, first doing a quick in-and-out check of the program, then puttering around finding things to occupy herself while she watched the ebb and flow in the store. Without realizing it, she had awakened from the dull routine she had been sleepwalking through for years. Now she had something to look forward to every day.

The following Saturday afternoon, Celine drove to Rellman Square to pick up a new chef's knife. With her errand complete, she leisurely strolled through the mall, jostled by gangs of teenaged girls and senior mall walkers, slowing her pace in front of the big display windows to examine the couture. Forever 21, Title Nine, Hollister, Anthropologie—from every shop window, the self-assured mannequins, static yet dynamic and decidedly underdeveloped, bore close resemblance to her own form. They silently beckoned her. Thereafter she abandoned her habitual work uniform of oxford shirts, sweater vests, chinos, and penny loafers in favor of more trendy outfits in fun colors that accented her trim figure, though never so tight or revealing to make them inappropriate for the office. She purchased striped socks, hoop earrings, and pink lip gloss at other mall shops and kiosks, and replaced her wide plastic frames with something more modern that, according to the optician, complemented her face.

One evening, as Celine sat safely working behind the counter, an older woman walked up to her waving a DVD box in her face: *Parrish,* an allegorical tale of the tobacco industry starring Troy Donahue. Jeremy had ducked to the back to gather a stack of videos for one of his regular customers, a young fellow with a handlebar mustache who often rented a dozen videos at a time. (When asked why he got so many, he explained he fast-forwarded through them all, hating most of the content but occasionally finding "a real gem.") She looked over her shoulder, but not seeing Jeremy, she grabbed the box from the woman and walked to the back, playfully shoving him with her hip as she retrieved the video from the shelf and, using her own homegrown system, completed the transaction. The woman was just leaving, movie happily in hand, as Jeremy returned with a dozen boxes of his own. He was impressed and appreciative. She was proud of her own resourcefulness and courage to simply jump in.

Ensconced in her cozy blind, Celine had become an avid people watcher. All types came through video store: boomers, hipsters, stoners, artists, office workers, musicians, gal pals, dads with kids, tweens and teens. All refused to subscribe to the notion that digital streaming could ever replace a little plastic disc you could hold in your hand. "You can't find everything on the damn internet," the diehards would say, and Jeremy's store was evidence of that. There was also something thrilling about shopping the aisles for rarities or old favorites, picking out a night's viewing, then hurrying home, full of anticipation, the boxed media in your purse or backpack like a Christmas present to yourself, to be opened and viewed only when the moment was just right.

She also keenly observed her host. Tall, a little awkward, with blondish hair in a ponytail, thinning slightly at the temples, he typically wore a variation of the same outfit each day: baggy jeans, slogan T-shirt with tiny holes, frayed flannel shirt, and canvas sneakers, also with holes. Jeremy tried to make Celine feel at home, never quite sure why she came over just to hang out. Her presence freed him from the front desk to do other things, for which he was grateful. He knew the value of her work and told her so often. She toiled quietly and diligently, and on occasion they'd share their day's experiences or crack jokes about the old-timey films that played on the monitor overhead. He was happy to have someone to chat with.

Jeremy assumed, based on little more than a hunch, that Celine was probably not interested in guys. She wasn't his type anyway (he preferred taller, blonder, with a little more heft), so no thoughts bubbled up in that direction. But he was ever kind, supportive, trustworthy, friendly, nonjudgmental, and funny, and she loved those traits in him. *He's nothing like Darla,* she thought, *except maybe for the funny part. But with her, it's a different funny, one that makes you feel a little unwell, like "this milk tastes funny."*

She avidly explored ways to improve the store—organizing the sales floor, relabeling the backroom inventory, changing the signage, enhancing their online presence—never asking his permission but simply starting in, then coyly cajoling him afterward to inspect her work. She completely redesigned the store's logo, then ordered T-shirts, ball caps, and bumper stickers with the new logo on them and put the cost on her own credit card.

Jeremy continually reminded her he could not formally hire her or pay her, but she swore there was nowhere else she had to be and loved helping out. She actually preferred working at the store to her regular job at Social Security. "Here you can almost always give people what they want, and they leave happy. At the office they never leave happy. Unrealistic expectations, a sense of entitlement, demanding things the government can't deliver. It's very frustrating." They agreed he would compensate her with free video rentals, and both seemed happy with the arrangement. She regularly carted multiple titles home, most on Jeremy's recommendation, and felt his obsession for the medium rubbing off on her.

Jeremy was becoming an obsession too. On hot summer days,

NEUTRAL, NO BRAKES

the late sun lingering low in the afternoon sky, Celine would leave the office immediately at five p.m. and drive straight into that blinding sun, rushing to arrive at Videodrome by five thirty, routinely staying till past eight, sometimes much later, when the streets had finally cleared and the stifling air began to lift its heavy pall. Heading home well past dark, she'd usually miss Darla's arrival from her day job and subsequent departure for her side hustle tending bar in Rellman. Even when construction started on the new traffic circles along San Sebastian Parkway, lasting eight months, she sat patiently in the queue, creeping past the flagger or halting abruptly as the opposing traffic snaked forward. This would delay her arrival until after six p.m., but on those days she'd stay even later, usually past closing time, reluctantly heading home too wound up to sleep, lying awake watching Jeremy's videos into the early morning.

Once a model employee on the path to supervisor, Celine began arriving late to work, by a few minutes at first, then later and more frequently; she'd always blame the traffic. Sitting in her cubicle musing vacantly about Jeremy and the store, her productivity slacked. She began to miss important details in her case summaries, disappointing her bosses and her clients as she hurried through her appointments, all the faster to return to daydreaming or the internet, where she would research old film stars (to keep up with Jeremy) or plan the next set of modifications to the Videodrome website.

Inevitably, she grew skeptical of her commitment to Darla, wondering why they'd ever hooked up in the first place, and distrusting her motives for staying together. She recalled their first encounter at a local pub many months ago.

Celine had been a late invite to the Wednesday Night Drinking Club, established by coworkers Deb, Kath and a few like-minded worker bees in the government services building. Celine stood within earshot as Deb described to Kath the new spot where they'd all meet the following night, complete with outdoor fire pit and funky house band. Unable to hold back, she surprised them and herself by saying she'd love to come along.

Celine struggled through the remainder of her work day, anxious at the thought of hanging out at a club with co-workers she barely knew. Full of dread, she dashed home by the shortest possible route, hoping to fix a quick meal before retiring to the shelter of her bed and a good book. She felt herself on the brink of one of her blue funks. As she hovered over the stove, mesmerized by the madly boiling water, she slipped a hard, tangled block of ramen out of its plastic sleeve into the pot. She watched it soften and unravel in the roiling heat and in it saw her life unraveling, all the twists and tangles and crooked places, compacted and tamped down in her soul for so long, spreading out randomly. She wanted to reach in, grab the whole mess, and fling it into space. She suspended her hand over the pot long enough for the steam to burn her, finally pulling away in agony.

The next night she found herself standing in a tight circle around a fire pit with Deb, Kath, and a couple of other Drinking Club regulars, trying to look casual. The heat was searing, the music loud, and the crowd raucous. She was finally out in the world and felt a disquieting sense of expectation mixed with terror.

She was working on her second margarita when she sighted Darla across the courtyard, engulfed in sparks rising from the fire pit, the flames licking her face in a diabolic visage, her explosive tangle of hair, her tan skin, her heavily muscled and tattooed arms fully exposed in her tight white wife beater, her haughty laughter, audible across the wide expanse even in the din of the Hump Night revelry. She was taller and bigger than the rest of her posse, her hips and belly subtly bumping in time with the music. To Celine, she looked a little dirty, as though she had not bathed, her undershirt sweat-stained, dark hairs poking out suggestively from her armpits.

The group chitchat fell away dully as she studied this imposing presence. Darla's eyes scanned the crowd and landed on Celine's, locking for an instant, Celine too slow to look away or not wanting to. Darla gave her a quick wink and a wry smile, then turned her attention back to her crew. Celine's face blushed a hot fiery red.

She had come out to her mother a year before, sitting her down for the long-form speech she had rehearsed. After a lengthy, dramatic windup, complete with extensive background information and supporting facts, culminating in the big reveal, her mom had responded with little surprise: "Yeah? What else is new?" Celine was relieved but puzzled, thinking she harbored an enormous, ugly secret, lugging it around for years, looking for a way to unloose her heavy load. Her decision to confess to mom—a confession it would be, not a celebration of a new life, nor the bliss of at last acknowledging her true self—had been fraught with self-doubt, self-abuse, and tears. But all those months of emotional upheaval were precipitously deflated with her mother's cast-off remark. She was so grateful when her mother had hugged her and called her "my little baby girl." Still she wondered: *Am I so obvious to everyone? Ugh!*

Celine watched Darla leave her friends and move in the direction of the sidewalk. After a slow beat she followed suit. "Whoo, so hot," she told her group, fanning herself with her hand. "Gotta step out for a breath of fresh air." She went through an opening in the iron fence encircling the patio.

Celine encountered Darla in the distance and inched slowly toward her, stopping about ten feet away, shyly leaning up against the fence, the music and idle babble muffled in the distance. There, Darla was hand-rolling a cigarette with focus and confidence, pulling the tobacco from a leather pouch, arranging it on the paper just so, carefully making the first fold, rocking it back and forth with speed and dexterity into a long symmetric cylinder, provocatively licking the paper's edge as she stared up at Celine, then completed the act with a decisive twirl.

It was the sexiest thing Celine had ever seen.

Their eyes met again as Darla lit up. "Hey," she said through blue smoke and a sardonic grin.

"Hey." Celine moved cautiously closer.

"I'm Darla. People call me Dee."

"Hi. My name's Celine." They bumped fists. "People call me Cee," she lied.

"No way!" She laughed and shoved Celine's arm. "Well, Cee, what do *you* do? Just come from work?" she said, looking her over.

She told Darla about her daily labors at Social Security. "It's OK. Decent hours, great bennies. And once in a while you feel like you're actually helping someone. I'm here with our little group." She pointed into the crowd. "We call it the Wednesday Night Drinking Club."

"Cute. Do you always wait till Wednesday?" Darla asked, raising her eyebrows.

Celine felt herself blush again. She was groping her way through the dark now, not knowing how she came to be standing here, about to hook up with this magnificent creature.

"No. I don't go out a lot actually. Way too expensive, you know. Drinks and tips, whoa, holy cow!"

"Holy cow!" she mocked, her eyes narrowing. "All you beautiful drinkers, throwing back my precious little cocktails. I couldn't make my rent without tips."

Celine fell mute. She had stumbled onto a new connection, one that seemed destined to save her from herself, and she'd managed to totally screw it up.

"Sorry. You're a bartender, then?"

"Part time," she said, now distracted by the music and the crowd.

"Hmm, must be interesting."

"Can be. Most patrons are kinda boring."

"But the pay's good?"

"It don't pay shit. Like I said, I live on my tips. All servers do. Most civilians don't understand that." She took a drag on her smoke. "I just love me my tips. So, I try to connect, you know, make everyone feel a little special."

"Sure. I get it."

"And once in a while, you feel like maybe you're helping someone." She smirked and winked. "Like you."

"Yeah. Like me." She felt back on track. The DJ played a thumping cut that made the iron fence vibrate and hum.

"Say, you got a ride?" she yelled over the music.

"Hmm? Like, a car? Sure."

"Think your friends would miss you if we jammed outta here? I could use a change of scene. And I'm so-o-o hungry! There's a burger place down the way we could pop into."

"Um, yeah, sure. I mean, no, they wouldn't miss me. We see each other every day, right? I'll just go tell them."

"Text them. I just gotta get outta here." Darla was already moving toward the parking lot.

Celine was in her car with Darla by her side going for burgers before realizing she didn't have cell numbers for Deb or Kath. She soon forgot all about it.

Darla spent that night at Celine's, then the next night and the night after that, then showed up Saturday morning with everything she owned in two large yellow panniers and a cardboard box.

At first they got along great, seeing each other only briefly in the evenings. Darla was always in high spirits, joking around, snarky, complaining about work, her bosses and patrons alike. The normally bland Celine, like tofu, took on the flavors she was steeped in, becoming a reflection of Darla's hard-edged sarcasm and annoyance with the imperfections of others.

They quickly settled into a routine: Celine would come home exhausted from work to find Darla, fresh and energetic, having slept in and chilled for most of the day, hurriedly preparing for work at LaFontaine Bar and Grill. They would kiss hello, then goodbye, and Celine, waving to Darla as she sped off, would settle in to read or watch TV until bedtime, invariably waking the next morning to a sleeping Darla and leaving for work without much interaction.

On nights Darla did not tend bar, she continued to hit the clubs with her friends, inviting Celine to join her. Celine felt reticent and awkward among them but tagged along anyway. Like Darla, they were coarse, cynical, and smug, treating her like an oddity. Next to their untiring snark and edgy fashion sense, she looked decidedly bookish in her schoolboy garb. Their pet name for her was Urkel. She had Black features with fair skin and freckles, "like the inside of a Whopper," joked Darla one night they'd all gone out to the movies. "See?" she said, biting into a malted milk ball and holding it up to Celine's dappled face, sending her crew into fits of laughter. Celine chuckled mechanically, having become inured to the many unthinking cruelties that were Darla's trademark, but it stung no less.

Darla's ethnicity, on the other hand, was a complete mystery to everyone, including Celine. Strangers would regularly try to guess her origins, even addressing her in foreign languages that reflected their own cultural assumptions. She did nothing to dispel the speculation or respond to their probing. Was she Hispanic? Asian? Middle Eastern? Sephardic? Black? Or a jumbled mix all whirled together in a genetic blender? It was impossible to tell, and Darla loved it.

Despite the slights and abuses, Celine reminded herself, the sex was great. It felt new, one of many novelties Darla brought with her. She referred to Celine as "my fun-size girlfriend." In the act, she would toss her around like a rag doll, her powerful arms and legs overpowering the scrawny Celine. She did not complain but submerged herself in the moment, secretly loving the attention and the directives. Sex for her had always been a tentative groping thing, a search for an elusive certainty. *Am I doing it right?* With Darla, there was no ambiguity as to who was in charge or the right way to do it. It was Darla who set the agenda, the pace, and the finish. And Celine was all in.

One evening over dinner Celine suggested to Darla that perhaps she "wasn't meeting her full potential." (Unlike Celine, who held a Master of Science in sociology, Darla had dropped out of high school and bounced around various table-waiting jobs, eventually getting her GED. Her highest education level was two weeks of bartending school.) After a cool stare, Celine showed her a flyer recruiting for temporary employment as a mail carrier for the US Postal Service.

"You're really smart, Darla, so strong and full of drive, with a real attention to detail," she said, using one of the new management tools she'd learned in a mandatory training session earlier that week. "Keeping all those orders in your head. Wow, I couldn't do it." She pushed the flyer closer. "Just think about it. I know the guy who does the hiring and can put in a good word."

"You bureaucrats all know each other, don't you?"

"Ha! No seriously, it pays well, good benefits, every holiday off, you work outside. You like to walk. Plus, I can also get you a little help on the exam."

Darla changed the subject, and though Celine prodded her periodically about the position to an irritated response, the matter was not discussed again until one night many weeks later. Darla was again complaining bitterly about her boss, who had "completely fucked with the schedule." But this time it was Darla who brought up the postal service job, and Celine could not have been happier. *Score one for me,* she thought.

Fulfilling her promise, Celine helped Darla pass the postal exam, known as the 473 Battery, by procuring copies of some old tests— she wouldn't say where—and tutoring her on the arcane though admittedly straightforward material. She also greased the skids with the local postmaster, who happened to be a close acquaintance. Darla waltzed into the position on her first try.

Having landed the post office gig, Darla insisted on keeping her night job at LaFontaine, calling it her "creative outlet." She was rarely home now, but Celine had by then gotten used to spending her nights alone and enjoyed the solitude. She started declining Darla's invitations to go partying with the gang, and eventually Darla stopped asking, simply announcing she was going out, without a protest from Celine. Again, all went well enough for a while.

Celine's newly discovered interest in Jeremy and the video store changed everything. The usually fastidious Celine had let the house go to hell. Dirty dishes piled up in the sink, fruit grew moldy on the counter, and the clothes hamper turned rancid.

Soon their respective roles—Celine, the longsuffering parent to Darla's reckless, impulsive child—became muddled. Now Darla routinely arrived from a long day at work to an empty house, on an empty stomach, expecting dinner on the table and the house picked up, with Celine nowhere in sight. She was forced to clean up after herself, wash her own clothes, fix her own dinner, none of which she did willingly or skillfully, tossing dirty laundry into a growing pile in the closet, zapping junk food in the microwave, and never quite able to locate the vacuum cleaner. She'd return in the early morning from the bar gig to find Celine sleeping on the couch, remote in hand, empty takeout containers everywhere, and some old flick still playing in the dark. The first time this happened, Darla roused her roommate and gently coaxed her to the bedroom. Now she simply blew past her to bed, leaving Celine to snore on the couch in the glow of the disc's main menu.

They begin to snipe at each other, exchanging unkind words about petty things, then evolving into acrimonious battles around more consequential matters. Darla considered Celine's new interest in old movies boring, her taste overly sentimental and outdated. She referred to her as "Grandma," casting a harsh light on their age difference, only twelve years. She accused her of falling in love with "that sad fuck Jeremy," which Celine stubbornly denied. Her favorite dig was to accuse Celine of being an elitist and a sanctimonious phony. "You don't fool me? I know you! You look down on people as much as I do. You're no better than I am." At least she, Darla, was willing to engage with the real world instead of trying to escape reality every night.

Celine in return called Darla frivolous, juvenile, dull, and ignorant, demeaning her lack of formal education compared to her own serious nature and scholastic achievements. "You'll never amount to anything. You're a fucking mailman, and you're too dumb to be anything else."

Finally Darla had had enough. "Clean up this filthy shithole," she yelled, tossing the broom in Celine's direction.

Celine turned on her, grabbing and shaking the broom in both fists with uncontrolled fury. "Clean it up yourself, you cunt," she shrieked. "Stop taking me for granted. I'm not your goddamn mother!"

Darla did not respond well to this line of reasoning. She stood in the hallway, breathing hard, then turned, stormed into the bedroom, and slammed the door.

Celine was immediately remorseful. She continued to make dinner for the two of them, assuming they would soon make up, though not a sound came from either of them. She had felt the stirrings of rebellion within her, an evolving awareness of their toxic relationship, and an irresistible drive to move on. But for right now, just for tonight, she wanted to patch things up and get back to normal. In an attempt at reconciliation, Celine sheepishly called out to the bedroom, "Hungry?" with no response.

In the bedroom Darla hurriedly dressed for work, picking a short, tight-fitting black knit skirt and white rayon blouse, then quietly stuffed the remainder of her clothes and other essentials into her two bike bags. She emerged silently from the bedroom, still unseen by Celine, with her mobile traveling show in hand. The door of the townhouse slowly opened and quietly clicked shut. She would not return.

12. RICHARD AND NIC BUILD A LIFE

Nic carried a sheaf of loose newspaper from the laundry room bin and dumped it on the study floor.

"Now listen." He shook a finger at Mr. Bird, already perched atop his antique cage. "I've got to change this damn liner for you, and I don't have time to put you in that ridiculous contraption today. So just watch yourself, or I'll . . ."

The mottled pigeon looked at him silently with his left eye, then his right. Cleaning the cage had become a familiar routine to both of them. Birdy looked forward to it as much as Nic dreaded it. Freedom to venture out of his cage was, according to Richard, critical to the bird's physical and mental well-being, but wearing the flight suit was mandatory.

Richard had taught Nic how to safely apply the colorful vest, and after many clumsy supervised attempts, he'd finally mastered it. Before the donning procedure, Nic would first place a fresh mini diaper into the rear poop pouch. He would then lay out the suit flat in front of the bird, placing him astride it so his feet were centered in the two holes. Then, gently lifting the elastic straps over each wing and guiding them through the holes, he would secure the Velcro tabs behind, sometimes making small adjustments to release Birdy's feet or set the vest more symmetrically. Then he was free to fly about the house while Nic changed the newspaper at the bottom of the cage, inspected the cuttlebone for wear, and provided fresh water and seed.

But today Nic was in a rush. A manic mix set thudded in his ear buds, turned up loud after his warning to Birdy. He had a long list of chores today: mow the lawns both front and back, plant new color spots in the flower beds, pressure wash the deck, order a yard of mulch ("not that awful red bark," Richard had warned, "but that nice black hemlock"), and arrange with the contractor to give an estimate on the bathroom remodel.

For four months Nic had comfortably nestled into Richard's spare bedroom and gotten on well with his new host. After twenty-eight months with his previous host, the State of Indiana, the new freedom and attention suited him. It felt good to finally have a home.

Richard for his part was thrilled with his new companion. He catered to Nic's every need, while indulging a few whims of his own. Richard arranged protracted shopping junkets to purchase trendy but tasteful clothing, footwear, and jewelry, state-of-the-art personal electronics, a new sound system for his room, an ayurvedic health consultation package, a chakra-balancing session, a home gym *plus* a gym membership that included a personal trainer, and a suite of pricey hair and skin products. He carted Nic to parties almost every week, where he was treated as an honored guest. They dined out regularly at Rellman's nicer bars and bistros. When tired of nightlife, they enjoyed gourmet meals at home, either intimately or with a handful of close friends. His hunky good looks, surly countenance, and enigmatic past gave Nic a dangerous and attractive mystique that was an immediate hit with the crowd.

But while any discussion of Nic's dark past remained an unspoken and rather sexy taboo, the question of his future came up frequently, whispered among the circle of friends or subtly implied with a knowing look or uncomfortable silence. Richard grew circumspect. Having a young live-in paramour was not unheard of, but he was "old . . . and a bit old-fashioned," and appearances mattered to him.

The stakes were much higher for Nic; finding employment was a condition of his parole. Initially subdued, even good humored and grateful for Richard's generosity, he'd grown increasingly aloof and touchy on the subject of work. So explosive and caustic were his reactions that at times Richard feared Nic might completely spin out of control. One particularly loud fight ended with Nic throwing a fork at Richard with enough force to embed it in the wall. It gave him chill bumps. A faint monologue ran through his head, warning him of another side to Nic, different from the person portrayed in his pen pal letters. But he refused to believe it, shrugging it off to jitters from Nic's recently acquired freedom in a strange new environment.

With Richard's encouragement (and network of connections), Nic tried out for several jobs in town, but could not land a position. Richard's good friend Chet, who owned a gas station and convenience mart on Copley Drive, had agreed to interview Nic but later confided his experience to Richard.

"I don't think your friend really wants a job, at least not the one I've got."

"Pumping gas and selling beer? My God, can you blame him? No disrespect, but—"

"Listen, he showed up to my place forty minutes late, gave no excuse, didn't give a shit about the job, kept looking out the window the whole time. And the mouth on him, boy—'fuck this' and 'fuck that.' You know I love you, Richard, but I have a very nice young man, my neighbor's kid actually, interested in the position. I simply can't take a chance on your friend coming in late, or not showing up at all, or picking a fight with a customer. I'm sorry, he'll have to try a lot harder . . . somewhere else. I wish him luck, but I am done."

"It's my damn record," Nic told Richard at the end of each unsuccessful day. "Everyone's polite to your face, but I know what they're thinking."

"Nonsense. You're letting your imagination run wild," Richard said without conviction, knowing he'd been largely responsible for promoting Nic's reputation as a sexy renegade. "You'll find something, I know it. You are very smart and talented and have lots of charisma. But there just aren't that many jobs here in the valley." The positive talk became a nightly mantra, as Nic missed out on one job after another.

As Richard went off to work each day at the salon, Nic busied himself around the house. He worked out on the weight set in the garage or rode Richard's street cruiser through the neighborhood, but increasingly curtailed these activities, sitting for hours at a time with the TV remote, snacking on Cheetos and pop in the morning, switching to beer in the afternoon or earlier as the mood dictated.

He began to shave and bathe irregularly. His lean, muscular arms began to soften and he grew a discernable paunch.

About three months into his stay, Nic had just positioned himself on the couch with a Monster Energy Drink to watch *Live with Kelly and Ryan*. Richard was in a panic. He was due at the salon in a few minutes but had double-booked the same time for the electrician to stop by and install some dimmers to replace the old-fashioned light switches around the house. He was about to cancel one or the other appointment, he couldn't decide which, when it occurred to him that perhaps Nic would not mind sticking around to let the electrician in and of course check to make sure everything had been completed satisfactorily and that "nothing was lifted from the house."

"Sure." He shrugged. "I can do that."

"Oh, you're a dear. I really appreciate it. I'll leave a signed blank check for him on my desk. Please fill in the amount and pay him when he's done?"

Other assignments of greater scope and complexity soon followed: watering the plants, painting a bench, hanging pictures, assembling IKEA furniture. As Nic slowly took on his new role of chief handyman and caretaker, Richard had a flash.

"Heck, why don't we just say you work for me? I'll be a good boss," he joked, "and it'll keep the parole people at bay." Nic saw the logic. He agreed to maintain the premises clean, neat, and in good working order, inside and out. He ran errands on his bike, or if the job required—grocery shopping, visiting the hardware store, or hauling cans to the recycling center—he would drop Richard off in town and take the car. For convenience, Richard arranged for him to have his own debit and credit cards, linked to Richard's business account, to make small purchases around town or pay for other household expenses. Nic performed odd jobs during the day, learned to cook simple meals in the late afternoons, and of course kept Birdy's cage tidy.

Soon enough, though, his duties included odd jobs both in and out of the bedroom, servicing Richard as well as Birdy.

Nic could not remember how or when their relationship had strayed into the physical, so subtle and incremental was the crossing over, but he suspected from the outset it would come to this. Richard had been verbally affectionate with Nic from day one, calling him "dear" and "sweetheart," which made Nic cringe inside. He kept a straight face, knowing that Richard was his only salvation, that if this didn't work out, his parole would be in jeopardy. He allowed Richard to touch him casually and did not pull away, first with a hand on his forearm, as a sign of manly friendship and encouragement, then a shoulder or neck rub after a long day. *Oh my, you're so tense. You must have been very busy today.* Richard's deep glances and lingering stares were more blatantly sexual than any physical contact.

One evening after they'd consumed a splendid home-cooked meal—chicken parmesan with roasted asparagus and new potatoes, harvested by Nic from their own garden, complemented by all of one and most of a second bottle of fine Côtes du Rhône red—Nic sat mellow and drowsy at the dinner table while Richard cleared. As he reached across the table, his hip leaned into Nic's shoulder, at first accidentally, then bumping him with more sassy intent. Richard pivoted, dishes in hand, slightly toward Nic and again pressed firmly toward him. He felt the light sustained pressure of Richard's crotch against his elbow. Nic kept his eyes fixed forward as Richard began to gently grind back and forth. He calmly reached down to Nic's hand and slowly placed it over his groin. Nic allowed his hand to stay and looked up at Richard, who was looking back with lids half-mast. *Now it begins,* he thought.

"You needn't do anything you don't want to do, dear," he said to Nic, who remained wordless as Richard set his plates down and unzipped his polyester slacks to reveal his penis, also at half-mast, guiding it into Nic's calloused hand.

Nic was no stranger to this sort of behavior. He'd had the occasional encounter in prison, on both the giving and receiving ends, in part to endure life among the rough-hewn inmates but also to find relief from his own pent-up tensions, sexual and otherwise.

Long before that—though it seemed all a dream now, like a phantom inhabiting some spectral province—a younger Nic had found himself catapulted into a wild, harsh world where all boundaries were blurred. He had impulsively lit out from home one night, attempting to escape the chaos and brutality of life in his father's house, without thinking much about the future or even the next moment. He felt bad about leaving Joan alone to survive by her wits but could not get her to come with him. Nor could she convince him to stay. He'd reached his limit of screaming, humiliation, and thrashings but knew Dad would never raise a hand to her.

On the street, he quickly realized there was little else a sixteen-year-old boy could do for money, food, shelter, and drugs. He had a pretty face, or so the patrons and other hustlers had told him, and he made the most of it. *Just play along for now,* he told himself. *Get enough scratch together to move on. This is just a stopover. I'm outta here soon.*

He easily fell back into the old ways with Richard, becoming a willing participant in the same old bargain, biding his time until he could find an escape route, except for one important difference. No money ever changed hands, and Richard intended to keep it that way. He considered the meals, lodging, and countless gifts he'd already bestowed on Nic sufficient recompense for all his labors. Thus Nic found himself unable to accrue sufficient resources to even consider making a move.

So there he stayed, day after interminable day, his freedom once again stolen. He spent hours in his room moping, emerging at night, sullen and short-tempered. He hated the arrangement but to his bewilderment was unable to break free. He felt his demons closing in on him as they had done before, his penchant for self-sabotage and self-destruction, familiar friends both, inching closer, threatening to overwhelm him.

His first glimpse at a way out occurred one bright, hot morning in downtown Rellman. He had dropped Richard off at the salon and stopped at the ATM to withdraw some cash for the day's errands: gassing up the car, buying a fresh sack of birdseed for Birdy, and driving out to "that cute little plant stand on the highway" to pick out some replacement shrubs for those that had succumbed to the scorching sun. Though he paid by card most of the time, he needed some ready cash for incidentals. But the ATM screen read Temporarily Out of Service. He went inside to make his withdrawal. The air-conditioning was jarringly frigid, but the cordial young bank teller greeted him warmly. She knew Nic by sight and was all smiles as she completed the withdrawal.

"Would you like your balance, Mr. Troxell?" she asked cheerily.

"Sure," he replied, studying his to-do list and scratching out the word *bank*.

"All three accounts?"

"Sure," he said again without looking up.

She wrote three dollar amounts on the withdrawal slip and handed it to him. The balances on the personal and business checking accounts were around fifteen hundred dollars each. The personal savings balance was $1,788,923 and change.

From that moment forward, Nic burned with the zeal of a man desperately scratching out of a deep pit, finally discovering a toehold he had not seen before. Emboldened by his discovery of Richard's wealth, the next day at the ATM he withdrew a few more dollars than he needed for expenses, this time from the big account. The following day he took a couple hundred more and more still the day after that. He was careful at first to make modest withdrawals in random amounts, where such activity might easily be ignored or offset by earned interest, but quickly ramped up his gleanings to the maximum of eight hundred dollars each day. Over the course of a month, his bounty flourished. Minus a tiny fraction attributable to actual expenses, he had accrued over $20,000 in cash.

Nic knew he was walking a tightrope but relied on Richard's less than diligent attention to money matters for cover. On rare attempts to balance his accounts, Richard always fudged at the end to make the numbers jibe, if he completed the process at all. He ignored the electronic bank statements that accumulated monthly in his email inbox, preferring to maintain in his head only a loose accounting of his income, expenditures, holdings, and financial obligations. Every day Nic felt himself a little closer to escaping from his imprisonment.

One afternoon Richard arrived home in a mischievous mood.

"I've been to the doctor!" he announced in a singsong voice. "Can't you tell?" He encircled his face with both hands. Nic's attention now fully captured, he discerned a softening to the crinkly brown skin he'd grown accustomed to seeing. Richard's usual countenance, aged but nonetheless animated, expressive and befitting his years, had been replaced by a masklike vacancy, its waxen immobility reminding Nic of an undertaker's work.

"Botox is my new best friend," he said.

"Oh, great."

"And here's my other new BFF." He shook a little white paper sack. Nic heard the unmistakable clacking of pills in a medicine bottle.

That night, a refreshed and invigorated Richard was feeling especially amorous. He wished to consummate their relationship anew, to celebrate his fresh, youthful appearance. Until then, their physicality had been limited by a few simple, albeit fluid, boundaries. It had started with mutual hand jobs, then progressed into Richard going down on Nic, and ultimately ended with Nic performing anal sex on Richard. Through it all Nic had steadfastly refused to return the favors. He would not perform oral sex on Richard or allow Richard to penetrate him from behind, and Richard was fine with that, having issues with hardness anyway: "like trying to push a rope through a keyhole," he'd joked, though he was allowed to "play around outside."

Tonight Richard was doing just that when, to Nic's astonishment and displeasure, he abruptly thrusted forward. It felt like someone had shoved a brick up his ass sideways.

"Hey! What the fuck," he yelled out in pain, trying to pull away. But Richard held fast and firm to Nic's hips.

"Hey, yourself!" He was now fully in place and gently rocking. "I took a pill! Isn't modern science wonderful? Relax, I'll be done in a minute."

"You're done right now!" Nic took a swing at Richard but was unable to land one from his awkward stance or loosen himself from Richard's surprisingly strong grip.

"Oh, am I now?" he said. "Maybe *you're* done . . . whenever *I* say you're done." He continued to slowly grind away. "You think I don't know what you've been up to? I've lived half of my life in this town. I know everyone, and everyone knows me. I got a little call the other day from my friend Tony, the manager down at the bank. He clued me in to your little scheme. Oh, don't worry, I lied. I told him I knew all about it, said it was just fine with me, told him you had full authorization and my complete trust." He pushed harder and faster. "I can trust you, can't I, Nic? What good is a friendship if there isn't trust?"

He shuddered, moaned, stiffened, and grunted softly, then rolled off Nic and stood up beside the bed, grabbing a few tissues from the box on the table.

"And I assure you, dear boy, you can trust me. You can trust that I won't call the cops, or tell your parole officer about your indiscretion. We both know what would become of you if I did."

"Please tell me you won't," Nic pleaded, curled up on his side, his back end still throbbing. Richard threw him a deadpan stare. In the soft light, Nic could appreciate it now; he really did look younger.

"Of course, you'll have to pay back the money you took from me or whatever's left of it. That's fair, considering," Richard said with a lascivious grin and raised eyebrow. "I'm not greedy or vindictive. I just want what's fair. Throw me my shorts, please."

Nic had been outmaneuvered on the field of battle. He drifted through the next day in a detached fugue. In the following weeks, Richard, with sardonic comments and biting asides, skillfully manipulated Nic, playing on his insecurities and past missteps, hurling cruel digs about his crimes, his abusive father, his estrangement from his family. They soon settled into a new normal: an unfettered Richard having his way, day or night, with the now subservient Nic playing dutiful houseboy and concubine.

Nic hurriedly rolled up the soiled newspaper from the bottom of Birdy's cage and was laying out a fresh layer, anticipating his full schedule ahead, when the disobedient pigeon left the top of his cage and happily took flight about the study, flying to the window, the grand piano, the mantel, and finally landing on the arm of the brocade couch, where, because Nic had failed to apply his vest, he deposited a multicolored runny poop.

"Oh, shit, no!" Nic cried out as he watched the misdeed transpire, rushing across the room and startling Birdy, who again continued his aerial survey and now gazed guiltily down at Nic from atop the bookshelf. Nic ran to the kitchen, returning with a handful of rags, and began wiping up the poop. But it had already seeped in and stained the silken material a dark brown. He quickly remembered Richard kept a small stash of housework supplies—furniture polish, window cleaner, WD40—in the bottom drawer of his desk.

Nic frantically rushed to the desk and rifled through the drawer, tossing items about. He located a small can of stain remover and squinted to read the small-print instructions on the back, but saw Spray On, Let Dry, Brush Off on the front, and that was enough. He ran back to the sofa and sprayed, let it dry, blew on it, waved his hand over it, and brushed it off with the cap, then repeated the process. To his relief, the stain was gone.

During all the commotion, Birdy decided he'd had enough freedom and excitement for one day and, seeing fresh newsprint lining his cage, voluntarily flew back to his perch inside. Nic breathlessly latched the cage door and flopped onto the couch. "Boy, we dodged a bullet there, didn't we?" he asked Birdy, without much reaction. Nic's attention again turned to his errands for the day. He collected the dirty newspaper and rags from the floor, then doubled back to restore order to the chaos he'd made of the desk drawer. He had neatly replaced its contents and was about to head out the door when he paused.

Nic looked with disgust at his hands, full of filthy rolled-up newspaper and rags soiled with bird shit. He recalled the list of dreary tasks that lay ahead for him, then cast an eye at Birdy blissfully rocking on his perch. He felt deeply mortified by the frenetic valet service he had just rendered, all to stay in Richard's good graces. Of the three inhabitants of this household, Birdy clearly outranked him.

Standing by the desk, curiosity mixed with a desire for payback suddenly overwhelmed him. He checked the driveway through the window. No one there. He reexplored the utility drawer, finding nothing but the household products. He slid open the other side drawer to find writing pads, pens, paper clips, stapler, letter opener, some loose keys, nothing more. He wiggled the top drawer. It was locked. He examined the keyhole, remembered the loose keys in the side drawer, and found a likely candidate. It fit.

On top in the middle drawer lay a stack of checks paper-clipped together. He examined them. Each was recent, made out to MRK Property Management, endorsed and ready for deposit. The checks were from retail shops and businesses whose names he recognized—ReddyCare, Dogg Life, Burger Basket, and others—all tenants of Morley Plaza, where Nic had many times dropped Richard off to work. There were also rent checks from at least a dozen homes and apartment complexes around Morley, concentrated in the streets immediately surrounding the plaza.

He explored further, finding family snapshots of Richard as a boy, a mini-pencil sharpener in the shape of a beehive, more pens and paper clips. Then, under all the clutter, some handwritten draft letters addressed to Mayor Howard Purnell and the Morley City Council, with strikethroughs and additions in the margins. He skimmed the text: "I strongly endorse the proposed development known as Morley Pointe Crossing . . . will bring economic prosperity . . . critical need for affordable housing . . . Morley's newest commercial engine . . . a jewel in the crown of the new Morley."

The letters were signed Maurice R. Kornbluth. Below his name, the words "President, MRK Holdings" had been crossed out and replaced with "Owner, Mr. Richard's Cuts and Color, Morley Plaza."

Comingled with the letters were two newspaper clippings, opinion pieces recently printed in the op-ed section of the *Morley Examiner-Post*, endorsing similar themes of economic development and affordable housing but also excoriating the NIMBYs in Morley who were "impediments to progress, backward in their thinking, who pine for a return to a Morley Valley that never was," and signed "MRK, a Concerned Citizen."

Finally, at the back of the drawer, half protruding from a small bubble-lined manila mailer, lay a Smith and Wesson .38 Special. Nic recognized the J-frame Bodyguard Airweight, its short barrel, slender wooden grip, and shrouded hammer designed for concealed carry. He carefully tilted the envelope and saw it was stuffed with cash. Careful not to touch the gun, he riffled through it, guessing it was about $60,000 in twenties, fifties, and hundreds. He gently slid the envelope and its contents back into its resting spot, then set the letters, clippings, and checks into place.

Nic's mind was racing as he tried to put it all together. *What does it all mean?* Richard had often made joking reference to arriving in Morley with a small nest egg, but now Nic wondered just how prosperous he had been. He'd apparently accumulated substantial real estate holdings over the past two decades, reaping a steady flow of monthly rent and sizable bumps in property values during that time. *This explains the big bank balance.* Nic now understood how his eccentric host could enjoy the high-placed connections he obliquely puffed about. Nic knew the small salon, catering to older ladies in dwindling numbers, could not be supporting his current grandiose lifestyle. He understood real estate well enough to know that the strip mall and dozens of houses would need to be leveled in order to make way for the "jewel in the crown of the new Morley" known as Morley Pointe Crossing, and that Richard stood to gain considerably from the sale of his holdings. He wondered if any of the business owners or families in or around the mall knew the hairdresser was their landlord and was aggressively selling them out.

Nic was certain Richard was at the salon with a full schedule this morning but mechanically checked the driveway again anyway. *Still all clear.* The low morning sun beamed brightly through the trees in the front yard, casting light and dark into the study. He sat down in the leather desk chair and focused on all that his explorations had revealed. The pieces of the puzzle were slowly falling into place, some firmly anchored, others still swirling freely.

His thoughts turned to those checks in the drawer, to the names of people who would be affected by Richard's ploy, unaware their lives were about to be upended by powerful forces they did not understand or even knew existed. He felt a burning resentment, not toward Richard or any individual, but a corrupt system that cared not one whit about people like him.

His mind for an instant flew back to a cold February morning long past, when he stood on a patch of broken sidewalk in shorts and a Superman T-shirt, his bare feet anesthetized by the cold, toeing a sprig of weeds pushed up through a crack in the pavement, clutching his blanket and stuffed bear in one hand and his sister's hand in the other. As their belongings were carried out onto the driveway, was he crying? No, his sister had told him to be brave, so he was brave, as stoic as a little boy should ever be. He asked her why the men were throwing out their stuff and if they could go back in now and have breakfast, because he was hungry and very cold, and his sister told him no but that everything was going to be all right as she clutched his hand more tightly. His father was arguing with the man in the green uniform, who had a paper in his hand and was waving it, shaking his head and looking at the ground with his fists on his hips, and the other man, the one who he had seen come around to pick up the rent before, was pointing at the other men and telling them what to do. And then his father told him and his sister to start putting all their crap in the car. So they did, big bags of it, and the back seat filled up quickly, so you couldn't sit back there any more or even see out the back window. The trunk filled up too and had to be tied shut. Then the men came out with a mattress, and they helped his father stack the mattress on top of the car, and his father took some rope and threaded it through the open windows and tied the mattress tight so it wouldn't fall off, but it was floppy and dipped down in front so that you couldn't see to drive, except through a narrow gap between the hood and the edge of the mattress. His sister got in front, and he sat on her lap, and she wrapped them both in the blanket. His father got in and slammed the door and lit a cigarette. Much of their stuff still lay on the lawn, but his father said, "Forget about it." As they backed out of the driveway, another car almost hit theirs, but his father slammed on the brakes in time, and the other car honked really loud and for a long time. They pulled out and drove down the street fast. He and his sister watched their house grow smaller through the side mirror, too tightly bound together in the front seat to turn and look back.

He shook his head and blinked his eyes hard. His mind snapped back from that February day to hard reality, the sun now crisp and brilliant, warming the walls, floor, and desk where he sat. He made one last inspection of the top drawer—yes, everything back in place—then slowly slid it shut and locked it, dropping the key randomly in the side drawer and closing it.

    He sat motionless for several minutes processing what he had learned. He knew something now, something secret and powerful. He could feel it. He was capable of doing some real damage but also—and with this, a peculiar sensation swept over him—correcting a terrible wrong that should be made right. But how? He had effectively isolated himself from the people in town since moving into Richard's place, and couldn't share this with any of the people in the strip mall. Not yet. If only he had his sister, Joanie, to help sort things out.

    Nic was desperate to release himself from Richard's ever-tightening hold even if it meant going back to Arkansas. He calculated his possible moves: threaten Richard, get some quick cash out of him and then split? No, there was the parole board to think about. He'd have to stay put for now but maybe on his own terms, just as Richard had made him toe the line with his own set of rules. Or he could call it "just their little secret," demand that Richard cut him in on a piece of the deal. Everyone would be happy and none the wiser.

But what did he have on Richard, anyway? Secret deals, buying low, selling high? Where was the corruption in that? Doubt clouded his mind. Anyone looking at it might say he was just a smart businessman, doing what made the most sense, and they'd be right. But why all the secrecy? There was still a missing piece to the puzzle. Richard was a big fish in a small pond, but not that big. There must be someone in the shadows, Nic concluded, with the real money, pulling the strings to make sure all the deals went through.

The rags and newsprint filled with bird poop still lay on the desktop, and alongside it his to-do list. The secrets in the drawer would need to steep awhile until the right moment. *In due time,* he thought. *Stay under the radar. Keep moving forward.* He gathered up the refuse and the list and made his way to the gardener's shed, disposing of the trash along the way. He pulled out the lawn mower and pressure washer. The new annuals sat in a row in the driveway waiting to be planted, speckled by the bright midmorning sun.

13. KONNICHIWA

Darla peddled hard up the hill toward LaFontaine. Her powerful legs and arms made short work of it, fired by a bitter rage after her tiff with Celine. She ran through the list of friends she might crash with tonight, swearing she would never go back. *Not ever!*

Tuesday nights were usually slow in Rellman, and night manager Cliff, with his penchant for austerity and a spreadsheet full of sales data, was experimenting with a new staffing model. Thus, on top of her regular duties as Chief Mixologist, Darla was scheduled to wait tables, a job she tolerated but thought beneath her. She was still seething about the new tip-sharing policy; having her schedule fucked with magnified her sour mood.

But it was not slow this Tuesday night at LaFontaine. As she coasted to the rear kitchen door, Darla saw the front lot filled with cars, while patrons struggled to find spaces on the street or in the bank lot next door.

"Hey, Jimmy!" she said, emerging into the loud, steamy kitchen.

"Turn around now, girl. Just go. Leave!"

"I know, right? It's packed out there. Something going on?"

"Nope. I guess people decided to get their drink on early this week. Can you blame them?"

The smell of charred meat filled the air. Smoke rose from the grill, sucked up by the whirring overhead vent. Skillets sizzled, sauté pans sputtered, capacious pots boiled. Sweaty waitstaff, dishwashers, and busboys moved energetically within the small space with elegant precision, defying the laws of physics by never colliding with one another.

Darla took a swig from her water bottle and checked her look in the mirror. "Gawd, I'm a mess!" She freshened her lip gloss.

"Oh, please. Sister, you'd look good if you spent the night at a gang bang. By the way, did you? Come here." He straightened her collar, fluffed her hair. "Now smile. Bigger! Atta girl. Now tuck your shirt in and get out there. I need you on the front line."

"You know I'm working the bar *and* the floor tonight."

"You need to tell me that? I'm on it. Already called Cliff to say we needed some help out there. He's calling around to find backup."

"Maybe he should drag his sorry ass in and work a shift himself for a change. Goddamn flex bullshit."

"Never mind that. Now go, go, go." He shooed her out the kitchen door.

Darla did a quick check-in with the harried waitress already on duty, grabbed some menus, and dove in. None of her patrons could have guessed she was anything but delighted to be at work. She never lost sight of her prime objective—boosting her tips—and was a master at it. She made sure she stood out among the other servers, always wearing something a little revealing or quirky. She was in total control of the verbal give and take at her tables and made you feel like an instant best friend: gracious, animated, engaging, sharing funny stories, allowing folks to talk as much as they wanted while nodding wide-eyed. She made recommendations from the menu and sometimes whispered that a particular dish wasn't her favorite, creating a secret conspiratorial bond with her customers. She always wrote a personal note on the check, like "Enjoy the movie! ☺ Dee."

Darla had taken her orders and was behind the bar mixing LaFontaine's signature drink, one of her own creation: The Bitterest Truth. Into a chilled rocks glass she combined a scant teaspoon of water, half a teaspoon of fine sugar, and three dashes of aromatic bitters. (Darla preferred sugar over simple syrup and never used commercial bitters, only her own house-made recipe.) She swirled in two ounces of Woodford Reserve and finished with a solitary round tennis ball-size ice cube and a wide swath of twisted orange peel set on top.

Jimmy emerged from the kitchen. "How goes it, princess? Keeping up?"

"You know it. I'm a highly paid professional."

"You're half-right. I'm gonna need about three of those Old-Fashioneds after this night. Can you hook me up?" He reached for the drink, and she slapped his hand.

"Mine!" She placed it on the serving tray and started on a Tom Collins. "Looks like the crowd is thinning out a bit."

"Thank you, Jesus. Say, why don't you hide behind your bar for the rest of the shift? These guys can handle the new traffic."

"Sounds good to me."

"Oh my my. Would you look at who just walked in."

She squinted toward the door. "Hmm? Where?"

"That twitchy guy in the tweed sport coat with the hunted look."

"Yeah, I've seen him in here before. Usually with a pushy blonde chick, a real ball-buster type. He always looks a little deflated afterward. What's his story?"

"That's the mayor of our fair neighbor to the west."

"He's the mayor of something? How could it be?"

"My guess is that he knows how to play ball with the right people, if you know what I mean." He rubbed his fingers together. "Some people will do anything for a few pieces of silver. And he's headed this way. Bye-bye."

Rusty Purnell checked in with the hostess and glanced about the room. Not seeing his party, he made his way straight to the bar. Darla set out a cocktail napkin in front of him. "Evening, sir."

"Hendricks martini please, dry, two olives."

"You got it." Rusty watched as she combined the ingredients in an old-style shaker. A cool blue light shined up on her face from below the bar. She briskly agitated the shaker overhead with a loud clatter and filled a frozen stem glass pulled from the cooler. Small ice crystals rose to the top as she skewered two olives and placed them carefully into the glass.

"Perfect. Nice and cold."

"Got a little extra here," she said, setting the shaker within his reach.

He took out his phone and thumbed through texts, finishing his drink in two gulps. He drained the shaker, downed that as well, and held up his empty glass. "Once more, please?"

"Rough day?" she asked as she worked on round two.

"The rough part is yet to begin," he said, still gazing at his phone.

She looked about at the busy bar and, seeing no new customers, settled in for what she knew would be a long conversation. "I'm Dee."

"Rusty."

"Nothing serious, I hope."

"No, no. Not a matter of life or death, if that's what you mean. No, much worse. I've just got some decisions to make," he mumbled to himself, "tough ones."

As he sat brooding, Darla was her most disarming, giving him her full attention, making light of his worries, fluffing his confidence, cracking wise, and getting a few laughs out of him despite his hard-faced mood. As the second martini began to creep up on him, he sensed a growing rapport with her, as if they were the only two people in that dark, clamorous room. And as most middle-aged men will do when a younger woman, even waitstaff, pays any attention to them, he thought: *Is she flirting with me?* And of course his answer was *Yes.*

A tumult was now brewing at the hostess station. Monica Sampson-Smith had arrived, with two well-dressed Asian men accompanying her: one younger, shorter, round-faced, and intense, the other older, taller, leaner, and more restrained. The hostess had just informed her there would be a slight delay in getting them seated. Monica's voice was audible throughout the restaurant.

"Let me speak to the manager, please. Who's on tonight?" She glanced around. "Do you know how much money I've dropped in this place over the years? I have a very important meeting with these two gentlemen here, and I do not appreciate being told we have to wait."

Rusty did not turn to view the commotion. He already knew. "My seven o'clock has arrived."

"The rough part?"

"Oh, yeah. Say, would you mind fixing up another one of these beauties, while I go make nice? Bring it to our table, please. I'm sure we'll get seated any second now," he said, seeing a pair of busboys furiously clearing and setting a booth for four in the corner. "You around later? I may need to debrief," he said as he placed two twenties on the bar. "This should cover me so far."

He eased himself carefully off the barstool and weaved his way to the front with open arms. "Monica, dear, how are you?" They exchanged brief hugs as she introduced the two gentlemen, whose deadpan expressions warmed immediately as they shook hands.

"Mayor Purnell, I'd like you to meet Mr. Xu and Mr. Huang."

They swapped pleasantries, Xu and Huang nodding approvingly at meeting a high municipal official. A moment later a contrite hostess arrived with menus and showed them smartly to their table.

The two visitors eyed their menus with bewilderment. Monica pointed to several items they might find appetizing, but Mr. Xu suggested they have a toast before ordering. Their assigned server had not yet made an appearance, so Monica summoned Darla to the table, snapping her fingers and motioning her over. Darla acknowledged her and an instant later arrived with Rusty's third martini on a serving tray, this one with four olives.

"*Konnichiwa,*" she said to the two Asian men, bowing slightly at the waist. They appeared perplexed, softly muttering to themselves in their native language.

"Dee, our esteemed guests are from China," offered Rusty in an attempt to salvage the moment. "Mr. Xu and Mr. Huang."

"Oops, sorry. *Nin hao!*" She placed the martini in front of Rusty.

The intense Xu, the restrained Huang, and the irate Monica looked in unison at the drink, then at Darla, and finally at Rusty.

"Mr. Mayor, were you planning on drinking alone tonight?" Monica said without a trace of humor. "Or did you plan to invite your friend here to join us?"

"No, of course not." He chuckled nervously, struggling to find a humorous out. "I was just getting a little head start on Monica here. She has a hollow leg, you know!" The gambit paid off. Xu and Huang apparently found his joke riotously funny and their demeanor brightened, though it was clear they knew not what the hell he was saying. Monica shot him a cold look, but he charged ahead. "Please, let us all order." Xu suggested something American—Jack Daniel's on the rocks—and all agreed. "Four JD rocks. Please take this away."

Darla curtly repeated, "Four JD rocks," as she grabbed up the untouched martini and returned to the bar, clearly rankled.

"Ugh, servants!" said Monica in a low voice, but loud enough to carry across the room.

After some small talk about their flight, hotel accommodations, and the problems of jet lag, the meeting began in earnest.

"While we wait for our drinks, Mr. Mayor, our guests would love to know more about your plans for development here in Morley."

"Yes, I'm proud to say the city has a long-range scheme for economic development that we think will be good for private investors as well as the people of Morley. Monica here can provide you the details, the financials, ROI, et cetera. In brief, we believe in a strong public-private partnership." He interlaced his fingers, forming a solid, two-handed fist. "Government can't do it all, right? One great example—Morley Pointe Crossing."

As though receiving telepathic cues from Monica, Rusty described the planned eight-acre development at the corner of Copley Drive and San Sebastian Parkway. "It's typical of the kind of development we're looking for. Four stories of high-end apartments, six if the developers apply for a variance, with nice retail on the bottom, right on the main transportation corridor. Light rail coming soon—we'll need some federal support for that. Bike and pedestrian-friendly, with flood abatement incorporated into a lovely watershed and greenway just off highway. Kid-friendly too, perfect for families."

"It will really turn the town around," chimed in Monica. "That corner is very centrally located; with a little infusion of capital, it can become the new hub of the community. Of course, some of the existing structures will need to be demoed."

"Forgive me. Demoed?" asked Xu.

"Sorry. Demolished." The two gentlemen nodded. "That awful strip mall, Rusty, what is it called?"

"Morley Plaza?"

"Yes, Morley Plaza, that will need to go away, and some of the smaller single-family homes surrounding it. Most of them, actually. They're no more than shacks really. The land is desperately underutilized at present."

"The owners will sell?"

"Excellent question, Mr. Xu," replied the mayor. "Yes, the owners will sell, I have no doubt of that. We have one very motivated landholder. For the others, we have something in the US called 'eminent domain.' We would not invoke this method unless absolutely necessary, but when a building project is for the greater public good, which this project clearly is, the government has the authority—the obligation, really—to procure the land for that purpose. At fair market value, of course. We're not pirates, after all!" He laughed but caught himself when he realized no one else was amused.

Darla quietly arrived with a tray of four tumblers of Jack Daniel's on ice and delivered one to each member of the party. Monica continued the conversation as though she were invisible.

"The market seems to be in motion right now. Lots of For Sale signs on lawns. And prices are a bit soft too, which is good for us."

"It's a buyer's market."

"Yes, precisely. Thank you, Rusty. A buyer's market."

"A toast," said Rusty, raising his glass as the others followed suit. "To prosperity and long life."

"*Gānbēi!*" said Xu with a smile.

"*Gānbēi!*" they responded in unison, clinked their glasses, and emptied them.

Mr. Huang, who had been silent until now, raised a finger. "If I may, who is to say the market will not continue to be soft after one makes an investment? I have noticed that many buildings in the town are old and in disrepair. The majority of your townspeople seem to be poor, and the most destitute, one may observe, are using drugs or living on the streets. Why should we have confidence in your project? Who will live here, shop here, when the project is complete? Your citizens cannot afford to live here now. What will happen when they are displaced?"

Monica was silent as Rusty cleared his throat. "Very perceptive questions, Mr. Huang. I have no excuses about the economics here in Morley. Yes, our community has fallen on some hard times, it is true. But the townsfolk are good, down-to-earth people. Not a lot of money but hardworking, with solid family values." He shifted into his canned speech. "We are committed to helping those without permanent housing to identify affordable alternatives. We certainly need to create more shelter beds in the short run, but it is difficult without outside resources and the political will to do so. Many of our attempts have been thwarted. 'Not in my backyard' is a phrase we hear often."

Huang held up his hand and smiled coolly. "Please. You need not be so quick to address your homeless difficulties. There will be much time for that. It is a very easy problem to address. You have laws already. Wait until these transactions have been completed. Meanwhile, it remains a strong motivation to sell; this will work in your favor. The best time to purchase a house with an ocean view is after the tsunami."

Darla stood at the next table arranging napkins and silverware, listening intently but focusing on the cutlery, trying to look disinterested. Rusty called for one more round. She looked up at him and languidly returned to the bar.

"Then there's Rellman," reminded Rusty.

"Yes, thank you, Rusty." Monica was now squarely in her element. "A key factor, gentlemen, is the continued expansion of the City of Rellman to the east. Rellman has enjoyed a real upsurge of wealth and status over the past decade. Many retirees from the bigger cities have found refuge there, with its safe streets, fine-dining opportunities, a community theater, art galleries, wine-tasting rooms, luxury townhomes and condos. Wonderful schools, a full-service healthcare system. It's really very nice."

"Then why should one not invest in that town?" queried Xu.

"Simply stated, cost," she explained. "Property values have soared there. Frankly, I believe they have plateaued, so return on investment is not what it used to be. Morley, on the other hand, is still affordable. It is a gold mine waiting to be discovered. Though it has not reached its full potential, it affords all of the same natural beauty, excellent climate, and recreational opportunities as Rellman."

"Shall we talk about the lake?" asked Rusty.

Monica's cool response immediately gave him the answer; the lake was still sub-rosa.

"Mayor Purnell is a true visionary. He sees opportunities like no one else can. Yes, for decades people have talked about bringing a reservoir to the valley. For now, though, it's only a dream. Who knows, perhaps one day?" She turned to Rusty.

"Perhaps. But working with wonderful professionals like Monica has opened my eyes to all the possibilities. I truly believe Morley's best days lie ahead."

The show of harmony and singular vision seemed to impress the investors. Mr. Huang delicately introduced a question. "With your permission, may we speak about the visa issue?"

Rusty took the reins now. "The E-2? Certainly. We've worked with other parties to obtain investor visas in the past. I can see no major hurdles."

"Unfortunately, our two countries do not have a treaty that allows this pathway."

"Hmm. You could take another route. Taiwan has a treaty with the US."

Huang sighed and smiled. "The Taiwan question is a complex one. The island that calls itself the Republic of China is a renegade regime based on an eccentric view of history. In reality it is still part of a single sovereign entity, the PRC. The government in Beijing is the sole legitimate authority overseeing Taiwan. We could not possibly—"

Monica, who had been searching the question on her phone, burst in excitedly, cutting him off.

"Have you considered Grenada?" She turned the screen to Huang, where a website described Grenada's "Citizenship by Investment Programme" and its required investment of $350,000 in a government-approved real estate project, or if not, simply a $200,000 "donation."

"No need to visit the country to complete the application, though I would highly recommend it. It is quite lovely." She smiled smugly.

"And this would open the opportunity for a visa to the US? I ask not for myself, of course, but for my son and his new wife. They strongly desire to emigrate to the US, but the process is so full of, as you say, 'red tape.'"

"Wow, it looks like we do have a treaty with Grenada," responded Rusty, examining the site with some surprise. "You simply establish dual citizenship there and then the path is wide open. And naturally we would welcome the involvement of any member of your two families in our project."

"Perhaps a job with a title, in addition to his investment?"

"He can be a project manager, no worries."

"Perhaps project leader?"

"Project leader it is!"

Their second round of JD rocks arrived via Darla, and again they toasted. "To new beginnings, and lifelong friendship."

Darla got out her order pad. "So what looks good?" she said tersely.

They ordered from the menu based on Monica's recommendations: Xu had the chicken fajita, which arrived sizzling with much spectacle and awe, and Huang ordered the grilled tilapia with much less. Rusty and Monica each opted for the porterhouse, medium rare, appearing also with great pomp, crackle, and hiss. The dinner shambled on, as such dinners will. More drinks were ordered and consumed, more stories shared—of families, travels, and deals both triumphant and challenging—as a new covenant was conjured by the smoke of burning flesh, annealed in the harsh fire of whiskey.

As the celebrants mellowed, their bellies and heads full of heavy food and booze, Darla brought the check—no personal touch, no emoji, no "thanks"—and placed it in front of Monica. She snatched it up. "My treat," Monica chirped as she extracted the corporate card from her wallet.

The two guests were still on Beijing time and full of energy, but Rusty was tired and eager to wrap up. "So next steps?"

"We will be in touch very soon. We have other calls to make in the area. I think I speak for Xu that we are both very interested. The timing will need to be perfect, but we will manage that aspect. We will be giving a very positive report about your town and its wonderful opportunities, and of course about the both of you."

"Thank you. That means a lot." They shook hands all around. "We have enjoyed your company immensely. We look forward to a long and productive relationship with you, your investors, and of course your venerable country."

Darla returned to the bar to run Monica's card. The restaurant had cleared out, and the party of four was the last table occupied. Jimmy again appeared through the kitchen door.

"Now there's an unsavory-looking bunch of criminals," he mused. "Looks like they're hatching some wicked scheme. Are they done plotting? I need to clean up and jet."

"Heinous. Just heinous," she fumed.

"Ooh, big word. I like it."

She ripped the credit card receipt from the machine forcibly, nearly shredding it.

"Hey, settle down, girlfriend. We're sharing tips now. Don't go messin' with my bottom line."

She slid the mangled bill into the faux-leather check holder, marched back to the table, and dropped it in front of Monica, stating in the customary fashion, "I'll be your cashier," but this time waiting tableside until Monica dealt with it. Monica was in midsentence when she realized Darla was still standing there. Rusty watched in awe.

"Yes?"

"Closing time."

"Very well." Monica smiled at the rest of the party while she signed the merchant copy, quickly calculating the tip. "There you go," she said coldly.

Darla slid the check holder into her waistband and noisily cleared some of the dishes from the table on her way back to the kitchen.

"I'll have to speak to the management about that girl. She won't have a job here tomorrow if I have anything to say about it." They were all silent.

"Well," said Rusty, changing direction, "again, thank you both." He moved toward the end of the booth to stand, and they each did likewise, followed by another round of handshakes.

Monica was the designated chauffer for the two gentlemen. "Shall we?" she said, indicating the exit.

"You are joining us?" Xu asked Rusty.

"No, no. Thanks, I've got my own car. We'll be in touch." Another round of cordial goodbyes, and they were off.

Rusty looked about the room. The busboys had swooped in, filling the space with the clang of metal on porcelain. He did not see Darla but ambled toward the bar, where Jimmy was arranging bottles, drying glasses, and refilling the garnish tubs.

"Good evening, sir. Thank you for joining us tonight. I trust everything was to your liking?"

"Yes," Rusty said, appearing distracted, "everything was fine. Say, is Dee still around? I wanted to thank her—and apologize for my colleague's bad manners. Monica can be a real piece of work."

"I believe Dee has left for the evening. Let me check." He

opened the swinging door to the kitchen and stuck his head in, speaking in a muted tone.

Dee appeared. She sauntered slowly to the bar, the top three buttons of her white blouse now opened, her hair mussed. She dabbed a cool wet bar towel to her face, neck, and chest.

"Hi."

"Hello."

"Listen, I'm a little embarrassed by the whole scene here tonight. I just wanted to say I'm sorry. She should not have treated you so shabbily."

"I can take it. You weren't exactly Prince Charming yourself. 'Come here, barmaid. Take this away, servant girl,'" she said, mocking him.

He scratched his head and smoothed his thinning hair. "Yeah, I guess I wasn't on my best behavior tonight. These guys, see, they have a lot of money to invest, and I really need this deal to go through. Maybe I pushed a little hard. It's only because I'm up to my eyeballs in it and trying to dig my way out."

"A little piece of advice? Lose the blonde. She's trouble on a stick. You'd do much better without her."

"Sure, maybe. But she's the rainmaker. She's connected all over the state, in DC, you name it."

"Whatever. Just sayin'. She also stiffed me on the tip. Not that it matters, since I have to give it all away anyway."

"Here, let me make it good." He placed a handful of cash on the counter.

"Thanks." She pocketed the bills without counting them.

"So you done for the night? Wanna get outta here and chill a bit? I could use a little down time after all that. You could too, I bet."

She shook her head. "Not tonight, Mr. Mayor. It's late. Besides, isn't it time for all you public servants to be home safe in your little beds, dreaming about how to make life better for all us common folk?"

"Maybe a rain check then? I like your style. You really know how to handle yourself."

She was momentarily flattered and again considered his offer, remembering her earlier pledge not to return to Celine's place tonight. She eyed him objectively now: four drinks (or was it five?)

and much the worse for it, the sport coat, the comb-over, the sallow skin and bloodshot eyes. Her imagination fast-forwarded to how the night would proceed.

"Save it, Your Honor. It's been fun. Good luck with your . . . issues." She spun around and was gone.

Rusty sat motionless at the bar, the cleaning staff now vacuuming around him. He got onto his feet and wobbled a bit, slowly regaining his balance, and moved cautiously toward the door.

He heard Jimmy behind him. "Thanks again, sir. Come again."

He waved without turning and disappeared into the darkness.

14. CELINE DINES ALONE

Celine uncorked the wine and carried it to the table, where she'd already arranged wineglasses, dinner plates, napkins, and silverware for two. She served up a smallish helping of stir-fried chicken and vegetables over rice onto each plate. Not too much; Darla was always in a hurry at dinnertime and didn't have an appetite until after her shift, when she was voracious.

She regarded the simple meal. A pedestrian dish, she thought, not her best but quick and satisfying, not just something to fill her sweetheart's tummy but a nightly ritual intended to warm her heart as she ventured out into the cold and dark, to protect her and see her safely home.

"Hey, hungry yet?" she called out in the direction of the bedroom. "Chicken and veggies. Gonna get cold." She sat down and played with her food for a while. "Listen, sweet. I'm sorry, really I am. Please forgive me. I shouldn't have said all those mean things to you. Can you forgive me, please?" No response. *Uh oh. The silent treatment. She must be really mad this time.*

She slowly rose from the table and treaded warily to the bedroom. "Sweetie? How long are you gonna be mad at me?" She leaned on the door jamb and cautiously looked into an empty room. *Hmm, must be in the bathroom.* "You're not doing something weird in there, I hope. Let's make up, right away, OK? Please, please, please? I'm starving . . . and I need a hug." No Darla.

In fact, she now realized, no Darla's clothes, toothbrush, make-up, or bike bags. She ran down to the carport. No Darla's bike.

Inevitably Celine grasped the obvious; Darla had snuck out the door while she was busy making dinner.

She sat on the stairs hunched over, chin in hands. She blamed herself. Why couldn't she hold her tongue? Just accept Darla for who she was, keep the peace, and reap the reward? A devil's bargain, surely, but worse than the alternative. They weren't the perfect couple, she'd admit that, and Darla was hell to live with sometimes, but she'd grown used to having her around, and for all her faults she felt protected when Darla was there.

The dread of being on her own intruded on her thoughts, immediately muscled out by a different dialogue: *That's so Darla!* she thought. *Such a drama queen. She just needs to cool off. She'll be back.*

She played a scene in her head: Darla comes home from the bar later that night. They are tentative with each other at first, then warm up slowly, apologize sincerely (mostly Celine), then touch, hug, and kiss tenderly. All is normal again.

And if not? Fast forward to scene two: Celine shows up at LaFontaine and sits at the bar in plain sight, forcing Darla to pay attention to her and convinces her, softly but firmly, that they're meant to be together, that she was totally in the wrong, she definitely could change, would change, be a better person, be more fun and less of a drag.

She climbed back up the stairs to the dining room, poured herself a full glass of wine, and tried to get interested in the stir-fry. She took a long pull of wine, topped it up, and took another long drink. After a moment things were looking better, the hurt and fear dissipating. She ate one snow pea and set her fork down.

Celine went to the living room and emptied her messenger bag. Out fell two DVDs from Videodrome: *The Haunting* with Julie Harris and Claire Bloom, and Billy Wilder's *The Fortune Cookie*. The horror movie, a psychological drama about two women trapped in a haunted house, had intrigued her in the store but now felt too dark and way too close to home. She opted for the Billy Wilder and slid it into the machine. Before settling down, she went back to the kitchen and doubled the helping of stir-fry on Darla's dish, covered it in aluminum foil, and placed it in the fridge. Darla could warm it up later when she got home. She was bound to be hungry.

The plot was simple: Jack Lemmon's disingenuous brother-in-law tries to run an insurance scam. Jeremy had called it "a morality play masquerading as a comedy." *I could use a laugh. I'll just ignore the morality part.* But she was fast asleep on the couch before any of the moral dilemma was revealed. She awoke two hours later, curled up, stiff-necked, and puffy-eyed, with *The Fortune Cookie* disc theme music playing over and over.

She quickly sat up and listened for Darla. Was that the click click click of bike gears she heard in the driveway? She looked out the window into the deserted street, saw and heard nothing, then moved quietly to the bedroom with anticipation. *Must be home asleep already.* There she saw the bed, tightly made and empty.

She lied down, coiled up in a tight ball atop the still-made bedspread, and stared at the clock. Now all her scenes played at once, one blending into the other in a crazy montage but with a new motif, louder and more dominant, coming rapidly into focus: Celine sits alone, night after perpetual night, her heart frozen and lifeless. She slowly perishes from the inside out.

Her alarm blared at 7:15 a.m., again at 7:20, then once more at 7:25, prompting her to finally roll out of bed. She showered lethargically, dressed without thinking. Minutes passed before she realized she was behind the wheel, driving the length of San Sebastian Parkway and pulling into her parking spot at Social Security. She berated herself for having blown it with Darla, still developing the talking points for their next conversation, editing her words, tossing out draft versions, honing her argument for their getting back together.

She arrived at her workstation at 8:59 a.m. The ticket dispenser was already up to eighty-seven, but only number four had so far been served. It was going to be a long day. She called the next one and greeted the young woman as she approached the desk, who told Celine a winding tale of a husband who had abandoned her and their two kids, leaving them destitute. She listened to the woman's protracted rant, tuning in and out while instinctively nodding and responding with "mm-hm" wherever she could fit one in, busily clicking through screens and typing in data.

"I'm sorry, what was that last address? And how old are the kids again?" The woman did not answer directly but continued to recite her bitter account, randomly interspersing the requested information while Celine feverishly tried to type in the data. "And your husband's age? Date of marriage? Do you have his social?"

"I told you, we're common law," she shouted. "He's thirty-four, and no, I don't have his social. Are you listening to me?"

Celine suddenly lost her focus and could not get it back. Her hands froze on the keyboard. She hung her head and sobbed silently, tears welling up.

"Hello?" The woman, who could not see Celine behind her computer screen, peered around it with a sneer. "Hey!"

"I'm so sorry." She was a quivering mess.

"Is there someone else here who can help me?" the woman demanded, looking around. "I need to speak to a supervisor."

Deb was the office lead that day. Sensing trouble from across the room, she rushed to Celine's side. There was often enough some kind of hubbub at the Social Security office, always plenty of drama, but this felt different.

"Are you all right?" Celine shook her head no, her chest heaving, unable to speak. "Ma'am, we can help you over here," Deb said, indicating the next counter over. "Calvin, can you please help this lady? Here, let me close your file." She saved the data Celine had entered and clicked the program closed. The woman gathered up her two kids and brusquely moved to the next counter. Deb put her hefty arm lovingly around Celine's shoulder and brought her to the break room. She seemed to crumple under it.

"I'm so ashamed."

"Nothing to be ashamed about, dear. Here." She handed Celine a paper cup of water from the cooler. "Now, what seems to be the trouble?"

"I don't know," she lied. She was not about to reveal any details of her private life at work. "I guess I didn't get much sleep last night, and that woman was so—"

"She's a miserable bitch," Deb whispered. "I'm not surprised the husband or boyfriend or whatever decided to leave her sorry ass." Celine giggled weakly, sniffling and dabbing her nose with a tissue from the box on the break room table. "There now. Feeling better?"

She nodded. "A little. But I can't go out there right now. I'm all nerves," she said shakily, her distress revving up again. "I can't do my job."

"Well, I don't know what's going on with you, but if you ask me, you need a mental health day. Also known as 'sick leave.'"

"Oh no, I couldn't. I'm not sick."

"Listen, I know how important it is to you to do a good job," said Deb, choosing to ignore the decline she'd seen in Celine's performance over the past few weeks. "I watch you with clients out the corner of my eye. My opinion, I think you care a little *too* much about this .place. But you can't work like this, honey. You are a disaster. You're no good to anyone in this state."

Celine reluctantly agreed. She was worthless to herself and anyone else, still reeling from the thought of losing Darla. "OK, sick leave," she nodded. "How do I do that?"

"You tell your supervisor, that's me, and then you skedaddle. Now, you OK to drive? You want me to give you a ride home?"

"No, no, I'm good. Just let me sit here for a few minutes." She sipped her water and folded her tissue.

"Good. You listen to Deb. She knows what she's talking about. Don't go back on the killing floor. You just sit here, and when you're ready, just sneak out the back."

Celine nodded docilely, and they hugged. She sat a bit longer but knew exactly what she needed to do.

At that moment Darla walked with purpose through the entrance of Videodrome. She had pulled herself together on little sleep and no makeup, showing up for work determined she would not be thrown off by the little dustup with Celine or her rough night at the restaurant. Her USPS uniform was wrinkly, having been stuffed into her pannier the night before, but her pith helmet and the blast of curls emerging uncontrolled from beneath it drew all attention away from her otherwise disheveled state.

Her mailbags felt heavy on her shoulders this morning. Samm had taken her in late last night—purely out of loyalty to an old friend, despite the protests of an angry Terri, who'd opened the door—where she'd spent the night on the couch. Samm and Darla had been an item before Darla left in a tempest and moved in with Celine the next day. Terri's icy stare, and Samm's curt note pinned to the couch this morning, confirmed for her that she was still on the prowl for a place to stay. Her mind was focused on this imperative as she encountered Jeremy.

"Hey!" He smiled.

"Hey," she replied absently, flipping through the mail.

Jeremy as always felt the presence of a powerful force when Darla entered the shop. Despite her cool indifference, her allure for him had never waned.

"Whew, hot out there, huh?" he said, struggling to get her attention. Without responding, she placed the usual stack of bills and advertisements on the counter and turned to exit, lost in her own thoughts.

"So, how's your friend Celine?" he said in a last attempt to make a connection.

Darla stopped and pivoted. Now he had her full attention.

"She's just fine. Why?"

"You guys are friends, right? She was super helpful to me, fixing up my tracking system and a bunch more. I just wanted to thank you for setting us up."

"She's here a lot, is she?" said Darla, feigning ignorance. She was, of course, acutely aware Celine spent most of her evenings at Videodrome, a habit contributing in large part to their breakup. As she looked around the store, she could see Celine's touch, appreciating a transformation in the space since her first time there.

"Oh God, yes. Almost every day after work and some Saturdays too. It's a regular thing with her, though I'm not sure why. Guess she doesn't have many friends or anywhere else to go."

Darla was half listening now. After months of delivering his mail, she finally examined Jeremy up close. Until then he had been invisible to her, a minor distraction from getting her route completed on time. She could see now how Celine might have the hots for this guy: tall, blond, gangly, but a nice body, high butt, sturdy legs, cute smile, kind eyes. A bit of a goofball, the little gray in his beard suggesting he was a bit older than he seemed, hiding behind a callow persona. Not very edgy, no tattoos or piercings. More Celine's speed than hers.

"Maybe she digs you," she offered slyly. "Ever think of that?"

"Uh, no, no, no." He waved his hands. "I don't think so. I mean, she's like wet leaves sometimes, hard to get rid of, but if I had to bet,

I'd say she likes girls."

"No! Really?" *Celine knows how to keep a secret*, she thought.

Darla took it all in. She still ached from her night on Samm's hard couch, a far cry from snuggling in her own cozy bed under an eiderdown quilt. She resented Celine for taking all that away from her: the bed, the quilt, the city view from the living room, the enormous, well-appointed kitchen, the massive Jacuzzi tub. *Well, screw her!* she thought, arriving at the obvious conclusion, an easy one really, based on her moral code and her sexuality, both of which were highly fluid.

She leisurely turned, pretending to look at a video on the shelf, then set her bags on the floor and slowly moved closer to the counter.

"And do *you* like girls, Jeremy?" She leaned her elbows on the counter, her eyes fixed on his, her breasts resting on her forearms, accentuating the cleavage visible through her open uniform top.

Jeremy was dumbstruck. He had longed for her attention, and now, for reasons he did not understand, here it was. But not the friendly, easygoing attention he had hoped for. In his personal fairy tale, he appreciated her thoroughly, and in return she appreciated him, with all his quirks and faults, odd fixations, and kindly gestures. In an instant his fantasy had been highjacked, transformed into something highly charged, wild, and terrific, his pretty reveries about friendship and understanding a thin camouflage for lust, all other considerations falling away and forgotten. Whatever they were, or were about to become, he knew in that moment they would never be friends.

She leaned in farther and he mirrored her, their breath comingling. They kissed gently, leaving no doubt what they both wanted. He felt himself pulled into a deep chasm, with nothing to grab hold of. What had brought on the abrupt turn? He couldn't fathom it, didn't care to. They kissed again, long and deep. He felt his blood surging.

"Warm in here," he said awkwardly after they broke.

"Mm-hm," she said, smiling up at him.

"Wait here."

He swiveled around from behind the counter, heading for the front door, where he turned off the Open sign and hung up the sign that read Back in a Few Minutes, Thanks! then locked the door and headed back to Darla, who had turned and was now leaning against the counter facing him, one knee bent up with her foot resting against the counter behind her, her short uniform skirt revealing her tanned muscular limbs. He took her by the hand and led her around the counter to a dilapidated couch on the far wall of the stock room.

Celine pulled out of the parking lot at Social Security and headed west. The sun was directly overhead. She gripped the wheel tightly, leaning forward, keeping her eyes on the road. She felt a burning imperative, having come face to face with the dark secret that had been nettling her for so long. She and Darla were over. She'd been living a lie. They had never really been close, not the way girlfriends should be. She'd allowed Darla to shove her around, physically and emotionally, and she had welcomed it. But no more. She felt emancipated, exuberant, ready for anything.

Her attention turned to Jeremy. *Beautiful, kind, sweet, gentle Jeremy. And smart too! Not like Darla, that dumb bitch. Jeremy and I can talk about anything really. He's so fun to be with, always joking around. He laughs at my jokes too, thinks I'm funny. And I know he appreciates everything I've done for him. He would never take me for granted. Not like Darla does.*

She bounded onto the lot at Morley Plaza, swerved to a stop in front of Videodrome, leaped from the car without locking it, and ran to the entrance. She tried the door, shaking it violently before she spied the Back in a Few Minutes sign. Perplexed, she checked the time on her cell: 11:40 a.m., definitely open hours. She cupped her hands around her eyes and looked in through the glass. The lights were on, *The Heart is a Lonely Hunter* playing on the big screen monitor. Even the miniature lava lamp was warm and burbling slowly. *Maybe he went to get some lunch. Sure, that's it. I'm never here in the morning; this is probably his usual routine. Grab lunch a few minutes before noon, before the crowd rush starts. He'll be back soon. Like it says, "Back in a Few Minutes, Thanks!"*

But Celine couldn't wait a few minutes. *He must be close by*, she figured. There was nothing within a mile of Copley and San Sebastian where he could get lunch and be back quickly. She looked around Morley Plaza for a likely place where Jeremy might be dining. She would go there, find him, and they'd have lunch together, or even better order to go, head back to the store, and have lunch there.

She crossed the lot to Burger Basket. But she did not see him in line or at any of the tables. She waited a few moments longer to see if he'd come out of the restroom. He did not. Her heart pounded. She again surveilled the plaza. Dogg Life, Mr. Richard's Salon, ReddyCare Urgent Care Clinic. None held promise.

"There. Of course, he's over there," she whispered aloud to herself, relieved that she'd solved the mystery. *I am so dumb. He loves to read.* She practically skipped with joyous anticipation toward Pickwick's Paperback Shack. *Gosh, I wonder what he's buying. I could get a book too. We could shop for one together, just the two of us. Then later, we could share what we read, and maybe even exchange books.* A sunny scenario, the brightest of them all, was writing itself as she arrived at the bookstore: Jeremy and Celine find lifelong fulfillment. They enjoy all sorts of intellectual things together: books, films, plays, music. They're the envy of all their friends. "Wow, she is so good for him." "And he's really brought out the best in her. I've never seen them happier."

The bell chimed as Celine entered the store.

A cheerful "Hi, there" came from behind the stacks. "Welcome."

"Hi," she replied distractedly. She searched the bookstore while trying to keep an eye on Videodrome across the lot, lest she miss Jeremy's return. She made a dash up and down the aisles, checking every crook and crevice of the store, believing each time she'd divined what section he would most likely be in but discovering only an empty row. She entertained for a moment that he might be behind the beaded curtain and stuck her head boldly into the Adults Only section but again saw no Jeremy. She felt as empty and flat as a crushed shoebox. The room spun, her heart raced, and everything seemed to be disappearing from her grasp. *Got to get back to the window,* she thought. *He may be back by now.*

As Celine turned the corner at the History section, Donna intercepted her. "Hello there. Help you find something in particular?"

"Yes, um, my boyfriend," she said, embarrassed by the word. "Has he been in? He's tall, blond, with a ponytail, really kind eyes."

"Oh well! A boyfriend is a very important thing to find. Sounds like quite a catch," Donna said kindly. "Sadly, I have not seen anyone matching that beautiful description today. Now, short, bald, scruffy, wacky, edgy—I can provide all manner of access to any one of those types if the other doesn't work out." She smiled wryly, telegraphing to Celine that she was pulling her leg. Celine finally got the joke and laughed out loud. She squinted out the window and could see the Back in a Few Minutes sign still hanging on the door. *I can pound on the glass,* she thought, *or maybe I should go home and come back later.* She chose a third option. *I'll just camp out right here till he shows up.*

"Now that you mention it, do you have any books on love?"

"I assume you mean 'romantic love' and not love of country, the human race, or God?" Donna escorted Celine to the Philosophy section. "Here's one." She handed her *The Four Loves* by C. S. Lewis. "There are five kinds of love in the Bible. The Greeks described eight, can you believe it? There's probably even more."

Celine glanced at the cover and flipped through the book. She was not interested in love as an abstract concept but the love of a man for a woman, a woman who was terribly flawed, a little gawky, emotionally fragile, sometimes sad, physically unimpressive but with the purest of hearts and deepest of souls. *That should be enough for any man, right?*

"How about something to make a man love you? I mean, love you even more than he already does."

"Ah, now that is something of a specialty of mine." She motioned Celine over to a darker corner of the store, where books glowed eerily under cool purple and warm red-orange lamplights. A glass skull sat grinning on the shelf. Donna selected a book and handed it to her.

"*Witchcraft and Love Spells*? Uh, no. Thank you, but that's not really the sort of thing I'm looking for," Celine said, returning it to her. She recalled her grandmother's constant admonition against falling prey to sorcery and devil worship, which included witchcraft, hypnosis, meditation, self-help, and yoga. She had attended a few yoga classes, true, but not without an overwhelming sense of guilt.

"I understand. It's not for everyone really. But, if I may make a suggestion by way of explanation? Witchcraft, many say and I do believe this, is a very practical skill, just a refined form of wishing for something—for love, as in your case, or for wealth and success, health, happiness, calmness, contentment, friendship, camaraderie, even enlightenment. All the important things each of us needs. A spell is just a way to make a formal request from the universe. 'Hey, Universe, Donna down here.'" She waved toward the sky. "Sorry, what was your name, dear?"

"Celine."

"Oh, how perfect! What a beautiful name. It means 'heavenly.' Anyway, it's like, 'Hey, Universe, Celine down here. Listen, Universe, I was wondering, if you could see your way clear to make—' What is the name of your beau again?"

"Jeremy."

"'Could you please make Jeremy really love, adore, and appreciate me? I would be ever so grateful. And to help you, Universe, to make your work easier, I am going to get myself together mentally and emotionally, think happy thoughts, stay strong and healthy, be interested in him, be interesting *to* him, and generally project so much lovability that he will have no choice but to adore me. Thanks very much, Universe. Amen.' See? Like a prayer, really. Very powerful stuff. I would not reject it out of hand before trying it at least once," Donna said and once more offered the volume to her.

But by then Celine she had stopped listening, having watched through the window as Jeremy unlocked the door of Videodrome to let Darla out, her mailbags slung over her shoulders, her blue-gray USPS uniform off kilter and needing adjustment. As the door swung closed, Jeremy switched the Open sign back on.

Celine wanted to dash immediately to his side, not to ask what the hell was going on but to simply be with him and confess her love. She realized Darla was still completing her route at Morley Plaza and didn't want to run into her, so she held back until Darla disappeared into ReddyCare Urgent Care Clinic.

"Sorry, gotta go," she said to Donna without looking at her, then darted out of the bookstore, head down, slinking along the storefronts.

She was about halfway across the plaza when Darla reemerged from ReddyCare, heading toward Burger Basket. Celine turned away, watching Darla's reflection in the window of the hair salon as she traversed the lot behind her. The proprietor, Mr. Richard, waved and beckoned Celine in, motioning to the empty salon chair in front of him. She did not acknowledge him but instead turned and sprinted to Videodrome as soon as Darla had slipped into the burger place. On the way in, Celine passed her own parked car directly in front of the video store. *Oh shit! She knows I'm here.*

She burst through the glass door, locked it, and flipped off the Open sign. Jeremy emerged from the back room.

"Oh hi, Celine. You're here early. Day off?"

She was hyperventilating, peeking out the window for signs of Darla before turning to him.

"Was that Darla I saw?" she asked. She was in free fall again, voice quivering, anguished tears flowing uncontrollably.

"Oh right, your friend who hooked us up on that computer stuff. Yeah, this is her mail route. You know that, right? Say, it's the middle of the day. What are you doing here?"

"What was *she* doing here?" Her eyes narrowed, burning holes in his.

"Delivering the mail, like I said. What?"

"I said, what was she *doing... in here? With the door locked?*" Celine yelled. "Since when do you need to lock the door to deliver the mail?"

"Um, she wanted to see something in the back. Some new videos I just got. They're still in boxes, and I haven't had time to inventory them. Man, it's been busy around here."

She felt her last measure of sadness and betrayal transform into pure anger.

"You're a FUCKING LIAR," she screeched. "She HATES your fucking videos. She tells me all the time. And she hates YOU. She thinks you're a LOSER."

The last twenty confused minutes with Darla had left Jeremy vulnerable, and Celine had landed a blow. "Wait, you talk about me, to her?"

"Yes. We talk about you. In our bed! After we FUCK! She's my girlfriend."

"I don't believe you."

"Did you fuck my girlfriend on that dirty old couch in back of your shitty little store? Ugh, you are such a fucking asshole!" she screamed with such loss of control that, for the first time, she actually scared Jeremy.

"You don't know what you're talking about. And by the way, dude, she's not gay, trust me."

"LIAR!" Celine marshaled all her anger and strength and was able to shove a full shelf of DVDs crashing onto the floor. She found it remarkably easy and satisfying. She wanted to do some real damage, to hurt Jeremy just where she knew it would. She shoved another shelf down with a thunderous racket, scattering DVD cases to the farthest reaches of the floor.

Jeremy rushed over and held both her wrists trying to restrain her. Still she managed to reach up and gouge his cheek with her nails, leaving deep scratches that bled freely. She wrestled out of his grip and pulled down the vintage *Casablanca* poster from the window, shredding it in the process. Finally, she yanked on the neon Open sign by the electrical cord and catapulted it across the room and into the opposite wall, where it shattered into a thousand pieces.

"Bastard!" She kicked the door but, forgetting she had locked it, left a spiderweb pattern in the glass. She unlocked it and ran out, fumbled with her keys, and drove off, leaving Jeremy standing speechless in the mayhem she had wrought.

Celine barreled down San Sebastian Parkway toward home, not certain if she'd run a few red lights on the way. The pain in her heart had subsided while she trashed Jeremy's store, but soon it returned harder and stronger. She had lost two lovers in a single day, one real and one pretend. She had burned her bridges down to ashes and embers.

Before long she was turning into her driveway. Her eyes stung, and her face was swollen and covered with tears and snot. She reflexively climbed the stairs to her door and let herself in. She saw no way out of the valley of despair in which she wallowed alone and forsaken, nothing for it but to go deeper still and pull the earth in over her. For the second time today, she knew exactly what she needed to do.

She went from the foyer to the bathroom, then to the medicine cabinet, where she took out a small brown bottle of Ambien and two white bottles of over-the-counter sleeping pills. She carefully transferred all three bottles to the dining room table, where the unused place settings still sat from the night before. She went to the fridge and brought back an almost full bottle of white wine, emptied the pills onto a plate, and pulled the cork from the bottle. She was careful not to overdo it, taking a small handful of pills at a time, followed by two or three swallows of wine. She finished off the last of the pills and had enough wine left for a few more swallows.

"There now." She took a deep breath and, for the first time since yesterday, felt an overwhelming sense of calm and clarity. She sat for few moments, reading the label on the wine bottle before her vision started to blur.

Celine stood up and wobbled to the writing desk in the living room, supporting herself with the walls and furniture. She pulled out some plain blank paper from the printer but, setting it aside, opened the top desk drawer and instead laid out a sheet of the nicer stationery with a faint pink cloud pattern. She wrote:

Darla,
By the time you read this I'll be dead. I realize I don't belong in this world anymore. I am so happy to leave it.
You treated me terribly, but I let you do it, so I don't blame you. I'm not as strong as you are. I can't do it anymore. You win. I hope you and Jeremy will be happy.
Tell my mother I love her.
Cee

She carefully folded the letter and slid it into a matching envelope, tucked in the flap, and wrote Darla across the front, then propped it up on the breakfast bar.

Her eyelids were very heavy now, the pills taking effect much faster than she had anticipated—she hadn't eaten anything that day—but she welcomed the feeling, the rush of oblivion comforting her in its deep bosom. She again navigated the room with great difficulty, her head spinning, and flopped down onto the bed. The sun was bright through the window. She groggily pulled the pillow over her head to shield it from the light.

15. CRIME WAVE

Geoff Saboteau cautiously cruised the parkway just below the speed limit. On the seat beside him lay paperback copies of *The Grapes of Wrath* and *The Philosophy of Moral Development*. Pink and blue Post-its poked out from between the pages, some with short, scribbled notes, others with only a word or two followed by question marks.

He drove with a copy of *Tortilla Flat* propped on the steering wheel. Every few hundred feet, he'd peek over the edge of the book to navigate the vehicle, but otherwise his eyes were down in the text. At each red light he read a few more pages before it changed to green. At one signal, in midparagraph, the motorist behind him grew impatient and tapped his horn. Geoff finished reading to the end of the page before driving off unperturbed.

Geoff was bound for his three o'clock shift at Dogg Life but had left his apartment early, planning a stop at Pickwick's Paperback Shack before work. He looked forward to seeing Donna again, to discuss the books she had loaned him and to pay for them. That was their deal. "If you like them, pay me later. Otherwise bring them back for a full refund." He liked them all right but had many questions he hoped to explore with her.

But Geoff lost his place as he pulled in. He saw the police cruiser first, then an EMS unit haphazardly parked in front of Donna's store, their red and blue lights flashing erratically. A tearful Donna stood on the walkway, attended by a young paramedic and, in her stiff white lab coat, her neighbor Dr. Sunita Reddy. Donna's left forearm was wrapped in white gauze. She was speaking with a female officer, the same one who had taken Geoff's report about the dumpster assailant some days ago. As the officer listened and wrote in her little notebook, she sometimes stopped to place a hand on Donna's shoulder to comfort her. Geoff parked the Bomb and rushed over to them.

"Donna. My God, what happened?" The group turned in unison, startled as Geoff's large lumbering shape darted toward them. Donna went straight to him, got up on her toes, and hugged him around the neck with her one good arm. The officer recognized him from several days ago by his Dogg Life logo shirt. She opened her mouth to speak, wanting to maintain control of the scene, but seeing Donna's reaction she held back.

"Oh, Geoff. It was just awful."

"What the hell happened?" he asked again. He looked with concern at a small circle of red already seeping through the fresh white dressing.

"I'm fine now, really," she assured him, "just a little scratch." She looked at the officer, seeking her permission to stop the interview and bring Geoff up to speed.

"I think I've got everything I need," she said. "We've got a pretty good idea of who we're dealing with here. Second incident in a week. Regular one-man crime wave. Here's my card. Call me if he comes back. We're going to take a look around." She walked back to the cruiser, where her partner was speaking on the radio.

Dr. Reddy broke in curtly. "Come over to my office when you are finished here. You will need that wound properly cleansed and examined. We'll update your tetanus as well. Don't delay."

"Thank you, Doctor. And thank you . . . Michael," she added, looking down at the paramedic's badge. "You are very kind."

"Glad to help. I guess we can clear now. Follow the doc's instructions. You folks take care." He packed up his heavy jump bag and lugged it back to the EMS truck.

Geoff finally put it all together: the cop car, the medics, the blood. "Somebody cut you," he stated bluntly, increasingly agitated. She nodded.

"Now, don't get all worked up, Geoffrey. I told you, I'm fine. I just don't understand it. I mean, what did I ever do to him, except show him respect and try to help?"

"Stop talking in riddles. Help who? You know this guy?"

"Sort of. He parks his cart over there sometimes and comes into the shop, wanting to barter for books. He just loves to read, I'll give him credit for that. Usually brings me some sad little item of no use to anyone, a broken statue or a cup with a chip in it. I usually take it and give him store credit, but never more than a dollar's worth. He goes right to the Sci-Fi section, or Biography, usually picks something interesting. Or he'll dig a couple of quarters out of his pocket and bargain some more. If it's not too expensive, I let him have it. Better to let it go to a good home, I say, than sit on the shelf."

"OK, never mind that. Jeez, Donna."

"So I show up this morning, and there he is, sprawled out right in front of the store, with his cart parked over there. I couldn't even get in the door. And then . . ."

She walked partway to the end of the storefront. Geoff now smelled the unmistakable odor of human feces, strong and pungent. They both instinctively placed their hands over their nose and mouth. On the walkway just below the window ledge was a mix of solid and runny brown waste. Amid the excrement lay several soiled napkins emblazoned with the Burger Basket logo.

"Ew, that's nasty," he said, keeping his distance.

"You think? I walked over to him and tried to rouse him, you know, so I could get in the door, thank you very much, and maybe have him clean up after himself. He was dead asleep, snoring, but I recognized him right away. Maybe I made a mistake, but I leaned over and touched him on his shoulder. Maybe I should have nudged him with my foot. It would have been safer, I suppose, but I just couldn't do it. So, anyway, I shook him very gently and said, 'Sir, excuse me, sir,' and just then, like lightning, he was on his feet. Before I knew it, he was lunging at me. I jumped back, then I felt a sting and something wet on my arm. I looked and saw I was bleeding. It was only then I saw the knife in his hand. I must have screamed, but by then he was off. He ran to his cart and pushed it around the corner. I was so upset, Geoff. I called 9-1-1 and just stood there bleeding all over myself. I didn't know what else to do."

He looked down and saw several drops of Donna's blood drying on the pavement. "I guess it could have been a lot worse. Come on, let's get you over to the doc's and have that cut looked at."

She allowed him to lead her passively by the hand, down the walkway and around the corner to ReddyCare Urgent Care. His hulking size and doting manner were comforting to her. She relaxed for the first time since the incident.

"Did you hear that?" she asked, "'Crime wave.' Wow! I wonder if it really was the same guy who attacked you."

"Yeah, I bet it was the same guy." He remembered the story he had recounted to everyone the week before about being attacked with a knife and having to defend himself, the incident growing more dire and dramatic with each telling, a story not unlike Donna's, except in his case it never happened. As they walked together, the memory of the actual event took shape in his mind—a shadowy gray form bursting out of the dumpster and disappearing just as quickly, as Geoff brandished his improvised weapon from a good distance. He was embarrassed by his tall tale now that his new friend had been attacked.

"Say, about that day. I may have overstated things. Just a touch."

"You mean, you made it up?"

"No, no, just embellished the story a wee bit to spur the cops into action. I don't think they believed me anyway. But now"—he pointed to her wounded limb—"they've got to do something, right?" He expected her to scold him or shun him. She did neither.

"Geoff, I'm sure you had your reasons for exaggerating. You were pretty shaken up, as I recall." Her soothing voice calmed him as it would a frightened animal. "Besides, you're right; now they've got to do something."

They walked into the urgent care clinic and presented themselves at the reception desk. A young woman greeted them; the name plate on her desk read Lori Cogan. She looked about nineteen. The right side of her head was shaved clean, the remainder of her hair the color of blue curaçao. She wore deep maroon lip gloss and heavy black eyeliner that came to a sharp point at the tips to resemble cats' eyes.

"Good morning, folks. How may we help you today?" There was a childlike simplicity in her voice, a contrast to her hard-edged appearance.

"Hi, I'm Donna. I own the bookstore across the way there. I have this cut," she said, showing her forearm. "Dr. Reddy said I should have it looked at."

Lori made no effort to acknowledge Donna as a neighbor, but simply handed her a clipboard with several forms attached. The ballpoint pen wedged under the metal clip advertised "ReddyCare Urgent Care Clinic. When you need care, we're Reddy!"

"Please take a moment to provide us with some medical history and your insurance information. The doctor will see you as quickly as possible."

Geoff and Donna looked at each other and took a seat in the empty waiting room. Donna's arm had started to throb, and she was having trouble holding the pen, so Geoff took on the task of completing the forms.

"Name?"

"Elizabeth Donatella Hart."

"Today's date? That's an easy one. Address?"

"4616 East Campagna Way."

"Date of birth."

"None of your beeswax. Here, let me see that." She took the form from him and began to stiffly fill it out, the discomfort showing on her face. He noticed for the first time she was left-handed. At that moment Dr. Reddy swooped into the waiting room and greeted Donna and Geoff in military fashion.

"Good, you've come." She took the clipboard from Donna. "We won't be needing this." She handed it to Lori and waved Donna into the back hallway.

Donna looked at Geoff. "May my friend come along?"

"Of course," Sunita said, addressing Geoff, "provided he does not faint. I do not need two patients."

She led them into a spacious examination room. The air was filled with the scent of aseptic cleanliness. The open miniblinds afforded a peek at the chain-link fence marking the rear boundary of Morley Plaza. In an attempt to conceal the ugly fence, Dr. Reddy had placed at four-foot intervals several potted creeping fig plants; some were lush and thriving, others brown and struggling. On the walls of the treatment room were displayed an eclectic mix of anatomical charts, South Asian travel posters, and photographs of flowers in extreme close-up. Below this was a stainless-steel sink and long counter stocked with examination equipment and supplies for injections, blood draws, and bedside lab tests.

Dr. Reddy sat down at her mobile workstation as Donna climbed onto the exam table, which was a little too high, forcing her to use the low footstool nearby. She allowed the doctor to slowly unwrap the gauze, exposing a fresh laceration at the side of her left forearm about three-eighths of an inch in length. The bleeding had stopped, though a bit of swelling was now evident around the wound. She cautiously palpated the area with gloved hands, spread the wound edges apart, asked Donna to move her wrist and fingers, and checked for numbness.

"A classic defensive wound. Your homeless man must be right-handed. You see?" She mimed blocking an attack with her left hand from an imaginary assailant.

"Good. That'll help us—I mean, help the police find him," Geoff said eagerly.

"Now, there are an awful lot of right-handed people out there," Donna reminded him, "but yes, it might help."

"Do you know when you received your last tetanus booster?"

"Gosh, Doctor, I have no clue. Maybe when I entered college?"

"Many years ago, then. I will update you today. You will be good for another ten years! Now, I will need to irrigate the wound. It may be uncomfortable for you. Would you prefer a local anesthetic?"

"No, that won't be necessary. Can I squeeze your hand, Geoff?"

"Sure." He smiled.

The doctor prepared her equipment: sterile gloves, a large syringe with an irrigating tip, a liter bottle of saline, a small plastic basin, two rolls of white gauze, and a roll of stretchy beige tape.

As she irrigated the wound, Donna winced at first but soon relaxed. She squeezed Geoff's enormous paw, causing him to wince himself. Having used most of the liter, she declared the procedure complete.

"The wound is very clean now. It is not very deep, and your function appears to be unaffected. Regarding stitches, you do not absolutely need them; it is your choice. You will have a scar there either way, perhaps a little smaller if we sew it."

"No stitches, please. Leave it open. I heal quickly. If there's a scar, maybe it'll remind me to be more careful in the future. Besides, I've imposed on you quite enough already."

"I will send you home with enough supplies to change the dressing daily. This tape adheres to itself, see? Perhaps your friend here can help you." Dr. Reddy wrapped the wound and delivered the tetanus shot under Geoff's watchful gaze. "Now, I must speak to you on another matter. May I discuss your medical history in the presence of your friend here?"

"Of course. I have nothing to hide."

"Except your birthday," Geoff said, and they both laughed out loud.

"OK, I'm thirty-eight, if you must know."

"Hey, me too!"

"Oh my God, that's amazing. Really?"

"No, not really. I'm thirty-two, actually."

"Oh, you . . ." She punched his arm. "Well, in that case, I'm forty-two, actually. So there!" They were now laughing uncontrollably, poking fun and leaning into each other, their heads briefly touching.

"Please, you two. I need your attention now."

"Sorry, Doctor. Please go on."

"Again, I am not concerned about infection in the usual sense."

"That's good, right?"

"But there are other types of infection." Dr. Reddy educated them about the risks of viral transmission. She was not worried about HIV, a fragile virus with little stamina outside the body. As for hepatitis, she explained, in theory it could survive on objects for a week, but there were no reported cases of transmission in knife wounds like Donna's.

"Now, if this individual had just stabbed himself"—she laughed—"or stabbed someone else, then used the same bloody knife immediately to stab you, then we might be worried. But I am not. I believe you are safe."

"You *believe* she is safe?'" asked Geoff, standing up nervously. He did not appreciate her humorous approach. "You're saying she could get hepatitis?"

"It would be rare. If you are worried, we could start the hepatitis vaccine series."

"OK, then, let's do it," he said.

"Stop! Geoff, please, sit. This is my body we're talking about. Now, Doctor, what I am hearing is that, while there is a slight possibility of contracting one these viral infections, you believe it is very unlikely under the circumstances." The doctor nodded. "That's good enough for me," Donna said, pulling down her sleeve and donning her jacket. "I really don't want to do any more tests or shots or pills or vaccines."

"Thank you for making your wishes clear. Sometimes when the science is not perfect, we rely on patient preferences. Some patients are very risk averse. I think you've made the right choice," Dr. Reddy said, then turned to Geoff. "I am sorry if I caused any alarm."

He did not respond. His mind was focused elsewhere: on the assailant, the one who had hurt his friend and who now roamed the streets freely preying on others or hid in some thicket, eluding the police, while he and Donna had to endure this trauma.

The doctor typed a few lines into the computer and printed out several pages of wound care tips and other instructions. She walked Donna and Geoff to the waiting room.

"No charge for today," Sunita said to Lori. "Professional courtesy."

Donna graciously thanked each of them. Geoff, staring at the floor, said nothing but rushed out through the open clinic door, with Donna following. She glanced back at Sunita and Lori apologetically and exited the building.

16. TASK FORCE

Donna caught up with Geoff outside the clinic, where a hazy afternoon glare greeted them. She clung tightly to his arm as they strolled back to the bookstore. Neither spoke until they'd reached the front door. The odor of feces still hung heavy in the air.

"Thank you for looking out for me back there," she said. "Lots to take in, huh?"

"Sure, no worries."

"I know you were getting upset. I just want you to know, I'm a big girl, and I can take care of myself. But it sure is nice to have someone like you in my corner."

"Look," he said, struggling to find the words, "you were pretty nice to me the other day. That doesn't happen to me much. I won't forget it."

"Aww," she said, placing her hand on his.

"Donna, I know we don't know each other very well, but somehow I feel like I've known you my whole life. Weird, huh?"

"No. Not really."

"You should also know, most days I'm kind of a mess. But somehow you seem to ignore all that. You're able to just look the other way when I'm acting up. Not sure how you do it, or why, but I appreciate it."

"It's magic!" They laughed, breaking the tension.

"I just . . . I don't want anyone or anything to hurt you."

She hugged his arm tightly. "No one's going to hurt me."

"That Dr. Reddy could learn a thing or two about bedside manner, boy."

"She's a little rough around the edges, it's true, but I really think she wants to do the right thing. She ran right over today when she saw the ambulance pull up. She was very gentle with me when I needed it. I was a total freaking mess. It was nice of her to waive the bill, don't you think? Since I don't have insurance."

"I guess."

"People like Dr. Reddy have pure intentions; they just have trouble expressing themselves. You've got to see them for who they really are down deep."

"Down deep can be just as ugly as what's on the surface."

"True enough, but more often you'll find a frightened child just trying to do their best and needing a little love."

A gentle breeze blew their way, and the pungent aroma of feces grew stronger.

"Oh, Geoff. What am I going to do with this?"

"Please, leave it to me. I'm used to cleaning up after animals." He tapped his Dogg Life logo. "You go open your store. I'll take care of this."

"Can't I help?"

"Go, I've got this."

"No, please let me help. Besides, I can't really open up until. . ." She pinched her nostrils.

"OK. But I don't want you dealing with any of the rough stuff. You've had enough abuse from that guy already. I'll be right back."

He jogged over to Dogg Life and returned arms loaded, carrying a length of hose with a spray nozzle, a shovel, a scrub brush on a broom handle, powdered detergent, a bottle of bleach, two pairs of gloves and a five-gallon bucket with a plastic liner. He donned his own gloves and gave the smaller pair to Donna. He deftly scooped up the waste and soiled napkins into the liner, tied the top tightly, and handed it to Donna, who deposited it in a nearby Morley Plaza trash receptacle. He then located a hose bib and, with Donna operating the spigot, filled the bucket with water, sprinkled in detergent, and added a generous splash of bleach. Geoff warned Donna to be careful, that the bleach may damage her shoes. He vigorously scrubbed the walkway and adjacent wall in front of

Pickwick's, working up a sweat while eliminating any remnants of the night visitor. He then hosed down the walkway and wall, sending a stream of frothy bubbles swooshing into the gutter. The foul odor was eradicated, replaced by the strong, reassuring fragrance of chlorine.

"What do you think?" he asked proudly. The concrete walk had already started to dry in the summer heat, sending up a steamy mist.

"Wonderful, just wonderful. I can't thank you enough." She seemed to fight back a tear. "You're quite proficient!"

"Like you said, it's magic—and a bit of practice."

"And hard work. Come on in, I've got some cold drinks in the fridge." She escorted him into the bookstore, where it was a shady ten degrees cooler, and opened the minifridge behind the counter. "Let's see, we've got Sprite, Coke, kombucha, OJ, bubbly water, coconut water, vitamin water, plain water—"

"Sprite'll be fine."

"Here you go." She opened a coconut water for herself. They each took a long draw, finishing with a simultaneous "aahhh."

"Hits the spot."

"I'll say." She prepared the shop to open for business, turning over the Open sign, arranging her sales log, and firing up her credit card reader. She rolled the cart of one-dollar books out onto the freshly cleansed walkway.

"So did you enjoy the little collection of books we sent home with you last time?"

"Sure did. I wrote down a bunch of stuff I wanted to talk about, but darn it, I left them all in the car. Here, let me pay you for them."

"Only if you got something out of them. Otherwise I'm happy to take them back." She perched herself on the high wooden stool behind the counter, then took out of the top drawer a stack of small paper bags with handles. With a red ink pad and rubber stamp, she methodically applied the bookstore's logo to the center of each one.

"No, I did, really. Here, I think I owe you twelve bucks. Two each for the Steinbecks and eight for the Kohlberg, right?"

"I believe you," she said wryly.

He turned to retrieve the annotated books from his car.

NEUTRAL, NO BRAKES

"Hey, wait. Come sit, relax. Enjoy your Sprite. It's hot out there. You've been working hard all morning, and besides, don't you have to do a shift at the doggie place in a little while?"

"I do."

"So chill a minute." She continued stamping her bags as he took the matching stool at the end of the counter. "I am curious, though," she murmured, faking as much indifference as she could muster, masking her true motives.

"About?"

"About those books. What did you think of them?" she asked casually. "Your general impression, off the top of your head."

He did not hesitate.

"The Steinbecks were great reading. He's a talented storyteller."

"Go on."

"OK, so I know we're supposed to sympathize with these characters, but don't you think he's asking a little much? Like Tom Joad. He's an ex-con, a murderer with a chip on his shoulder, pissed off at the world, suspicious of everyone, a tendency toward violence, can't hold a job, hates authority, always looking for trouble, and guess what, it finds him everywhere. The rest of the family, they're borderline dysfunctional. Short-sighted, small-minded, generally cussed, no education, few transportable skills, overdependent on religion, their faith misplaced in institutions that don't come through for them in the end, big surprise. OK, it's not *totally* their fault, dust bowl, et cetera. They're shrewd and wily, and Mother Joad seems like a kind soul. But don't they own some of the blame for the fix they're in? Is he suggesting that no one's responsible for any of the bad shit that happens to them, that it's always someone else's fault?"

Donna took out a next-size stack of bags and continued rubber stamping them.

"Same with *Tortilla Flat*. Couldn't put it down. Finished it literally on the way over here. But same deal again. Lazy bums all of them, drunkards, petty crooks, self-centered, self-serving, duplicitous, justifying any act in the name of immediate gratification. And that ending? Sitting there letting the house burn down? Retarded! I will say this, though, it was a brilliant exploration into the workings of the criminal mind. Anyway, I really enjoyed them both. Thanks."

"Hmm" was all Donna could utter in response. She had lent him the two Steinbecks after his run-in with the hooded vagrant, hoping he'd glean some insight into the plight of the desperate and destitute. Instead, Geoff's point of view hadn't softened but solidified. But how could she fault him after her own violent encounter and his touchingly sympathetic response? Her throbbing arm caused her to doubt her own humanistic leanings.

Donna had one other motive. Despite his ham-handed crudeness, gruff talk, and ungainly form, Geoff was one of the few persons she'd ever considered her intellectual equal. She had long sought a sparring partner with whom she could debate the big questions, one she could convince, firmly but gently, of the rightness of her own well-considered views. She pined for a safe harbor where she could reveal her true soul and was ready for anyone who might go there with her. The book assignments had been an experiment to determine if Geoff was truly a Neanderthal or just pretending to be one. Alas, she had revealed the brute in him—a clever brute but a brute no less. But in spite of it, she'd begun to feel a nascent and unfamiliar awareness in her breast that brushed away all his shortcomings. Inexplicably and overwhelmingly, she wanted to be with him.

"And the Kohlberg?" she asked.

"OK, now tell me the truth. Were you trying to teach me something when you recommended that book?"

"Maybe. Did you learn something?"

"It is an interesting treatise. A little thick, so I'm still plodding through it. But it strikes me that his system is not so much a hierarchy as a practical toolbox for dealing with a complex world."

"How so?"

"Sometimes doesn't it just make sense to be obedient to authority? Like when you're sitting at a four-way stop. You don't really need a lofty ethical principle to guide you, just obey the rules. Or when someone stabs you and takes a crap on your doorstep. Isn't it better to be selfish than altruistic?"

"Makes it hard to be a humanitarian, I'll give you that."

"My point exactly."

"Well, very thoughtful comments, I must say."

"Thank you, Teacher."

"I don't happen to agree with a single one of them."

"We're all entitled to our own opinion."

"And entitled to be wrong."

"Hey, now hold on a minute. I thought you were the free-thinking, open-minded librarian type. No wrong answers. Everyone welcome to feast at the smorgasbord of ideas, et cetera."

"Librarian type? Gee, thanks." Geoff immediately regretted the mocking dig. He was no good at filtering himself and knew it. He'd given up trying to tame his insufferable side and instead used it as a test to see who could tolerate him and for how long. *Take me as I am or leave me alone.* The strategy, while revealing in the short term, had left him alone most of the time, which he considered the price of intellectual freedom.

"OK, mister, here's why you're wrong. First of all, there *is* a high moral principle at work in every human encounter, no matter how trivial. It's called unconditional positive regard. At the four-way stop, you've got to care about what's best for your neighbor, or else the social contract falls apart. And while I don't appreciate someone crapping on my doorstep, and certainly don't delight in the idea of being stabbed, I refuse to let it to harden me. If I do, I am forever diminished. Look, we all sit on a little speck of dust, hurtling through space, all made of the same stuff. And yet we spend our days focused on ourselves or our little tribe."

"We've got to protect ourselves and our tribe."

"I'm sorry, I don't believe in tribes. There is no difference between me and that sorry soul who stabbed me. If I hate him, I hate me. And I certainly don't hate me. As for the Joads, it's a sympathetic portrayal, true, but why shouldn't we sympathize with them? An otherwise well-meaning person might do anything under the right stressors—live in a tent, panhandle, steal, shoot drugs, even kill."

"There but for the grace of God?" he scoffed.

"Yes," she insisted, "that's right."

Geoff conceded without protest. He wanted to argue his point more decisively but recognized she could not be swayed from her position, nor would she have any luck dislodging him from his.

"You make a persuasive argument," he said. "I'll be the first to acknowledge your 'speck of dust' theory. We are just one step up from the muck."

"That's not what I said exactly." But she was grateful for the small concession and a momentary truce. They'd both had a hell of a morning and were worn out.

"How's your arm?"

She rubbed it. "A little throbby."

He drank from his Sprite and said, "So, what do we do now?"

"God, I don't know. There must be some way to lift these people up, get them back on their feet."

"Right, enough is enough."

Their back-and-forth continued for a few more passes, aimed in completely different directions. She spoke passionately about awakening the spirit of the community, encouraging everyone to lend a hand, recognizing the homeless as our legitimate neighbors. He in turn reiterated his unwavering view that vagrancy, crime, and chaos had run rampant for too long, and that productive citizens should not be forced to deal with trash, needles, or car prowls. The homeless were a drag on society and should be driven out.

"Wait, what? No, you've got it all wrong."

"Do I? I thought we were brainstorming here. Besides, you know I'm right."

Geoff continued at length to remind her of her injury, proclaiming the rule of law was the bedrock of our way of life and that civil society could only endure so much.

As Geoff's meandering diatribe drew to a close, Donna was lost in her own thoughts. She continued stamping the paper bags with robotic efficiency, completing another forty before finally speaking.

"The universe will always tell us what we need to know," she said softly. "All that's required is for us to be still and listen." Geoff took this as a request for his continued silence and complied.

"What if . . ." she said.

"What if what?"

"What if we formed a committee? No, wait. Not a committee. A task force! What if we formed a task force? One that could really tackle this problem."

"Committee or task force. What's the difference?"

"Oh, big difference," she explained. "A committee is a perpetual bureaucracy that never achieves anything; it's just an excuse for more meetings. But a task force. Now that's a thing of beauty. A task force has vigor and intensity. It has balls. And a finite lifespan, that's very important. The clock is always ticking for a task force. And once it meets its objectives, it disbands into thin air."

"OK, so what's next?" he asked, sensing she was about to woo him into something very big.

Donna was energized now. She went on about affordable housing, wraparound services, and community policing; about recruiting members, giving testimony, and holding meetings at the local coffee house. The talk of social interaction made him queasy.

As she listed her projects in rapid succession, Geoff felt his neck muscles begin to tense. Donna's voice seemed to come from a far distance. The skin across his forehead felt prickly and moist. His breath became rapid and shallow; his heart thumped heavily in his chest.

"So, what do you think?" she asked. "Geoff?"

He could not hear her now or answer her. He felt dizzy and weak. His vision grayed in and out. His hands had gone into a contorted spasm. He could not feel his fingertips.

"Geoff, are you OK?"

He kept his eyes closed and took slow, deep breaths through his mouth. *Get hold of yourself, boy,* he thought. *Come on, you're OK. You're not dying.* He planted his feet firmly on the floor, wiggled his toes in his shoes, gripped his thighs, felt the texture of his khaki slacks. He opened his eyes a crack, but, instead of looking at Donna, he focused on the red ink pad, noticed its porous surface, the sheen of wet ink, the slightly worn and compressed spot in the middle, the hinged metal case randomly stained with red, all the while breathing more slowly, more deeply. *I'm here,* he told himself, *I'm alive, here in the bookstore, in Morley, with Donna.* He heard her calling his name from a distance. He blinked a few times, then turned to her.

"Hi," he said weakly.

"Hello. Welcome back."

"That was a little embarrassing."

"Not at all," she replied patiently. "Seizure or panic attack?"

"Panic attack. How'd you know?"

"Seen them before. Better now?"

"Yeah, better. That wasn't a bad one." He took a sip of Sprite. "I never know when they're going to come on, but they're getting a lot shorter. I've learned a few, what do you call, techniques? Helps me to focus and break the cycle early, if I can. God, I'm so sorry."

"Hush now. I'm the one who should be sorry. Did I say too much too fast? I didn't mean to bowl you over. I know I tend to get a little excited."

He was still lightheaded but felt less anxious, more in control. "No, you're fine. My fault totally. I told you I was a mess."

"You're not a mess, my friend." She slid off her stool and hugged him. "You are a beautiful soul, Geoffrey, so smart and thoughtful, so passionate about what you believe. And most important, you are kind." She grabbed his shoulders, held him out at arm's length, and looked him straight in the eyes. "There is nothing wrong with you. Don't ever think there is."

"It was a bit overwhelming, I'll admit. These are big issues, Donna, bigger than us. How are two little people going to make a difference?"

She thought for a moment, now laying her head on his big chest.

"Here's how I see it. We both know there's something terribly wrong here, something that really troubles us but something we think can be fixed. We could just say, 'Screw it, it's not my problem, someone else'll fix it,' or 'This is way too much trouble to deal with.' And what would that make us?"

"Lazy, weak, punk-ass slackers?"

"Not my choice of words, but basically yes. We could get on with our lives, save ourselves a lot of trouble, continue to bitch and moan, maybe even get bored doing that and look the other way and become embittered, cynical, defeated old shells."

"I couldn't see you doing that."

"Or we could light a candle in the darkness, as the saying goes, and recognize one immutable fact about the world: a little focused effort by a few committed people can move mountains. And that's when the magic happens."

"The magic?"

"Yes. Like magic, we become empowered, fully engaged, and much happier people, even if we end up not moving the whole mountain but only a single pebble or a grain of sand."

He sighed and thought about it. Donna needed his help and protection, and he was ready for the job. He would keep his ideas to himself for now, like temporarily suspending the Fourth Amendment, if it meant more time with her, away from his dark apartment and the white glow of a computer screen.

"OK. I guess I'm in. But you're in charge. I'll just load the trucks."

"You have a deal." They shook on it. "For now. I have big plans for you."

"Oh goody," he said.

"So, what should we call ourselves?" she asked, jumping right back into it.

"Huh?"

"A name for our organization, a unique identity, something catchy that'll get people's attention and tell the world what we're all about."

"How about Bumbusters.org? We even have a theme song. 'Is there something strange . . . in the neighborhood,'" he sang with enthusiasm, bobbing his head to the familiar rhythm. "'Who you gonna call? Bumbusters!'"

"OK, funny, but I don't think that'll get us any positive press or, more important, any grant funding."

"Something with a more humanitarian spin? I get it. How about the Joad Foundation? It's got name recognition, promotes family values, and sounds like we already have tons of money."

"OK, let's skip the name for now. I'll work on some stuff today, but I'll need your feedback when I'm done." She placed her hand on his. "We're a team."

"Yup," he said, smiling shyly. "This'll be fun. We can even recruit that lady doctor if you want." Then, looking over her shoulder through the store window, past the children's books and the one-dollar cart across the mall parking lot, he saw old Dan emerge from Dogg Life, look around, check his watch, then angrily shake his head.

"Oh shit! I'm late."

"Uh-oh. Sorry. Tell him it was my fault."

"He won't give a crap. Gotta go. Bye." He waved and was around the counter and out the door in an instant, where he discovered the cleaning supplies and equipment he had inadvertently left on the sidewalk. He clumsily gathered everything up and sprinted across the lot, making sloshing sounds as he ran.

17. DEB LOOKS FOR CELINE

For the second time in a week, the Hassan family snaked up the ramp of the Social Security office. Briskly in the lead walked their patriarch, Pete Hassan, wearing a pink button-down shirt purchased yesterday at T.J. Maxx, fresh out of the package with the folds still visible. His young son and daughter followed in their American schoolkid gear, also from T.J. Maxx. His wife and her mother, in their traditional dress, slowly brought up the rear. They had become a fixture at the office the past few weeks, but today, Pete assured them, they would finally be successful.

Their stride slowed instinctively as they approached the door. Sprawled on a blanket directly in their path lay a thin, gray-bearded man in olive drab camo fatigues, his hair matted, his skin weathered and tan. He leaned his back against the wall with legs splayed out, appearing so relaxed he might have been mistaken for a vacationer sunning himself in a poolside chaise. Next to him lay a languid hound, looking healthy and well groomed but bored. The man held a faded cardboard square with worn edges and a message in orange crayon:

> Disabled Gulf Vet
> Anything Helps
> God Bless You

Affixed atop the sign fluttered a miniature American flag and, fastened below with twist ties, a color photograph depicting a young marine in full dress uniform, looking out toward a distant but unseen threat to the left of the camera's lens. The man on the blanket, now wizened and world-weary, bore the same uninviting countenance, the name on his tattered fatigue jacket matching the one in the photo: Tomlinson.

As the family approached, the veteran made no attempt to pull in his limbs, forcing the group to either step over or navigate around them. When the young boy raised his foot to avoid treading on the vet, the indolent hound let out a deep rumbling growl, causing the boy to jump back and hide within his grandmother's black cloak.

The languid old marine suddenly came to life.

"Goddamn rag heads," he mumbled to himself. "Here for some US taxpayer money?"

Mateen Abdullah "Pete" Hassan was a proud new American who believed in blending seamlessly with his adopted culture. To that end he had chosen a Western-sounding name, one that he later learned meant "rock," hoping it would make his compatriots more at ease. (His wife refused to call him Pete; she thought it an abomination and referred to him only as Hassan.) Despite his new moniker, the family had encountered rough treatment since arriving in the States, mostly unfriendly stares but at times elevating to near violence. One young man had approached him in a shopping center, vehemently shaking his fist and yelling so closely that droplets of spit had landed on his cheeks.

"Please, sir," said Pete, positioning himself in front of his family. "We mean no trouble."

"Screw you, Osama," the vet yelled. "Get back to your own fucking country." He refused to move from his declared spot. "Goddamn hajji."

Pete knelt and spoke softly to his children. "This poor man will not do us harm. He has only the energy to insult us. Go now. Do not speak to him. Do not look back." The family scurried around the vet, who produced one final "Fuck y'all!" as they safely entered the noisy waiting room.

"So what are we doing today?" asked the triage desk officer, a soft-spoken young man with spiky hair and a nose ring.

"We are here to obtain benefit for my mother. We spoke with Miss Johnson last time. She is here today?"

"Can't say," he replied, clicking information into his computer. "Please have a seat. You'll be seen at window number nine."

"Yes, window nine. This is where we were the last time. Miss Johnson's window." He looked in anticipation in that direction but could not see who was staffing the counter. They all took a seat. So full was the waiting room, they had to split up, the grandmother sitting next to the two children, who shared one seat, and Pete and his wife sitting opposite one another a good distance from them. Pete was wedged between a young woman with a baby in her arms to one side and a large red-faced woman on the other. He looked at his number—thirty-three—then up at the display—thirty-one.

"Ah, we will be helped soon, see?" he said, enthusiastically showing the number to his wife, Jahidah, who, in the face of his excitement, remained blasé. Jahidah had grown tired of these pilgrimages to social service offices. The prodigious efforts by her husband had yielded SNAP and WIC benefits, Medicaid, disability payments, and Social Security disbursements but, she believed, only through her persistent prodding and haranguing. She was not above using guilt to motivate a man she considered overly deferential and a little submissive, invoking his paternal obligation to provide for them. She allowed him to relish the feeling of accomplishment these small victories engendered but, having come from a prosperous family in her homeland, hated groveling like this.

"Thirty-three."

"Yes, here." He motioned to his mother-in-law to stay put and mind the children while he and his wife proceeded to the window.

"Good morning, folks. My name's Brian. How may I help you today?" asked a tall man in his late fifties in a white open-collar shirt and blue cardigan stretched tightly over his protuberant belly. He peered down at them over readers perched at the end of his nose.

"We are to see Miss Johnson. She helped us and my mother," Hassan said, pointing to the waiting room, "to get Social Security benefit last time. Very helpful. We can see her now?"

"Sorry, folks, Ms. Johnson is not available today. But I'd be happy to help. What is the name please?"

"Hassan." He spelled it slowly and spoke the name once more. "Sir, Miss Johnson, she knows us, was very helpful." He produced a thick manila folder with the forms and informational pamphlets

Celine had given them on their past visits. "We are very comfortable with her. We can please see her now?"

"Mr. Hussein," he said imperiously. "As I said, Ms. Johnson is not available today. I'd be happy to help you if that's what you would like. Otherwise I would ask you to move back to the waiting room so I may help all these other folks."

Pete and Jahidah exchanged words, the wife urging him on. "Sir, I insist," he said finally.

Brian spun on his stool and walked to one of the many desks in the work area behind the counter. At the largest desk sat Deb, the office lead. Brian spoke with her in low tones, frequently motioning to the couple standing at his window. Deb quickly reviewed their record on her screen, slowly pushed her chair back, and motioned for Brian to follow, her wide thighs swishing as she walked.

"Good morning, Mr. Hassan, ma'am," she said with kindness and authority, offering her hand to the man and deferring to the woman, who did not offer hers but placed her hand over her heart. "Brian here tells me you would like to speak with Ms. Johnson about your case?" They both nodded. "I'm sorry to tell you that, unfortunately, Ms. Johnson is out sick today and will not be able to help you. However, I see that she made very clear and complete notes on your previous visits. I can understand why you want to continue working with her. She is one of our best, very caring and respectful, very thorough. Now Brian here is also one of our most trusted senior agents. I have the greatest confidence in him. He will simply take over today from where Ms. Johnson left off, and if there is any further work to be done, Ms. Johnson can be involved again when she returns from her sick leave. Now, how does that sound?" she said with a smile, handing the file back to Brian. "And I will personally let Ms. Johnson know you were here today. She will be happy to know you asked for her by name." They again nodded, and with that Deb wished them a wonderful day and turned back to her desk.

"One moment, please," said Brian as he pivoted and followed a step behind her. "You're actually going to discuss this with Celine? There's no need."

"See to your customers, please," said Deb, and walked away.

"Of course," he said, stopping in his tracks.

Deb returned to her seat and pulled the cell phone from her purse stored neatly under the desk. Over a week had passed since the morning Celine broke down at her workstation and needed Deb's coaxing to take some time off. She had expected Celine to check in with her a couple of days later, though she could not recall specifically instructing her do to so, and now she was vexed. She searched her phone contact list and discovered Celine's number was not there. She then opened the HR file for Celine Johnson, plugged in her headset, and clicked on the number.

"This is Celine. You've reached my voice mail. I'm so glad you called. Please leave your name and number."

Deb left a short message to call her at work, then searched for an alternate number. A Camille Johnson was listed as both her next of kin and emergency contact. She called the number and left another voice message. She then perused Celine's HR record, seeing nothing but the usual generic information. No red flags. No vacation time used. Still plenty of accrued sick leave. She returned to the home page, feeling an unwelcome tingling sensation at the back of her neck. Was her blood sugar low again? She pulled a KitKat from her desk drawer and munched on it while searching for Celine's home address, then mapped it. She nervously made circles on the screen with her mouse as she deliberated. *Not that far*, she thought and, without thinking a moment longer, grabbed her purse. She informed Trudy, her second in command, that she needed to be out of the office on official business for at least an hour and left the building by the side entrance, glancing one last time at window nine. The couple was fully engaged with Brian, the husband and occasionally even the wife smiling and nodding. *Good,* she thought. *Well done.*

As she walked down the ramp, she encountered the angry veteran, forced to stop short by his legs blocking her path. He looked up, feeling her irritation, and pulled his legs in so that she could pass.

"What's your dog's name?" she asked.

"Tracker." He caressed the dog's nape.

"Does he bite?"

"Only when I want him to."

She slowly bent forward and held out her hand, palm down, allowing Tracker to first sniff her, then lick her hand. She gently petted the dog's head.

"You know you're blocking a public right of way here. Do you think you can move your operation down to that area, please?"

He roused himself. "Yes, ma'am. Thank you."

It took her but eighteen minutes to drive from the office to the address listed in Celine's employee file. Midmorning traffic was light. On the way she texted Celine and called her number again but got no response.

She pulled up to a row of townhomes, all jammed together in repetitive shades of pale gray, pastel blue, and muted tan, differentiated slightly more by the colors of their doors. Celine's was black. Like all the others, it featured a sunken garage on the first level and exterior steps leading to a miniature porch on the second. The third level loomed high overhead, affording a view from the bedroom windows of the distant street below. The curtains were drawn shut. She looked around for Celine's Toyota with its dangling government-issued parking placard, but it was not to be seen.

With great effort, Deb slowly climbed the stoop to the landing above. She was not accustomed to second stories, having opted for single-level living in her own home. Winded, she paused at the top to catch her breath. Mailers and parcels of varying sizes littered the entrance. A couple of doorknob hangers swayed in the wind. She looked around the placid neighborhood, sniffed the air scented with pine and clematis, felt the warmth of the sun on her face, heard the gentle hum of bees hovering around the potted lavender, noticed the heavily treed streets and the panoramic view of Morley Valley to the west. She peeked through the living room window, where she saw a rumpled couch, throw pillows askew, and a flat-screen TV that had been left on. The remote lay on the floor. She could not see what was playing from the landing.

She glanced at her watch. *Better be getting back soon.* With some trepidation, she knocked quietly on the front door, then more loudly, calling "Celine" in a low voice, her lips close to the door. She looked again through the bay window and, seeing no movement, rapped vigorously on the window itself, so hard she feared she might break it. She called the cell number again and saw it light up and vibrate on the coffee table inside. Now she found herself yelling, "Celine! Celine!" to the windowpane. A pair of kids skateboarded by in the street below, looking up at her quizzically without stopping. Deb felt a little sick to her stomach. She had progressed from curious to worried in a matter of moments. She turned away and called 9-1-1, not sure what she was about to tell them. She was put on hold for what seemed like several minutes. She tapped her foot, paced back and forth, looking up and down the street for a police car she knew could not be responding already. She heard the weather seal on the black door creak open behind her.

"Deb?" she heard in a weak voice.

Deb gasped and wheeled around to face a gaunt, pale, and thoroughly wrung out Celine, in a dirty T-shirt and underwear, her hair sticking out in all directions, her lips cracked and dry, and a strong, complex stench emanating from her, a mix of unwashed body odor and stale urine. Down the front of her shirt was a brown substance that resembled dried vomit.

"What are you doing here?" she said blankly, rubbing her eyes and yawning.

"What am I doing here? What are *you* doing here?"

"I live here," she said, confused by the question.

"My lord in heaven, look at you." She was genuinely shocked. "You're an absolute mess." Dispensing with etiquette, Deb did not wait to be invited in but pushed past Celine, pulled her inside, and closed the door. Celine had no gumption to resist.

Deb impatiently ministered to the disheveled, smelly waif before her, angry and disappointed but mostly irritated at herself. *Guess I'm not the judge of character I thought I was. Makes me so mad!*

"In here," she yelled from the bathroom. "Take those rancid clothes off. Put them in a pile." She turned on the water to fill the tub, making sure there was soap, shampoo, a washcloth, and towels on hand. Celine stood naked and shivering, obediently following commands. Deb was surprised at how boyish Celine's body appeared—small bony frame, barely visible breasts, skinny arms and legs, no butt to speak of. "Now get in there. Make sure it's hot enough. Scrub yourself. I'll get you something clean to wear."

She walked into the bedroom, where clothes and pillows were strewn on the floor. The room smelled like Celine. Bedsheets lay twisted and dangling off the bed. In the center of the bed was a large dried yellow stain. On the nightstand stood three empty medicine bottles. Deb tore the sheets and blankets from the bed, pulled off the pillow slips, and gathered the whole mess in one spot on the floor. She delicately dropped Celine's dirty underthings on top, holding them by the unsoiled parts, and went looking for clean clothes, which she found in the bureau—a long-sleeve top, underwear, drawstring pants, and socks.

On her way back, she detoured into the living room, tossed the throw pillows back on the sofa, and shut off the TV. She stopped in the kitchen, ignored the dirty dishes and decaying food for the moment, and hastily made a pot of coffee. On the breakfast bar, she saw a near-empty wine bottle and the envelope addressed "To Darla" propped up against a basket of molding oranges. Fruit flies circled above it. She snatched it up and proceeded to the bathroom.

Celine had immersed herself in the tub, water still running, looking passively at the ceiling. Seeing the pathetic form before her, Deb's tone toward Celine softened a bit.

"Here you go," Deb said, handing her the washcloth. "Scrub yourself." But Celine responded like a waxen figure. Deb sat on the edge of the tub, soaped up the washcloth, coaxed her forward, and began scrubbing her back so hard the skin glowed a bright red, which seemed to revitalize her. "Here, you finish. Do your face and neck." Celine took the soap and slowly went through the motions of washing her face. "There, now you're getting it. Go on, scrub good. Your privates too."

Celine looked up at her. "Thank you," she said, smiling meekly.

"Don't thank me. I saw what you tried to do in there."

"One more thing I failed at—"

"Save it," Deb interrupted, shaking her head in disapproval without a trace of sympathy. "Why the hell didn't you call me, girl? I would have come. You're valuable to me. I don't want to lose you." Celine shrugged. "It seems you've been on a long, dreadful journey this past week. Somehow you managed to return. But you still look like a zombie, not quite dead, which is no way the same as alive. You've got to come back to the land of the living. First we've got to get that stink off you. You smell like a corpse. That won't do. Then some clean clothes. I've got them right here. Finally"—Deb looked around in disgust—"we have to decontaminate this house. Degauss it good. Whatever went on in here, we have to chase it out." Celine nodded, now more engaged in cleaning herself. "I suppose this has something to do with it," she said, waving in the air the envelope addressed to Darla.

"Give me that." Celine tried to grab the suicide note from her hand, sloshing soapy water onto the floor, but Deb was too fast for her. "That's mine. Don't you read it," she cried.

"Read it? I'm going to burn it. No one should read this, especially you!" She tried once more in vain to take the letter, but Deb crumpled it in her hand.

"Nothing but ugliness and sorrow in this letter. I can tell. Just look at you. Whatever this Darla person is to you, you'd better run away from her as fast as your little feet can carry you."

Celine was taciturn. "I thought I loved her."

"Heard that one before," Deb said cynically. "Let me tell you something, miss. I've been around the block so many times, I'm about to lap myself, and I've learned a thing or two. First, there is no one who can fill that hole in your heart. You've got to do that for yourself. No one can make you a complete person except you. You've got to shake off all the bullshit everyone's been handing you, all their negative energy, just so *they* feel better about themselves for a split second by shitting on *you*, then go on their merry way, and now you're walking around covered in *their* shit. Nope, that won't do."

Celine had made a passable effort at cleaning herself in the bathwater. Nodding approvingly, Deb commanded, "Now get up and do your private area and your backside like I said. Go on now. I'm not going to do it for you. I'll turn around so you can have your privacy." Embarrassed, Celine complied, standing in the tub scrubbing her groin, legs, and behind. Deb pulled the shower curtain closed. "Now wash your hair. Wash it twice, then shower off. Put on these clean clothes. I'll be in the front room."

Deb could hear the shower running as she tidied up the kitchen—rotting food into the compost bin, dirty dishes rinsed and into the dishwasher. She swooped back to the bedroom and stuffed the soiled linens into a big garbage bag she had found in the kitchen, dragging it out to the porch to be discarded. She gathered up the empty pill bottles, dumped the remaining wine down the drain, and threw all of these into the garbage bag as well. Finally, she looked at her watch and called the office, telling Trudy she'd be back in half an hour, asking if everything was OK. *No problems? Good.*

Celine emerged from the hallway, timidly making her way to the living room where she sat on the couch facing the bay window. Deb had set out two cups of coffee on the table. She took the chair opposite her.

"Now then," Deb said, appraising her, "that's a little better. OK, what are we going to do now?"

"Do?" Celine still seemed inert.

"Yes, do. I mean, do I have to sit here on suicide watch with you all day or what? I've got to get back to the office."

"No, I'll be OK. I won't do it again."

"Damn right, you won't do it again. Do and I'll slap you silly. I've got my eye on you now, girl. What the hell were you thinking? And don't talk to me about 'Oh, I loved her, but she didn't love me.' That is the oldest damned story there is. You may not know it—or maybe you do now, and it's about time—but love is almost never returned in equal share. One always loves more than the other. Usually just a tiny bit more, nearly equal, and that can be good enough. But sometimes one person loves way too much and the other hardly at all. And that's just the way it is. You can't be thinking, 'Oh, I love you so much. Why don't you love me back?' Just stop it, or you will go to your grave asking that question and be frustrated every minute till then."

"Makes sense, I guess," Celine said, sipping her coffee, starting to revive.

"You don't look too sure about it."

"No, no, I get it. I'm trying to make a change. But it's hard, you know?"

"Mm-hm."

Celine stared out the window. "Don't you want to know why I did it?"

"Nope."

"I did some pretty awful stuff that last day you saw me."

"So you're going to tell me anyway?"

"I had this big fight with my girlfriend, you know, Darla, the night before. Looks like we're split for good now; she left and hasn't been back. The next day after work, I went to my other friend's store to, you know, talk to him about it and found out that *they* had just hooked up. Right there in the store. I got really mad at him, because I have, like, a serious crush on him. I went a little crazy and kind of trashed the place."

"Go on."

"Mostly knocked things over, but I tore up all of his prize posters and broke his neon sign. Smashed in his door too."

"That'll all cost some money to replace. You'll be lucky he doesn't sue you, or worse."

"He won't have to sue me. I feel terrible about it. I'll pay for everything. I've got a little money saved up."

"I said 'or worse.' He could have you arrested."

"Really?"

Deb had heard about enough. She looked at her watch, rose from her chair, and sat next to Celine.

"Listen, I've got to get back to work now. I need to tell you something before I go." For the first time today, she struggled to find the right words. "I placed a lot of trust in you, Celine. I hired you with big, big hopes. I have schooled and molded and mentored you over the past couple of years, so that you might be first in line to take over for me. From our previous talks, I believed that was something you wanted as well." Celine nodded. "You've really come along, showed a lot of promise. But now I'm wondering if you're suited for a position of authority and responsibility."

"Oh, I am, I am, I promise."

"We'll see. I'm not getting any younger, you know. I've got a few health problems, which let's not talk about right now. I've got to take my retirement before I'm too old to enjoy it. But today, miss, today you have really let me down," Deb said emphatically. "I have never in my life been so disappointed. Disappointed in you, and even more in myself, for not seeing this coming, for not being there for you, for not doing whatever I should have done. I am very, very sad, Celine."

"I'm sorry," Celine said, averting her eyes, full of remorse.

Deb continued matter-of-factly. "And do you know what I do when someone disappoints me and makes me sad?"

"What?"

"I put as much distance between them and me as possible. I shut them out, shun them, banish them from my mind entirely, forever. I've got to stay on the right path, walk in the light, and, frankly, take care of myself. There's too much negativity and darkness in this world to bother with it or let it weigh me down."

Celine was crying now, but Deb would not relent.

"Right now, you're contagious. You've fallen into a bottomless pit and you will pull anyone down who gets close to you because you've had all the life sucked out of you. I simply cannot have that kind of energy around me, dragging me down. I will not."

"Are you firing me?" she whimpered.

"I can't fire you. Not for this. No, this is technically off the record. You're still on sick leave. I shouldn't even be here, since this is none of my business. But your supervisor would appreciate you checking in with her now and again. Formally, that is. Send me an email, so we can make this longer term if we need to. And get some help, or medication, or religion . . . something, anything. Whatever it takes. My God, woman, you're young. Are you going to throw your life away over some tragic affair? Please!"

"I will get help, I will, I promise. I know what to do. This—this has happened before."

"Big surprise." Deb had shaken off her anger and was now a little ashamed by it. She wrapped her arm around Celine's shoulder. "Now, be a big girl. Take care of yourself and get back on track. I'm counting on you." Deb gathered herself up and headed toward the door. Celine followed her.

"Call me tomorrow. Let me know how things are going. You have my cell. Off the record, of course."

"I will."

Deb walked onto the landing and grabbed the big garbage bag with the soiled bedding and empty bottles. "Where is your rubbish bin?" Celine pointed over the banister to the alley behind the townhouses. "OK, then." She began dragging the bag down the flight of stairs, one step at a time.

"I can get that," said Celine as she watched Deb grunt and struggle with the bag.

"Already got it," Deb said, raising her hand. "But you'll need to put some clean sheets on the bed. Let it air out first."

"OK, I will. Bye, and thanks again."

Deb's breath was heaving as she made it to the bottom of the steps. She dumped the bag into the bin and went to her car. Before leaving she checked her phone. There was one call from a recent number: Camille Johnson, Celine's mother. There was a voice message. Forty-one seconds. She looked at the phone, then up the stairs, and made a decision. *Not my business.* Without hesitation, she swiped it left, deleting it.

On the drive back to the office, Deb could not keep her mind in check as she replayed events. Over the years she had learned to act decisively, without regrets. This morning was different. She was full of regret, full of doubt. *Why did I come here? It's not like me to get in deep with someone this messed up.*

Her misgivings continued to occupy her head as she arrived back at the office. The Gulf War vet had moved with his dog to a lesser traveled section of the sidewalk as instructed. He impassively held up his sign as each pedestrian ambled by, not bothering to make eye contact. The office waiting room was loud and full, typical for this time of day. Families huddled together taking turns at sitting in the curved plastic chairs. She checked in with Trudy, who smiled and pointed over to Brian's window. The Hassan family was still occupying the space, the grandmother and two children having now joined the younger couple at the window.

"I've been over there a couple of times already. I think Brian will need some combat pay for this one," said Trudy.

"Can you handle it, please? I've got to catch up on a couple of things."

"Sure thing."

She sat down at her desk with a groan, happy to take the weight off her feet, and opened up her computer. There was already an email from Celine, sent a few moments after she had left the townhouse.

Dear Ms. Ethridge,

Thanks again for facilitating my sick leave last week. My sincere apologies for not contacting you sooner. I was very ill at the time but am happy to report I am much better now. I have received some much needed attention from a wonderful, caring friend and am on the mend.

I will be back in the office in the morning. I promise you, I am not contagious! (I know that's our office policy—and a good one it is too!)

I have copied HR here and will make a full accounting with them tomorrow.

See you soon,
Celine Johnson
Eligibility Specialist II

Deb closed the email without responding. She would do that later. For now she needed to clear her head and get back to business. She clicked through a few more emails, then mechanically looked over the staffing roster for the rest of the week. Having Celine back in the office would certainly make her job easier; otherwise she would need to start calling around for additional coverage.

Her back and feet ached. *Not sure how much longer I can do this,* she thought, her eyes scanning the office. *Got to get free of this place.* She still harbored doubts about Celine, her ability to come back, her very sanity, and remained irresolute about her own judgment.

Deb reached into her purse and pulled out the wadded-up envelope addressed to Darla. She had not burned it as promised but rather had stuffed it into her pocket while Celine was in the shower, then transferred it to her bag. She now carefully placed it on her desk, smoothed out the paper, and tried to divine the contents within. Overwhelmed with curiosity, she turned it over, noting that the letter had not been sealed but the flap simply tucked into the envelope. Without reaching in, she carefully pulled the edge of the envelope back slightly but could not read any of the writing and set it down on her desk. She held it up to the light, hoping that would reveal the intended final words of a cuckolded lover, written from beyond the grave to a lost and errant sweetheart. But nothing could be discerned.

"Whatcha got there? Who's Darla? Does she work here?"

Deb turned to see Trudy standing over her shoulder. "No. Found it on the street. Trying to see who it's sent to so I can get it to them."

"This one of those morality tests? 'You find a letter with a stamp on the ground next to the mailbox. What do you do with it?' Gee, tough one."

"Yeah," she said, placing the letter in her top drawer. "So what's up?"

"Oh, just wanted to let you know the Afghani family finally left. I think we figured it out."

Trudy went on to explain in great detail the error that had been made on their application forms, the one digit that had been mistyped and the cascade of bureaucratic processes that had been marshalled to correct it.

But Deb was not listening now. She only thought of Celine, the young woman in whom she had placed her trust and faith, whom she had pulled back from the edge, who was returning tomorrow from her terrible journey, and who, thank you, Jesus, was going to be her salvation.

18. CUTS AND COLOR

Richard Kornbluth stroked his straight razor across the thick leather strop attached to his barber chair. It made a soft *shishing* sound. Nic Troxell sat motionless, facing the mirror.

"How do you like my handiwork? I used a number six up here," Richard said, working his fingers gently through Nic's hair, "and a three on the bottom. I really like it." He applied warm lather from the dispenser to Nic's neck and defined a sharp border with his blade in short, determined strokes. "My God, when are you going to do something about this dreadful tattoo?" he asked, his razor revealing by sections the black-and-red swastika flag under the lather.

Nic did not comment. "Are we done here?"

"Not till I've finished slitting your throat. Now hold still," Richard said, carefully dragging the sharp edge across the skin behind his ear. "Is this a Van Gogh moment or what?"

"Ha ha."

"Shhh, don't talk, or I'll have to cut the other one off to balance your sideburns. There." He toweled off Nic's neck, applied lilac vegetal, and gave him a quick shoulder rub. "All set. Now, what little chores do you have on your list today?"

Nic dared not tell Richard his real plans; he made up something believable. "I have to see about a new garden hose. And I'll stop by the market on the way home."

"Yes, the cupboard is indeed bare. Oh, please get the 'no kink' kind."

"Huh?"

"The new hose. I just hate it when my hose kinks," he said in a suggestive tone.

Nic ignored him, now bored of his perpetual attempts at double entendre. He doubted if Richard even knew where the garden hose was, let alone ever used it to actually water something. Since he had moved in, that was exclusively Nic's job.

"And not one that's too thick and heavy, please. Such a bother to lug around. How about one of those wind-up hose caddies, you know the kind?"

"OK, sure." Nic said, growing impatient.

"I don't want you to hurt yourself, Nic. I'm just thinking of your welfare."

Nic had spent a lot of time thinking about his own welfare lately, since the day he stumbled upon the locked desk drawer filled with financial records and correspondence implicating Richard's involvement in the proposed redevelopment of Morley Plaza. The handgun and sixty grand in cash were on his mind too, but he was after bigger stakes, millions perhaps, though a plan had not yet crystalized. He needed more information for all the pieces to fall into place. This was the goal that dominated Nic's to-do list most days.

Across the Morley Plaza parking lot, Geoff Saboteau examined his own image, reflected in the window of Pickwick's Paperback Shack. His locks cascaded over his ears almost down to his shoulders. He remembered his commitment to Donna—to attend next week's town council meeting looking "clean and legit." To this end, he'd visited the Play It Again resale shop in Rellman and purchased a blue cotton dress shirt, a red-and-blue-striped tie, and a pair of navy relaxed fit Dockers. Other than the laundry mark on the collar—Bronfman, the name of its previous owner—the clothes were like new and fit him well. To complete the look, he had polished up an old pair of black oxfords he had last worn to his grandmother's funeral. A haircut was all that was left. But where?

Every month for three chaotic years, his stepfather, Donald, had dragged young Geoff to Svenson's Barber Shop. The shop had managed to stay open through thin years, but now, thanks to gentrification, it was situated in a popular section of Rellman known as Old Town. There, a declining Sven Svenson routinely asked his customers, "So what can I do you for?" and regardless of the response invariably delivered the same signature cut: white walls and flat top with a faux part on the left or some variation of it. It had become a destination spot for tourists and hipsters to watch the decrepit but lovable Sven do his thing, but the prospect of sitting in that chair again made Geoff uneasy.

The answer appeared to him just over his shoulder across the mall parking lot, reflected in the bookstore window.

He had passed Mr. Richard's Cuts and Color daily on his way to Dogg Life but had written it off merely as a ladies' salon catering to "old blue-hairs." Now as he walked across the lot he definitely saw a man, a very manly one, sitting in the barber chair.

He entered the salon and was hit with the pungent odor of industrial chemicals used for perms and acrylic nails. On glass shelves, displayed in an orderly array along a gold-veined mirrored wall, sat colorful bottles of high-end shampoos and conditioners, and several large containers he could not identify marked "To the Professional Only." Overhead played a bluesy '50s tune, also one he could not name, the singer's heavy vibrato filling the room, asking fortune if this would be her lucky day.

"Why, hello there. How may I help you?" echoed a voice from the far end of the salon. In the distance he saw a thin, gray-haired man with a closely cropped beard and remarkably taut skin busily brushing the stray hairs from Nic's neck and shoulders. He wore a Hawaiian shirt unbuttoned at the chest and too-tight white polyester slacks that accentuated his male anatomy. He smiled broadly at Geoff, showing inordinately brilliant and uniform white teeth.

"I think I need a haircut?"

"Why yes, indeed you do," said Richard. "Well, you've come to the right place. We're just finishing up here. Have a seat." He gestured to the row of chairs opposite the mirrored wall. "So what do you think?" he asked, proudly spinning Nic around to face Geoff.

"It's . . . nice. Good work," Geoff said.

"Yeah, good work," said Nic, mimicking Geoff.

"Thank you and fuck you!" murmured Richard. "Listen, I've got a paying customer here, so be on your way please, and try not to get into trouble." Nic stood up and forcefully yanked the brown plastic smock from around his neck in one motion. Geoff now saw he was well over six feet, with rough features, tattoos, piercings, and muscles evident under his tight-fitting T-shirt. He walked toward the front of the salon, throwing the smock in the general direction of Richard, who caught it midair.

"Watch your backside," said Nic to Geoff as they passed.

Geoff felt suddenly uneasy. Hoping to escape, he checked the time on his phone, about to suggest that perhaps he should come back in a little while, when Richard beckoned him to the now-empty chair.

"Next. And you are?"

"Geoff."

"So what are we doing today?"

"I'm going to the town council meeting next week, and I need to look 'legit.'"

"I can do 'legit.' I'll make you look like a goddamn junior Republican."

Outside the salon, Nic started up the Impreza and drove out onto Copley Drive toward the Morley True Value. There he purchased a medium-weight, fifty-foot NeverKink garden hose with a lifetime replacement guarantee, along with a NeverLeak hideaway hose reel in an enclosed box with a side crank, in a traditional design that would blend well with the existing patio furniture.

Before leaving the True Value parking lot, he opened the trunk and took from the spare tire well a pair of license plates he'd recently stolen, to which he'd affixed magnets. Making sure the tags were still current, he snapped the plates over his own. From there he drove four miles into Rellman and parked across the street from the office of Ms. Monica Sampson-Smith, in a spot that allowed a clear line of sight to the entrance of Rellman Realty Group. He called the office asking for Monica and was told she was not in but would return in a few minutes. So there he sat, waiting to see . . . what? He wasn't sure.

About a week after rifling Richard's desk, Nic had broken into his phone by watching him key in his access code, which Richard made no effort to conceal. He hoped checking Richard's recent calls and contact list would shed some light on the conundrum of his financial activities. There he discovered frequent calls to and from Monica Sampson-Smith, his current pursuit, and others too, most notably a caller identified as RP, who turned out to be Morley mayor Howard "Rusty" Purnell.

On a whim one evening, after completing his daily chores, he'd followed Monica from the office to her home, convinced it would reveal something about Richard's real estate dealings. It did not, but he soon discovered that shadowing Monica added zest to what at times could be an otherwise dull day. He'd grown to appreciate her shapely figure, meticulous grooming, and the forcefulness with which she attacked her objectives. Now he tailed her around town as often as he could find the time, just for the thrill of it.

After several minutes Monica pulled up in her white Lincoln Navigator and entered the building unaccompanied. He savored her walk from the car to the building, then waited around another twenty minutes but, having had his fill and noting nothing more, drove off. From there he doubled back to Morley and stopped at the Joint City/County Complex, pulling around back to the employee entrance. Again, he engaged in a waiting game, hoping to discern some relevant intel, as he had done on another such sojourn a month ago when he'd watched Mayor Purnell emerge from the building with Monica accompanied by a pair of dark-suited Asian businessmen with serious faces. He rolled down the window and strained to make out their words. He could not but heard them end their conversation all happy and congratulatory as the two strangers drove off with Monica. *Who are these guys?* thought Nic, never having seen them before, *and what do they have to do with the old man?* They might have been college professors, engineers, goodwill ambassadors, or even yakuza. But his gut told them they were nothing more than money guys in nice suits, about to pass some cash from one hand to another.

Seeing nothing of interest at City Hall today, he drove to the Hensen County Library, parked, and went inside, situating himself at one of the public computer terminals available to library patrons. He was forced to do so since Richard had, to Nic's consternation, figured out how to operate the History function on their laptop at home and, despite being fastidious about erasing the sites he visited, had the Virginia census web page pop up one day unexpectedly. Often as not, Nic had to wait for a spot occupied by one of the library's regular complement of dispossessed drifters, identifiable by their sun-exposed skin, poor grooming, bags of ragtag belongings stuffed under the desk, and personal paraphernalia, sometimes including a take-out lunch spread out on the carrel table. He was not shy about walking up to these desperate souls and pointing menacingly to a sign affixed above each screen stating the one-hour time limit, which would invariably lead to a terminal being vacated. Once seated, he continued what he called his "research."

Ensconced and undisturbed at his workstation, he could comb the electronic archives, with particular attention to Morley Plaza, the surrounding area, and the proposed Morley Pointe Crossing. He began with the Hensen County Office of Building and Design Standards, searching for any recent building permits, applications for variances, code and zoning data, property tax records, corporations operating in Morley and their associated parent companies, corporate charters, board memberships, financial statements, and bankruptcies. From the County Recorder site, he pulled up deeds of trust, quitclaim deeds, inter vivos trusts, wills, and other estate information, though he soon learned many of these documents were never duly recorded with the county.

He probed deeply into the lives, past and present, of Monica Sampson-Smith and Howard "Rusty" Purnell, examining the usual social media sites for education, degrees, and employment histories and all of Monica's current real estate listings.

Finally, he dug up anything he could on Maurice Richard Kornbluth: birth records, ancestry and lineage, past addresses, military record, criminal record. Having noted his date of birth and Social Security number from documents he'd found in the desk drawer, Nic was able to pose as Richard to access personal records or establish novel online accounts ostensibly in his name. To join sites with an associated cost, he used a prepaid credit card he'd squirreled away while still on his illegal cash withdrawal spree, before Richard had caught him. Any desired hard copies he'd either print at the library or request by mail and have delivered to a free-standing mailbox at the UPS Store across the street from the library.

He labored diligently on his rounds during these stolen moments, a discipline he'd developed during twenty-eight months in the Indiana State Prison system. He considered the hours spent a wise investment in his education. He took copious paper notes, not risking an electronic folder that might be discovered. As he built his secret dossier, he kept his findings in a nondescript grease-stained paper sack stuffed under the spare tire of the Impreza, where he knew Richard would never look.

But as stimulating as his investigatory pursuits were in their own right, Nic had fallen back into another habit since arriving in Morley, equally engrossing, that made his daily grind all the more tolerable.

Nic knew from long experience how to spot a meth dealer. Given the number of sellers dotting the map between Morley and Rellman, it was not long before he found one he trusted. Because of his tall stature, edgy appearance, and close association with Mr. Richard, Nic had become quite conspicuous on the streets of Morley. In order to avoid being seen with shady characters, he employed a tested procurement method. Spotting a likely source, he would drive by slowly, make brief eye contact, and telegraph a subtle signal, like a tug on the brim of his hat, then duck onto a quiet tree-lined side street and wait patiently. Soon the merchant would appear. He got comfortable with one, known only as JJ, and soon their routine was seamless. With the contraband in his possession, he would then drive another few blocks to a deserted road and fire up, the whole process taking about four minutes.

The drug energized Nic to the point of sheer exhilaration, while fear of detection raised his vigilance out of proportion to any real threat. Naturally circumspect, he now wore blackout sunglasses even indoors and kept the rim of his ball cap pulled low over his eyes. On his street rounds, he eyed the rearview mirror compulsively, taking circuitous routes to allude anyone who might be trailing him, pulling into alleys abruptly to wait for traffic to clear. Some days, he was convinced, he was being followed by Richard, which he knew was impossible. He made certain of this by secretly activating the find-a-friend function on Richard's phone and confirming his location with his own phone frequently. With regularity, he sighted what he believed to be one of his surveillance targets at a distance headed directly toward him and would speed away only to find he had been mistaken as he passed them on the street. He had full appreciation of the drug's effect on him but was comfortable with it. Besides, he just loved being high.

Meanwhile, back at the salon, Richard indulged himself in his own favorite addiction: spilling his innermost thoughts to a random customer.

Once seated in the barber chair, Geoff immediately noticed around the styling mirror an arrangement of framed photos and snapshots that Richard had hung, a sort of shrine to himself. Given their location just opposite the cutting station, clients could not help but see them. There Geoff viewed images of a trim, almost gaunt young man, in one photo wearing a red calypso shirt tied at the midriff and sporting a broad straw hat and maracas, in another the same youthful figure laughing, drinking, and smoking with friends. Some photos showed him suspended in midair, lithely performing a leap or twirl. Geoff squinted at the framed pictures and pointed. "Is that—?" he asked.

"Oh yes. I'm afraid it is."

"Wow, you were really something," replied Geoff, genuinely impressed without a hint of irony. He had always admired fitness and athleticism, possessing neither trait himself.

Richard pulled one of the framed photos from the wall that depicted him and two other dancers as circus aerialists, admiring it. "I was so beautiful then. That's me there," he said, pointing to the third dancer on the right. He had eye-catching angular features and a vigorous bearing. "And this one," Richard said, exchanging photos, "was from my Margot Fontaine days." The photo showed Richard, backlit in starkly contrasting gray tones, wearing a black leotard and tights, white face paint, and a white cape, holding a skull and striking a Mephistophelian pose.

"Very nice."

"Ancient history, my boy." He gently nudged Geoff's head forward, the electric clippers now vibrating the back of his skull.

"So how did you end up—"

"In this God forsaken place?" They both laughed. "The usual rags-to-rags story. You really want to hear this?" Richard said hopefully. "Well, if you insist. I grew up a tiny village in Virginia called Onaqua Springs, about an hour out of DC. I'll spare you the details of the first sixteen years, but could I write a movie!" He spoke dramatically now, pitching the plot: "'Boy dancer, stuck in Mayberry. Eccentric, slightly off plumb, trying to be true to his calling and not get himself killed.' Well, that wasn't going to work, so first chance I got, I lied about my age and joined the navy."

As Richard prattled on, Geoff uttered an "mm-hm" or a "wow" with polite regularity whenever it seemed appropriate. He was not much for chatting when held captive in a barber's chair and was happy he'd picked one who did most of the talking.

"I said my final goodbyes to Tobacco Road, and off I went. I couldn't have been happier. I suddenly found myself floating on an aircraft carrier in the Sea of Japan, scouting for Reds. Such a waste, but it was a step up for me."

"Uh-huh."

"For entertainment we'd put on little skits and shows, making fun of the navy or our CO. Everyone loved it, and I discovered my true calling was 'in the theat-ah.' I was sure as hell 'never going back to Old Virginny.'"

"Sorry." Geoff shook his head. "Is that a song?"

"Forget it, and hold still. Anyway, I got out and headed straight to New York City. It was the Golden Age of Theater, I tell you. The Golden Age. So many shows, so many opportunities, if you were willing to work hard. I learned my trade and started getting jobs right away. I was pretty good too, but let me tell you, we sweated our asses off! Because it meant something. Not like today," Richard complained. He switched to a short pair of scissors and began snipping Geoff's hair at the top in quarter-inch cuts.

"So, um, why Morley again?"

"I followed my heart, dear boy, and my poor knees came hobbling behind." He mimed a crippled walk. "Let me tell you something, Geoff, youth does not last. Does. Not. Last! That's why we worship the young so. Even when everyone *tells* you it won't last, like I'm telling you right now, no one listens. I didn't, not till it was too late. You think you're going to be nineteen forever. Forget it. That leap you made," he said wistfully, pointing to his photo, "so effortless, like floating through time and space. But time doesn't give a damn about your young body, and gravity is all around us. It never sleeps. Soon it grabs hold of you and pulls you right back down to Earth."

"Bummer."

"Yeah, bummer. At twenty-eight I'd get up in the morning and everything hurt. A stiff joint turned into an ache, an ache into a pain, and a pain into pure hell. I could barely climb the stairs to my flat in the Village, let alone fly through the air. I didn't need a brick wall to fall on me. So I went back to school for cosmetology and got my license."

"No regrets?"

"Are you kidding? Many regrets. If I had just taken better care of myself . . ."

"Boy, I can relate to that," Geoff said, grasping his own spare tire.

He looked Geoff over. "You have a very nice body, my friend. Sturdy, well proportioned. You should treat it better. I watch you over at the Burger Basket every day," Richard scolded, wagging his finger.

"Guilty!"

"No, I'm talking about real debauchery, the self-destructive variety. Like chain smoking or binge drinking or partying all night, which is *all* we did, by the way. And fucking. Don't forget the fucking. Endless fucking. Fuck, fuck, fuck, and always with a new boy every night. It was a wild time. There was no such thing as HIV then, or even herpes. We all felt invincible. You could still catch something, though, if you weren't careful, believe me. Horrible disgusting things. The clap, syphilis. Why, I knew one fellow . . ."

As Richard chatted gleefully about syphilis, Geoff again began to harbor the same trapped, anxious feeling as when he'd first walked in. He quickly changed the subject. "You say you followed your heart?"

"Yes, yes. I had kept up with a fellow named Dale, one of my old navy buddies, long distance, you know, just letters back and forth. And one day he just showed up in Manhattan and said he was on his way out to California to work in pictures, and would I come along."

"And you said . . ."

"'Fuck yes!' is what I said. I was ecstatic. You know, secretly—and I never told him this—I had always had a thing for him, though nothing had ever happened between us until then. I guess we started out as friends and became lovers. Romantic, don't you think? Believe me, having a good friend is much better than good sex, especially after all those one-night stands with nothing to show for it.

"So we moved out to Hollywood, and right away he got a job at Paramount, doing some extra work at first, you know, man-in-crowd stuff, but eventually he fell into the production side and was really good at it. He had a head for business. I kept doing hair, and fast forward thirty years we became everyone's favorite married couple. Not legally of course, not back then, but just as good as. Oh, the parties we threw. Massive affairs. Movie stars, producers. We were happy as two old queens could possibly be. It was a wonderful time."

Richard offered to trim Geoff's eyebrows. A strange idea, Geoff thought but acceded anyway.

"But everything grows stale at some point, doesn't it? Suddenly the mirror cracked."

"How do you mean?"

"AIDS, of course. You've heard of it?"

"Oh, right."

"All through the eighties, we watched our friends get sick. It was a very sad time. We all felt so helpless. Thank goodness Dale and I were monogamous, or pretty close to it. Catching something wasn't a huge issue for us, but God, it was hard to take. Just heartbreaking."

He lathered Geoff's neck, just as he had done Nic's, and shaved a clean line.

"Eventually the dust settled. I suppose people figured out how to be safe. They were so full of fear. And life just went on and on. The parties got a little tamer, a little less frequent, and broke up earlier. Then a funny thing happened. Suddenly we were old fuddy-duddies. All our friends, the ones who had made it through the worst of times, just kept getting, you know, old! Then we realized, for God's sake, *we* were old. And then *they* all starting dying off, and we thought 'Oh-oh, we're next!' We looked at each other one day, Dale and I, and at the very same moment said aloud what we'd both been thinking: 'Let's get out of here, out of the city.' And so we did. We had a nice little nest egg squirreled away by then, plus we sold our home in Silverlake, at a tidy profit too. We found our cozy little country cottage right here in Morley, along with some spending cash. Not a bad deal.

"Dale was so happy. We were both small-town boys, you see, but I loved the city, and he'd always hated it and wanted to get back to his roots. He loved the solitude, the quiet, after all those years of dealing with studio types, who are, I'll have you know, the lowest form of life on the planet. He just wanted to get away from it all, to go for walks in the woods, bicycle to the grocery store, stare at sunsets, blah blah blah, that sort of shit."

"Sounds nice."

"You think so? I was bored to tears immediately. I never said anything, though. Dale seemed so happy, and that made me happy. But the solitude didn't last. People were naturally drawn to him. Maybe it was all the years he'd spent in show business. He had such great stories to tell. They thought he was exotic. Can you imagine? Between the two of us, now *he* was the exotic one. He couldn't seem to get out of public life, no matter how hard he tried. They just adored him. He was so popular in our little village that eventually some of the town leaders approached him to run for town council. So he did, and he won! I couldn't believe it."

"Wow."

"I'll say *wow*. But he made a lot of positive changes. The flower baskets along the parkway? That was him. And those Morley Pride neighborhood signs? Him too. Me, I just got more bored. He was spending more and more time away from the house, and I had to do something, so I dragged myself back into doing hair. I opened this little shop to keep myself from going stir crazy, and voilà, here we are," Richard said proudly, "my little domain, to which I welcome my new best friends every day." He made an exaggerated theatrical bow.

"And Dale? Is he still on the town council? Maybe I'll meet him next week."

"Dale had the bad manners to up and die on me about six years after we got here. Can you believe it?"

"Oh, sorry. He sounds like a nice person."

"Well, it wasn't very nice of him to leave me alone here in our 'home on the range.'"

"I'm sorry," Geoff repeated, not knowing what else to say.

"Too late now, son. He's been cold and underground for years. It was a tremendous blow to me *and* the town. That's him there." Richard pointed to a photo of him and a young Dale from the '70s, Dale clean-cut and conservative, Richard bearded and flamboyant, both much younger, with wide lapels and ties, cocktail glasses in hand. "I'll admit, I went a little nuts at first, I missed him so. Started drinking again and carousing. Doing risky things. I didn't really care about what happened to me. Maybe I wanted to join him on the other side, I don't know. Or maybe just to prove to myself I still had a little life in me. And boy, did I. I burned the candle at both ends, till I ran out of candles entirely."

"Looks like you made it OK." Richard showed him the finished haircut in the handheld mirror. "Thanks, looks great."

"I finally came to my senses, got involved in volunteer work, helping prison inmates transition back to civilian life. It's very rewarding."

"Sounds like it would be," Geoff said, hoping to not open the topic further.

"And then, almost as if it sensed that Dale had died, the town itself started to die. Who can say why exactly. Businesses started closing up. Good people moved away or died themselves. Plus they'd overbuilt so much during the boom, it seemed like every property was all of a sudden underwater. Homes went into terrible disrepair. The lawns were permanently yellow. Once Dale was gone, no one seemed to give a shit about getting involved or about anything else. The whole reason people had moved here had vanished. Our sense of community was gone. Morley became a ghost of its old self."

"That explains a lot," Geoff said, finally jumping into the conversation on something he felt strongly about. "The place has really taken a downturn since I've lived here."

"Have you seen the tent camps springing up down by the river?"

Before Geoff could answer, Richard took a colorful bottle down from the shelf and splashed a generous handful across Geoff's neck and cheeks. He smelled the heavy scent of lavender, cinnamon, and clove.

"What's that?"

"Two Girls Florida Water. See?" Richard showed him the bottle with two smiling Asian girls in traditional garb. "And how about all the petty crime that's going on—drug use right out in the open, needles everywhere, broken windows, cars being ransacked."

"Right! And violent crime too. My friend got stabbed just over there, at the bookstore."

"Yes, I saw the commotion. She's all right? I saw she's back at work, hopefully paying her rent . . . I mean, able to make her rent."

"She's fine, thanks."

Without asking, Richard gently massaged Geoff's temples, moving down to the muscles at the base of his skull. He then leaned his elbow into his trapezius muscles on each side and worked out the knots in a circular motion. Geoff could smell Richard's breath, heavy with the odor of cigarettes and . . . was it vodka?

"Don't you think the mayor and city council are totally turning a blind eye?" Geoff asked groggily as his whole body relaxed.

"They're probably all on the take. What other explanation could there be?" Richard replied softly.

"They refuse to back up the cops."

"With all these court decisions, they're totally hamstrung."

"Since when did sleeping on the street become a First Amendment right?"

"Did you hear about the bum who's suing the city because they removed his tent and all his junk on one of their sweeps?"

"I know. How do these people find lawyers willing to take on these cases?"

"The ACLU. They always seem to crawl out of the woodwork."

"Scum," said Geoff lethargically.

Richard continued his shoulder massage, now more vigorously pressing his right fist deeply into Geoff's upper back muscles, wrapping his other arm around to the front of his chest for counter pressure.

"If it's any consolation, I think we're about to be eaten alive by Rellman in one big swallow. They seem to be coming down on us hard." Richard enunciated each word in the same tone he had used with Nic: lascivious, suggestive.

"Sure, and we're just rolling over and taking it. They're selling off the town in huge swaths."

"I understand they want to erect a huge apartment complex right here."

"Which no one will be able to afford," interrupted Geoff.

"They've got to satisfy the market in Rellman. It's exploding right now and has nowhere else to go. They're coming, and we can't stop them. Who knows, maybe an injection of money is just the juice we need."

"For more high-end housing? I see perfectly good homes in beautiful neighborhoods being condemned and demolished. It's killing the character of our town. That's why we're going down to the council meeting next week."

"I can tell you've been practicing your little speech," he said softly. "You sound a little stiff." Richard now casually fingered the short-cropped hairs at the back of Geoff's neck. "Why so tense?" He moved in close from behind, his hairy chest tickling Geoff's skin. "You need to relax."

Geoff leaned forward automatically, turning around with a puzzled look. He stood up abruptly and Richard backed away.

"Oh, never mind," Richard said, crestfallen.

Geoff hastily grabbed his coat.

"Oops, gotta get back. Listen, what do I owe you?"

"Twenty."

Geoff handed Richard a twenty and four ones.

"Thanks. Anyway, mixed use."

"Huh?"

"You asked what kind of development. Not high-end housing. Mixed use. Business on the bottom, bedrooms on top. Are you familiar?"

"Yeah, I'm familiar.

"Put that in your speech."

"OK. Bye."

Geoff walked briskly toward the door.

Richard dusted away the hairs from the barber chair with a snap of his smock. He took down the photo of himself and Dale from the wall, sat in the chair, and lit a cigarette. He flicked his ash onto the floor and examined the young couple in the picture with a long exhale.

"Alas, no one wants to fuck me anymore."

19. NEUTRAL, NO BRAKES

Monica prepared for her very busy day. She checked her look in the mirror, having opted for the blue-and-white-striped epaulet blouse, black knee-length skirt buttoned down the front, red patent-leather belt, and matching wedge sandals. Her naturally blonde hair was pulled back in a tight French braid and coiled into a bun, and her flawless nails, all twenty of them, shined a fire-engine red. She skillfully applied concealer and foundation, curled her lashes, brushed on eye shadow and mascara, penciled in her eyebrows, dusted crimson blush onto each cheekbone, powdered her forehead and nose, and blended it all with a big brush. She finished with bright red lip gloss and examined her work, satisfied with the transformation.

Monica gathered a stack of brochures from the dining room table, each with her card stapled to the upper right corner. The glossy cover depicted a full-color rendering of the proposed Morley Pointe Crossing development, where fit, young, happy, computer-generated urban dwellers could be seen walking their computer-generated dogs, window shopping, dining out, or simply enjoying their idyllic new lives at the Pointe.

At the breakfast bar, she checked her laptop for two important folders: the first, her presentation on the project for the Rellman Construction Guild luncheon later that day. *Piece of cake*, she thought. The second folder was more troublesome: a dossier on Clean Up This Mess!

The local organization had been a real headache for Monica and her associates lately. Its manifesto demanded an immediate solution to the problem of homelessness in the valley, favoring low-cost tiny house villages, accessory dwelling units, organic farm collectives, and self-governing shared communities. It rejected the conventional notion that Monica and her colleagues had worked so hard to promote: to simply build as many housing units as the market could absorb. The dissenters especially loathed the high-rise dwellings, tony restaurants, and exclusive shops planned for Morley Pointe Crossing.

The dossier contained bios on Elizabeth Donatella Hart and Geoffrey Saboteau, the group's apparent masterminds, along with a screenshot from the website's About Us section depicting Pickwick's Paperback Shack, where they often met. She'd also gathered photos of the store's Adults Only room, obtained clandestinely by an unnamed source, documenting what she referred to as "prurient titles and lewd images." An aerial map of Robert T. Whitehead Middle School, with concentric circles emanating from it, showed the largest one of a thousand-foot radius just clipping the southeast corner of the Morley Plaza parking lot.

Monica's attempted anti-porn spam campaign had fallen flat. She was now determined take her campaign to the streets. To that end she'd preloaded clipboards with flyers and petitions, each headlined with "Protect Our Children! Shut Down Pornography Sales!" across the top, followed by brief details of Pickwick's proximity to the middle school, the alleged adult literature being peddled there, and the detrimental effect such sales would have on the well-being of the community's children.

She stuffed her laptop, thumb drive, laser pointer, and Bluetooth mouse into her computer bag; loaded her oversized purse with brochures, clipboards, petitions, flyers, and a roll of Scotch tape. With her travel mug, sunglasses, key ring, wallet, pepper spray, cell phone, purse, and bag in hand, she jangled out the door.

Monica headed up San Sebastian Parkway in her S Class, en route to the Construction Guild. About halfway there, she pulled in at her favorite drive-through car wash. She heeded the hand directions of the handsome young attendant in his short-sleeve shirt and bow tie, carefully maneuvering the sedan up the ramp toward the gaping maw of the wash tunnel. Finally the young man held up two fists, formed an X with his forearms, and shouted, "Neutral, no brakes. Premium today?" As always, she gave him the requisite ten dollars plus a two-dollar tip, then rolled up her window as he sprayed her windows and wheels. She relaxed as she felt the roller beneath her grab onto her tire, tugging her along into the sudsy, sloshy portal.

Monica pulled out her laptop and opened the file for her Guild luncheon talk. She was very comfortable with the content, having given it before; she knew when to speed up or slow down, crack a joke, or be sincere but clicked through it anyway. She finished her review just as the green light came on, both she and the Mercedes feeling renewed.

She decided to make a brief stopover at Morley Plaza to use Mr. Richard's salon space as a staging area for handing out posters and petitions after her talk. At the salon she and Richard exchanged warm hugs and laughter. He set her up at the manicure station near the window, where she unloaded and organized her clipboards, petitions, flyers, and Scotch tape. She wiggled her coffee mug playfully in the air. Richard took it from her with a smile and returned from the back room with a steaming hot beverage.

Once situated, her paraphernalia neatly sprawled out, Monica decided it best to first visit the shops and businesses of Morley Plaza, then return after the Construction Guild talk to canvass the surrounding residential streets. She taped a flyer to the front door of the salon and left a clipboard and petition for customers to sign, then, with a wave to Richard, exited the building.

On her way out the door, she nearly collided with USPS mail carrier Darla Skornik and her bulky mailbag, who was busily delivering letters, small packages, and throwaway ad circulars to Morley Plaza. Monica muttered, "Pardon," as she passed Darla, not registering that the wild-haired mail carrier was also the young server who had waited on her meeting with Rusty and the two Chinese gentlemen at LaFontaine. But Darla had not forgotten. She fixed her eyes on Monica as she walked out of range.

The kids at Burger Basket were harried and distracted, and Monica's visit was met with mixed enthusiasm. When she asked to see the manager, the sixteen-year-old lass staffing the counter summoned to the front an eighteen-year-old lad who was filling small bags with french fries. He introduced himself and nodded politely, as he would with any woman of his mother's age, and said, "Sure," to posting her flyer on the door, trying to hide his impatience. He thanked her and went back to filling orders at the fry bin, setting the clipboard high up on a shelf of hamburger buns. After she had taped her flyer to the window, Monica looked at him sternly, eyeing the clipboard. He quickly grabbed it, ducked into the back room and tossed it on the small desk next to his staffing roster, where he remained until she had left the building.

Dr. Sunita Reddy of ReddyCare was more reserved, nodding silently as Monica prattled on about salvaging children from smut. She took a flyer and petition from Monica, ostensibly "to study them further."

At Videodrome Jeremy was quite agreeable, pointing to the window where Monica could post her flyer, a space already cluttered with event posters, band announcements, and theater playbills. He eagerly took the petition from her with no intention of signing it or having it sit out at the store, smiling dumbly as she preached at him. He did make mental note, however, to definitely visit Pickwick's Adult Only section at the earliest opportunity.

Monica avoided Dogg Life and Pickwick's in her initial rounds, intending to confront the two troublemakers Donna and Geoff later and on her own turf. That her own sweet girl Stacie sat at Dogg Life right now, under the care of Geoffrey Saboteau, was an uncomfortable fact. She had considered immediately pulling the dog, but there was no other daycare as convenient or affordable. For many years she'd enjoyed a good relationship with the owner, Dan, and did not want to raise any questions that cancelling might provoke.

But as she passed the doggies in the window on her speedy rounds through the mall, something familiar—large, white, and fuzzy—caught her attention and drew her to a stop.

Geoff slouched listlessly at a small cluttered desk in the back of Dogg Life, figuring out how to fill the empty stapler. The room was suffused with a musty canine smell. The clicking of nails on the cement floor echoed from beyond a waist-high partition separating dogs and humans, punctuated intermittently by an abrupt surge of high-pitched yips and throaty barks that died out just as quickly.

Most of the four-legged patrons enjoyed their playful sniffing and poking, but a few inmates sat glumly at the periphery, abstaining from playtime, watching the door for any sign of their humans' return; none had given up hope of rescue.

Geoff brooded along with them, feeling as low as the saddest deserted dog. *I really need to get these bills out,* he thought, regarding the stack of invoices before him. But he could not concentrate on the chore, his mind crowded with a hundred unfinished tasks in anticipation of the upcoming town council meeting, while Donna continued to pitch forward like a supercharged juggernaut.

He thought too of the brief encounter at the hair salon, of Nic's unsettling presence followed by the inelegant come-on from Richard. It had cracked the door open just a slit, casting light onto a dim past he had kept sealed for years, one he did not wish to resurrect, not now or ever. Geoff felt a wave of nausea. He shut his eyes, used his mind trick, the one he'd employed at Donna's, to force his attention back to the mundane, concrete present, back to the empty stapler, the invoices needing his attention, the dogs . . . He breathed deeply, then breathed again, a tranquil, restoring breath. It was working; he could smell them now. He was back, and the vault was sealed once more.

Geoff got up enough steam to process the first dozen invoices, printing and folding the paper bills, inserting them into envelopes, addressing them by hand, and stacking them by the postage meter.

He had only ten invoices left, but it was coming up on noon, and he was getting hungry. He decided to do a few more before breaking for lunch. He read the next bill very closely.

Client……………..…………… Stacie
Breed/Color………………Labradoodle, white
Human Friend………….. Monica Sampson-Smith
                              1405 Rising Glen Terrace
                              211-223-6867
Special Diet……………….. Ask my human

Geoff recognized the name of the human patron, had seen her picture on bus benches around town, advertising her real estate business. The silly honorific stuck out in his mind—"Ten Million

Dollar Club." He easily picked out the only white labradoodle in the place, snow-white head to tail, carefully groomed, tall, and self-confident. She looked back at him long and hard, then continued to aggressively jostle a chihuahua-dachshund mix half her size.

Geoff, spurred by boredom and anxiety, was suddenly ravenous. He stood and walked unthinking past the forty-pound bags of dry chow stacked in high rows along the wall to the glass cooler where the special diets were kept, like a mindless trip to his own fridge at home, just to see what was there.

Feeding time was not part of his regular duties. That was Dan's job, and he could see why. While most of the regulars received standard kibble for lunch, for a few dollars more, a self-identified elite merited concierge service. In the tall cooler he saw a diverse assortment of plastic containers and vinyl lunch sacks, organized alphabetically, each meticulously labeled with client and human names, precise feeding times, and any special considerations such as portion management, food allergies, or microwave instructions. The containers bore cheerful puffy stickers, five-pointed stars, or smiley faces next to the dogs' names.

He went to the *Ss* and found the small green tub labeled "Stacie." Through the clear plastic lid, he could see chopped white-meat chicken, peas, carrots, and brown rice beautifully presented with some sort of white sauce and even a sprig of parsley. He stared at it for a long time. It looked really good, and he was so hungry. For an instant he considered sampling the meal, maybe just a little bite of chicken, but feared Dan would somehow be able to detect his tampering. He set it back into place, grabbed his keys, and walked out into the damp, cool daylight, locking the front door behind him.

On the way to Burger Basket, he did his best to avoid the hair salon, turning right instead of left, walking around the rear of the mall complex. The lunch crowd hadn't descended yet, and he was able to get his usual order in just a few minutes: a double Philly cheesesteak burger, medium fries, and a Diet Coke. He retraced the same roundabout path on the way back.

Geoff always felt a pang of guilt eating in front of the dogs, but he needed to get those invoices done before the outgoing mail at 1:00 p.m. He worked on them between bites. The first few mouthfuls of the burger were, as always, satisfying, heavily laden with salt and fat, but about halfway through, he felt logy, and it became an effort to go on. He set it on the desk and gulped his Diet Coke.

Stacie watched him intently through the fence. They again regarded each other eye to eye, having previously established a connection. The dog made it clear she was interested in his burger. "Hey, girl. You want some?" he asked, not wanting his uneaten lunch to go to waste. Stacie whimpered and pawed the floor. Geoff rose from his chair, opened the gate to the Rustle and Tussle free-play area, edged in, and slipped a short lead around Stacie's neck. "Come on, girl. I have a treat for you!" He brought her out of the common area, closed the gate, and led her over to his desk, to the puzzled stares of the other dogs. "Look what I have for you. Mmm, good."

He spread the remains of his burger and fries out on its blue-and-white-gingham wrapper and set it on the floor in front of her. She sniffed it apathetically, looked up at him, poked it with her nose, shoved it with her paw, sniffed again, then sat upright, staring as if to say, "What else you got?"

"Go on, girl. You'll love it." He waited. Nothing. "Jeez! Has every ounce of dog has been bred out of you? Are you even a dog anymore? Gimme that!" He kneeled down before her, grabbed the food off the floor, which by now had devolved into disorganized debris with each snooting and pawing, and wolfed it down, chasing it with the remains of his Diet Coke.

Geoff was on all fours and out of breath by the time he'd consumed the meal. He was just getting his bearings when an insistent *tap tap tap* at the glass door startled him. He'd apparently locked up on his return from Burger Basket. He poked his head up over the partition and saw a tall blonde woman about forty-five, smartly dressed head to toe. She jiggled the door impatiently, pointing to the lock, then to her watch, silently mouthing, "You're supposed to be open."

Stacie whimpered giddily, moving to and fro with exultant beast energy, sensing who was out front. Geoff quickly led her back through the gate to the common area before opening the door.

Monica's heels clicked briskly on the concrete floor. She was fit and self-assured. He was impressed by her starched blouse, with creases so sharp they could cut. Geoff wondered how a garment could be made to be so stiff.

"Was that Stacie with you? It's not mealtime yet." She glanced at her watch with the red wrist band. Geoff quickly thought of an excuse.

"No, no. I mean, yes, it was Stacie, and yes, it's way before mealtime, of course. No, we have a new service. It's called Cuddles and Kisses. A little extra affection in the middle of the day. We're trying it out for some of our favorite clients. No charge, of course."

"Oh, really," she said suspiciously.

"You must be Stacie's human. How can I help?"

She thought a moment. "I'm here on a very important matter. I'm canvassing the mall to let our business neighbors know of a situation that requires immediate action."

"Oh, right, the multiplex." He referred to the proposed conversion of a small neighborhood theater off the parkway to a ten-screen complex. Citizen reaction was polarized; for that reason it had received repeated coverage on the evening news. Neighbors cited concerns over cut-through traffic and noise at night. "I'm still kind of undecided," he said. "God, I really do love Dollar Night. On the other hand, it would be great to have more movies to choose from. I mean—"

"No," she interrupted, "that is not why I'm here. I've a much more urgent mission." She showed him a flyer attached to one of her clipboards that depicted a street-level image of Morley Plaza. He immediately recognized Pickwick's Paperback Shack at the center of the photo, a red arrow pointing to it, as if God had flung it down Himself. Burger Basket sat off to the left, and to the right, Dogg Life.

"Are you not aware there is a pornographic bookstore operating within this mall?" Monica showed him the aerial map. "As you can see, it's less than one thousand yards from Whitehead Middle School, a clear violation."

"A pornographic bookstore?" he said, acting ignorant as best he could. "Why, no, I didn't know." He examined the map. The thousand-yard circle barely clipped the far corner of the parking lot. The bookstore itself sat a good fifty yards from that. *A bit of a stretch*, he thought but said nothing.

Geoff cherished the Adults Only room. The curious time capsule cloistered behind Donna's purple bead curtain featured color pictorials along with hard-to-find paperback novels from the '60s and '70s, when one could actually *read* pornography rather than merely look at it. He had personally purchased copies of *The Tang's All Here* and *The Adventures of Lady Areola Muffington*, mundane reads but nonetheless rousing.

"We are asking concerned business owners and their patrons to help bring this issue before city council. I'd like to post one of our flyers on your door and leave a petition here on the countertop for your patrons to sign," she said, handing him a clipboard with a certitude that left little room for disagreement.

"Well," he hesitated, "I just work here. Dan's the owner. If you leave the petition here, I'll ask him about—"

"No need." She pointed to Dan Chesney's signature on line one at the top of the page. "I've already talked it over with him, and he's on board. I can't tell you how important your support is. The neighbors and businesspeople of Morley need to work together on these issues."

Just then, mail carrier Darla Skornik swung open the door in a flurry and briskly walked to Geoff's desk, her black rubber-soled shoes squeaking noisily across the floor. She set the incoming mail down without a greeting, then turned and stared dead-on at Monica. Still not a glimmer of recognition.

"Any outgoing?"

"Oh shit!" Geoff ran to gather up the envelopes that contained the billing statements he had completed and handed them to Darla. She looked at them indifferently and shook her head.

"No postage." He had forgotten to put them through the Pitney-Bowes. "Sorry," she said, handing them back.

"Please, can't you wait a minute?" He clumsily started up the postage machine, while Darla tapped her foot.

Monica intently watched the drama of the unpaid postage play out and decided Geoff would be no match for her. *They'd better have something more on their side than this guy, or else they've got nothing.*

"Listen," Monica broke in, "I've got to get going. I'll just put up that flyer now." She fished out her roll of Scotch tape, attached the flyer neatly to the window, and unceremoniously sprinted out the door in a whirlwind.

Darla, without Geoff's letters, exited immediately behind her.

A half hour later, Donna landed at Dogg Life with a sheaf of papers under her arm and immediately filled the room. Geoff sat at his desk staring blankly forward. She balanced herself on the corner of the desk and began an expansive monologue.

"Whew, what a day! You wouldn't believe what I've had to deal with. The printer got our order all wrong, and I had to stand there and sort out all the pages and restaple them. It wasn't their fault, of course. And he was so nice; he helped me get everything back in order. Plus, the posters turned out beautifully. So I tipped him. Just five bucks, that's all, to say thank you. Then I had a very nice meeting with some of the neighbors." She motioned to the residential streets surrounding Morley Plaza. "Did you know they've all been given no-cause evictions? Thirty days! Who would do that? I tell you, something is definitely coming down the pike." She took a break from her reportage, finally noticing the state he was in. "Hey there! How's my partner in crime?"

"We've got trouble." He handed her the petition.

"What, the multiplex again? God, I would hate to lose Dollar Night."

"No, worse than that. Here." He got up and pulled the flyer off the glass, tearing one of the corners Monica had so diligently aligned, and handed it to her.

"Oh." She shook her head as she read. "Oh my."

"I can't believe it," he said, grabbing the flyer and crumpling it. He recounted his run-in with the imperious and demanding Monica. "This really pushes my buttons. There is no porn in your store. Those are vintage . . . whatever you call them."

"Americana.

"Right!"

"True cultural icons."

"Absolutely!"

"Geoff," she said hesitantly, "I have a confession. I knew this was coming."

"You what? How?"

"Last week Dr. Reddy came by. She showed me an email she'd gotten from Monica. She's been planning this for a while."

"And you didn't tell me."

"I didn't want to worry you."

But Geoff was worried; Donna had become a target. He wanted to warn her and to plan how they could fight back. But Donna was no longer listening. She wore that faraway expression that had become so familiar to him now. She was churning through a problem, and he knew to best let her be. Finally she spoke.

"Geoff, this has nothing to do with my little vintage erotica alcove."

"It doesn't?"

"Nope. Not one thing. This is payback."

"Payback? For what?"

"Retribution—for our group and the website."

"Yeah, I guess. We must be doing something right. What do they say, you take the most flack when you're over the target?"

Geoff's assessment was accurate. Clean Up This Mess! was gaining momentum. Donna and Geoff made a good team, complementing each other's strengths and styles. In workmanlike fashion, Donna had designed and launched their internet presence, with supporters accruing daily. She wrote letters to Mayor Purnell and each member of the Morley City Council. She sent editorials to the *Morley Examiner-Post* and *Rellman Daily Sentinel*. She, along with Geoff, Dr. Reddy, and a group of irate neighbors, had stood all day on the I-14 overpass holding an enormous banner that said:

HEY, MAYOR PURNELL!
FIX HOMELESSNESS IN MORLEY NOW!
ENOUGH IS ENOUGH!
CLEAN UP THIS MESS!

The event, called a crazy stunt by some, received national news coverage for a week, deeming it a major grassroots crusade.

For his part, Geoff was an essential contributor to the success of the website. Donna told him this often, and her praise was not unmerited. Geoff proofread all the outgoing correspondence and position statements issued under their logo, adding a little bite wherever needed. He maintained the Contribute Now section of the site. He screened membership enrollments, insisting on adding an I Am Not a Robot button. Most important, he sat with her while she worked, bringing her tea and snacks without being asked, rubbing her shoulders, and telling her she was amazing with a frequency that was truly endearing.

Geoff watched with pride as Donna was transformed into a local celebrity. She had tremendous crowd appeal, even among her detractors. Into her middle years, she remained strikingly beautiful but now possessed an air of wisdom, self-knowledge, and inner calm that made her hypnotically appealing. She was positive, open-minded, collaborative, and refreshingly plain-spoken in her communications. She called out with candor all the shortcomings of the city government as well as the failure of the business community, churches, and nonprofits to take seriously the problem of homelessness. She indicted sanctimonious NGOs for tacitly maintaining the status quo, implying they would derive the greatest benefit if their espoused objectives were *never* fulfilled. She subtly suggested collusion between local officials and outside investors who were buying up and bulldozing older neighborhoods to erect unaffordable high rises, while depressing property values and driving out longtime residents with intentional neglect and disregard. She insinuated that the homeless were drawn to Morley by its implicit hands-off policy while being driven out of Rellman and other nearby towns by strong community policing practices.

Their concepts and recommendations were getting traction among the townspeople and beyond. In a short time, Donna and Geoff's website flourished into a full-blown resistance movement. The mayor and city council now received dozens of written and voice communications a week, demanding action to address the homeless crisis, spurred on by a letter-writing campaign sponsored by CleanUpThisMess.org. More protests were organized. Attendance boomed at city council meetings to standing room only, and the delivered testimony grew more incisive and impassioned. Spontaneous rallies outside City Hall could be counted on at least weekly, and calls arose for the impeachment, recall, or resignation of the mayor. The people demanded a town hall meeting, and finally one was scheduled.

But an ugly truth had materialized for the fledgling movement. As their coalition formed, Donna and Geoff discovered a spectrum of opinion about the homeless from the darker recesses of the web.

Most posts on the board were measured and compassionate, but some were rash, vindictive, hate-filled, or downright crazy. Geoff tried to screen these and protect Donna from them. When she did discover them, she was prone to reject the divisive voices immediately and counter their arguments with cries for inclusion and empathy. But Geoff had another point of view, pragmatic if not wholly principled.

"These may not be our friends, but they don't have to be our enemies either. Consider them bedfellows."

"What?"

"Allies of expediency. Every great movement has to deal with unsavory supporters who help move the agenda along. We need to be sure of our footing before we start to jettison our crew."

"You're mixing your metaphors again, friend. Besides, these are creeps, and I don't want to be associated with them."

"Can we at least wait till the town hall? We can disavow them then. For now, let's play innocent. We can be shocked and dismayed after that. I want to go into that meeting with a loud voice. We can fine-tune it later."

Donna reluctantly agreed with Geoff. She saw his logic but remained troubled. Had they known what lay in wait for them, they might have strived to scrub their ranks more thoroughly.

Monica headed out of the Morley Plaza parking lot. As she bumped and bounced through the lot's many potholes, she congratulated herself on missions accomplished: she had delivered all of her petitions, posted all her window flyers, had gotten a close-up look of at least one of her opponents, and was emboldened by his manifest incompetence. She'd even gotten a few signatures. Feeling good, she clicked on her mix set and turned it up loud. She sang along to "We Are the Champions."

Her attention now turned to her luncheon address at the Rellman Construction Guild. She paused Queen and practiced aloud her opening remarks, imbuing herself with confidence and a touch of cheek, rehearsing the names of the Guild's principal players, imagining their positive reception.

As she moved toward the exit, she passed a 1999 Subaru Impreza parked at the far end of the lot. She'd been oblivious to it following her around town, only now catching a full glimpse of its driver, slumped back in the car seat fast asleep, mouth agape, audibly snoring, the bill of his cap pulled over his eyes. She noticed the offensive tattoos going up his neck.

"Ughh!" she said in disgust. "Note to self. In the future, stay the hell out of Morley!"

20. RAPPROCHEMENT

Celine stood frozen outside the Videodrome window. She watched as Jeremy waited on customers, engaged and happy as always, and flashed back to the horrible morning a few weeks ago. Since that day Celine had been submerged in a dark pool of self-loathing. With Deb's help, she'd managed to pull herself together enough to return to work. She seemed to be doing all right, but a feeling of anguish stubbornly filled her days. She ached for Jeremy's forgiveness and, until she got it, she would not forgive herself.

A bright LED display had replaced the old neon Open sign she had destroyed; Celine watched as it cycled through the colors of the spectrum. An errant fragment of curved tube glass (part of the O perhaps, or maybe the P) sat on the windowsill, a remnant of the mayhem she had caused. The *Casablanca* poster had been pieced together and mounted on a sheet of foam core board, the rip lines barely visible, including a jagged tear across Bergman's exquisite face.

The remainder of the store looked about the same. Better actually. Jeremy had rearranged the upended shelves into a diagonal pattern, making better use of the square footage and improving what she understood as feng shui. Other little enhancements had been deployed, making the store more welcoming, more interesting. She was impressed by Jeremy's industry and creativity, forgetting for a moment that her frenzied outburst had been the impetus for the transformation.

She cleared her throat and walked in.

"Hey," she said, forcing a half smile as she crossed the threshold.

Jeremy looked up briefly with blank eyes.

"The store looks great. Nice arrangement." He did not respond. "I was standing just outside and—"

"I saw you," he muttered coldly, keeping his eyes on his work.

"I was afraid to come in. Afraid you hated me." She cautiously approached the far end of the counter toward the snug little space where she'd spent so many warm afternoons in the comfort of his company. "Look, you have every right to despise me. I've had a lot of time to think about what happened that day—"

"What *happened*?" he snapped, finally breaking his silence. "You mean *what you did*?"

"OK, what I did. I acted horribly. I was so mad—mad at you, at Darla. I felt so betrayed, I don't know what came over me. It was like I was possessed. But I am so, so sorry. I just hope you can find it in your heart to forgive me."

"Forgive you. Why? There's nothing to forgive. We cleaned up your mess. Now please go make a mess somewhere else."

"We?"

"Yeah, Darla and me. We did all this. I had to close for two weeks, buy a new sign, build new shelves, get shit repaired. And it wasn't cheap, your little tantrum. All because of—what'd you say? Your feelings?" he scoffed. "You're a menace, Celine. You need help. I think you should leave now." He went back to his screen and pretended to concentrate on his work.

His words hit her like a gut punch, shaming her anew, causing her to doubt whether she deserved forgiveness for her absurd foray into madness and self-indulgent wallowing. Had her sincere apology not been sincere enough? Why had she even come here?

Her last hope was for him to be kind. The blowup had confirmed what she'd long suspected—she simply was not made for a relationship with a man. She just didn't have the constitution. If they could rebuild a friendship out of the wreckage, she would settle for that. Anything but the disgust he obviously felt for her now. But with Darla in the picture, Celine feared that she and Jeremy might never be close again.

She dawdled silently among the shelves, ducking behind the Staff Picks where Jeremy couldn't see her. *Walk out, move on*, her head told her, but she refused to concede. She pulled a title from the shelf and warily crept to the counter.

"Can I at least check out a movie? I hear this one's pretty good."

"Sure, why not." She handed him the box for *Atonement*. He looked up, completely aware of the inference. Try as he might, he could not stop himself from commenting on the film. "Book's better."

"Ian McEwan, right?"

"Yup."

"Saoirse Ronan's in this one. I like her."

"Me too. And Vanessa Redgrave. Brilliant." He read the liner notes. "Have you seen *Julia*? She's in that too."

"Of course. I rented it here. From you."

"Sure, I remember."

"I couldn't stop crying."

"That's about repaying a debt as well. About making things right."

"That's just what I want to do. Make things right."

He looked full on at Celine now for the first time since her arrival, his expression softening. Without intention, they had gracefully wandered back into their old routine, and neither of them fought it.

"I'll pay for everything," she offered. "The sign, the shelves, even the poster, if I can."

"The poster had more sentimental value than anything. It was pretty wrecked before you tore it to shreds. It has more character now."

"Me too." She smiled. "What about the other stuff? Please let me reimburse you."

He chuckled to himself. "Like after a barroom brawl?" he asked.

"You mean a donnybrook?" she said with a giggle.

"Yeah, a donnybrook, where the bartender grumbles, 'Who's gonna pay for bustin' up my saloon?' And the hero throws down a handful of silver dollars and says, 'That oughta cover it.'"

"I don't have a handful of dollars, but I do have a checkbook."

"Thanks, but I suppose I still owe you for all the work you did for me. Let's call it even."

"Nope. I insist. Please, it'll be good for me to make it up to you somehow, good for my soul. And to find a little closure."

"Closure. That's a funny word."

"It's exactly the right word," she lied; she didn't want closure, not with him. She wanted to make everything right, wanted them to go on and on. "I'm trying to move forward in my life. If I'm going to do that, I've got to drop a lot of baggage."

"Hmm."

"I don't mind telling you, Jeremy, I tumbled pretty far after our little fracas. I almost didn't make it out alive. I never want that to happen again."

Never an overly analytical person, Jeremy tried his best to follow her, but she was traveling into the deep recesses of her psyche. It made him uncomfortable.

"I've been pretty self-centered most of my life. Guess I've had to, to survive. I was like a broken toy, barely functional, moving through the world half-conscious, not truly connecting with anyone. I was so fucked up."

"Hmm."

"Hanging out here with you made me feel more normal than I'd ever felt before." She touched his hand. "You were a good friend to me, Jeremy. You accepted me for all my quirky faults and shortcomings. Then I went and hurt you anyway. That was wrong."

He did not want to hear the details of anyone's descent into hell or subsequent rise from the ashes and was eager to change the topic. "I get it. So now what?"

"I'm back at work now and actually loving it."

"Good."

"Turns out, when you've hit bottom, you can actually connect with people much better."

"Empathy, right? The whole 'I've walked in your shoes' thing."

"Exactly. And I'm getting a promotion too," she announced proudly. "Looks like I'll be working for the government for the long haul. I've finally found my calling."

Jeremy didn't know how to respond to this declaration but simply gave her a belated thumbs-up.

"So what about you? How's the business?"

In the aftermath of Celine's destructive rage, Jeremy had been forced to develop his online business, and since then it had mushroomed. He spent mornings dubbing and packing web orders, then carried the entire day's mailings in his messenger bag to the UPS store. Most days he was done by noon, in time to open the store for the peak afternoon and evening hours.

"Darla convinced me there was a whole universe of movie nerds out there just waiting for my expertise, and that I was wasting my time waiting for people to randomly stumble into Morley Plaza."

It stung to hear Darla's name again. "I guess she should know," she replied, wanting to say something supportive. "She delivers all kinds of packages to all sorts of people."

"Yeah, she helped me figure out the whole shipping piece, kind of streamlined things for me." Confronted with the realization that Darla had taken her place as Jeremy's support system, Celine felt a pang of jealousy; it faded quickly with his next words.

"But this whole vintage culture thing? It's sort of lost on her."

Ah, she doesn't get him . . . not like I do. With this small victory, she was feeling magnanimous.

"No, but she does have certain endearing qualities. I can see why you'd fall for her. I sure did."

"Yeah, well, that ain't all it used to be either."

"Oh?"

"I don't think she means to hurt people," he confided in a low voice, as if Darla were listening from the next room, "it just sort of happens. She's like a wild child, totally self-centered. She turns on the charm when she wants something, and she usually gets it. It's hypnotic."

"God help us if she ever figures out how beguiling she is."

"Amen."

"Are you saying you're not an item anymore?"

"What I'm saying is that she's still staying with me but not 'living with me,' if you get my meaning."

"Oh. Sorry."

"No biggie. I actually soured on the whole thing myself a while ago. She helps with a rent. Not regularly, of course, but a bit. It's a mutually beneficial arrangement. She'll probably fly the coop someday. I gather that's her MO."

"At least you have the online business to thank her for?"

"That may be *all* I have soon." He handed her an official-looking letter on MRK Management, LLC stationery. "I've gotten notice from the owner that the whole block is slated for redevelopment. My lease won't be renewed when it runs out in a few months."

"Oh no."

"Oh yes. It's fine, really. Video stores are kind of a relic nowadays. It's a wonder we even still exist."

"Aren't you going to fight this? What about the other businesses here in the mall; are they being thrown out as well?"

"Yup. Thence cometh the wrecking ball. Boom!"

"But you've got to do something. Can't you all get organized?"

"Funny you should mention it. We are organized, or more accurately, *they* are organized. I'm just along for the ride." He opened the CleanUpThisMess.org website and turned his phone toward Celine, where she read the About Us blurb.

"Hey, I know her. That's the bookstore lady. They're closing too?"

"Mm-hm, forced to close, along with the burger place, the dog daycare, Dr. Reddy, the hair place, everything. The hair guy doesn't seem so broken up about it, but the rest of us are really stressed. There's actually a town hall in a few days. Everyone's gonna go, to testify and show support."

"That's great. Support for what?"

"For some better alternative. Or at least some citizen input. They're pushing this demolition and rebuild idea pretty hard. Besides the strip mall, they're bulldozing the whole neighborhood to put up luxury condos and apartments six stories high, retail on the bottom, with a promenade and a fountain. Supposedly there's already a Starbucks and Whole Foods showing some interest. And not a word yet from the city to any of us."

Celine was still fired up from her newfound dedication to purposeful living and reconnection with the human race. She burned to do something selfless, instead of coddling her own despair.

"Can I go?" she blurted. "I mean, I'm not a neighbor or a property owner or anything, but I am a concerned citizen."

"Yeah, why not. I'm sure you'd be welcome. There's a planning meeting over at the bookstore tonight. Gotta wear the T-shirt, though. Can't be a neighborhood activist without the T-shirt." He reached down to his right and pulled a shirt off the top of a stack, holding it up to assess the size. It was an extra small. "Looks about right," he said, handing it to her. She immediately pulled it over her head and shoulders, and stuck out her chest proudly, showing off the Clean Up This Mess! logo. It fit her well.

21. A SPELL IS CAST

With the town hall just days away, Donna focused all her attention on assuring the Clean Up This Mess! team would make a strong showing before the city council. Every detail of the approaching event passed through her hands and before her eyes to receive its final approval.

She would arrive at Pickwick's each morning before six o'clock to answer and send emails, polish her own compelling testimony, or review written statements from other members of the organization to assure theirs would be equally persuasive. To strengthen their arguments on equity, justice, or social reform, she would browse the stacks of the bookstore unearthing incisive remarks from the works of great minds and learned thinkers, and either paraphrase or outright quote them in their testimony. She paused each day at ten a.m., right on schedule, to open the store doors, but would immediately return to her desk, taking short breaks only to perfunctorily guide her customers to the works they requested. Otherwise they were on their own to roam the stacks without her usual personal attention. Her prep work left little time to straighten the shelves or curate her incoming books, which lay in boxes in every corner of the store.

But each day seemed to bring a new wave of calamity that threatened to upend the peaceful order of the bookstore and pull her away from the town hall preparations.

First came Monica's petition about pornography sales on the premises, which she completely blew off. *How could she make such an accusation?* Donna thought. *It's just silly.* She was certain it would come to nothing and so banished it from her mind, refusing to let it disrupt her flow.

But soon another shock wave struck. She received in the mail one morning an official notification from the Hensen County Bureau of Developmental Services cataloging several code violations at Pickwick's. Puzzled, she could not recall any county personnel visiting the store for an inspection, at least none identifying themselves as such. Later she would recall a youngish fellow with a notebook, who had silently visited every recess of her retail space, including the restroom, without purchasing anything or asking any questions whatsoever. As he was leaving, he had lingered outside the door scribbling notes, which at the time she thought strange.

The laundry list of violations in the letter included lack of an ADA-compliant restroom (the grab bar was one inch too high), no GFCI outlets (three of these were missing), a seismically unsecured water heater (unstrapped, that is), inadequate bathroom ventilation (phew, she could vouch for that), and a lack of Exit signs (also true, though she thought anyone who couldn't figure out how to leave through the same door they had just come in might need to visit a different sort of establishment).

Wasting no time, having none to waste, she plunged into the county's website, confirmed that the violations had been duly registered and appended to her business license, then followed up with a direct call to Lead Code Inspector Harley Timmons to pick his brain about corrective remedies. She was a natural respecter of rules and, rather than being defiant, wholly supported the intent of the regulations. *God forbid someone should receive a shock from an ungrounded outlet or that the water heater should wiggle loose from its footing and tip over in an earthquake.*

Harley was genuinely impressed by her proactive response. After a long career in code enforcement, he'd had his fill of scofflaws and whiners. He assured her that these violations, usually complaint-driven, had likely come from someone with an ax to grind but could easily be corrected. While Harley would never openly admit it, her call had charmed him and virtually guaranteed a speedy resolution to her code violations. He recommended—not officially, of course, for in his position he could not ethically do so, but informally—a few excellent small-jobs contractors who could complete the needed repairs in one afternoon for somewhere in the low three figures. She thanked him profusely, happy that she now had a new friend at the county. Still, she wondered: who could have lodged such a complaint?

But Monica's petition and the noncompliance letter were mere gnat bites compared to the hideous events that occurred just two days later, when a sheriff's deputy arrived at Dogg Life and summarily arrested Geoff.

Donna saw the commotion unfolding from her desk, not realizing at first who or where or what was involved. *Did someone try to rob the Burger Basket?* she thought. Only when she saw Geoff being expeditiously led out of the building in handcuffs and hustled into the police cruiser did she halt her work midedit and rush to his side, or at least tried to.

"I'll call you," he mouthed to her through the closed cruiser window as it sped off, which he did an hour later, asking her to pick him up from the courthouse where he had been released on a personal recognizance bond. She had to come and vouch for him, assuring the judge that he would not leave the area or pose a danger to society and would show up for his court date.

A reticent Geoff sat silently in the car on the drive home. By now she'd already read the story headlining her local news feed, but Geoff could not garner the courage to explain things to her any further.

At home Donna flipped on the news to see Geoff's shocked and innocent face in a mournful, starkly lit mug shot, the sheriff's seven-pointed badge emblem in the lower right corner. *Oh God!* she thought, as evening anchor Todd Diaz related a bizarre and disturbing account of suspected animal abuse and endangerment.

Geoffrey Saboteau had been accused of animal cruelty by an undisclosed dog owner, a patron of the well-known local business. The woman was interviewed in fuzzy focus, her speech altered for anonymity. Crying in a computerized Darth Vader voice, she described watching in horror as Saboteau offered her beloved companion, a labradoodle mix with severe food allergies, a spicy burger and fries from Burger Basket, then consumed the dog's own specially prepared low-allergen meal on his hands and knees like a dog himself. Saboteau had been booked and released from custody.

The station then cut to a live on-air report from Morley Plaza by field correspondent Maddy Brewer. Dan Chesney, owner of Dogg Life, expressed to reporter Brewer his dismay at Saboteau's admittedly bizarre behavior but wanted to assure his clients that no other dogs appeared to be involved, and all of them were safe and in good health. It was not clear why Saboteau singled out this particular animal, but as a result of the incident, he had been relieved of his job duties and no longer worked at the daycare center.

Bystanders in Morley Plaza, unaware of the event, were collared by Ms. Brewer and interviewed for the news spot, each more appalled than the last at the thought of animal abuse. They expressed deep concern for both the victim and her human owner and fear for their own dogs' safety, repeatedly using the word *scary*.

For days afterward Geoff wandered about ashamed and afraid. He perseverated on his tribulations to Donna. He'd been harassed at the grocery store by random patrons who had seen him on the news and received vitriolic calls from unknown numbers. Repeated demands for his dismissal from the Clean Up This Mess! leadership board had been posted on the site's community forum page. And of course, there was his firing, leaving him without paycheck or prospects in the small parochial community of Morley in which he had achieved sudden notoriety. He fell quickly under a sickening malaise that haunted him in waking and sleep. He became reclusive, unwilling to show his face in public, engage online, or, worst of all, concentrate on preparations for the town hall. Donna was worried she would lose her beloved new partner and most valuable collaborator.

"It's such a dreadful accusation, Geoff. I just don't understand who could have done such a thing or why? I'm sure there's not a shred of truth to it." Sensing Geoff might be able to provide an explanation, she gently opened the door for him. "Is there?"

"Well, actually . . ." Reluctantly Geoff recounted the events at Dogg Life the day he faced Monica and her petition, including his impulsive interaction with Stacie and his failed attempt to share his cheesesteak burger with her. He theorized Monica must have watched this drama play out through the window but said nothing to him at the time, reserving it for deployment later.

"But I swear to you, I did not eat that dog's chicken dinner. She's totally making that part up."

Donna listened until Geoff ran his story to the end. While another soul might have ripped him a new one—and a part of her wanted to—she needed her cohort intact and at full strength.

"I am grateful for your honesty, Geoff," she said, placing her hand reassuringly on his. "I'm sure you had your reasons for—"

"Nope. I did not," he blurted out. "There wasn't any good reason for what I did. There never is. I just . . . get weird sometimes, and things happen."

Only a few weeks into their friendship, she knew he was speaking the gospel truth. He did get weird sometimes. "OK, I'll accept that." She hugged him. "We're all allowed to make bad choices once in a while."

Geoff hugged her back. He knew he'd really fucked up this time, the latest in a lifetime of stupid choices. He regretted the shit storm he had brought down on them and was embarrassed by her forgiveness yet so relieved she was willing to let it go. For that, he loved her.

"So now what?" she asked.

"Don't know but looks like we're at war with this Monica person."

"My thoughts exactly."

"But why? I mean, first the porn petition, which was totally ridiculous. Then the code violations. I'm sure she was behind it. She probably knows someone downtown and put in a complaint. Now this bullshit charge."

"She must have figured the chaos would discredit the organization and take us off task."

"Yeah, and she was right." He was thoroughly dejected now.

Donna sat quietly for a short moment, then with head erect and backbone straight, smacked her hand down hard on the desk.

"So it's war, is it?" she declared. "Well, I'm sorry but we're not going to cower here in some ditch waiting to be overrun," she said, poking her finger straight at Geoff. "We're going to attack!"

"But how? With what?"

"I haven't figured that part out yet," she said with a calm confidence that reassured him. "Give me a minute."

In the days that followed, instead of being driven to distraction by the misfortunes that had befallen them, Donna demonstrated the equanimity and singularity of purpose for which she was so admired. She continued to line up her speakers, paint her placards, and put the finishing touches on everyone's two-minute testimonies as well as her own. While Geoff remained flustered and tense, she assumed his duties as webmaster and chief communications officer, fielding every text and phone call, posting every update, answering every question, putting out every fire.

She promptly scheduled one of the recommended contractors (having screened them all first) to complete the store's code-compliance repairs, then just as quickly invited Inspector Timmons to come out and give the work his stamp of approval. They got along splendidly. He even bought a book: Isenberg's *Conversations with Frank Gehry*.

In response to the pornography petition, which Donna felt compelled to share openly on the website, a group of her loyal customers had started their own petition in support of Pickwick's Paperback Shack that had already gathered over three hundred signatures. And unbeknownst to Donna, for she would not have approved had she known, her acolytes had gone from power pole to brick wall to storefront, ripping down Monica's flyers and meeting notices, and had even surreptitiously pilfered signed petitions from the businesses in Morley Plaza.

She carved out time to help Geoff write out a statement that he posted on the Clean Up This Mess! site, explaining with profound contrition the events of that day at the dog daycare, apologizing for any hardship or distress his actions may have caused. It seemed to find purchase, garnering several supportive replies and quashing his critics.

As Geoff's court date approached, Donna gently reminded him he was still without legal representation. Only then did he confide to her that, in a fit of foolhardy libertarianism, he had imprudently spurned the assignment of a court-appointed attorney, reckoning he would represent himself. Acknowledging now that neither of them possessed the meagerest legal skills nor the money to retain private counsel, she immediately combed the Legal Aid site and pulled down a referral to what seemed a competent attorney: Caleb Cole, Esq. Caleb, as it turned out, was already acutely familiar with Geoff's case, having followed it in the media, and was eager as hell to defend him pro bono, asserting that Monica's complaint was completely baseless. (A judge eventually agreed, dismissing all charges.)

Still, Geoff continued to wallow in a state of listless melancholy. Donna was convinced that Monica, in her effort to derail them, had conjured a dark spell and that Geoff remained under the influence of her psychic siege. The only way she knew to counter such a wicked force was to build a stronger force for good around them, a virtual wall of protection, grounded in compassion, decency, and love.

"You know, voodoo only works if the victim believes in it," she cheerfully informed him, "so we can't afford to believe in her spell, only in our own magic."

Geoff nodded in rapt agreement. He was sufficiently well read to be familiar with the concept of spells, dark magic, and mind control, and while he had never actually gone to battle with the forces of evil, he felt wronged and ready to fight. He also found the idea of casting spells exhilarating.

So, while diligently carrying out all her other obligations, Donna spent every spare moment at Geoff's side, attending to his shifting moods, observing his language, and tracking his movements, ready to jump in to ward away any wicked influences on him. They frequently paused during the day to pray together, expressing their thanks for perfect health, prosperity, and harmony among themselves, their friends, and associates, and asking for guidance, wisdom, and a perfect outcome to all situations.

While ministering to Geoff, Donna also employed tricks to defend herself from malign intent. She meditated frequently throughout the day, sometimes for just a few seconds while she worked on other tasks, closing her eyes, clearing her mind, and focusing on her breathing. She lit orange and yellow candles at her desk—yellow for optimism and energy, orange for enthusiasm and connectedness—and "breathed in" the colors to infuse her mind with those attributes. She scrupulously maintained her to-do list, adding new items and gleefully crossing off old ones as they were completed, each time with a whispered, "Thank you, Universe." She kept a trinket on her desk, a small black porcelain seal balancing a crystal orb on its nose, a gift from Dr. Reddy, who had been impressed by Donna's equipoise in the face of chaos. She deflected the compliment but was moved by the gesture and now and then would glance at the statue as a reminder to always stay in balance and in control. She ended each day with a prayer of profound gratitude, affirming that everything everywhere was already all right.

By the day of the town hall, she had achieved a state of serene calm and clarity. Her measures were working. She felt Geoff at last pulling back from the dark edge, into the light and once more at her side. Her town hall speakers were briefed, testimony buffed, signs artfully rendered, and T-shirts delivered. She was square with the city development bureau, confirmed by a clean record on the county website. And the petition campaign against her and the bookstore had fizzled and flopped like a spent balloon. Her focus was impenetrable. She wore an expression of beatitude, as if she were listening to a distant celestial choir. She had done all she could do. She was content and ready for anything.

22. UGLY TRUTHS

Richard tossed the herringbone jacket onto the bed. With each rejected outfit the mound grew: the camel hair, the houndstooth, the plaid twill, the cream silk, along with their complementary trousers and accessories. In the end he went conservative, settling on the navy blazer, gray windowpane slacks, black tasseled slip-ons, and a crisp white shirt. For added flair, which he refused to do without, he added a bright red pocket square and matching bandanna tied around his neck with the knot turned to the side.

He examined his face in the three-way mirror, tugging his cheeks and eyelids up and back, then letting them ooze forward. He took a closer look through the concave mirror and noted a mild crinkling since his last treatment. *Better call Dr. Amal on Monday*, he thought, *time for a tune-up.* He applied a hydrating toner and concealer to mask his bags and shadows, plucked a few stray hairs, threw some gel into his hair and combed it straight back, adding a little pompadour flip in front, as much as could be managed with the few remaining strands.

As he emerged from the bedroom, he heard Nic pull into the driveway. He was late, and Richard hated to be late, preferring to arrive early to all events grand or mundane. He loved to surveille the scene before anyone arrived, a habit he had picked up in the Hollywood years with Dale, planning his entrance and exit and where to linger in between, scrutinizing people as they streamed in, cherry-picking who to shun and who to woo.

Nic lugged four heavy bags of groceries through the door and set them on the counter. Richard met him in the kitchen and did a quick turn.

"So what do you think?"

"What's with the cowboy neck wear? You look like a gay Roy Rogers."

"Philistine! I've got to do something to liven up this preppie costume. Besides, red always gets people's attention. I want them to remember me. You'll see; it'll be spectacular."

"Oh God, tell me you don't still want me to go to this thing with you tonight." He emptied the bags onto the counter. Richard noticed Nic was in a dark mood again, lately his predominate state.

"But I need you there, Nic. For moral support."

"I'll take a pass, thanks."

"Can you at least drive me? You know I don't like driving after dark." He grunted in the affirmative.

Nic had grown sullen and aloof over the past two months. He still did all the shopping and most of the cooking, ran daily errands, took care of the yard, and, of course, pandered to Mr. Bird. But recently he had allowed odd jobs around the house to languish in varying stages of completion, claiming he would get to them as soon as this part came in or that other thing was done. He'd often leave the house before dawn, not returning until after dark but offering no explanation of what he'd been up to, except as evidenced by the groceries, hardware, or other supplies he'd cart home in the Subaru. In the evenings he was cold and irritable, snapping at the least provocation. Rather than withdrawing from Nic's brush-offs, Richard's response was to hover over Nic and amplify his gadfly sarcasm with attempts at witty bon mots, inevitably leading to a fiery escalation.

They had long since stopped sleeping together or engaging in even the most casual physical contact. At the outset, Nic seemed to Richard a perfectly willing, if not an especially eager, participant in his playful sexual antics, a willingness facilitated by his position as Nic's parole sponsor and prime benefactor. He'd become even more grudgingly compliant after Richard had discovered and quashed his clumsy attempt at grand larceny. Now Nic seemed disinterested in pleasing Richard in any way, including in the bedroom.

The estrangement hurt Richard deeply, propelling him into some old habits. He began bringing young men—"my little strays," he called them—to the hair salon for quick encounters, usually for modest sums of money with a haircut thrown in gratis. Occasionally he would meet men just for sex with no expectation of payment. Richard dreaded these romantic trysts. Uncomfortable about his advancing age, he was forced to endure well-intended compliments on how youthful he looked for his years, how wise and experienced he was. He felt out of touch when his dated cultural references fell flat and much preferred to pay for physical intimacy outright. The exchange of money created clear rules and unspoken boundaries; those boys never brought up his age.

One afternoon Nic had finished the day's shopping and stopped by the salon. He walked in to find Richard in the back room on his knees, hungrily devouring the cock of a tall barely legal man-child. Richard hadn't heard Nic come in and kept on.

The young man—thin and haggard, his pimply face full of boyishness yet already hardened by life—looked dispassionately at Nic, then with a half smile lightly tapped Richard on the shoulder as Nic, shopping bags in hand, stood silently.

It was nothing Nic hadn't witnessed before. The scene felt uncannily familiar: a wretched street urchin, doing what was necessary to get on in the world, indulging the dirty little obsession of a customer willing to pay for the privilege, each of them at once both hunter and quarry.

The boy gently pulled Richard off him and pointed over to Nic, who now viewed him in all his fullness. He was impressed. *Kid was made for this job*, he thought. Richard stood up as quickly as he could manage, the stiffness in his knees evident, the boy offering his assistance. Not sure what to do next, Richard made introductions as if they'd all just met at the coffeehouse.

"Oh, hello, Nicky. Nic, this is Trey. Trey, Nicky." The two nodded toward one another. Trey somehow managed to remain at full attention while unselfconsciously making small talk.

"Hey, how's it going, man?"

"I see you've done the shopping for the salon. Did they give you any trouble at Sally's? You got the professional discount?"

"Yeah. No problem." He set the bags down on the floor.

"Trey was just leaving," he said as he motioned for the boy to pull up his pants.

"What about my haircut? And, uh . . ." He rubbed his fingers together.

"Oh shush. And please put that thing away." He turned and stepped in front of Trey to shield him from Nic's judging eyes. "I'll take care of you, don't worry," he said in a loud whisper. "Now, Nic." He turned back around, but Nic had vanished. He ran toward the door but could not catch him. The Subaru pulled away with a roar.

"Dammit!" he muttered to himself. At that moment he could not gauge the damage done but knew a fragile vessel had been shattered, and nothing he could do would ever piece it back together.

Trey, now fully concealed, walked out of the back room, sat in the styling chair, and played with his own curly hair in the mirror. "That your boyfriend?"

"No," he said, still gazing out the window. "Just a friend. Just a very good friend."

Nic paced the floor, waiting for Richard to complete the final touches of his look. He landed with a *woosh* in the overstuffed leather chair in the living room, lit a cigarette, and squirmed in his seat, his foot bouncing nervously.

Nic ruminated on his situation. His weeks of self-styled research had proven quite an education. He knew all the principals: the officious real estate broker Monica, her weak-chinned partner and occasional paramour Mayor Rusty, the enigmatic Chinese backers Huang and Xu, the well-intentioned but naive Donna Hart and Geoff Sabateau, their committed cadre of do-gooders, and a sundry cast of minor players. But he remained uncertain what to do with his newfound knowledge.

Morley Plaza and its surrounding neighborhood would be razed; of that, there was no doubt. The concerned citizens of Morley may well express their opinions pro and con at tonight's town hall, provide facts and heartfelt testimonials, but none of it would affect the outcome one whit. The juggernaut was too vast, too powerful to be stopped by the likes of the socially awkward Sunita Reddy, the submissive Jeremy Kelner, or the ragtag collection of neighbors living month to month on their disability payments, social services, and trips to the food bank. Their gumption had long since been wrung out of them by poverty, sickness, and the inability to imagine a different future for themselves.

Then there was Richard, making last-minute micro-adjustments to his red neckerchief and pocket square, brim full of gumption and imagination, who at every stage of his life had conjured up a new reality to suit himself. And here he was, doing it again.

Nic had tracked down the history of MRK Holdings and MRK Management, the two companies that, respectively, owned and managed Morley Plaza and twenty-four other properties within a quarter-mile radius. Originally called Kornbluth/Gantry, LLC, it had been created by Richard and Dale, jumpstarted by Dale's retirement money. In a turn of tongue-in-cheek irony, the name was shortened to KG Enterprises, but when Dale died, Richard split the company's activities between acquisitions and management and renamed them. The corporations were healthy—no bankruptcies, strong financials—with Richard as sole owner and CEO.

And while Richard talked endlessly about his youthful exploits, influential friends, and hairdos, he never once mentioned a word about his holdings to anyone, keeping the real estate business at arm's length. In so doing he was able to move surreptitiously among the townspeople and his tenants, portraying himself as just "a regular working-class hairdresser," if there could ever be such an animal. In that guise he planned to testify tonight on the benefits of the Morley Pointe Crossing development.

Nic had no interest in attending the town hall, considered it at best a circus act, but now was stuck driving Richard, who finally emerged from the bedroom, having discarded his neckerchief in favor of an ascot.

"Better?"

"Bringing back the L. Ron Hubbard look, I see."

"Classic neckwear never goes out of style. Want to hear my speech?" he said gleefully.

"No."

Richard sat on the hassock opposite Nic anyway. He launched

into his main talking points, reading from a sheaf of rumpled handwritten papers. He spoke in a grand oratorical style about improving the livability of Morley, affordable housing, something called "workforce housing," all the jobs a massive building project would bring to the valley, the strong community support, and the state-of-the-art design of Morley Pointe Crossing. He finished with an expectant glance to his imaginary listeners around the room and waited for a response.

"So?"

"So what?"

"So what do you think?"

Nic stood up, towering over Richard.

"I've never heard a bigger line of bullshit in my life." He grabbed the papers from Richard and pitched them across the room, scattering them in all directions. Richard cringed and held up his hands defensively, convinced Nic was about to throw him across the room next. When that didn't happen, he slithered to the floor and crawled around the room gathering up his speech, finally hiding behind the sofa tremulously rearranging his pages into the proper order.

"You don't give a fuck about this town," yelled Nic, "or about jobs or housing or the goddamn community. When were you going to mention you stand to make millions on this deal?"

"You needn't be so rough." Nic could hear Richard's voice and the sound of papers rustling behind the couch. "Besides, what do you know about it? About anything? You stupid ex-con!"

"I happen to know everything about it. About MRK Holdings, your meetings with that real estate agent and the mayor, those two shady bag men. All of it! You're not fooling anybody."

Richard emerged, speech in hand, from behind the couch and smoothed his jacket.

"Well, it seems our little felon has done some homework. I wondered what you were up to when you disappeared for hours. And so what! Do you honestly believe this town is better off with that depressing little strip mall? Or those rundown shacks I pass every day, all those crackers hanging out on their lawns waiting for their welfare checks? Ugh, it makes me want to vomit. Besides, who's going to listen to you? I know everyone in this town, and—"

"Yeah, I know. And they know you, blah, blah, blah. I'm sure your friends on the city council are all in on it, and God knows what arrangements you've made to sweeten the deal for yourself. But what if all those crackers you despise were to get wind of it tonight at the town hall? I don't think it'd go over very well."

Richard walked to the full-length mirror and performed one final adjustment of his pocket square that had been jostled loose in the altercation.

"Don't make threats, dear boy, if you're not ready to follow through," he said nonchalantly. "As for arrangements, you know I could make this very worthwhile for both of us. No reason not to share, right? That's what you're getting at, isn't it?"

Nic had anticipated every possible reaction from Richard and was not surprised by the offer in exchange for keeping quiet. A tidy sum could be his way out and would exact some well-deserved revenge on Richard for his shabby treatment. But in the next instant, Nic felt an unseen force sweep over him. He heard himself speaking now. It was his own voice, without a doubt, but he could not believe the words coming out of his own mouth.

"I don't want your fucking money!" *Goddammit,* he thought, *shut the fuck up.* But it was too late. The deal was lost, and he could not turn back.

"You don't?" asked Richard, bewildered, his tone softening. "But that's the way things are done, my boy, the way they've always been done. That's how the world works." He was conciliatory, even avuncular in his counsel. "You're absolutely right, there *is* a lot of money being passed around to get this deal done. It'll be a very good investment for everyone concerned. Why should your objections be treated any differently from anyone else's? You deserve to wet your beak. It's the right thing to do, don't you think? Won't you reconsider? I insist."

Nic got ahold of himself, stood erect, arms folded, his back turned to Richard. Again, the voice shouted to him: *He's begging you. Take it!*

"Keep it," he said curtly.

Richard was truly disappointed. He actually admired Nic's industry in digging up the truth on him and his willingness to call him out on it. He wanted to reward him for that, and for much more.

"So are you taking me or what?" he asked meekly.

"Drive your own damn self," Nic mumbled. He stormed out the kitchen door to the garage, where he straddled the street cruiser propped against the wall, activated the garage door opener, and coasted down the driveway. The streetlights were just coming on in the advancing dusk. He accelerated along the quiet street to top speed, his fat knobby tires whirring in rhythmic unison with each pedal stroke, his breath setting the pace.

Richard stood for a moment in the dining room, his body full of nerves but his mind devoid of thought or emotion. He fumbled for a cigarette and lit it, taking a deep drag, picking a stray strand of tobacco from his tongue. He mechanically moved to the breakfast bar, pushed open the lazy Susan cabinet where the liquor was stored, and poured himself a slug of Popov vodka. He downed it, then drew and downed another. His nerves began to steady. He took a hip flask from the drawer, filled it, and slipped it into his breast pocket.

He took one last look at the mirror, smoothing an errant lock of hair back into place, and grabbed the keys to the Subaru from the key caddy.

OK, Dick, here goes.

As Richard backed the car out from the garage, his front left tire first pushed then rolled over the plastic recycling bin full of empty wine and booze bottles Nic had placed out on the curb some hours earlier. The collision made a loud crash. The sound of glass shattering and rigid plastic being bent, snapped, and crushed reverberated through the quiet neighborhood. He pulled out onto the street and was off.

Down the deserted block, Nic had slowed to a coast. *I should go back,* he thought, more out of habit than anything else. Loyalty, charity, and gratitude were still foreign sensations to him. He U-turned in the middle of the street and was heading back to the house when he heard breaking glass and crunching plastic and knew intuitively what had happened. He then heard a more familiar sound: the Subaru, its undersized engine gunned and winding noisily in protest, rapidly approaching. He quickly ducked behind the trunk of a fat old oak, where he sheltered in shadow as Richard sped through a stop sign and made a too-tight right turn. As he rounded the corner, both passenger side tires thudded loudly up onto the curb and briefly took air, returning to the asphalt with a jagged scrape. Nic watched the Subaru pull away at full throttle, headed for San Sebastian Parkway.

23. CARNIVALE

A festival atmosphere filled the streets of downtown Morley as Donna and Geoff pulled slowly along in the Bomb. From blocks away they heard the thump and jangle of drums and tambourines, barely audible above the thunderous rumble of his breached and riven muffler. Rhythmic chants of "Hey, hey! Ho ho!" echoed off the sides of buildings, the familiar cadence clear; much less so was the crowd's plea for what "has got to go."

Oversize placards filled Geoff's back seat, along with an equal number of five-foot wooden garden stakes densely bundled together. They had hoped to arrive early to attach the signs to the sticks but were having no luck getting near the already-full parking lot and had to park on the street four blocks away. It was dusk, and a breezy shower kicked up as they walked toward the main building. Donna, concerned her signs were getting wet, asked Geoff to slip them up under his coat, which was impossible since they were far too large. Doffing his coat in an act of true chivalry, he wrapped the signs against the rain, turning the lettered sides inward on themselves for extra protection.

"Careful, don't bend them."

"OK, got it," he replied as the wind blew the arms of his coat in all directions, nearly buckling the cardboard signs. Donna carried the stakes, along with a heavy-duty stapler to attach the placards, a stack of flyers securely tucked under her sweatshirt, a grocery bag of healthy snacks for her crew, and a teetering tower of chartreuse

T-shirts with the Clean Up This Mess! logo silkscreened onto the front.

Folding tables lined the sidewalks in front of the City of Morley office complex. Vendors huddled under ponchos and makeshift rain shelters, hawking coffee and hot spiced apple cider, cookies and muffins, specially treated health-assuring water, tie-dyed T-shirts, handmade necklaces, and organic draw-string pants. Passionate advocates beckoned the throng to sign this petition, learn more about that issue, or otherwise demonstrate their solidarity with an array of progressive causes, candidates, and products.

Donna and Geoff made their way through the parking lot and into the main lobby of the city building. Giant arrows, printed by the office staff earlier that afternoon and festooned with Mylar balloons, pointed the way to the meeting hall. They had to wait in a long line for the security check. Supporters farther ahead recognized them, turned, and waved. Geoff was sure they were making direct eye contact with Donna only, while still regarding him coolly after his recent legal troubles, though he made sure to smile broadly anyway and wave as if nothing was wrong.

Donna opened her bag for inspection, and both passed through the metal detector without a problem. But the security officer prohibited the sticks she had brought for the signs.

"The signs are fine, ma'am, but no sticks allowed."

"But why?"

"Too easy to turn into a weapon. Same if you tried to bring in a baseball bat or a machete." The officer was kind and polite. "Your people can hold up their signs and wave them, no problem."

She thanked him earnestly but asked what she should do with the sticks. "I paid money for these stupid things," she said, balancing the large, round bundle on its end. "Please don't make me cart them back to the car in the rain. We had to park three, four blocks away and it's getting close to seven o'clock."

The guard scrutinized the pair, whose heads and clothes were still damp, and deemed them harmless. He looked around and made an executive decision. "Set them just over there, inside the door. You can keep an eye on them and pick them up on the way out."

"Oh, thank you. You just saved me forty bucks. I know I can use them some other time."

"In the garden maybe?"

"Yes, in the garden."

They walked past more balloons into the brightly lit Great Hall, the size of a gymnasium. Despite its vastness, the room was close and musty, the odor of human beings heavy in the air, flooded by the din of two hundred conversations, their volumes dialed up in an effort to be heard. A few members of the committee had already arrived and greeted them warmly. Some familiar faces—Dr. Sunita Reddy; West Morley Neighborhood Association Chair Shannon Wise; Mona Cummings and her husband, Jim, from the Presbyterian Church—and some new ones Donna did not recognize. They had turned out in respectable numbers but had felt a bit lost while waiting for their leaders to arrive and give them direction.

A gaggle of boisterous young people in red T-shirts representing the anti-police contingent had staked out the middle of the room, all tattoos and piercings and blustering anger. The shirts featured a stylized letter A encircled by barbed wire, symbolizing their allegiance to the principles of anarchy, along with some words too small to read. They were here to protest the $14 million recently approved by the city council for new cops and to ply their case in favor of more mental health specialists and drug outreach workers.

To their left was the booster squad for the community rec centers, once again on the budgetary chopping block. From preschoolers to the very old, they wore light blue hooded sweatshirts and ball caps with their own logo. They had signs too, a little smaller than Donna's, all professionally printed and all the same: "Save Our Community Centers." *At least mine are unique,* she thought. (Hers were hand-lettered, with as many clever slogans as there were signs, like "What's Wrong With Our Town?!?!" "Wake Up, People!" "Take Back Our Streets!" and their signature catchphrase "Clean Up This Mess!")

Donna immediately took charge. She set her bundle of sticks in its designated spot by the door and started distributing the awful yellowish-green T-shirts to the members of her team, who held them up to themselves appraising whether they would fit.

"They're basically all large or extra-large. Just pull them over your regular clothes. We want to be a sea of green," she said. They complied with varying results, some swimming in the baggy shirts, others tightly bound by them as if wearing corsets.

She handed Geoff the flyers and instructed him to place one on each folding chair, starting with the section of the room where they now stood, then spreading out to use up as many of them as he could. The flyers depicted a tent camp on the front, with bulleted talking points on the reverse side. There were hundreds of chairs, but Geoff had enough to cover nearly the entire room. He conserved flyers by rationing them to every other chair as he moved out to the farthest reaches, instinctively avoiding the red-shirted gang altogether.

As she passed out tangerines and KIND Bars to her followers, Donna reminded them to sign up to give testimony. They would then receive little numbered tickets, she explained, and their numbers would be drawn randomly, like a door prize raffle. She also requested, if one of their lead speakers had not been selected, that the "winner" pass his or her ticket to a different speaker so their most compelling stories could be emphasized. The members agreed.

From a side door in the far corner of the room now emerged a ragtag phalanx of souls numbering about a dozen, led by a young administrative assistant, who, in her smart blue dress and kitten heels, contrasted sharply with the little troupe. They shuffled warily to their reserved seats in the front row, huddling close to one another and eyeing the amassing crowd. Unique among them was a wide-eyed young woman accompanied by an obedient little girl at her side and an angelic newborn in her arms. Next, trailing the group out of the cloistered space, appeared City Councilor Deirdre "Dee Dee" Coffey. She carried her impressive girth with strength and vigor as she took in the packed room with one glance, then spoke individually with each of her guests. In low tones she thanked and reassured them all, spending extra time with the young mother, who despite her potential vulnerabilities appeared determined and self-assured.

The woman in the blue dress tapped the microphone, and the crowd quieted slightly. "Thank you all for coming. If we could all take our seats . . ." A few people moved slowly toward chairs, but most continued their conversations.

Richard, who had been among the first to arrive (thus gleefully snagging a prime parking place just outside the door) stood off to the right alongside Monica Sampson-Smith. Both looked out into the crowd as they spoke.

"I see Dee Dee's brought her army of the forgotten," he said, leaning conspiratorially toward Monica, who had to pull back to avoid the overwhelming stink of Pall Malls and vodka. "They should be able to squeeze some tears out of the gallery."

"I suppose. It all depends how Rusty and the rest of the council are feeling tonight. Getting the crowd on your side is fine, but it's not everything."

"Worried?"

"I don't worry," she said, clicking her pen nervously. "But I don't like to count my chickens."

"Rusty's in the bag, of course. Well, isn't he?"

"Of course he is," she insisted, still reconnoitering. "I meant the others."

"Dee Dee must be a sure thing." He caught Dee Dee's eyes across the room and waved with a broad smile. *Fat sow!* he thought. She returned his greeting enthusiastically, waving simultaneously at Richard and Monica with both hands. "What about Bill Devereux. I've never seen him take a stand on anything. He always goes with Dee Dee, and we only need three votes."

"True," she replied without conviction. "But then there's Fran and Hank to deal with. Fran's pretty hard core, sees herself as guardian of the people's money. Inclined toward a 'no,' I'd say, but who can tell? She tends to feed off the crowd and so could go either way."

"And Hank, what's his story?"

"Also a fiscal conservative. To him it's always about what it will cost, not whether it's a smart idea."

"It's not going to cost the town anything as far as I can see." He rubbed his hands together. "Then there's all that beautiful tax revenue."

"You're forgetting the SDCs, my friend. You know, system development charges, for putting in things like streets and sidewalks, water, sewer, schools, parks, all that stuff. They're all waived."

"Really!" He tried to appear riveted but had already lost interest, again surveying the crowd.

"We made our case for the project, then convinced them we needed an incentive to bring it to Morley. An incentive! Can you imagine?" She laughed out loud.

"And if they're waived?" he asked. "Who pays for all that?"

"Why, our fair city, of course. Hank will hate that."

"He'll learn to love it, I'm sure. Oh, look." Richard pointed to the stage as Mayor Rusty Purnell found his way to the dais. "His royal highness has arrived." Purnell settled into the middle chair and tested the microphone. Councilor Bill Devereux sat to his right. They exchanged bland pleasantries, then Bill went back to his phone and waited for the show to begin.

Rusty was uncomfortable among crowds, had always been more of a one-on-one guy, and the room tonight made him particularly tense. Too many unknowns, too many factions. His head hurt. He had taken a couple of pain pills earlier, but they hadn't kicked in yet, except for the queasy feeling they gave him. He dutifully chewed on his nicotine gum, which seemed to jangle his nerves even further. *I would kill for a drink right now*, he thought.

He had attended all the charrettes, pre-meetings and happy hours, taken all the phone calls, listened to all the voice mails, read and reread all the emails, and yes, cashed all the checks made out to Reelect Purnell Campaign. He discovered everyone knew precisely what to do and told him so without a hint of uncertainty. Drawn in by the swirling interplay of eclectic demands and desires, he approached decision-making as if sampling from a buffet table of ideas. The strategy had proved wholly impractical. He'd never mastered the skill of simply stepping away and deciding. More than a drink, all he really needed tonight was to do the right thing.

The town clearly needed a leg up; everyone agreed. Morley Pointe Crossing promised to be that but also threatened to disrupt the very fabric of the community, its culture and history. Not that any of that was so wonderful. Unemployment, drug abuse, alcoholism, crime, domestic violence, dependency on government aid—the status quo was hard to justify. But no matter how hobbled their chaotic lives might be, no one in the path of the project was clamoring for their world to be upended.

Rusty spoke civilly into the microphone. "Hello, people. Let's take our seats, please. Lots to talk about tonight." Again the volume in the room dimmed slightly as attendees made halfhearted efforts to end their conversations. Unintelligible shouts and laughter emanated from the boisterous red-shirted anarchists, whose banter seemed to escalate rather than quell. Rusty held his hand over the microphone and called down to the front row. "Councilor Coffey, can we please . . ." She did not respond but continued to confer with her minions. Councilors Francine "Fran" Mayhew and Henry "Hank" Ward had come to the stage but remained standing, speaking with one another behind Rusty's back. "Guys?" he said, motioning them to their seats. Dee Dee Coffey finished pep-talking her special invitees, hoisted herself up the steps, and sat with a grunt at the left end of the councilors' table. A few attendees made last-minute runs to grab cookies and punch, and the room finally settled.

Mayor Purnell officially called the town hall to order, welcomed the crowd, and thanked them for attending, remarking on the size of the turnout. He reminded them of the lottery process for providing testimony. Any issues that affected Morley were appropriate for discussion, he explained, but comments would be limited to two minutes per person. "If you don't get a chance to speak tonight, I promise your voices will be heard." He drew their attention to the email and phone number appearing on the screen above. "I personally review all your feedback on any issue before the city council, and it becomes part of the public record." He set some other ground rules for the discussion: Speak Respectfully, Let Others Have Their Say, No Profanity, No Shouting, Hold All Applause. "Instead, express your agreement silently with a thumbs-up or your disagreement with a thumbs-down."

He assured everyone he was acutely aware of the problems of homelessness, drug use, housing, unemployment, and crime that had befallen Morley over the past two years, then continued by listing all the innovations the mayor's office had launched and the progress that had been made: more shelter beds in the pipeline, more money for drug rehabilitation and mental health outreach, more police officers on the street, and tougher anticamping laws.

With the last two accomplishments, a woman's booming voice arose from among the seats.

"Fucking fascist!"

The crowd gasped collectively, cracking the dreariness that had shrouded the room since Purnell had started speaking. All turned see a tall, substantial, densely tattooed woman in a tight-fitting red shirt that accentuated her feminine build. A red ball cap barely concealed a tall tuft of black curls sticking straight up, cropped close to the skin on both sides, the brim pulled low over her eyes. Rusty squinted into the crowd to see the offender. Something in her tone, her shape, her carriage struck him as familiar, but the lights were too bright to make out details.

One older woman turned to the disruptor and yelled, "Oh, shut up, you foolish child." A few in the room cheered, most vocally her fellow Red Shirts. A group of Morley Middle School students, here with their current events teacher to see real democracy in action, tittered uncontrollably.

Rusty had feared it would be this kind of night. Verbal outbursts and profanity had reliably accompanied all of his recent public appearances. *I oughta be used to this by now*, he thought, but nevertheless it troubled him. His self-doubt lingered like a bad cold. What was he doing wrong? Did he carry some invisible mark that made him the target for abuse? Even his fellow town leaders had begun to distance themselves from him, their conversations courteous but cool. He gazed out from the stage at two hundred angry townspeople and wished in that moment to be transported away to anywhere but here. The scene took on an illusory aspect. His heart pounded as he held fast to the microphone, gripping it tightly in his sweaty hand.

"Come on, folks, this isn't going to get us anywhere," he said in a slow cadence, lecturing them as if they were all misbehaving middle schoolers. "We all know the rules. Please follow them. Not for my sake but for all of you, the engaged citizens of Morley who came out in the rain to participate in this important town hall. The public safety officers are prepared to escort anyone out of the building who continues to be disruptive. I hope this is fair and sufficient warning."

A security force of half a dozen uniformed men and women, armed with pepper spray and Tasers, had already taken positions dotting the room, ostensibly ready for any potential disturbance. They clustered at a safe distance around the Red Shirts, where the profane comment seemed to have originated.

The remainder of the crowd, through their nodding silence and murmured conversations, tacitly rallied around the mayor. These were not anarchists. They believed in participatory government, valued the role of the governed—themselves—in shaping society's future and their own. They respected cops and the rule of law, and hence the Mayor's Rules would be followed. They were not about to let their meeting be hijacked by a gang of police-hating thugs.

"All right, now let's continue. Councilor Coffey, you have some special guests who would like to give some testimony?"

"Yes, Mr. Mayor, thank you. Mandy, would you like to come up first please?" As Dee Dee Coffey introduced the young woman, she pulled the suckling child from her breast, covered herself, and rose to take a seat at the table arranged with microphones for public testimony. Her remarkably well-behaved toddler sat quietly next to her, gawking at the row of councilors before them.

Geoff had been checking and rechecking his raffle ticket, impatiently awaiting his chance to testify. He leaned over to Donna. "She's jumping the line? What the fuck?"

"I don't know," she whispered. "Shhh."

The woman composed herself. At first she spoke so quietly the assistant in blue had to move the microphone closer to her. "Mayor Purnell and council members. My name is Mandalit Delacruz. Thank you so much for allowing me this opportunity. I'm a little nervous, so please forgive me." She shifted the wriggling hungry infant from one arm to the other and inserted the binky tethered to his onesie, juggling her handwritten notes. "Thank you especially to Councilor Dee Dee Coffey for inviting me."

Mandy Delacruz told her story, one of hardship and struggle but ultimately success and salvation. She had dropped out of high school in the middle of her junior year, pregnant, working a minimum wage job to subsist. Then six months ago, thrown out of her home by an alcoholic mother and her abusive boyfriend, she found herself homeless and living in her car, with one child to feed and another on the way, no job, no daycare, no training or education, not knowing where their next meal would come from, not even decent clothes to look for a job. She began to cry; the assistant quickly brought her a box of tissue.

"I was ready to do almost anything to survive." She paused to dab her nose as the crowd imagined just how far she might have gone. "Finally, I was directed by Councilor Coffey to the New Beginnings women's shelter. It was made for people just like me. They understood my situation immediately, knew exactly what I needed to thrive and not just survive."

The shelter, she went on, afforded her a safe environment, along with nutritional support, daycare for her little one, prenatal care for the one on the way, training on how to search for a job, and even the right wardrobe to be successful.

"Soon I was able to find stable housing at Mary Beech Home. I got a position working with at-risk moms like myself. I eventually gave birth to my beautiful son, and now I'm saving money to finally get a place of our own. None of this would have been possible, Ms. Coffey, without you and your support for New Beginnings and Mary Beech. You literally saved my life, and I want to thank you for that."

The room erupted in supportive applause, every faction moved by her compelling story and turn of good fortune. The mayor gently reminded them to hold their applause and give the thumbs-up if they approved. They all did.

Geoff anxiously eyed the clock and fingered his raffle ticket, thinking the young mother, now well past her two-minute limit, had finally finished. She hadn't, and he threw up his hands in frustration.

"But my story is not unique. There are dozens of girls like me in Hensen County. They all need our support, and we need to do more, much more." She cited the affordable housing units planned for Morley Pointe Crossing. "It's something we desperately need. And for that reason, the project has my strong support. I urge you each to vote for its approval."

She gathered up her brood and went back to her seat in the front row. Dee Dee Coffey blew her a kiss as she left the testimony table. By the end, Mandilit Delacruz had sounded more like a seasoned politician than a forsaken waif. The crowd again applauded wildly, this time with whoops and hollers. The mayor did nothing to silence them.

Mandy was followed by several more sympathetic characters invited by Councilor Coffey, each more rumpled and less articulate than the young mom. To a person they called for more shelter beds, lunch lines, warming centers, and a broad range of social programs and finally praised the effort to build affordable housing units in the proposed development.

Amid the enthusiastic hoots and shouts, Jeremy and Celine now appeared at the rear doors of the hall, wearing their bright yellow-green shirts. They had no difficulty finding the rest of the team in their matching color. They awkwardly rushed to Donna's side, embarrassed by their lateness.

"Hi, Donna," said Jeremy, introducing himself to jog her memory.

"Ah, yes, the young man from the video store."

He nodded. "This is my friend Celine."

"Celine, so nice to meet you. Thanks for coming. It's quite a rowdy crowd tonight. We may be in for some fireworks. You know, you feel very familiar to me, Celine." She dug into her bag for a snack. "Tangerine?"

"I was in your store once. You showed me a book on spells."

"Nutty bar?"

"No, thanks."

"Yes, of course, I remember now. But then something came up as I recall, and you had to dash off in a big hurry."

"Um, yeah, sorry about that," Celine said, not wanting to recount too many details of that terrible day.

"I've still got that book, if you're interested."

"I might be."

Geoff broke in. "Shh, shh. They're calling people." Nine numbers were announced by the woman in blue. She wrote them on a dry board to the left of the stage and invited the ticket bearers up to the speakers' table in groups of three.

"Well?" Donna asked Geoff, looking at his ticket and hers.

"Nope."

"Don't worry; it's just the first volley." But Donna fretted as she watched people she did not recognize in chartreuse T-shirts moving about the room. She thought she had screened all the potential presenters from Clean Up This Mess! but now wondered who these people were, where they'd gotten the logo tees, and what they planned to say. She quickly reminded herself that theirs was a democratic organization not ruled by any one person or clique and that all voices should be heard. Still, the loss of control made her uneasy.

The next person to give testimony was an older gentleman in a blue hoodie. He and his wife attended the community center around the corner from Morley Plaza, directly in the path of the proposed development. With somber sincerity, he touted the after-school reading program, music and art classes, writing and theater workshops, and seniors' singles dances. There was no plan to replace the center, already scheduled for demolition, and he begged them to consider including a new one in the long-term planning for Morley Pointe Crossing. The councilors, careful to avoid making any commitments, only nodded compassionately.

Next up was a woman from the anarchists' ranks, telling the story of her young cousin who had been paralyzed by a police officer's bullet in a gang unit raid. She depicted him as an innocent though troubled fifteen-year-old who had made some bad choices but still "had his whole life ahead of him, until a rogue cop cut him down." She graphically described his feeding tube, tracheostomy, urine catheter, bed sores, diapers, and the daily care required for each. She railed against the police bureau's "stop, talk and frisk" policy and demanded the council reverse their decision to fund additional police officers in favor of more field-trained mental health workers and addiction specialists.

The Red Shirts fervently supported her, ignoring the mayor's prior warnings for silence, loudly chanting slogans, stamping their feet, and banging their folding chairs on the floor. One of the drums from the rally outside had been smuggled in, and now a slight young woman stood pounding on it violently. They eventually settled down when the security force moved in. The drum was confiscated, and the young woman escorted out, to the jeers and fist-pumping of the Red Shirts. Her screamed obscenities could still be heard echoing from the lobby.

After a few moments, the room again quieted and public testimony resumed. More boluses of citizens were called up. The next several speakers raised no hackles whatsoever. They used the open forum to concentrate on personal gripes and grievances with the city, delivered in lengthy diatribes, straying far from their subjects as often as addressing them, and boring the audience and council members alike. But no one complained. Everyone seemed grateful for the respite. More cookies and punch were enjoyed.

Geoff listened intently as the woman in the blue dress called the last batch of raffle numbers. So far Donna and Geoff's group had been sparsely represented. He leaped up joyously when his number was announced. But his elation wore off as reality set in. He now admitted to himself that he wasn't ready to speak, didn't even want to. He'd barely practiced his remarks, the ones Donna had ghostwritten for him, and when he had practiced, he'd often flubbed his lines and gotten panicky. He looked at Donna sheepishly. There she stood, crestfallen, holding her neatly typed missive in both hands, eloquent words that would never be heard.

"Here," he said, "you'd better take this."

"Are you sure?" she replied as she took his ticket. He nodded.

"Go on. Knock 'em dead." She hugged him around the neck and rushed forward to take her seat at the speakers' table.

24. THE SHOE DROPS

"Guess I'm next," said Richard, his cheeks flushed bright red. Monica eyed him with foreboding as he held his ticket up for her to see. All evening she had watched him slip behind the expansive comment board, scattered with three-by-five cards, to take short nips from a steel flask. She had said nothing but now wished she had.

As he advanced to the front of the room, he steadied himself on the backs of chairs, unwittingly bumping the heads of people with his elbow along the way, once hard enough to be heard in back of the room, for which he did not apologize. He eased himself down to Donna's left, and they exchanged nods.

To her right, reviewing his notes, sat the third speaker, a bearded young man wearing one of her chartreuse T-shirts. His was among the faces Donna had never seen before. She tried to make eye contact with him, but he was the picture of concentration.

The mayor motioned for the first speaker to begin. After a moment's confusion, the two men deferred to Donna. She rustled her papers and tapped the microphone before beginning.

"Good evening, all. I'm Donna Hart, owner of Pickwick's Paperback Shack in Morley Plaza. I have a few sobering thoughts to share with you about our city and the project currently under consideration. We've heard lots of stories here tonight, so let me begin with one of my own."

"Oh, good," Geoff whispered excitedly to Dr. Reddy, "she's going to talk about being stabbed!"

"One very cold night last November, I came out of my shop to find a man lying on the hood of my car. 'Sorry,' he said, 'just trying to stay warm.' I looked at him first with fear, then anger and finally pity. He told me his name—Danny—and said he was just leaving, since my car was getting cold anyway. He looked so gaunt and forlorn, I asked when he'd last eaten; it'd been a couple of days. Now I can't really explain what happened next or why, but something in his humble manner touched me. I decided to take him to the Burger Basket across the way and get him fed. We spent the next hour driving around Morley, trying to find him a place to stay, somewhere warm and safe. Eventually we found a shelter that would take him in. All he had to do was behave himself and follow a few simple rules."

Geoff sat on the edge of his seat, mouth agape. *She never told me any of this. Why isn't she talking about the bum who knifed her?*

"Unfortunately, I saw Danny sleeping on the street the very next night and many more nights after that. I went to the shelter where I'd dropped him off to ask about him. The attendants were at first hesitant to give out any information, so I made up a story, told them I had a personal item of his and wanted to return it. 'Afraid you won't find him here,' they told me. 'He's banned for life.' It was then I learned that some people behave so poorly, they are permanently denied access to a shelter bed. Can you imagine? What a tragedy."

The crowd murmured their apparent agreement.

"Street camping is a difficult and inhumane way to live. None of us would allow a friend or loved one to exist in such a manner. So why do we let people like Danny live this way? It's unsafe, uncomfortable, unhygienic, and very stressful. Yet every night, shelter beds sit empty, and motel vouchers go unclaimed. Why?

"For one, shelters and motels require residents to abide by certain rules—no stealing, no dealing, no drugs, no drinking, no fighting—but for whatever reason, God love them, many aren't able to do so. Even a very organized and sober person could spend hours applying for a motel voucher or waiting all day for a shelter to open its doors, all the while still struggling to find enough to eat, or battling street violence and the elements.

"With Danny's story in mind, it seems to me our obsession with erecting more high-rise apartments in Morley is quite misguided. Of course, people need a safe place to shelter and sleep. But if homelessness were simply a matter of housing, it would have been solved by now. For years we've foolishly believed the same old canard from developers that we're in a 'housing crisis.' They've been given the green light to build, build, build on an empty promise that they would construct so-called 'affordable housing units.' But they've leveraged their political influence quite effectively and so are required to dedicate only a tiny percentage of new construction to low-cost units in exchange for enormous tax breaks and other financial incentives, while the vast majority of units are designed for high-end tenants paying top-of-market rents. We've placed our trust in developers to do the right thing, and year after year they betray that trust.

"This is at its core a public health crisis, not a housing crisis, and it requires a public health solution. We've got to understand why a person becomes homeless in the first place; otherwise we'll just be kicking the can down the road. Success in life is never guaranteed. It relies on individual qualities like resilience and grit, self-respect, respect for others, delayed gratification, the ability to imagine a better future, and a sense of your place in the world. But if you look into the histories of folks on the street, you will often find a lifetime of poor choices, coupled with economic hardship, negligent parenting, bad role models, traumatic childhood experiences, mental illness, addiction, or incarceration. If these factors are not addressed, we will forever be housing a broken and dysfunctional population doomed to failure. Society can help—through education, vocational training, racial and gender equity, a living wage, kickstart loans, and other incentive programs, thus creating a tide of economic justice that will raise all boats.

"We want our communities to be safe, clean, and healthy as well as compassionate and welcoming. But it is neither healthy nor compassionate to allow people to camp on the street, relieve themselves in the bushes, use needles, and leave trash while making everyday people feel uncomfortable and unsafe. I feel the pain of the homeowners and businesspeople in our town who work hard to maintain their properties. They are understandably frustrated.

"And to you folks here tonight who are struggling with homelessness yourselves, let me just say: we see you, we hear you, and we know how to solve this. Tonight we call upon the City to demonstrate the moral and political courage to tackle this problem in the right way, not by building high-rise apartments but by investing in people. Thank you very much."

Celine, Jeremy, Dr. Reddy, and the rest of the Clean Up This Mess! crew rose from their seats to cheer Donna, with a handful of citizens joining in. Geoff sat dumbfounded, still reeling from Donna's odyssey with the bum. The Red Shirts sat with their arms crossed muttering among themselves. Most were taciturn, too respectful of Donna's sincerity to jeer her, perhaps even in silent agreement with some of her logic but blindly committed to opposing any position not their own.

Mayor Purnell gave the crowd a minute to vent and settle down, thanked Donna, then invited the next speaker to begin. "Your name, sir?"

"Why you know my name, Rusty," said Richard coyly, leaning forward so close his lips touched the microphone, sending ear-piercing feedback reverberating throughout the hall. He recoiled, then continued with a heavy slur, "It's me, your friend Dick Kornbluth. Mr. Richard to everyone else," he said, laughing wheezily. "Hi, Dee Dee." He waved with a flourish at Councilor Coffey, and she waved back.

"Hello, Dick. How are you feeling tonight?" she asked, her voice portraying genuine concern for his tipsy state.

"Damn good, Dee Dee. Damn good." He absently fumbled in his shirt pocket and pulled out a Pall Mall.

"No smoking, sir," the mayor admonished. Richard did not seem to hear him as he shakily struck a match. "Please, Mr. Kornbluth," the mayor said more loudly, "this is a nonsmoking venue. Please refrain." Richard complied after getting off one good puff, defiantly crushing the burning smoke to bits in his hand and onto the table. He started to tidy up the fragments.

"Never mind that mess, sir," the mayor said sternly. "Please make your statement."

Rusty indeed knew Richard, from their many joint meetings with Monica to discuss plans for Morley Pointe Crossing. He found the old fellow amusing, full of stories, a little ribald at times, always designed to entertain. But tonight he wished to avoid even the appearance of a cozy relationship with anyone giving testimony, fearing it could cast a cloud on decisions made by the council. To contain Richard, Rusty would need to snub him.

"Make your statement, sir. You have two minutes." *The deal's nearly done,* Rusty thought. *Don't make an ass of yourself. Everyone knows these meetings are just for show.* In his brief career in public service, Rusty had learned a cold fact: people needed these staged performances to prevent them from losing faith in the democratic process or feeling completely trampled upon, even while knowing down deep that their fate had already been sealed. He recalled a quote he'd heard more than once—"bread and circuses"—not knowing its origin but fully appreciating its meaning.

A subdued Richard stared glumly at the microphone while the crowd waited. "All right, all right," he said with a dismissive wave. "I'll have my say, then you can be rid of me."

"What is your comment, sir?"

Richard pulled his crumpled speech from his breast pocket and read the text slowly and deliberately. "I am here in support of Morley Pointe Crossing. And I'll tell you why. This town is on the skids, and we all know it."

The room drew a breath in unison.

"The place needs a kick in the pants before it goes completely under. This development—*my* development—will be the boost it needs. Imagine shops and restaurants, beautiful greenways, fountains, piazzas, condos overlooking a lakefront promenade. If you have any sense you'll approve this deal. Otherwise the likes of them will take over"—he pointed his thumb in the direction of the Red Shirts—"and you'll be living in Detroit!"

The crowd, having listened quietly in disbelief and now hearing something new to be angry about, again found its voice. The Red Shirts jeered him, tried to shout him down. Donna and her group displayed their silent thumbs-down most vehemently. Even the gray hairs in their blue hoodies booed. Richard shot them an icy stare and went on.

"When we first moved here, Dale and I, Morley was in the middle of a renaissance. Good weather, cheap land, old folks with lots of money, and a bank on every corner. Then all those old fuckers died off. And who replaced them? Joe Six Pack with his fat house frau and their ne'er-do-well kids, their dented cars and toys all over the lawn, the whole family medicated one way or another. Now, Morley's in free-fall. Bums on every corner, panhandlers, meth heads, and all their filthy mess.

"Most of you don't remember Dale Gantry. He loved this town, though God knows why. Would do anything for it. He finally died for it, and for what? For what? This place drove him into the ground." Richard's face screwed up in a tortured grimace; sobs and tears soon followed. "He was the love of my life. And you killed him. Now he's gone, and I hate all of you, you provincial clods. I've seen London, Paris, Rome. I've lived in New York City *and* in Hollywood. Let me tell you, that's living—beautiful creative people doing beautiful creative things. Morley is a dump and I can't wait to get out. Cannot wait! So you can all go to hell." The next instant he was spent, sobbing noiselessly in a heap.

Donna placed her hand on Richard's shoulder and stroked it tenderly. Every soul in the room sat silent and unsettled, as will happen when sensibilities have been stripped to the bone. For the first time tonight, a consensus had formed among the disparate assembly. A sense of deep shame consumed them for what they had witnessed and with it an overwhelming desire to look away, shake it off, and simply keep going. So after a few moments of Richard sobbing, that's just what they did.

The mayor considered a recess to reestablish decorum but instead motioned for the final speaker to begin. The burly young man, who'd ignored Richard completely, pulled the microphone close to him. He sported a bushy red beard and navy-blue bill cap depicting an aircraft carrier with USS Hornet CV-8 embroidered across the top. His blue-gray eyes were impersonal and distant; they did not blink. As he spoke, Donna immediately recognized his tone from blog comments she had read.

He started slowly, his voice restrained, almost a whisper, though powerful and enthralling.

"We have a problem here, people." He breathed noisily through his nostrils. "I don't know where I live anymore. The place where I grew up, where I raised my kids, that place is gone, and it's never coming back. We are living in a human cesspool, and I want to know right now what the city council is going to do about it."

"Sir, can you state your name for the record, please?" asked the mayor, unperturbed.

"Rudolph Cerney, sir. My wife and I have lived here most of our lives. We love Morley, unlike some people," he said, casting a cold glance at the dispirited Richard. "All we ever wanted was a peaceful place to raise our kids. But our world was shattered one evening when my wife was attacked on our own street. Walking home from the store, she was shoved to the ground, groceries flying everywhere, overpowered by a man in a gray hoodie who grabbed her purse and ran."

A few murmurs passed among the throng; otherwise they sat engrossed and silent. Demonstrating a thirst for excitement and appreciation of a good story, they had already moved on from the spectacle of Richard's public breakdown. They wanted to hear more.

Geoff leaned over to Jeremy. "Hey, I like this guy. He knows what he's talking about."

"Our neighborhood was once among the safest in Morley. Now we're too afraid to walk alone after dark. We're the victims of car prowls, break-ins, and armed theft. Packages are routinely snatched right off our porches. We've been accosted, intimidated, threatened, even spat on. There's graffiti everywhere. The Walmart on 122nd Street is crawling with bums living out of RVs, which the store actually encourages, always loitering in front or circling on bikes through the parking lot like a pack of wolves, menacing good people. You'd have to be blind not to see the decline that follows wherever the tents go up. These people just waltz in, camp anywhere they please, then turn the neighborhood into an open sewer. If these people want to live in Morley so badly they're willing to freeze in the winter, then why do they do everything to make themselves so unwelcome? It makes no sense. I'm all for freedom. I fought for it." He touched the brim of his cap. "But we've got to balance individual rights with what's best for everyone else. Shooting up on the street, relieving themselves in public. They destroy the very community they lay claim to. It's outrageous. When we report these crimes to the police, there's no meaningful response. They claim they can't be everywhere at once, can't arrest someone unless they catch them in the act. Well, I am here to tell you," he shouted, "we have had enough!"

The polarized crowd began to stir in earnest again, half of them cheering, half booing. The mayor tried in vain to quiet them, but Rudolph Cerney went on, and the chatter died down. For better or worse, they wanted to hear him out.

"Given the absurdly high property taxes we pay, we deserve better. Unfortunately, we see no sense of urgency from our city leaders, meaning all you people." He pointed an accusing finger at the councilors. "Either you're completely out of touch, or you don't give a shit. Take a walk anywhere in this town, if you dare. It's turned into frigging Calcutta.

"How do we dig our way out of this? First, we need more police presence on the street. They're eager to help but feel hamstrung by your so-called humane approach, to the point of neutering them. Get out of their way, and let them do their job. Let's bring back the old-fashioned beat cop, someone on the front line who can keep an eye on the neighborhood and prevent bad things from happening in the first place."

The Red Shirts had found Cerney, with his military cap and cesspool talk, objectionable from the start. Now fueled by his apparent disdain for the disenfranchised poor and a call for more law enforcement, their shouts rose and echoed throughout the hall.

"Check your white privilege, dude!" screamed someone from Red Shirt territory.

"Check your own BS, dude," he retorted. "Get a clue. We're at a turning point. The time for tolerance and compassion is over. It's time for some old-fashioned vigilante street justice. You're either with us or against us."

The councilors sat motionless, their deadpan faces revealing nothing. Mayor Purnell reminded Cerney that his time was up. The public safety officers nervously eyed the Red Shirt brigade, wishing they'd had more manpower.

"It's time you started representing the people who actually built this town: hardworking, property-owning, tax-paying, stable families like ours. *We* built this! This is *our town*. This is *our* struggle. *We're* the victims here, not them. And if you don't do something about it, we're going to take it back." He slammed his open palm onto the table.

Geoff Saboteau shot to his feet applauding, along with a handful of red-haired, ruddy-skinned townspeople who all could have been related to Cerney. The mayor shouted into the microphone, but his voice could not compete with the rising din, the Red Shirts now pumping their fists. A few of them stood and boldly swaggered through the aisles toward the speakers' table, ready to confront Cerney. The outnumbered security force frantically called for backup.

As the crowd was stirring, two of the Red Shirts inched unnoticed toward the rear door. Crouching behind the chairs, they undid the bundle of heavy garden stakes that Donna and Geoff had carefully left there earlier. A few more of the rear-guard Red Shirts formed a human chain and clandestinely passed the stakes forward to one another through the distracted crowd. Suddenly the advancing force held weapons in their mitts, waving them overhead.

The townsfolk of Morley reacted impulsively to the brewing melee. A significant plurality attempted to gather their things and hurry toward the doors but were blocked by the throng shoving forward toward engagement. Alliances of necessity quickly formed without negotiation, either to defend Cerney's ideas or oppose them. The racially diverse Red Shirts were joined by the mostly white cadre of the homeless and their nonprofit advocates in defense of the defenseless. The blue-hoodied oldsters aligned with the Clean Up This Mess! crowd, shouting and waving their placards. The otherwise unaffiliated citizens who remained, defenders of liberal democracy and outraged by the idea of violence, were determined not to submit to mob rule. They expressed their dissatisfaction from their seats, fighting not with sticks but with words. Other folk, less principle-driven, felt themselves sucked into what promised to be a good fight on a Friday night.

Donna watched the scene unfold with alarm. Sensing danger, she immediately stood up from the speakers' table and edged her way back through the noisy crowd toward the relative security of her own pod. She determined all were safe and accounted for, except Geoff, whom she had passed, fire in his eyes, moving into the fray. She called out his name, but he had already disappeared into the crowd.

A long-haired, gap-toothed, extra-large member of the Red Shirt brigade, more flab than muscle, advanced forward, swinging his stick in wild circular movements in the fashion of a samurai warrior. He charged Cerney. Two others followed, hoping to coalesce into a three-on-one assault, but were cowed as they watched Cerney grab their massive comrade by the neck and hair, throw him over the table toward the stage, then turn and charge into the crowd himself, beet red and damp with sweat. The duo stood their ground and made feeble attempts to defend themselves against a thorough thrashing by Cerney.

The polite young public safety officer who had helped Donna and Geoff shouted into the talk radio attached to his epaulette. He removed the pepper spray from his duty belt, armed his Taser, and, with his cohort of five officers, darted forward into the skirmish.

Richard, drunk and oblivious to the ruckus surrounding him, sat slumped over the tabletop, resting his head on folded hands like a napping child. The table was jostled as bodies slammed into it, eventually knocking it completely away, causing him to fall forward onto the floor. Dazed and disoriented, he slowly turned to see a large female form looming over him, silhouetted in the glaring lights and wearing a red ball cap. Next he heard a resounding *thwack* as his head exploded with pain. Blood poured from his forehead into his eyes and down his cheeks. He was again thrown to the floor. He made an anemic attempt to right himself, finally getting up onto all fours and crawling weakly toward shelter under the table. He gazed down at a puddle of his own blood and was again kicked and pummeled to the ground.

Before he could raise himself up, Richard felt his entire body elevated aloft by the scruff of his jacket. He moved through the crowd now toward the back doors, not under his own power but as a limp passenger on an effortless ride, one strong arm holding him by the waist, his own frail arm thrown over a pair of broad, muscular shoulders. His rescuer cleared a path through the crowd, shoving bodies to the left and right, even as the weaponized garden sticks continued to swing toward them.

Richard turned and looked into the eyes of his hero.

"Nic?" He rubbed the blood from his face. "Nicky, is that you?"

Nic did not answer, but continued to maraud toward the exit signs.

"Oh, Nicky, you saved me. What—what are you doing here?" They were now past the doors, into the foyer, then into the parking lot. He felt the cool air on his face and heard an approaching siren's blare.

"Keys," said Nic bluntly, spotting the Subaru so conveniently parked.

"I—I don't know where . . ."

Nic dove into Richard's front pocket and pulled out the car keys, unlocked the passenger door, and gently eased Richard into the seat, then got in to drive. He squealed out of the parking lot and barreled toward the center of town.

Richard's head lay against the headrest, looking out the window, finally recognizing this was not the way home. "Where are we going?"

"Hospital."

"No hospital. Take me home."

"Forget it," he said, surveying the wounded mess that was Richard.

"No hospital, I said," in as loud a voice as he could muster. Nic ignored him and sped on for another quarter mile. "Please, Nic, I beg you. No hospital. Please."

Nic looked over at a bloody Richard once more, then made a sharp U-turn in the middle of the highway and headed for Dahlia Lane.

25. WHERE ARE THE KEYS

Nic rolled up the driveway and into the garage, avoiding the broken glass and shards of plastic strewn about by Richard's violent exit. Small solar path lights dimly illuminated the chaotic scene. Richard lay asleep in the seat beside him, head askew, mouth open, blood and snot trailing from his nose. Only the rhythmic sound of snoring assured Nic he was still breathing. Whenever it paused, Nic gave him a little nudge, causing him to startle and snort.

"Home," he said gruffly. No response. "Home," he repeated a little louder, shaking Richard's arm.

"Hmm?" Richard moaned weakly. The sweet, heavy fetor of blood and half-metabolized vodka filled the car, despite Nic's having rolled all the windows down the last half of the drive.

"Come on, let's get you inside." Nic came around and opened the passenger door. With his prompting, Richard grabbed the doorframe with both hands, feebly lifted one leg at a time, and pivoted slowly, planting his feet on the concrete floor.

"Attaboy, come on, you can do it." But Richard's body wouldn't budge; he went limp with a sad whimper. Nic threw both of Richard's arms around his own neck and grabbed his belt. "There you go. Got it? OK, now step, step . . ." Richard was on solid ground once again. Nic held him by the armpits as he shuffled slowly toward the mudroom door, then into the kitchen. He sat with a lurch at the breakfast nook, took out a cigarette, and lit it.

Nic walked to the bathroom, grabbed the peroxide and some hand towels, then returned to the kitchen. He ran warm water on the towels, splashed them with peroxide, and sat in front of Richard, cleaning his face and examining his wounds. In the short drive home, Richard's eyes had swollen into two puffy purple slits. A deep jagged laceration extended from midforehead to the bridge of his nose. Nic heard a soft crunching sound with any contact in the area, causing Richard to wince and yowl with pain.

"It's too much," he said, shaking loose from Nic's ministering. "I need a drink." Richard turned and deftly grabbed the half-empty plastic bottle of Popov from the counter where he'd left it earlier this evening, along with two shot glasses.

"Oh no, you don't." Nic attempted to snatch the bottle from Richard's hand. "You've had enough."

"Oh yes, I do," he said, yanking it back. "I've been through a lot tonight, dear boy."

Richard poured two shots and pushed one toward Nic, who continued to clean him up, gingerly avoiding the gaping wound between his eyebrows. *Yes, you've had a rough night, old man*, Nic thought, *all of your own making*. The wound began to ooze afresh, and Nic dabbed his cheeks and chin with the towel to absorb the trickling blood.

"I know what you're thinking," said Richard, raising his glass and pointing an accusing finger at Nic. "I can read you like a book. You're thinking, 'You got yourself into this mess. You shot off your mouth, embarrassed yourself, then got your head bashed in. And for what?' Cheers!"

Nic waved off the booze. "You did look pretty foolish up there."

Richard emptied his own glass, then Nic's, in two quick swallows, took a drag off his Pall Mall, and poured two more. "I suppose I did play it all wrong. Could have been more 'discerning,' as my mother would say, and kept my mouth shut. I just wanted to go out in a splash, tell everybody to go screw themselves. Guess I blew it."

"Yup" was all Nic could say. He wanted to lay into him, but Richard looked so pathetic he could not mount an attack. It just wasn't in him tonight.

In their brief time together, the two men had settled into a familiar pattern—bitter mockery and acerbic comebacks, aggressive dominance and grumbling compliance—a lopsided equation that usually tilted in Richard's favor. Despite all that, and in spite of himself, Nic had slowly developed a begrudging loyalty to Richard. Loyalty, or was it just habit? He could not be certain. But after everything that had happened tonight, suddenly his plans for an exquisite revenge had fallen away. He thought of the greasy, rumpled dossier on Richard and company he had compiled and stashed in the spare tire well of the Subaru and vowed to discard it. It all seemed pointless now.

"I'm just so tired, Nicky," Richard confessed without emotion. "Very, very tired."

Nic had never heard from him such utter resignation. "Hey, don't be morose. You're just drunk."

"And I'm going to get a lot drunker." Richard downed the two shots and poured himself one more. "I am done. Done, done, done! I don't want to go on. I can't. The money doesn't mean a thing to me now. I miss my friends. I miss being young, miss having the strength to do whatever I want, whenever I want. And I miss Dale. He was the love of my life."

"Yeah, so you've said." Nic dropped the towel and retreated to the living room.

"Now, Nicky, please don't think that I—"

Nic had heard enough of Richard's fixation on the departed Dale. In all his lovesick yearnings, Richard never bothered to mention his current housemate. Hadn't Nic taken care of him, been his Man Friday, worked like a bracero, serviced him on demand, responded to his every whim? Had their time together meant anything? Apparently not.

Richard called out to the living room. "Nic? Nic, are you coming back?" Silence. "Nic, I'm bleeding again."

"Bleed to death, motherfucker!" he heard from beyond the door.

Fresh blood dripped slowly down his nose and onto the table. He picked up a paper napkin, left over from Independence Day, with American flags and fireworks depicted in grand celebratory kitsch. He indifferently wiped up the blood on the tabletop, then dabbed his face as he puffed on his smoke. The vodka shots were working. His face felt warm, his nerves calming for the first time since his ordeal tonight. Events blurred together in random order. He remembered cracking wise with Monica and publicly flirting with the mayor. After that, nothing. He must have done something bad to be in the shape he was in, but could find no memory of it to latch on to. *Oh well, no regrets. What's done is done.*

"Nicky, please come here," he pleaded, trying to sound desperate. "I need you."

After a moment, Nic reappeared at the door, leaning ominously against the jamb, arms crossed and head cocked, his eyes full of loathing.

Richard smiled and chuckled softly. "Aren't we a pair? Look at me," he said, examining the bloody napkin. "I'm in an absolute state. And you—you look like Satan's evil twin." Nic turned to leave. "Oh no, please, Nic. Come sit here with me, just for a minute. Please?" He patted the chair next to him. Nic considered his options, which at that moment were exactly none. He slowly returned to the kitchen and sat across from Richard.

"Look, don't ever think I take you for granted. I owe you a lot. You've been a good friend to me these past few months, and I know it. You've taken care of the house, and Birdie . . . and me, of course. You've been a wonderful companion, and for that I'm very, very grateful. I could never repay you for that."

Nic rolled his eyes and shifted his weight to get up.

"And you saved me tonight. My Rosenkavalier! I at least owe you something for that." Nic sat wordless, his glower softening. "As for all my boo-hooing about Dale—well, he was quite a guy. You can't live with someone like that and not miss him. We were just a couple of punk kids when we met. We grew up together, grew into men." He sighed. "Then we grew old together, and boy did we." His face again twisted in disgust. "God, I hate being old. I always told him, 'You'd better outlive me.' I knew I couldn't get on without him. Guess it was true. I've done everything I could to get my mind off him. Chasing after money, property, boys. Nothing helps. I've been pursuing a ghost." He checked his face with the napkin. The tears had started, but the bleeding had stopped. With a deep breath he composed himself. "We're all running, I suppose . . . toward something we'll never catch or away from something we'll never escape. What fools we are."

Nic sat forward, elbows on knees, gazing at the floor morosely. "Speak for yourself. And mind your own fucking business."

"Ew, so testy. Just trying to help."

"I don't need your help. I'm fine."

"Oh, really? Admit it, dear boy. We both know perfectly well what you're running from."

"Listen, no one gives a shit about you or your sad stories. 'I'm so old, nobody loves me . . .'" They could care less."

"Couldn't."

"Huh?"

"'They *couldn't* care less.' 'They *could* care less' means—"

"Hey, know what? I could or couldn't give a flying fuck! Take your pick. Neither did any of those assholes tonight. You're lucky you're playing ball with them. Otherwise you'd be ground down under foot, just like everyone else. 'My development will be so great.' Are you blind? This isn't *your* development. It's not your *anything*. They'll build this thing with or without you, dead or alive. Have you seen those two Chinamen lurking around? They look like a couple of lizards sunning themselves on a rock. They'll eat you like a bug. And how about your little blonde friend Monica or your boyfriend the mayor? He really shut you down tonight, acted like he'd never seen you before. You're nothing but a speed bump to them. I should have left you back there lying in your own blood."

"You would never do that. You care about me too much." Nic sneered. "Yes, you do. You see, you really do love me, Nic, in your own perverse way. At the very least you admire me. A misfit, just like you, who somehow managed to do what few people ever do. I've made a good life for myself. How did I do it? It's called grit, and I've got it in spades." Richard made a tight fist and shook it. "With grit, the world will bend to meet you. Without it, it will crush you." He lit another smoke. "Oh, I know I'm a handful sometimes, a real pain in the ass."

"Literally."

"But I hope you've learned a thing or two from me these past few months. You came here so full of rage and resentment, so eager to take advantage of me and of all this. But that all melted away, as I knew it would. I watched it happen. We've had a good life together, don't you agree? I gave you a home, a sense of security. And you gave me . . . I'll say it, friendship.

"Hold the sanctimonious speeches. I see what you're all about. I know what you are, how you think. I can only imagine who you sucked and fucked or walked all over to get ahead. Hell, you stole most of what you have from that dead husband of yours."

"Listen, you ungrateful bastard. You know nothing. Nothing! I've worked hard for all of it, and I've got the scars to prove it. Life is not for the meek. It's a blood sport! You've got to have two sets of balls in this world: one pair dangling out where everyone can see them and a spare set in case the first pair get cut off. Besides, you have nothing to brag about, boy. Or should I say *old man?*" Richard's voice now took on a biting clarity. "You're not as young as you think you are. You won't be using those looks of yours as a weapon for much longer. Prince Charming's charm is fading."

"You oughta know."

"It's true. My time is over. I know what it's like to be hot, then not. But I'm going down kicking. I'm not going to let you stand in my way. You think I'd let an ex-con, a two-time loser, a murderer live in my beautiful home without doing my homework. You think I was born yesterday? I read the court transcripts. I know exactly what happened in that bar that night. You were high, with a chip on your shoulder. You picked a fight with a guy because you didn't like how he looked at you. You egged him on, hoping he'd come at you, then you killed him with that switchblade you're always packing. You're lucky you're not still rotting in that jail in Indiana."

"Thanks to you, I suppose. Is that what you're saying?"

"Yup, thanks to me. And I could have you back there in a flash. Oh, did I mention the rest of your ugly past? That night your father died and you were stuck in juvie, picked up at sixteen on a hustling charge. Let go, of course. Then that check-washing operation of yours, that poor girl taking the rap for you, spending fourteen months in prison while you went free. You must be very proud of yourself. Shall I go on?"

Nic could only respond with a bitter "Fuck off." He retreated again to the front room, as Richard prattled on with his stinging observations. Nic didn't need to hear any of it. It was all true. He'd lived life on a knife's edge, had been an unrepentant taker and bullshit artist. For someone who suffered periods of dark self-loathing, he had an outsized ego. He considered himself special, entitled, willing to have others cater to him, pissed off when they asked for anything in return. He could read people masterfully, discerning in an instant who might help him and who he could disregard. He learned to tease out their most impenetrable secrets and vulnerabilities and use them to gain an advantage, fend off a threat, or simply manipulate lost souls for the fun of it.

Richard struggled to push himself to his feet and stumbled to the kitchen doorway. He had more to get off his chest.

"Oh, there you are. As I was saying, you blame everyone for your misfortunes but yourself. You don't take any responsibility for all the bad luck that's befallen you, for all the hurt you've inflicted on others."

"Shut up. *Shut up!*" He grabbed his jacket. "Are you done yet?"

"Nope. Just getting started."

Nic saw the car keys on the kitchen table. He tossed on his jacket and tried to squeeze past Richard to get them. But Richard held fast to the doorjamb with wiry tenacity and would not let Nic pass.

"Where do you think you're going?"

"Away from here. Away from you." He reached behind Richard for the keys, but Richard's body would not allow it. He shifted his hips, trapping Nic's arm.

"Wait, Nic. I want to talk some more." Richard grabbed on to Nic's wrists; his grip was remarkably tight. As Nic struggled to break free, Richard pushed him with all his strength, sending Nic a few feet into the living room. Nic now rushed Richard, making contact and hurling both of them against the wall with a thud that quaked the house, knocking a picture to the floor. Nic saw his opening and dashed for the keys, but Richard again lunged into his path. Both men now occupied the kitchen doorway. Their bodies roiled and twisted, grunted and heaved. Nic broke free from the hold and shoved Richard even harder. His body flew like a rag doll into the stainless-steel refrigerator, his spine hitting first, then his head whipping back and landing on the freezer door with a loud crack, leaving a bloody dent. Richard's eyes lost expression as his body stiffened and tipped forward, first slowly, then, a slave to gravity, accelerating toward the floor and landing with a thud.

Nic leaned on a chair to regain his equilibrium. He gazed down at Richard's motionless body and gave it a soft kick with his foot.

"Wake up, you old fucker. Don't play possum with me." Seeing no response, he kicked again, this time a little harder. "Wake up, I said." Richard lay there facedown as blood pooled around his head and inched toward Nic's feet.

Nic had been at enough bar scuffles, overdoses, and street scenes to know what to do next. In one sweeping motion, he flipped Richard's limp carcass onto his back and grabbed his chin, pulling it forward. His lower plate floated loosely in his mouth. Nic grabbed it, flung it aside, and again yanked up on his now toothless gums. With that, Richard took a loud, gasping breath. His body gave a shudder then began to flail aimlessly.

"Don't you die on me, fucker. Don't you do it."

Richard's movements became more purposeful. He swiped at Nic's hand, knocking his fingers out of his mouth, then spat out the blood that had trickled in, creating a pink plume that dotted Nic's face and clothing.

"Where's my goddamn teeth?" His speech was indistinct and mushy. Nic searched for them on hands and knees, retrieved them from under the table, and handed them to Richard.

"Rinse them please. And help me up."

Nic dowsed the teeth at the sink then lifted Richard up onto the chair.

"Why are you so mean to me?" Richard said as he reinserted his plate. The teeth clacked and shifted as he bit down to test them, finally seating themselves with a squish.

"You can take it, you old bird."

"I'm not an old bird. Besides, shush, Birdie will hear you. Don't listen to him, Birdie," he called to the next room. "You hurt me, Nic. After all I've done for you. You hurt me terribly. Does it give you pleasure to see me suffer? Why?"

"Because you talk too much."

Richard began to cry again. His wound had opened up and bled freely. He fumbled for the vodka bottle and sloppily poured himself another drink, missing the glass and making a wet mess on the table.

"Why don't you slow down there, buddy?"

"I've got some demons to kill," Richard replied, gulping the drink.

Nic was not ready for another round of Richard's invectives. "I'm out. Where are those goddamn keys?" he said, looking on the table and underneath.

NEUTRAL, NO BRAKES

"I have no idea."

Nic grabbed him by his shirt front and flung him back and forth. "Gimme those keys."

Richard cowed and cringed, fearing Nic was about to hit him again. "I told you I don't have them," he whimpered. "They were sitting right there."

Nic desperately overturned every item in the kitchen, looked under the fridge, checked the sofa and table in the living room, searched Richard's pockets and his own, then started all over again.

"Fuck!" he finally screamed, then turned and stamped out the door to the garage.

Richard exhaled and sat expressionless for a moment. He could hear the garage door open as Nic, muttering loudly to himself, strode down the driveway and out onto the street.

Richard waited long enough to be sure Nic had left. He felt the heat of his cigarette as it burned down to his fingers, snuffed it, and lit a fresh one. He then slid his hand down the front of his pants, deeply into his crotch, and delicately pulled out the key fob for the Subaru. He had snatched the keys off the table as Nic was searching for his dentures. He dangled them, then dropped them onto the table. He laughed loudly then grimaced in pain.

"Oh, my head," he groaned. He caught his reflection in the kitchen window, touched his swollen, tender face and assessed the gaping wound between his eyes. "What a catastrophe I am."

26. BALLOONS

The clock ticked over into morning. A forensic photographer moved silently in the Great Hall, snapping shots of toppled furniture, makeshift weapons, and the gory floor. A saggy, half-spent purple balloon bounced into his view, causing him to shift attention in search of other images. He'd already captured most of the blood, and the wounds had all been bandaged. Stoic security officers debriefed with distraught public servants and unsettled citizens in pods of three and four. A pair of detectives in tweed sport coats and wool slacks, their pistols holstered at their waistbands and badges dangling from leather lanyards around their necks, circulated among the witnesses. Angry, afraid, silent, or chatty, all were thankful it was over.

Two alleged perpetrators of the violent outburst had been detained. The rest had either scattered or had been released after questioning. The first, a thin, wild-eyed creature wearing a red T-shirt, stood motionless in zip-tie handcuffs, immersed in a crowd of uniformed law enforcement personnel. His dirty jeans hung low on his hips, exposing his butt crack and grimy underwear. His long hair was clumped together, and he appeared not to have shaved for several days. Neither had he bathed, obvious from the smell emanating from him.

The second was a defiant young woman, also cuffed, who was described by several witnesses as "that big woman over there." They had identified her as having wielded a wooden stake, though no one could say for sure if she had assaulted anyone. She refused to answer any questions, choosing to glare defiantly at police officers and bystanders.

At the center of this activity, surrounded by his support staff, stood Mayor Rusty Purnell. He addressed his team pointedly, his words made more emphatic by vigorous gestures. His hands trembled slightly, and his voice cracked. He wanted answers, and he wanted action . . . now! Who was responsible for this disaster? How do we prevent it from happening again? He wiped his brow and kneaded the back of his neck, struggling to maintain focus as he listened to their ideas.

The young staffer in blue took furious notes on her tablet. One city administrator demanded strict enforcement of the rules of conduct at public meetings, while the city attorney warned about First Amendment encroachment. Others nodded silently to both propositions. Posed with this conundrum, Rusty again felt confused, as he had through most of the proceedings. He lamented the succession of events that had led to the meeting deteriorating before his eyes and his failure to avert it. He could not get in front of his own thoughts racing furiously in his head. His gaze repeatedly drifted to the tall, sturdy red-shirted woman in police custody. She seemed so familiar to him. Once during the town hall, his gaze had met hers and they stared at each other for a bit too long. *Where have I seen her before?* But nothing came.

In the next huddle stood Donna Hart, backed by her supporters, all of them wearing their signature bright yellow-green. She looked directly into camera lenses and spoke eloquently into handheld microphones in response to questions from live-on-scene reporter Maddy Brewer and others from competing stations. Her coherence, confidence, and beauty were natural magnets for the media. Dismayed by the violence but encouraged by the outpouring of community involvement she'd seen tonight, she praised "this tangible demonstration of the people's will." She looked forward to "working with city officials to sort things out and find a compromise solution" everyone could live with.

Geoff stood in a third pod a bit farther down alongside Jeremy, Celine, and others in the Clean Up This Mess! crowd, speaking with one of the detectives, who jotted details in his little flip-book. Geoff's lip was swollen and his hair mussed, but he wore the correct affiliation colors and so successfully blended into the crowd of innocents who had stayed on scene to pick up the pieces. The surveillance video might tell a different story later, but for now he felt safe assuming the role of defender of the peace and not aggressor.

Some of the less vehement members of the red-shirted brigade had hung around after the disturbance and now joined ranks with the green shirts, blue hoodies, and civilians in plain clothes indicating no particular affiliation. Individual Red Shirts were quick to remind others of their heartfelt support for the marginalized who happened to be houseless and actively distanced themselves from the more bellicose members of their tribe. The grandpa who had testified earlier in favor of community centers stood silently nearby. He was not ready to excuse the actions of the Red Shirts, nor the omnipresent street vagabonds they championed, always in crisis yet somehow organized enough to pitch elaborate tents and commit petty crimes. He had as little regard for their nonprofit NGO advocates, but in the moment, he chose to ignore his own contrarian thoughts and nodded in solidarity.

They all comforted one another with nods and smiles, handshakes, and A-frame hugs. After their shared ordeal, they affirmed they were, in the final analysis, all Morleyites and in this together. A moment of consonance had emerged, a bond borne of a mutual need for harmony and healing, denying any former discord as an unfortunate fluke.

Jeremy and Celine tried their best to participate in the conversation, but they were too distracted to concentrate. Soon after their arrival at the town hall, both had been simultaneously startled by the same realization.

"Hey, isn't that Darla?" asked Celine, referring to the woman who had cursed the mayor. Jeremy scrutinized the woman; it was unmistakably her but somehow different.

"Boy, she's really packing it on." She had shorter hair now, cut high and tight, military style, most of her kinky curls gone except at the top. Her face was fuller, the sharp lines softened at the cheek and jaw with the slightest hint of a double chin. Her still-sturdy arms and legs were rounder and plumper, no longer lean and well muscled. She filled out the red T-shirt amply. A little pooch was prominent at her belt line that could have been a little belly flab . . . or something else? Neither of them could bear to gaze upon her long enough to be sure; the thought made them both too uncomfortable.

The mayor conferred with the two detectives. They had done all they could tonight and agreed the remainder of the investigation would be continued in the morning. The yellow tape barriers had already closed off two of the doors and would be strung across the remaining entrance once everyone had vacated. The two detainees were led out the last open door in the close custody of uniformed officers. Another officer wearing purple nitrile gloves followed, carrying the alleged weapons that had been bagged and tagged for evidence: two bloody garden stakes, one intact, the other splintered into pieces. City personnel began directing folks out of the building.

Rusty needed air. He left his staff in their semicircular tribal council to conjure up the City's next move and strolled with the chief detective toward the door, stopping for a final exchange in the foyer. He absently kicked a balloon that skittered across the floor.

For the first time since the ruckus, Rusty saw Monica leaning against the City of Morley Memory Wall looking at her phone. He said goodbye to the detective and instinctively walked toward her.

"Well, now, how about that?" he said, exasperated. He leaned against the wall, facing her in a relaxed posture.

Monica shook her head, declaring it "a total mess." She hated disorder and confusion. The outcome of this hearing, she thought, had already been wrapped up in a tidy package ready for delivery. Now the unthinkable had happened. What did she do wrong? Had she underestimated the passion of the crowd? Perhaps she should have stopped Richard from speaking at all or been more aggressive over the past weeks to shut down Donna and her crew. Maybe the timing was off, with the anti-cop bunch letting their cauldron of violence bubble over at a most inopportune time.

"Have you let our two friends know?"

"Yes, I just called them. They were awfully polite, didn't seem at all upset. They're no strangers to public discord, you know, but of course, hard to tell. I think they're in it for the long game. We'll probably see them again."

"Uh huh." He did his best to reassure her but was certain they would evaporate—and their support along with it. Too much scrutiny and commotion, too much bright light shined into dark corners. "But assuming the worst case, just for a moment, if there isn't any more outside money—what then?"

"Depends. Let's see what Richard has to say. It's his property; he might be willing to wait it out, or maybe he'll want to look around for another deal. I don't know."

"Have you seen him around, by the way?" Rusty said, scanning the hallway up and down.

"Nope, last I saw him, he was crying in his beer about his departed boyfriend, then passed out at the speakers' table."

"Let's ring him up, get his take on this. Hopefully he's sober by now." Rusty pulled out his cell and scrolled to find the contact number for Richard. Without looking up he asked, "My God, how long has he been dead now?"

"Who, Richard?" She let out a high-pitched giggle at her own wisecrack, finally breaking under the strain, letting her guard down with the only real friend she had in the city.

He laughed along with her. "No, no, Gantry!"

"Oh right, Gantry." She laughed out loud again. "What was his name? Dale?"

"That's right, Dale Gantry," Rusty said, not taking his eyes off his phone. "I've actually heard of him. He's a name from, like, back in the '80s."

She shrugged as her mind wandered to other matters. Her feet hurt in the heels she had chosen this evening. As she slipped off each shoe to give herself a foot massage, her gaze slowly panned over to the Memory Wall. She now realized they had been standing directly in front of the plaque commemorating Councilor Gantry, his strong profile emerging in faux bronze.

"Hey, looky here. It seems Mr. Gantry has been spying on us all along." She patted the bust on the forehead and bent to read the plaque. "'Dale Wilson Gantry, 1933 to 1989.' Wow, he died pretty young. 'City Council Member '84 to '87. Council President '87 to '89. Our beloved friend and colleague. We can never thank you enough.' Hmm, way before my time."

"Mine too. Ah, here we go." He put the phone on speaker as it rang Richard's number. The three of them—Monica, Rusty, and Dale—all listened intently.

"Hello, this is Mr. Richard. I'm sorry, I'm a little inconvenienced right now and can't come to the phone. If you're calling about a hair appointment, honey, please leave your name and number, and we'll get you scheduled right away. For any other matters, leave a detailed message. Please ee-nun-see-ate clearly. Thanks!"

"No answer. Damn! We're running out of options here." Rusty thought for a moment. "Hell, let's go over to his place. We need a strategy, and now."

She looked at her watch. "Rusty, can we please put this bed for now and take it up in the morning? It's twelve thirty. The old guy's probably home asleep, and I'm completely beat."

"Yeah, sure, I guess you're right. Nothing we can do about this tonight anyway. But let's definitely get over there first thing tomorrow."

"Good, will do. And in the meantime, boy, I could sure use a drink."

"Amen to that, sister. Usual place?"

"You read my mind. Mind if we take one car?"

"Not at all. Let's take mine," he said, moving in closer. One car. He recognized this ploy, her way of tipping her hand discreetly. It had been a while, and he was very pleased. "We can swing by and pick yours up tomorrow morning." He could smell her hair now, felt her breath on his face.

Her tone was rapidly warming. "My, you are quite the mind reader."

"Mm-hm."

Rusty regretted suggesting LaFontaine, but it was close and familiar, and the possibility of scoring with Monica crowded out any hesitation. *I need to get some drinks into her before she changes her mind,* he thought. It had been weeks since their meeting there with the Chinese backers, and he had not returned since. For weeks he had thought about his encounter with the waitress. *That waitress... God, what was her name?* He could not retrieve it. Exhausted and unable to handle any more complexity tonight, he turned his focus to the singular objective at hand: the handsome and sensual Ms. Sampson-Smith.

They stopped to chat with Milton, the night security guard, as he unlocked the main door to let them out. "Some big doings tonight, Mr. Mayor," he said, laughing. He had missed most of the good action, his shift having started at eleven o'clock, though the officers with whom he was chummy had filled him in. He was at least able to witness the perp walk and watch the crime-scene investigators gather their evidence.

Rusty Purnell put on his public face and made warm eye contact. "Yup, you could say that."

Milton shook his head in wonderment. "Boy oh boy, sir, I don't know how you do it. Week after week all these angry folks coming here with some beef."

Rusty smiled. "Heavy is the head that wears the crown," he said. Monica had to turn away to hide her eye-rolling.

"Hell, I'd tell them all to go you-know-where."

"Can't do it, but I'll take that advice, Milton."

"Anytime, sir."

They exited the building into the cool night air. Both felt exhilarated and oddly triumphant. Sure, the town hall had been a debacle, but here they were, still standing, squarely at the epicenter of a great fault rupture, surrounded by destructive forces but oddly not affected by them. They would come out clean, no matter what the aftermath, and they knew it. Their shared sense of omnipotence and impregnability also fueled their fervor for one another. They liked being seen together, knowing each looked better with the other on their arm. If there was ever a power couple in Morley Valley, they were it.

Partisans and peacemakers still milled about the plaza, consoling one another, sharing commitments to do better next time, though shy on any concrete plans. Too early for that; too much untidiness to absorb and process. An animated older woman was lecturing a small crowd, then broke away and headed straight toward the mayor.

"Uh-oh, here comes trouble," Monica warned.

"This'll just take a minute. Don't worry, I'll have us out of here soon." They kept walking but slowed when they could no longer politely pretend to be in a hurry.

The woman wore the light blue hoodie of the community center boosters, complemented by a broad-brimmed straw hat with a matching blue flower. She moved with an intensity that, for her age, propelled her at an unnatural clip.

"Mr. Mayor? Mr. Mayor!"

"Yes, hello again. It's Judy, right?" Rusty recognized the woman immediately, having encountered her at previous meetings. He knew her to be a vocal advocate for any number of eclectic policies and issues: graffiti abatement, afterschool art programs, and fare-free streetcar zones in downtown Morley. Tonight she had come lobbying for community centers but at this moment wanted to talk to him about something else altogether.

"Mayor! Mayor, I have a solution for this terrible homeless problem. If you have a minute."

"Well, I . . ." He glanced at Monica, then toward the parking lot, but hesitated too long, and the woman stormed into the gap.

"Are you ready? A CSA!"

"I'm sorry, a . . . ?"

"A CSA," she repeated slowly. "You know, community-supported agriculture. Brilliant, right?"

He pretended to know what she meant, nodding approvingly. "And how would—"

"Simple," Judy interrupted vigorously. "It's a terrible life these homeless folks are living out here, right? They have to use every resource, every opportunity just to survive, right? You've got to be clever to live on the streets. It takes ingenuity and a lot of hard work. Why, you've got to find your spot, pitch your tent, scope out the closest hot food line, forage in a hostile and dangerous environment to find enough cans to turn in, or bikes to chop, or goods to pilfer and resell."

"Hey, now hold on a minute," he said in mock outrage, while Monica suppressed a laugh.

"Just kidding. Bottom line is they are very hardworking and resourceful people, right? Just a little, you know . . ." She pointed her finger at her own head and twirled. "Nutso! So here's the plan, and if I say so myself, it is a magnificent one. Round up all these clever, industrious folks and put them to work as—wait for it—organic farmers! Genius, right?"

"Why would they ever want to do that? You can't just round up people."

"Give them a choice. Either to go jail—which of course nobody wants, and hopefully it would never come to that, but let's keep it as an option, just for argument's sake—or come work on the beautiful and peaceful organic farm," Judy explained, wistfully gazing into an imaginary, bucolic future, "where you get a warm bed to sleep in, clean clothes and a shower, kitchen and laundry privileges, a library, a rec room. Not to mention"—she gave him a nudge with her elbow—"free internet. Plus you learn valuable skills, while you recapture your dignity and earn back your place in the world rather than living like an outcast."

The crowd had migrated toward Judy and Rusty and gathered behind her as she spoke to the mayor. His first inclination was to cut her off by dredging up the usual dog-eared objections to similar ideas that had been floated in the past: exploitation of vulnerable populations, forced labor tantamount to human trafficking, abusive and unsafe working conditions. But the audience of citizens had quickly encircled them, so he chose to remain silent and look attentive, sensing the only way to end this conversation was to let the woman have her say and move on.

"Then you create a CSA, which I'm sure, as mayor, you know all about, right?"

He still didn't but would not admit it. "Go on," he encouraged.

"It's brilliant, if I didn't say that already. People like you and me, see, we buy shares in the CSA in advance. This is kick-start money, see? There you go, financing up-front. Don't you love it? This lets you lease some land, get all your tools and equipment together, do your soil amendments, buy some starts or even heirloom seeds, et cetera. Crops get planted and are tended by the homeless folks, see, who are now no longer homeless but gainfully employed, earning a living wage plus food and lodging. Then all that wonderful organic produce is harvested, then allocated to all of us, the happy shareholders. You haven't lived till you've received a big box of fresh organic produce at your doorstep. It's like Christmas every week! Swiss chard and red chard and beets and lettuce and potatoes and … Well, you name it. And whatever's left over you can sell at the Saturday farmer's market. After a year or two, the program is totally self-sustaining, which I'm sure is music to any politician's ears, am I right?" She chuckled loudly at Monica, who could do nothing but simply nod and chuckle back at her. "Everything is excellent quality, completely organic. And eventually you can get into other products, like homegrown eggs or local honey."

"Sounds expensive."

"A little more than the local Ralphs. But think of the quality. And most important, think of the warm feeling you'll get knowing you're helping people get off the streets." Judy winked, then leaned forward, whispering to Rusty and Monica, "There isn't a single person of means in this county who wouldn't pay an extra dollar or two to clean up this mess."

Monica inched close behind Rusty and, keeping her gaze locked on Judy, discreetly tugged on his sleeve. When that failed to move things along, she gave his right butt cheek a firm pinch, causing him to startle, which Judy misinterpreted as his wide-eyed interest in community-gardening methods. But when Monica grabbed his ass a second time and wouldn't let go, Rusty had to jump in.

"Um, Judy, wow, so many good ideas. Thank you. Why didn't you testify tonight?"

She pulled out a small paper ticket from her pocket and held it in front of his nose. "Your damn lottery," she answered with a wry smile. "Never got the chance."

"Well, I want to hear more. Could you please contact my legislative assistant, Mellie Chown, to set up an appointment?" He handed her a card. "Just leave your name and contact info, and she'll get you on the schedule."

She examined the card. "I will, Mayor. I definitely will, you can be sure of that. It's really a good idea. Other towns are doing it and having great success."

"Great," he said, sensing Judy was getting her second wind and ready to launch into another soliloquy. He looked at his watch. "It's been a long night and—Oh my, is it really almost one? I've got to get some sleep so I can get back here early and sort all this out."

He started moving with Monica toward the parking lot as he waved back at Judy and the gathered crowd.

"Can't let Morley fall behind," she yelled across the increasing gap.

"Looking forward to it."

They quickly found his white Cadillac Escalade in the spot designated "Hon. Howard Purnell." He clicked open the locks and politely held open the passenger door for Monica as she slid onto the white leather seat. She returned the courtesy by pushing the unlock button for him. It was redundant, but he thought it a sweet gesture. As they buckled themselves in, she turned and confronted him with a smirk.

"Seriously?" she asked in a cynical tone. "'Heavy hangs the head…?' You have got to be kidding."

He did not respond but stared forward in silence.

"I thought she'd never stop talking," Monica continued, ignoring his reticence. "God, don't these people every sleep? Anyway, to the bar, James." She pointed forward. "And don't spare the horses!" But Rusty sat quietly. She scrutinized him. "Oh, now wait a minute," she said incredulously. "You're not going to let that mob get to you? That's not the Rusty I know. Come on now, it's getting close to last call," she cooed as she slinked toward him. "Monica wants a drink, and Monica is feeling very cozy tonight." She rubbed his inner thigh, with no reaction. He finally spoke, monotonously and without a trace of guile.

"Monica."

"What?"

"Monica, what if—" He again stopped short.

"OK, I give," she said after a long pause. "What if *what?*"

"What if—what if we really *could* do some good around here. Make it so everyone could get a little bit of what they really wanted. Not everything, of course, because nobody gets everything they want, but just enough so that they wouldn't feel so exploited, like the government despised them."

"Stop talking nonsense. First of all, how do *you* know what everybody really wants? Half the time they don't even know what they want till they're told. Second, if you haven't noticed, these people want it all, and they're not ready to settle for anything less. Everyone's got some grandiose idea to change the world and in the process get more goodies for themselves. It's a zero-sum game, friend. Your gain is my loss."

"An endless war, everyone versus everyone else? Why does it have to be like this?"

"Because that's the way it's always been. Everyone want's what they want, either for themselves or their little tribe. Enlightened self-interest. That's how we managed to crawl out of the jungle and stand up on two feet while we went looking for someone's head to bash in." She smiled at her own joke as she touched up her lipstick in the visor mirror.

"Maybe there's a way to make things different, you know, better for everyone. There's got to be a way to . . ." His voice trailed off as he gazed absently out the window.

She grew impatient. "Hey, you're breaking the mood here. Snap out of it, or Monica may want to go home."

"Sorry. It was just a thought." He turned to kiss her gently on the mouth. "Let's get out of here."

27. A LIFE SIMPLIFIED

A pair of gray eyes peered over a well-manicured boxwood at the edge of the city hall parking lot. They lingered long enough to watch Rusty and Monica drive off, then disappeared behind the shrub.

Nic's instinct was to remain out of sight. He was certain none of the citizen throng would remember him from the commotion earlier tonight but nevertheless waited until the stragglers had broken up before emerging. Once they'd cleared out, he moved cautiously toward the rack where he had stored Richard's bike.

Earlier that evening he'd watched Richard barrel past him in a drunken frenzy. Disregarding their quarrel, he'd followed Richard by bike to the town hall, arriving in time to hear the first testimony. He remained out of sight near the hall's rear entrance, where he watched Richard milling about, chatting with Monica, and sneaking pulls from his flask. At the close of Richard's melodramatic testimony, Nic had stepped outside, intending to secure the bike in the Subaru and drive the drunken Richard home, when he heard the riot erupt. He ran back in as everything was going to hell. Impulsively he rushed to Richard's aid and dragged him out to the car. Sirens were already blaring in the distance. With the brawl inside roaring full force and the cops arriving imminently, Nic and his bloodied charge surely would have drawn attention, so he left the bike behind. When the Subaru keys went missing at home, walking the three and a half miles back to the city hall became his only option.

As he emerged from the bushes, he immediately recognized the solitary bike in the rack, a purple-and-black street cruiser he had ridden around town for the past few months. He remembered securing the frame and rear wheel solidly to the rack with a heavy cable and U-lock. As he approached, though, he saw that the front wheel and saddle were missing. What remained of the bike lay askew in a pathetic heap.

"Goddammit!" he screamed in a loud whisper. He kicked the bike, still tethered by the cable and lock, which sent it flipping onto its other side. He paced about wildly, flailed his arms, cursed some more, but to no avail. The seat and front wheel did not reappear.

He saw headlights in the distance. Realizing he must look a spectacle to any passing car, he scuttled behind the building, just out of the security light's intense glare. *Now what?* he thought. It was nearly two a.m., and there was a pervasive chill in the air.

The one-wheeled bike frame was junk to him. He squatted against the wall and deliberated on how he might restore it. During his months with Richard, he'd fallen into the habit of fixing broken things, or at least planning to fix them. The repair would be an easy one, but he'd need to grab a couple of hours' sleep and at sunrise scope out some parts.

But the problem of the ransacked bike withered in comparison to the broader implications of the evening: the breakdown of order in Morley, the Bloody Town Brawl (as the papers would later call it), the assault on Richard, followed by their own violent scuffle and apparent falling out, the cold realization that he had come to rely on Richard for everything. An undeniable truth slowly took shape amid the chaos in his head: starting now, nothing would ever be the same.

He considered a long trek on foot back to Dahlia Lane and all that awaited him there: apologies, reconciliation, a hot meal, a warm bed. And why not? Hadn't he built a sort of life with Richard? Not perfect, but . . . All his stuff was there, too, including the heavy jacket he acutely wished he'd brought with him.

But pride and anger would not permit him to return, even if it meant staying out all night. *Hell, I may never go back!* he swore, *just to teach that bastard a lesson!*

A cool breeze cut through his light clothing. He hugged himself for warmth and pulled up his collar as far as it would reach. It was not enough. He looked around for shelter and saw none. He spied at the far end of the parking lot a massive bin the size of a shipping container, placed there by the city for recycling newspaper. It would surely be warmer inside than out. But there were only two ways in: a pair of swinging doors at one end, locked and impenetrable, or the narrow slits along the top of the box for depositing papers, too narrow for a human of any size. By luck, some ecologically minded Morleyites (having found the bin full, or perhaps too short or too lazy to reach the slits) had piled their recycled newspaper on the ground alongside it. He grabbed a thick stack, then scanned the grounds for the darkest spot within the landscaped bed, locating a faraway clump of dense bushes that would shield him from headlights and prying eyes until sunrise. He crouched behind the bin once more as a car passed at the end of the block, then scurried into the brush.

Nic efficiently laid out a thick palette of newsprint on the ground. He slipped additional layers between his shirt and skin. With the leftovers, he fashioned a sort of blanket over himself to keep the chill off. It worked remarkably well. He was quite comfortable, given his dire circumstance, and congratulated himself for his ingenuity. He shivered just for a moment while body heat warmed his little cocoon, then was overcome by a deep and silent sleep.

After what seemed like only a few moments, Nic abruptly awoke to a loud hissing sound near his head, followed by a frigid wetness soaking through his newsprint shelter and trickling down his neck and back. He shook his head out of its torpor and sprang to his feet, surrounded by an army of foot-high black sprinkler pipes sending out circular sprays of misty water in all directions.

He dashed for dry walkway by the shortest route, leaving his newspaper bed disintegrating on the bark mulch. His wet socks made a squishing sound in his shoes as he ran. He watched as water pooled in the depression his body had made in the mulch. In the soft light of early dawn, he recognized many of the species he had planted in Richard's yard—bee balm, hyssop, periwinkle, hearty fuchsia—all perennials now established and in bloom in the late spring.

The rising sun came winking over the horizon and through the big leaf maples; it hurt his eyes. He assessed his miserable state: dripping wet, saturated to the skin, and shivering cold. He found scant privacy at the rear of the building, where he peeled off his light

NEUTRAL, NO BRAKES

jacket and shirt and wrung them out while cursing his soggy circumstance.

Moving half-naked toward the rack to reassess the dismantled bike, he discovered the remains of the one-wheeled frame were now gone too. Only a severed cable and pieces of a smashed U-lock remained. He examined the shredded ends of the cable and laughed dryly. He sat dejected and shirtless atop the bike rack.

Early morning traffic was proliferating. *Can't stay here,* he thought, *can't be seen.* He shook and billowed out his shirt and jacket and started walking. He found his wet socks were an uncomfortable burden; he stopped to pull off his shoes, wrung out his socks, and carried the lot in both hands. He made good time walking barefoot through downtown on the grassy median strip, while he probed his memory for some public space where he could hide in plain sight undisturbed, lay his clothes out to dry, and get some sleep.

He headed in the direction of Riverview Park, a large multiuse recreational area on the highway leading out of Morley. On weekends and holidays, clusters of families would picnic there, the smell of grilling meat and sounds of children's voices filling the air. Basketball hoops, tennis courts, an outdoor pool, and a baseball diamond were all in frequent use. Importantly, it had grassy open spaces for frisbee or touch football and plenty of trees at the periphery, large enough to afford some shelter from the elements and prying eyes.

Nic had come to know Morley well in his short time there but only by two- or four-wheel conveyance. Never had he walked its streets for any distance, but he soon discovered its geography was much larger on foot than he realized. Moving out onto the highway, he was forced to leave the comfort of the grassy strips in favor of rocks, burrs, gravel, and broken glass. He slipped his shoes back on, which helped, leaving his still wet socks dangling from his back pockets. His thin polyester jacket had dried sufficiently to put back on as well, making him less of a curiosity to the inquisitive eyes of passersby.

The morning mist was burning off, and the traffic had by now fully blossomed. Cars sped past him at seventy miles an hour, more than once shouting indecipherable jeers at him to get off the highway. He was grateful to finally see the signpost indicating the turnoff for Riverview Park, though the walk from that point to the park entrance seemed interminable. He hopped a low guardrail and found a shortcut to the gate.

Nic had hoped to find the park deserted at this early hour, where he could claim a private spot to hunker down in relative peace and anonymity. It was not. There along the perimeter, skirting the wooded area, were innumerable tents and makeshift shelters. A few resembled backyard camping setups, a bit soiled and worn but otherwise intact, like a dad might pitch for his kids on the lawn. All the others were sad undertakings cobbled together of blue and brown tarps, cardboard cartons, ropes, and bungee cords, using every manner of solid and semi-stationary object, commonly a shopping cart, as an improvised tent support. Garments hung on slack clotheslines. Stacked at one site was a large and diverse collection of bike parts: frames of every size and color, tires, wheels, seats, gears, cables, derailleurs, even helmets for the safety minded. A set of handlebars, with pink and white streamers still attached, lay prominently on the pile. An unseen boombox softly played an '80s rock mix.

The most notable feature of the settlement was its trash. Everywhere the landscape was peppered with debris, as if it had been sprinkled out of a passing aircraft, low on fuel and forced to either abort its mission or release its cargo of crap to make itself lighter, which had wafted randomly onto the grass, some objects identifiable—clothing, plastic jugs, drink cups, crumpled napkins—but most nondescript and all of dubious value, save for the fact that someone had deposited them there and felt they were important enough to never clean up. Absurdly, pristine empty trash receptacles dotted the park within twenty steps' walk. The scene reminded Nic of a dystopian Scout jamboree, one in which a lax Scoutmaster had failed to impress upon his charges the importance of maintaining a clean campsite.

Nic swung in a wide arc to avoid the densest concentration of roughhewn dwellings, toward an unclaimed patch of grass near a grove of Douglas firs where he could monitor the approach from any direction of marauding bands or rogue actors. He mapped out at least two escape routes, then laid out his damp T-shirt and socks on the grass to dry. His jeans and underwear were clammy and stuck to his skin, so he wriggled free of them and spread them out as well. It felt good to let the cool air circulate around his private parts. He wrapped his windbreaker around himself for decency. The sun was now glinting through the high trees, and he arranged his belongings where they might be hit by a random ray of sun before it moved on. He hadn't peed since the night before and made a quick run to the forest's edge to take care of that, hiding behind a fir tree wide enough to shield his entire body.

A profound sense of relief flooded over him, not just because his overfilled bladder had finally found release. For the first time in a day he felt a measure of safety. He had been running since he rescued Richard, his one brief respite interrupted by a thorough dousing of sprinkler water. A deep exhaustion set in. He leaned against the trunk for support, able to fight off sleep only by heroic effort. Having finished his business at the tree, he pushed himself back to his newly declared territory and laid himself down, his loins covered by his jacket and his arm flung over his eyes to keep the sun out.

In the quiet of the morning, his body was bone tired, but his mind raced unwillingly through the events of the night as he tried to make sense of it all—how to get things back to normal, if that were even possible, what to say to Richard, whether to apologize or be defiant, or to go back at all. *Dude, you have to go back,* he muttered to himself, *otherwise parole violation.* To this reality he was finally resigned.

As he floated toward sleep he heard a song he knew by heart, wafting from a distant boombox somewhere in the tent village, of paradise lost, a world turned upside down.

He mouthed the words and was drawn far away, back to his days on the street, the faceless tricks, the cruel connections, the rough nights and rougher mornings, the tender girls who saw something in him, all of whom he eventually proved wrong.

What the hell happened at the town hall? he wondered. It was never supposed to be his fight, but somehow he got pulled in. To defend Richard, he supposed, but that wasn't all of it. No, he was already feeling jumpy when the ruckus broke out. Something was fermenting in him as he listened to the posturing government officials, smug testifiers, and over-aroused onlookers. He instantly recognized that human trait he had long come to despise—the ability to dress up selfish motives in bullshit. He understood pure self-interest better than most but could not stomach it cloaked in pious pronouncements and false sincerity. He accepted it for what it was: simply their attempt at snatching a bigger piece of the pie for themselves. He'd done the same thing hundreds of times, but never deluded himself that it was anything but greed or survival. Having listened to an evening of this, who wouldn't want to bust some heads?

With his heart pounding, it took him but a moment to fall into a deep sleep.

Nic stirred and opened his eyes to a glaring overhead sun. For a moment he wasn't sure where he was or how he'd gotten there. The grass was soft and warm, and he let it enfold him. He turned and reached out to feel his clothing, now dry and stiff to the touch, and silently vowed to put them on, but this would have required standing up, and the sun's warm rays were too comforting to interrupt their sweet embrace. He slept.

As he drifted from dream to reality and back to dream, an eerie vision emerged, not so odd as dreams go but nonetheless disturbing. He observed himself as he walked down a long corridor, while in the opposite direction marched the parade of all those in his life he had wronged or who had wronged him. His father, his mother, his sister, the dead man in Indiana, the man he had knowingly sold a car with a cracked block, the old woman he had watched fall on a bus as it lurched forward and did nothing to help, all the women he had allowed to fall in love with him before hurriedly moving on, the girl who gave up everything for him to whom he had given only herpes in return. And now Richard, whom he imagined sitting at home, by now sober, showered, dressed, and rested, wondering where Nic was and missing him.

All the mistakes, the betrayals, the broken promises, the pain inflicted by him or suffered by him, all were gathered here in this one place. As the procession passed, he whispered his secret admonition to each of them: "*Shhh, don't tell . . . Tell not a soul. Hush now . . . Hush.*"

Again he dozed.

Nic was jerked out of his reverie by a gravelly voice. He looked up to see a dark form silhouetted by the low sun radiating behind it.

"Better get yer stuff 'fore someone grabs it. Nothing ain't nailed down don't last too long around here. Where's yer grip?"

He propped himself up on his elbows and noticed his windbreaker had blown up, leaving him no modesty. He quickly adjusted the fabric to regain it.

"No grip. I left in kind of a hurry."

"OK, just lettin' you know. I'm Harry. They call me New York Harry, but I ain't never been to New York, so you got me." He extended his hand. He wore a black leather vest, tan cargo shorts with a long rip up one side, frayed blue Tevas, and a tall-crowned straw cowboy hat with a red, white, and blue flag bandanna, from which dangled several large bird feathers. He was otherwise shirtless. His shorts rode low over his buttocks, revealing the upper reaches of his groin. He wore a white Fu Manchu mustache and long gray hair that cascaded down his shoulders. His face, neck, arms, and torso were deeply tanned. He moved with an energetic urgency, eyes flitting, jaw busily gnawing on something.

Nic artfully wriggled on his underwear while still flat, then stood up, pulled on his jeans, socks, shoes, and finally his shirt and jacket, then shook hands with Harry.

"Hungry?"

"Hell yeah."

"Too late. Church just shut down their lunch table for the day. Hot lunch everyday around noon. Like clockwork. Good people."

"What time is it?"

"About four." Nic could not believe he had slept the whole day. "No worries, man. Dinner line starts in an hour. I'll show you where. Here, want some Cheetos?" He extracted a crumpled red-and-orange bag from his pocket. Nic took the bag and ripped it open. He filled his mouth, then offered the bag to Harry.

"Naw, can't eat the things. Reflux," he said, pointing to his epigastrium. Nic scarfed the remains of the bag. It was his first meal since noon yesterday.

"You live here?" Nic asked New York Harry.

"Just passing through. That's my gear over there. Come on."

Harry led Nic across the wide grassy meadow toward the densest collection of shelters. No human inhabitants emerged from their nests as they passed through the settlement, though one or two crude dwellings heaved and shook, showing signs of life within. They arrived at a large blue tarp, hung over a rope tied taut between two stout trees. Harry swung back the cover, revealing another smaller tent ensconced beneath, and bade him enter. Suspicious but hungry, half-asleep, and with literally nothing to lose, Nic followed him in. Both men had to hunch over and almost crawl through the opening.

Inside the shelter he saw an elaborate and remarkably well-organized space tricked out like a general store, with every manner of supply, gadget, or survival tool neatly attached to the wall, hung from the ceiling, or bundled and tucked tidily into a corner. A small battery-operated lantern gave off an electronic glow, casting purplish white light around the tent.

"Nice setup," said Nic. *Just passing through?* he thought.

"My man cave!" he exclaimed, laughing with his entire body. "It's cozy. Make yourself at home."

He plopped down onto the floor, seeing nowhere else to land. He could feel the spiky grass just below the GORE-TEX fabric. Harry came over to kneel in front of him. He dipped into his deep cargo pocket and pulled up a charred glass pipe about four inches long, along with a small plastic bag and torch-style lighter. Nic recognized the crystalline substance—meth, or at least a mélange of tainted ingredients compounded into a white crystal intended to mimic it. With a wide grin that revealed more gaps than teeth, Harry held up the baggie for Nic to see and shook it, as if to say, "Look what I got."

Nic lodged no protest, thus tacitly granting his approval to fire up. Harry pinched off a few small chunks of the dirty crystal from the bag and dropped them into the top of the bulb pipe. He heated up the bottom of the bulb with the lighter, gently rotating the stem back and forth to distribute the heat, then sucked in the white cloud as it emerged from the pipe's orifice. He offered the pipe to Nic, who took it from him like a pro. Harry held the flame under the bowl for him as he inhaled the smoky plume. Both men went immediately mute as they gazed into the void. After several minutes in that state,

Harry sat on the tent floor cross-legged while Nic lay on his back looking at the ceiling.

Neither man was aware of the passage of time, but when Harry decided to top himself off with another hit, Nic perceived the tent was noticeably darker. He was still high so this time declined Harry's offer. It had been several weeks since he'd last used, and his tolerance for the drug had waned. He looked around the tent, studying the environment for the first time. All the paraphernalia meticulously bundled and hung, he decided, must be the product of a focused mind. He felt his guard soften slightly, believing, or hoping, that a man demonstrating this level of commitment to task completion would not senselessly rob, rape, kill, or otherwise harm him.

Nic examined Harry's gear in detail: a length of nylon rope, multicolored bungee cords, a heavy wrecking bar and a lighter pry bar, a large standard screwdriver, a set of jiggle keys, and a can opener and corkscrew on a string. Along the back wall were lined up several pairs of footwear: flip-flops, sneakers, boots, and hard-soled oxfords. Nic mused that Richard would probably appreciate Harry's organizational skills but not Harry himself.

He regretted his tiff with Richard last night. Without thinking, he checked his tracking app to see where Richard was, not because he was in any hurry to head back. He wasn't quite ready but getting there, as his one night on the street had reminded him just how hard life could be. No, it was more out of habit, as he repeatedly hit the Search button. Richard had bought the phone for him, and it was a nice one, fast with lots of connectivity. It had not taken him long to adopt the modern fetish of habitually fingering it. But the pinwheel kept spinning as the app searched for Richard, finally flashing "location not available." *Must have forgotten to charge his phone again, let it run out of juice. Typical Richard!* he thought. It was then he noticed his own device was down to 8 percent power and knew he'd better do something about it soon or be completely isolated. For the moment, though, he slipped the phone back into his pocket and dozed off.

The air was getting thick within the close confines of the tent. He discovered Harry was prone to passing gas, letting loud ones rip with some frequency. After a particularly rumbling one, Nic opened his eyes to see New York Harry in the full throws of a meth jag, grimacing and twitching, mouthing words and gnawing incessantly, his hands pantomiming some macabre tale that only Harry understood. He had evidently continued to smoke as Nic dozed and was now staring menacingly at him. Nic cautiously sat upright to assume a nonchalant defensive posture. He had witnessed this sort of freak-out before and knew the protagonist at any time could explode unpredictably into a frothing paranoid mania. To avoid this, he needed to appear completely at ease, neither threatening nor threatened.

"What's up, man?"

New York Harry did not answer but continued his fidgety dance, listening to the wild inner dialogue clanging in his head.

"Dark out," Nic said finally. "I better get going. Gotta find a place to stay tonight."

"Stay here, man. I got plenty of room." The inaccuracy of that statement troubled Nic, as did the thought of spending another moment in the rank chamber. He doubted whether there was adequate oxygen to support the two of them, let alone sufficient space or sanity to keep them off each other's throats all night.

"Phone's dying, man. Gotta find some power to—"

"Covered!" he interrupted. "Got my charger set up right here." He lifted back a corner of the tarp to reveal four car batteries linked together in parallel, jury-rigged to the bare wires of a car phone charger. "Here, lemme see it."

Nic hesitated a moment, then reluctantly handed the phone over to him, hoping to at least put some charge on it while he figured out his next move toward freedom.

"Nice one," he said, fingering the buttons. He set about trying to plug the power source into the phone but could not quite get it to fit. He hunched over it, struggling and grunting, turning it this way and that, finally shoving harder and wiggling it into the slot. It occurred to Nic at that moment that it shouldn't be that hard.

"Here, let me take a look."

"No, no, I got it, man. Look, see?" Nic looked closely at the phone and saw that Harry had strong-armed a micro-USB plug into his lightning socket. "Wait, hold on, it's not working." Harry would not give up the device but proceeded to wiggle the wires and check his connections. He intentionally shorted the wires from the battery and got a spark, proving to his satisfaction that his setup was not at fault. "Damn! Sorry, man, your phone's not taking a charge. Must be broken."

Nic took his cell phone back and quickly slipped it into his pocket. He felt the imperative to bust out but could not let it show. "That's cool, man. Thanks for trying. Anyway, thanks for the hospitality. Gotta jet."

"Hey, where you going, man? Too good to hang out with me? You're not too good to smoke up my drugs, then split. You owe me, man." He actually sounded hurt, but was more ominous as a result.

"Hey, you offered," Nic said with a cautious smile. He realized Harry sat between him and the exit, a tactical error on Nic's part. It was good to get a buzz on, but now he regretted hooking up with this crazy vagrant in the first place, regretted smoking his meth, regretted all his foolish choices, too many to number.

But Harry's countenance was stern, his tone all business. "Fair is fair."

"I got nothing, man." He shook his head. "I'm broke."

"What you got to trade?"

Nic mentally inventoried his belongings: a wallet with a defunct ATM card and seventeen dollars, one dying and likely damaged cell phone, the out-the-front knife he kept in a cutout recess of his shoe, a set of housekeys to Dahlia Lane, and the clothes on his back. At that moment he determined not to give up any of it to Harry but instead to call his bluff.

He had been in tight spots like this before, in prison and out, and knew that while a show of resistance carried risk, sometimes deadly risk, it could be the best option, like making yourself look big when you encounter a cougar in the woods. His face hardened into an angry grimace. "I got nothing to trade, and I ain't trading nothing!" he said, delivered in a harsh basso profundo voice, pointing at Harry accusingly and making sure to sound a little crazy, as a pro wrestler might while showing off his bravado for the camera. "You handed me the fucking pipe. I ain't owe you shit." He whacked the side of the tent for emphasis, sending all of Harry's paraphernalia dancing and shuddering. He got up to exit the tent and found he could only crouch low without hitting his head on the ceiling but continued to rise and thrash about, causing a tempest within Harry's little world.

Harry moved back an inch or two. "Hey, man, I was just shittin' you, OK, man? Can't take a joke?"

Nic ignored him and continued his egress, pushing past Harry to find the opening in the tent, then throwing back the tarp to reveal the park shrouded in twilight. Lights had begun to flicker on in the distant parking lot. He deeply breathed in the cool, clean air, the first full breath he had taken since descending into Harry's dank realm. The speed had nearly washed out of his brain, and he made some quick decisions. First, to move as far and quickly away from the tent as possible. He made a calculation that there may be other campers in the park who were less fucked up than Harry and perhaps found him loathsome as well, so he walked briskly toward the center of the settlement, a sort of village square that had formed by the encircling tents and tarps. As he did, he could hear Harry noisily clamber out of his shelter and bellow, "Hey, fuck you, man."

He did not turn around but proceeded to the large collection of bikes and cannibalized parts he had seen earlier. A young dark-skinned man in a gray hoodie was busily working by lantern light on a frame with journeyman's dexterity, assembling a bike from disparate parts that all seemed to come together into a variegated yet functional whole. He regarded the young man, who kept to his task, with a cursory nod. Alongside the jumbled pile of parts stood an orderly row of finished bikes reminiscent of a display at Walmart. There, he unmistakably identified the purple-and-black frame of Richard's street cruiser that had gone missing from the city hall bike rack last night, now with a new seat, handlebars, and front wheel. Rather than raising a fuss about a transgression he knew would go nowhere, he felt it altogether fitting that he should barter back his own bicycle. He needed a means of getting the hell out of there to reestablish some order to his life that had been completely overturned in the past twenty-four hours.

"How much?" he asked, pointing at the purple one. The hoodied young man continued to work on his project bike as he eyed Nic suspiciously.

"Two hundred," he mumbled.

Might as well be two thousand, he thought, remembering he had only seventeen bucks on him. He decided to bargain with the entrepreneur.

"A hundred," he offered.

"One fifty," the man answered without looking up. "That's it." He made the cutoff sign; he was done.

Nic dug the phone out of his pocket. "How about ten bucks and a phone?"

The seller looked at the phone and shook his head. "Got a hundred phones just like it," he said, handing it back to him. Apparently high-tech devices were not coin of the realm on the street.

He slipped off his shoe and extracted the fighting knife from the recess in the foam sole. It featured a clean blue anodized aluminum grip and a matching blade. Nic showed it to the bike dealer as he worked the in-and-out mechanism, making a satisfying *schlick schlick* sound. Out-the-front knives had been banned in the state, so concealable and deadly were they, making them high demand and very tradable.

"Mini-Infidel," said the hoodie, holding it in his hand. "Haven't seen one in blue yet. Nice." He offered a deal. "The phone and the knife, plus ten bucks cash, and it's yours."

Nic examined the bike, making sure the tires were plumped up and the gears and brakes worked. "Ride it around?" he asked, twirling his finger around the open space in front of the encampment.

"Leave the knife."

He slipped his shoe back on and rode the bike in a broad circle and returned to the bike hawker. "Brakes are a little soft. Knock off ten bucks?"

"Deal."

Nic was reaching for his phone to close the transaction when the hoodied man looked over Nic's shoulder with a startled glare, then turned terrified and ran. Nic spun around to see Harry barreling toward them, eyes afire, fists flailing.

"You muthafucka," he yelled. Harry had been watching the commerce transpiring at the chop shop and in his drug-stoked condition had taken offense, feeling disrespected and abandoned by his newest, and now lost, best friend. Nic did not wait to find out what was on Harry's mind. He leaned hard into the pedals, throwing up grassy divots and loose dirt behind him with his fat rear tire. Harry lit out after him screaming gibberish through the camp. Nic had to slalom around several startled onlookers who had emerged from their tarp shelters to see about the disturbance, then pedaled out into the open flat and rode in a wide expanding curve, evading Harry but still able to catch a glimpse of him. Harry's unsecured shorts had now fallen down around his ankles, which hindered his stride severely. He had to hoist them up with one hand, while he continued to give chase and shake a fist at Nic with the other. Two inhabitants of the camp, about the same vintage as Harry, materialized with exasperated looks. They evidently had seen this script play out before and now were in close pursuit of Harry to subdue him.

Focusing on a speedy and enduring escape, Nic directed his bike toward the park entrance, then onto the frontage road paralleling the highway. He rode in and out of the orange light cast by the streetlamps overhead, back to familiar territory and instinctively heading toward Dahlia Lane, abandoning his previous resolve never to return. He noticed now that the bike actually rode better than in all the weeks he had used it. *That guy knows his shit*, he mused about the hoodied capitalist back at the camp. Only then did he realize he had never given the fellow his full price as he felt the phone still in his pocket, pressing hard against his thigh. He regretted shorting the man but refused to return to the camp. He was a solo agent again, at least for the moment, until he could get himself safely home. He had nowhere else to go and knew it.

Home. The very notion felt foreign to him. As he rode through the streets of Morley, he passed more lost souls occupying crude dwellings. Overnight, he had become one of them. Perhaps he'd always been, living in desperation, bouncing from crisis to messy crisis, surveilling the world, furtively avoiding its dangers or capitalizing on its fragility. But in his ignorance he had miscalculated life on the street as existence reduced to its most basic elements. He beheld it now with open eyes, in all its painful complexity, its murky ethics and shifting boundaries, everything magnified and looming. Rather than simplifying life, it merely cheapened it.

Nic sensed a calming familiarity as he turned up Persimmon Terrace heading for home. He again ran through his mind how he wanted the make-up scenario to play out with Richard, what to say to him, whether to be contrite or defiant, kind or sharp-tongued. He decided on kind and just a little contrite. *Richard's a crusty old bird. He'll get over it! Apologizing won't help anything.* Besides, he thought, Richard was his own worst enemy most of the time, a real nuisance, irritating as hell. He deserved to be knocked down a peg once in a while.

Nic slowed his pace as he rounded the corner, the house just in view. In the distance flashing red and blue lights reflected brightly off wet asphalt and the windows of two police cruisers and a plainclothes detective car in front of the house. A handful of neighbors lined the street, talking among themselves. Once again, the ubiquitous Maddy Brewer stood at an allowable distance outside the yellow police cordon, speaking via handheld mic into the camera. She read notes off her tablet screen. Nic noticed that she was unexpectedly short, much shorter than she appeared on the evening news, and rather oddly shaped, like a pear. She wore tight yoga pants and pink sneakers, though waist up, in her white blouse and blue station logo jacket, she looked well put together for her medium close-up shot.

At first disoriented by the confused scene, it took but a moment for Nic to recognize it was his own house—Richard's, technically—that the police tape encircled. He then watched two attendants wheel a gurney with what appeared to be a covered body from the house down the driveway and to the rear of the coroner's van, removing any doubt of what gruesome event had taken place there.

"Richard?" Nic whispered to himself. "Oh no—no." He stood immobilized as the body disappeared into the gray van. He waited in shadow for the vehicle to leave the cul-de-sac, which seemed to take forever. He reached out and gently touched the side of the van as it slid past him. He could see the attendants inside joking with each other.

The gathered neighbors had turned in unison to watch the van depart, then hovered around Maddy Brewer to catch a glimpse of behind-the-scenes television in the making. From his remote vantage point, Nic recognized people from the neighborhood and was sure they would soon recognize him as well. Real busybodies, he thought, who habitually stood out on the street, yakking with one another about who was sick or getting well, who had moved in or moved out. One surly retiree, who fancied himself the street's unofficial mayor and regularly accosted Richard to chat him up, now stood three feet from Maddy Brewer, eagerly awaiting his chance to speak with her. All of them must have known of Nic's residing at the house for these past months, and would certainly inform the police and the press. Whatever events had taken place tonight, Nic saw far enough into the future to realize the police would soon be seeking him out for questioning.

Nic backed himself deeper into the shadows, then silently turned his bike around and sped off. *What could have happened?* he thought. *Was that even Richard's body they wheeled out? Someone else's, maybe?* His imagination overtook him. Had Richard invited one of his boys to the house, perhaps to get even with Nic after their spat, waiting for him to come home and be discovered, just like that time at the shop, but then something went wrong and an altercation ensued? He remembered the Smith & Wesson Richard kept in the desk drawer in the study. Richard was not his best that night, and anything could have happened. Would they soon be leading the perpetrator Richard out of the house in handcuffs? He did not want to wait to find out. He rode on.

Then it all came streaming back: their fight, the kitchen spattered with blood, his own shirt still bearing the signs of the struggle, the dent in the fridge door, his amateur CPR.

"*Oh God! I killed Richard! I killed Richard. I killed him, I killed him, I killed him . . .*" The cadence seemed to taunt him in rhythm with the bike's pedals. Anguish and grief tore at him. For the second time in his life, an innocent man had died at his hands. The wind blew cold and hard in his face, filling his eyes with tears. He made tortured grunting sounds with each new wave of shame that flooded his mind.

He felt his soul careening into a black pit, further and further into a relentless, unforgiving darkness. Still he rode on. What would be his fate? Where could he wander now? It didn't matter. Nothing mattered. His life of bad choices and selfish disregard had finally caught up with him. He had crossed the line, passing through that thin veneer that separates living souls from the haints, those empty vessels that walk the earth in a masquerade of life, banished from the light and all that is good yet unworthy to find rest among the peaceful dead.

Still he rode on. Where could he go to shelter, to escape? He recalled the denizens of the tent colony at the edge of the woods. Were they his people now? New York Harry with his pants around his ankles, the cagey hoodied bike salesman, the crazy old fucks running around the park? Was this to be his purgatory, shared with his kindred outcasts, brushed aside by time and circumstance awaiting their final oblivion?

No. Even his most cutting self-condemnation could not bring him to return to the camp. Head down, eyes on the pavement, without thought or plan, he pedaled with all his strength through the dark backstreets and brightly lit boulevards of Morley, sweat soaking through his clothing as he rode.

When he finally looked up, he was in front of Mr. Richard's Cuts and Color. He coasted cautiously through the deserted parking lot a couple times, then through a gap between buildings leading to the alleyway behind the beauty salon. He wondered why the police had not staked out the shop. Perhaps, he thought, they had already been here and, finding everything secure, simply left the scene. Or maybe they hadn't figured out that Dick Kornbluth was also Mr. Richard. No, that couldn't be. As he'd always said, Richard knew everyone in this town, and everyone knew him. Perhaps the cops were just being lazy, especially after last night's cage match at City Hall. This was way too much police work for a hamlet like Morley, and they needed a break, figuring they would circle back to the shop tomorrow, making a few other stops along the way, gathering what evidence they could for their investigation.

Whatever the reason, he found himself quite alone in the alley, accompanied only by the crickets that chirped warily in the tall brush by the river's edge. He desperately needed a few survival provisions and knew he could find them in the shop. He usually kept a set of back door keys with him, but these were somewhere back at the house behind a line of yellow police tape. He remembered Richard typically kept the bathroom window ajar, "to let out the bouquet" he would say. Sure enough, there it was, open. *He should know better*, Nic admonished, before recalling that Richard was probably lying dead, by his hand, in the morgue. He shook it off and got back to work. He pried the screen from the frame ever so gently—*pop, there you go*—and let himself into the window, in the old days a task he would have accomplished in one smooth movement, his strong arms, legs, and trunk acting in unison and landing on his feet. Now he had to hoist himself up, turn sideways, squeeze, and wiggle his way through, in the final stage walking his hands along the sink and tumbling down onto the floor, scraping his thighs and ankles on the windowsill.

He quickly rifled the cash register at the front counter, pulling out one hundred twenty-five dollars in small bills, the exact amount Richard customarily left in the till each night, along with a fistful of quarters. He then grabbed a kitchen-size garbage bag and filled it with hygiene supplies—toothbrush and toothpaste, soap, some bath towels and washcloths, and a change of socks and underwear, all of which Richard kept on the bottom shelf of the backroom storage unit. He also grabbed two comforters from the waiting room couch and Richard's warm winter coat from the hook behind the door, a spare he kept there, and threw it on over his windbreaker. It was tight around the arms and belly, and the sleeves were just a bit short, but it was serviceable. He finished by snatching some crucial items from the cutting station—scissors, brush, comb, and most important, having given up his cherished fighting knife to redeem his own bike, a straight razor.

As he busied himself, Nic now saw headlight beams course slowly across the ceiling, then heard the crunch of tires on the gravely pavement outside. He had underestimated the cops' diligence and industry. They had not been there yet, but here they were now. He moved expeditiously to the back door, this time opting to exit the building standing erect like a human rather than a slithering snake. He opened the door but in his haste had forgotten that Richard had asked him two months ago to retrofit an alarm, the kind that lets out an earsplitting whine when the circuit was broken. The shrill noise at first disoriented him, but with added alacrity he was out in the alley and on his bike. He rode along the uneven pavement, through deep puddles and potholes, staying close to the undergrowth, until he saw a narrow trail to his right that split the tall grass. He pedaled down the jarring slope without turning around, branches slapping him in the face as he flew. In a few moments, when the cops came around the corner to check the rear of the building, the alarm still piercing the air, there was no trace of him, only the shallow ripples that remained in the puddles, fracturing for an instant the reflected moonlight, then dying away.

28. DONNA NOBIS PACEM

Deeply ensconced within the Biography section of Pickwick's Paperback Shack, Geoff sorted volumes into their proper alphabetical order, carefully aligning each book's spine with the edge of the shelf. He savored the task, not because Donna's love of order had rubbed off on him (though it had). The routine also allowed his imagination to wander. It was a job without end. *Why can't people to put books back in their right place?* he complained silently, affirming his opinion that humans were a lazy species with limited attention and little regard for doing the right thing.

He deliberated whether the Steve Jobs bio should come under *J* for Jobs or *I* for Isaacson. He opted for the latter, which matched the scheme in the Autobiography section. While sorting, he leaned against the shelves for minutes at a time reading the forward, liner notes, or even whole chapters of interesting books, while Donna worked industriously around the corner. If she knew of his innocent sloth, she never acknowledged it as a deadly sin. She so loved having him around the bookstore, as he loved being there with her.

At her desk Donna archived her new arrivals and flagged them with little summaries to enlighten her customers. For her, books had never been merely inventory. She loved divining their wisdom and sharing it, guiding her clients as a skilled apothecary might prescribe herbs and potions from an arcane pharmacopeia. Every malady, she believed, had a literary remedy.

Besides Donna's company, working at Pickwick's also provided Geoff a brief respite from the complexities of the outside world. Despite no legal consequences arising from the dust-up over Stacie, he had not been invited back to his job at Dogg Life. Dan simply could not have him caring for his canine clients after the notorious incident, and Geoff was fine with that. The constant yipping and yapping had not fazed him initially, but toward the end he'd felt himself reaching a breaking point. Had he stayed on, perhaps he would have done something more terrible than offering a labradoodle a hamburger. Gradually he migrated to the bookstore and made himself indispensable by performing for Donna any small but necessary task she requested and literally all the heavy lifting. Without ever saying so, Donna soon came to regard him as her business partner. A few weeks later he moved out of his sad studio apartment and into her ornate Victorian home, mandated by his lack of a steady paycheck but also a testament to their burgeoning romance. Since then, their lives, activities, and finances were completely comingled.

Geoff and Donna had been profoundly shaken by the events of the disastrous Town Brawl, but like all of Morley, they remained at a loss for what to do next. Two weeks had passed, and luckily no fallout had manifested from Geoff's mixing it up with the Red Shirts. The city had failed to post anything on its website about the violent clash, as though it had never happened. Gradually Geoff's hypervigilance was replaced by a more sanguine composure, and for that Donna was profoundly grateful. They both poured themselves into their work, choosing to avoid the subject entirely.

All official dialogue about the proposed Morley Pointe Crossing development, now called MPC, had also evaporated. As a result, everything the townsfolk thought they knew or remembered about it, they had to glean from the nightly investigative reporting of young Maddy Brewer. Maddy had stumbled onto Morley's biggest news story in decades: the Town Brawl, followed by the suspicious death of a principal player in the doomed land deal. It was a gift from heaven, and she seized the opportunity, becoming an instant local celebrity and Morley's most trusted news source. So pleased were the station bosses that they pulled her, bundled and shivering, from her evening news assignments on the cold streets of Morley into the warmth and comfort of the studio. With a few phone calls and web searches, she had uncovered "the link between Dick Kornbluth, known professionally as Mr. Richard" and the eight-acre property slated for demolition to build MPC, as well as his long relationship with former City Council president Dale Gantry. Maddy had set up outside Morley Plaza to get the public's take on the death of Mr. Richard. She stopped by the bookstore twice, the first time finding Donna too fact-based, sensible, and solutions-oriented on the subject to be interesting. She followed up on different day, only to hear Geoff, alone for a few minutes while Donna ran to the bank for change, spouting a disjointed ramble about cosmic forces. Maddy did not return.

The public were also treated to nightly photos of Nic Troxell, a person of interest sought by the Morley Police whose criminal past and parole sponsorship by Richard were now common knowledge.

As for the Clean Up This Mess! coalition, after a three-day break it again stoked the boiler and chugged forward under the strong and sure hand of its leader. Outreach stepped up, and long-range planning continued. Neighbors who had been apathetic were now fully engaged, with Donna as their charismatic, relatable champion.

Despite their return to a degree of normalcy, the tumult had triggered a subtle evolution in Donna, imperceptible to her followers though obvious to Geoff. He had always depended on Donna's bright-line distinction between right and wrong, her purity of analysis and unwavering pursuit of the good. Now swirls of gray formed the boundary between good and evil. She still believed that human beings, given the chance, would eventually do the right thing. But the violence and bloodshed, the lies and backstabbing, the persistence of selfish motives, the unrepentant commitment to personal gain over the greater good—all of it had hardened her just the tiniest bit. She remained true to her principles, but part of her soul had crystalized. "Call it my new pragmatism," she told him.

The shopkeeper's bell rang cheerily as the next patron walked through the door. He wore a short, ill-fitting plaid sport coat in the modern style that inadvertently accented his gut. For a man of his age and body type, it was decidedly unflattering.

"Welcome in, friend," called out Donna, barely looking up. "How are you doing today?"

"I'm good," he muttered after a long moment's pause.

"Great! If I can help you find something, just holler."

The patron did not respond but silently strolled the aisles, pulling down his shades to read the titles and catch curious glimpses of Donna working at her desk. He had come in search of answers to questions not yet fully formulated but also to check out the competition and plan his next move. As he rounded a corner, lost in thought, he almost collided with Geoff, who was ostensibly organizing the US History section but had stopped to read a chapter entitled "The Conquest of the West." Geoff jumped when the patron walked into his view. As they stared at one another, a recognition slowly unfolded.

"Hey, wait, you're—you're the mayor. Am I right?" Geoff quickly closed the history book and replaced it, out of order, back on the shelf.

"Guilty as charged," he replied. To Rusty's disappointment, the sunglasses had not worked.

"I think you want Donna," said Geoff, dashing out of the stacks to the front desk. "Donna! The mayor's here to see you."

"Sorry, what did you say about the mayor?" she said, still concentrating on her work.

"He's here to see you." He pointed over his shoulder, whispering, "He's right over there, between History and Biography."

The mayor emerged from around the corner.

"Why, hello, Mr. Mayor." She stood and smiled as he approached, her words respectful and warm without a hint of snark.

"Please, call me Rusty."

"Hello, Rusty."

"Hello. I remember you from the Town Hall. Great testimony. I've reread the transcript a couple of times. I may actually plagiarize some of it, with your permission of course. I'll give you due credit."

"Plagiarize away. I like to think it was all pretty common sense to anyone who's paying attention."

"She's really good, isn't she?" Geoff beamed.

"Yes, very good. And actually, I've been paying a lot of attention lately."

"That's usually a good thing, as mayor. What brings you to our little shop?"

"I happened to be driving by and wondered if you had any books on"—he scanned the shop for any other customers—"on leadership."

A little late for that! thought Geoff.

"Hmm, let me think." Donna's eyes widened. She welcomed the opportunity to lead another lost book hunter on an expedition through the store. "Why yes, yes I do," she said, turning and motioning him to follow her down the aisle. She disappeared behind a shelf. Geoff and Rusty stared at one another in astonishment, then followed in a scramble. As they caught up with Donna, they found her hunched over the bottom shelf in the Business section.

"Here you go," she said, rising with a tall stack of books in her hands. "Let's see what we've got here." She handed him one title after another: *The Tribe and You, Getting the Most Out of the Daily Grind, Merrily We Get Along, Ouch!! Learning How to Fall and How to Bounce.*

"Oh, here's a good one. *Empty Your Trough and Fill Your Heart.*"

"Hey, whoa there, I can't manage all of these."

"Choices, Mayor, you have many, many choices."

"I don't want choices, I have far too many choices as it is. I need someone to tell me what to do."

"Oh? Ohhhh, right!" She grasped for the first time the real reason for his visit. "You mean about the, um . . ."

"Yes, about the, um . . ."

"Well, if you don't mind my saying, Mr. Mayor—"

"Please, Rusty."

"If you don't mind my saying, Rusty, this is not a leadership problem at all, not in the conventional sense." She handed the stack of books to Geoff, who deposited them on the nearest convenient shelf. The safari set off once again, this time headed for the Literature section. She stopped in the *G*s and pulled a dog-eared paperback from the shelf.

"Here you go."

Rusty took one look at the cover and burst into a loud cackle. A bloody pig's head impaled on a stake stared back at him. "*Lord of the Flies?* Are you kidding me?"

"Oh, great book, Mayor, great book," declared Geoff, himself looking a little bewildered.

"Yes, it is a great book, Rusty."

"I saw the movie a long time ago. Disturbing to say the least. But what on earth does—"

"Does this have to do with your current situation?"

"Yes. What indeed?"

"It has absolutely everything to do with it."

Geoff chimed in helpfully, doing his best to sound erudite. "I think what she's getting at, Rusty, is . . . what kind of leader do you want to be? Are you a Ralph or a Jack?"

"Yes, that's part of it," said Donna, "but more important, it forces you to ask some fundamental questions."

"Like?"

"Like what is your true north, and who is your master, who will you serve?"

"The truth or the beast?" offered Geoff.

Rusty sighed, shaking his head. "OK, it's getting a little heady in here. But if you think it'll help, I'll take it. What do I owe you?"

"That'll be three dollars, please."

"Cheapest leadership seminar I've ever attended," Rusty said as he handed her the cash, "though I have my doubts."

"It's OK to be skeptical. But you must promise to do the homework; otherwise, no certificate." She winked.

He crossed his heart and held up his right hand. "I promise."

"OK then."

"OK then!"

Rusty loitered uncomfortably with Donna and Geoff in the deep stacks, beyond the time when another patron might have already departed. He looked down at the floor, while Donna studied him discreetly.

"Something else, Mayor?" she asked gently.

Timidly he confessed, "Actually, I was wondering if I could have a word . . . alone?" He shot a quick glance at Geoff.

"Geoff is my right-hand man, my trusted confidante and partner in all manner of crimes and misdeeds. Whatever you say to me, you can say to him."

"And it'll stay right here," Geoff added, holding up his left hand in affirmation.

Rusty kneaded his neck muscles, his habit when feeling tense and gloomy, and took a deep breath. "By now you've probably figured out from my topic of interest," he said, holding up the Golding text, "that I've got a bit of a problem and no way out of it."

"Go on."

"This whole mess at the town hall. I never saw it coming. I thought everything was all sewn up. A big new building project, with lots of new jobs into the area, more housing, nice retail spaces. Now, one riot and one mysterious death later, and everything's gone off the rails."

"Yeah, we're all waiting for something to happen," said Geoff, "but nothing does."

"Well, I'm waiting too, damn it," Rusty barked, immediately regretting his tone. "Despite popular opinion, I actually want to do the right thing, I want this town to thrive and prosper. Hell, I was born here, I don't want to hurt these people any more than I already have. And yet . . ."

"And yet?"

"It seems every way I turn, every possible option, creates a few winners and a whole lotta pissed-off losers. I'm stumped."

"Meanwhile," said Geoff, again trying to be helpful, "we're turning into a tent city."

"Thanks! Like I hadn't noticed."

"I was just agreeing with you!"

"OK, settle down, you two," said Donna.

"You seem to have your head screwed on straight," Rusty continued. "You've got your finger on the pulse of this town, know what they want. I was hoping perhaps you could, you know, help me see a way out of this mess. In an advisory capacity. We can make it official if you like. We have room in the budget for a consultant's fee. Whatever you think is fair."

She was now in all-out creative mode, looking past the two of them and off into the distance at nothing in particular, nodding slowly, automatically, hearing the mayor but listening to an inner voice, like the voice of an angel whispering in her ear, ready to convey its interpreted wisdom to the mortal beings abiding in the material universe.

"Well, Rusty . . . By the way"—she turned to him—"is Rusty your given name?"

"I'm Howard originally. Rusty was my nickname growing up," he said, pointing to his thinning red hair, now streaked with silver.

"Mmm, Howard. The brave watchman, the high and noble guardian. They say, 'What's in a name?' I say everything. May I call you Howard?"

He nodded.

"Howard, listen to me. Your problem is an all too common one."

"Oh?"

"You are trying to please everyone, and it simply cannot be done. No one in your position could, not with all the money in the world, nor all the advisors, consultants, well-heeled backers, or, frankly, any superpowers you may possess. So to begin with, you must first stop trying to do the impossible."

"But what then? I've got to have a plan, make a decision. I've got to do something."

"Yes. And something you shall do. The moment it comes to you, your path will be clear. You simply need to trust that it can be so, then the magic happens."

"The . . . ?"

"The magic," said Geoff. "She taught me that."

"Oh, great." Rusty sighed in desperation. He thought of Monica Sampson-Smith, the Red Shirt brigade, the Chinese moneymen, the untimely death of his principal landowner—and now this talk of magic. "So, you're not going to tell me what to do then."

"That's not what you need, Howard. You need to turn off your head and open your heart. Trust that you already possess the wisdom inside you to do what is right and necessary. Don't allow yourself to be pulled one way or the other. Look into your soul for the answer. That's where you'll find it."

"Into my soul, eh? Hell, I'm not sure I even have one anymore. If I ever did," he said, making a fist at his chest and yanking, "this job'll steal it right out of you."

"Oh, you have a soul, friend. A very beautiful one. Otherwise you wouldn't be so tortured."

The tinkling bell announced another visitor. Through the door, with sharp and confident moves, walked Monica. Even the thick carpet runners could not mute the certainty with which she thudded up the aisle to where the group now stood.

"Ah, Rusty, there you are," Monica said, making eye contact with the mayor and no one else. "I've been looking all over for you. We're about done out there. Time to be going?" she asked, looking at her watch. "I'll be in the car." She pivoted and was out the door as quickly as she had arrived, leaving only the fragrance of Chanel Allure lingering behind.

Rusty looked sheepishly at Donna and Geoff. "We're doing a little surveying of the area, in case anything should move forward with the MPC project."

"Just won't let it go, will you?" said Geoff, unable to further restrain his characteristic bluntness. "Can't you see, no one in town wants this development except your oligarch cronies?" His filter had fallen away completely, triggered by Monica's brash arrogance, and he was becoming visibly angry. Donna quickly intercepted him, moving between the two men before Rusty could respond.

"Listen, boys," she said, "I think we've probably discussed this project enough for one day." She walked the mayor to the door, stopping at the window overlooking the parking lot. "Don't want to miss your ride." Monica sat at the wheel of her white Lincoln Navigator while two workmen wearing hardhats and orange vests climbed into a large pickup truck. "But I will make one suggestion. Maybe a cooling-off period would be good for the whole town. A building moratorium, perhaps? No new projects for a while. That has a nice ring, doesn't it? You wouldn't need to make it about this venture specifically but for the whole town, and only temporarily, to allow some time to recalibrate and for wounds to heal. It might take the pressure off everyone if they knew nothing was hanging over them immediately."

Rusty reflected on her suggestion. "At least it would be some kind of a decision, I suppose, even if it was a decision to do nothing."

"Doing nothing is still a decision, and this is far from doing nothing."

"I'll think it over. Sorry, I've got to be going. Bye for now. And thanks for the book recommendation."

Donna and Geoff watched as he walked to Monica's car and drove off. The clock struck four.

"What a creep," said Geoff. "I don't trust that guy. And that blonde steamroller. You know she was the cause of all our troubles, right? Her and her stupid dog. You remember that, don't you? And he's still hanging around with her? Asshole!"

Donna did not answer but again looked into the remote beyond, past the parking lot and the Burger Basket, the trash and the weeds, the parkway traffic, and the distant hills. Geoff knew she was in her quiet state now. It was time to let her be. If he persisted, he would only upset her.

After a moment she silently returned to her desk and began labeling her books for the New Arrivals shelf. Geoff went back to sorting the History section but first found the chapter on "The Conquest of the West" and skimmed it all the way to the end.

29. REX

Nic dozed peacefully amid the soft stirrings of the forest at dawn. He lay on the damp ground bundled head to toe, save for a small aperture just big enough to breathe through, in blankets he had commandeered from Richard's salon. Three weeks had passed since Nic had encountered another soul up close; to avoid the curious or malign, he'd moved well away from the urban glow and deep into the bush. Nevertheless, he'd been roused nightly by rustling noises in the woods. Spooked at first, he learned to disregard the disturbances, ascribing them to some foraging deer or family of raccoons.

Suddenly as he slept, a jet of hot, stale air blew into the opening of his cocoon, awakening him abruptly, his arms flailing. It was no deer. *Bear maybe?* he thought. *If it is, I'm dead.* He instinctively pulled into his shell but not before something warm, moist, and rank touched him on the nose and lips.

"Rex!" he heard in a hoarse whisper. "Rex, no! Come." The onslaught abated as Nic heard loud panting and heavy paws moving through the leafy detritus, followed by footsteps unmistakably human. *Fucking dog walkers,* thought Nic as he pulled the blanket down over his eyes and fell back asleep.

Several more hours passed before Nic emerged fully from his swaddling. He'd awakened hungry, a daily affair. Remembering he'd finished off the last of his provisions the night before, without enthusiasm he gathered his essential belongings—those items he could not afford to have boosted—into a black garbage bag, concealed the remainder in a hollow under a bush, and prepared for the short walk to the highway.

Since the night he'd ridden into the tall weeds behind Richard's salon, Nic had refused to fraternize with the primitive society of dispossessed inhabitants that had sprung up around the city, preferring to go it alone. He routinely slept until late afternoon, then spent the waning daylight hours foraging. He would return at twilight to guard his campsite and tally his haul, only feeling safe to sleep around five in the morning, when even the most stalwart thieves and insomniac pillagers had too closed their eyes. He learned to make himself invisible while moving about town by hiding in plain sight—just another slow-moving, dirt-encrusted bum haunting the alleyways and underbrush of Morley.

But before long the cash from Richard's till had dwindled to nothing, and he was forced to barter away his beloved bike. He needed a sustainable strategy to keep himself fed. He discovered that, by hanging around fast-food joints at a safe distance, he could spy on patrons as they dumped their half-eaten fries or burritos into trash barrels, then move in promptly to grab them before the birds had their chance. Accustomed as he was to fresh, hot meals prepared in Richard's kitchen, he soon wearied of the lukewarm, half-nibbled cast-offs rejected by strangers. The teeth marks were the worst; no matter how empty his gut, he refused to comingle his spittle with that of others, eating around the ragged edges of their bites as best he could.

If this plan failed, he simply sat down at a lunch spot and looked pathetic, waiting for some godly patron in the spirit of St. Benedict to transfer the unfinished portion of their meal to Nic's table. One time he'd even walked up to a teenage couple enjoying each other's company at Taco Time and started nibbling on their chips. The grossed-out teens immediately abandoned their uneaten fish tacos for him to wolf down. When truly desperate, he would venture into a local grocery store, leisurely fill his cart, then simply roll out the door without paying for anything. He'd gotten away with it a few times, but it had become risky. The loss prevention thugs soon came to recognize him and would follow him around through the aisles, forcing him to leave the premises and move on to more vulnerable targets, where the cashiers were not interested in confronting the grimacing, broad-shouldered, unclean figure over a lousy bag of groceries. If they did happen to inform the authorities, he knew the police would listen to them politely, promise to send a car around, then do nothing.

No one said a thing to him except little children, who had to be admonished for walking up to the dark figure and pointing in awe. He looked like the zombies they'd seen on TV.

Every successful food run affirmed for him once more that he was fated to live the rest of his life on the streets.

As Nic threw his garbage bag over his shoulder, into the clearing galloped a heavy, fat-pawed muscular brown mutt, first at the corner of his vision, then rushing toward him. He crouched into a defensive posture and waited for the forthcoming attack, but none came. Instead, the beast whimpered excitedly, moving in a figure-eight around his feet, sniffing his legs, and finally jumping up on him with both paws to greet him. The huge hound nearly knocked him over. Nic stood motionless to avoid provoking any turn toward violence, but this was a wholly friendly greeting.

"Rex, down!" The dog immediately complied by sitting on his haunches and staring up at Nic. "It's OK. He knows you. Rex, come!"

The dog on command moved immediately to the side of his master. Nic turned to see a spindly but robust young man with short-cropped hair and several days' beard stubble, wearing a jean jacket and carrying a hefty backpack, which he removed and set on the ground.

"Knows me? How does he know me?"

"He's been sniffing you for the past three days." He laughed. "Last night he got a little personal. Sorry about that. Hope he didn't startle you."

Nic dismissed the comment with a grunt. He liked dogs fine, and the young man seemed harmless. He was well spoken and mannerly, attributes Nic suspected came from money, education, or both. But this closeness of quarters was violating his primary code: no contact! He grew increasingly eager for his visitors to be on their way. The dog, on the other hand, made a couple of tight circles, then settled down between the two humans with a contented sigh.

"This is his turf, you know," the man said with a smile. "We've been staying in this little clearing for quite a while, Rex and me. We don't get many guests. None, really. It's nice here, quiet, isolated. Then three nights ago we got home and, boom, there you were. We didn't want to disturb you. Everyone's entitled. So we bedded down just over there, beyond those trees." Nic looked in that direction but could not see more than ten feet into the woods. No wonder he had not seen them.

The young man dug into his backpack and pulled out a plastic bag of beef jerky, taking a piece for himself and tossing one to Rex. He offered the pack to Nic, who did not respond but continued only to look at the prostrate dog relaxing in his glade.

"Been on the street long?"

"Not long," said Nic.

"Four years for us, off and on. Used to sleep in my aunt's garage, till she started asking for rent. Had to get outta there fast, boy, I'll say." He laughed out loud. "Stayed at my grandma's house for a few weeks, but she died so had to move on again. I tell you what, in some ways it's easier being out here. Open air, freedom, never have to, you know, justify yourself to anyone. 'Course, you have to learn a thing or two. It's not something that comes natural to most people." He looked at Nic's makeshift campsite, his black plastic garbage bag. "You gotta figure out your resources and where to find them. Hot meals, clothes, blankets and tarps, water. Warming center in the winter, cooling center in the summer. Most important, you gotta know who's a friend and who's not. Sometimes it's hard to tell. Everyone's got a hustle. Job number one out here is survival, so if that means taking advantage of a fellow human being, so be it." He again offered the jerky to Nic, who now motioned to toss him the package.

Nic wondered if the young man was a friend. He'd been fooled before. But his empty gut protested too loudly to care. He reluctantly ate the jerky—*job number one, right?*—conceding there might be strings attached.

"You need a tarp under there," he said, pointing to Nic's now soiled and damp blankets. "I've got a spare. Here you go." He reached into his backpack and tossed him a rolled-up blue tarp.

"Don't worry, I can get another one down at the Social Services office. They give out all kinds of free stuff. I'll take you there tomorrow. You'll be amazed. Closed now, but first thing in the morning?"

Nic was annoyed by the thought of tromping across town to the Social Services office for any reason, let alone first thing in the morning. He took the tarp and nodded.

"Let's go grab some dinner." The young man lifted the straps of his heavy backpack onto his shoulders with ease, to which Rex responded by immediately standing at the ready. "Gotta make one stop first, though," he said, then walked off. He did not try to cajole Nic to follow them but simply assumed that he would. Nic was relieved to be alone again as he watched the duo exiting his tenuously claimed territory. But his relief was short-lived. The jerky had not sated his profound hunger. He grabbed his garbage sack and was off at a trot.

The young man weaved his way through the brush like a native, every landmark and feature, every zig and zag seemingly engrained in him. Nic kept up about ten paces behind. His guide moved with a vigor that reminded him he was out of shape. They had just begun to see the lights on the highway when the young man ducked behind a tall thicket and emerged with two large black bags. From the sound of them, Nic knew they contained cans and bottles, gleaned from who knows where, ready for redemption. The man hoisted both bags onto his back, one on each shoulder, and continued toward the highway.

Rex appeared to derive great joy from his master's mission. Perhaps he recalled from other trips that there was a treat waiting for him at the end. In any case, he must have truly felt he was being of help to the pack, which had now grown to include Nic, for a sense of canine fulfillment was evident in his wagging tail, flopping tongue, and airborne stride.

The three travelers arrived at the highway and crossed as a group, Nic having closed the gap between himself and his two new companions. They approached the bottle drop around back of the supermarket, a grimy, poorly kept space with a sticky floor and the yeasty smell of remnant beer. The two humans, each using one of the available machines, quickly emptied the plastic bags and received their redemption slips while Rex watched. Their take was just under eighteen dollars.

Nic handed his slip to the young man, who refused it, saying, "Three way split, man. That's only fair. We all helped. We'll get something yummy for Rex, and splurge a little on ourselves before dinner." They walked around the front of the building and into the market, where the young man purchased a sautéed beef bone and four cans of dog food for Rex and two bottles of kombucha for himself. "Whatcha gonna get?" he said with childlike enthusiasm.

"I could use some deodorant. And some toothpaste, maybe?"

"Go for it."

They checked out and were left with a balance of a dollar fifty, which they split three ways, Nic taking two quarters and the young man keeping the remaining dollar. "Dinnertime," he said, and led the way out the door, across the street, and up four blocks, stopping in front of St. Michael's Episcopal Church.

When the three arrived, church personnel were still setting up the serving tables in the parking lot, though several dozen persons had already convened and formed a long queue in anticipation of receiving a hot meal. Nic had heard about the dinners provided by the well-meaning religious group but was wary of crowds that might result in his being spotted so had avoided the scene. Something about the young man had boosted his confidence. Still, he reflexively kept his head low and his hoodie pulled far forward as he moved through the church lot.

The young man led his small group to their place in the queue, occasionally having to redirect the dog to behave himself. He nodded to faces he recognized or that recognized him as they passed but mostly diverted his eyes away from people. Only one person approached him, nonchalant and smiling, a man in his middle years with gray in his beard wearing a tattered olive fatigue jacket. He shook the young man's hand affectionately and embraced him with a hearty backslap.

"Yousef, my man!"

"Charles. So good to see you."

"How you been, man? How's that beast of yours?"

"Good, man, really good." Rex whimpered and offered his paw to Charles.

"Atta boy," he said, nuzzling Rex behind the ears. "Ready for some good chow?"

"You know he is."

"So am I. I got to get in this line before it's all gone," Charles said, eyeing the growing crowd. They embraced again. "OK, man, be seeing you. You keep that ferocious dog in check, now." He walked off laughing to take his place in line.

Nic turned to the young man. "Seems like a good guy," he said.

"Yeah, good guy. Tough story. He's been out here longer than any of us, since right after he got released."

"From . . . the service?"

"Nah, jail, man."

"For?"

"Gang banging, drugs, armed assault, attempted murder, you name it. Hasn't been able to get off the street since. Can't seem to get a leg up. Too bad, too. He's a really great guy."

Nic changed the subject. "Yousef? That's your name?"

"That's what they call me. I guess we haven't been properly introduced."

"I'm Nic."

"Good to know you, Nic." They shook. "You, of course, know Rex," he said, playfully petting the hound, who barked gleefully. Rex was feeling the bonhomie intensely.

The line started to move. As it did Yousef extracted a plastic bowl from his backpack and gave it to Rex, who carried it carefully in his drooling mouth. The smell of hot food was working on Nic's senses too. His stomach growled in earnest now, and his mouth watered. He didn't really care what was being served. He would eat it and right away try to get another helping.

Yousef said, "Mmm, chicken mac and cheese. Great! There should be enough for seconds. And look, fruit salad and a big sheet cake. Man, it's our lucky day." He let Nic go ahead of him to get his plate loaded up, then got his own, requesting an additional clean paper plate for Rex. They found an empty spot just at the far corner of the lot and sat down. Yousef pulled a can of dog food from his backpack and emptied it onto the plate. As Rex dove in, the young man excused himself and went to fill the dog's water bowl. Rex was done eating before Nic had barely started his meal. The dog looked up at him plaintively, and Nic had no choice but to share half his mac and cheese with him.

Rex had just polished off his extra ration when Yousef returned with the bowl of water. Yousef expressed his disappointment in Rex by admonishing him sharply, but the dog's heartfelt contrition was so evident in his sad eyes, he quickly forgave him with a hug and a scratch.

"So sorry. Rex has such bad manners sometimes."

"No worries. He's a good dog." Nic was petting him now too.

"The best. Good to have a companion out here. We look out for each other, don't we, Rex?"

"You say you've been on the street for, what, four years? You seem to be getting along all right. What's your secret?" Nic was keen to learn some pointers to help him adapt to his new way of life.

"My secret. Hmm, that's a tough one. Stay away from bad influences, for one. Like that guy over there. See him?" Yousef said, pointing to a slight young man sporting a massive head of blond hair in a top knot, who sat alone and shirtless with a menacing look on his face eating his dinner. "That's John the Spitter. He wanders up and down the street and randomly spits on people as they walk by."

"That's not right."

"No, that's real fucked up. Rumor is that if someone passes him and they avert their eyes, he'll spit. But if they acknowledge his existence in any way, like with a flash of eye contact or a quick nod, or say, 'Z'up?' or something like that, he'll leave them alone. I guess being ignored really pushes his buttons."

"Guess so. But they can't be all degenerates." He studied the assembly of humans. "What about her?" He pointed to a full-faced woman in a peasant blouse and floor-length skirt. At her feet sat two small children of preschool age, each picking at their macaroni by hand. Nic was silently moved by the scene, harking back to his own destitute and hapless childhood.

"Ah, yes. Those poor kids, living on the street, hand to mouth. God bless them. A pitiful sight, no doubt."

"I admit, I hate seeing kids subjected to the bad decisions of adults."

"Yes, of course, but you understand, these children are here on the street quite voluntarily. For them it's all a great adventure, like playing make believe. You see, they're not homeless at all, and they're certainly not penniless. They're not even her kids."

"What?"

"Sure. They all live in an apartment not five blocks from here. The kids call her Auntie. She borrows them from her neighbor for a few hours every afternoon, then she sets up their little diorama in front of the bank by the ATM to do some panhandling. Children are a tremendous draw, I must say, even better than a dog. It's a very sweet scene. The kids occupy themselves with their little games on their phone or whatever the hell children do, then afterward they all stop here for dinner on their way home, whereupon she drops them off to their mother and splits the take, sixty forty. The kids are fed and happy and tired, Auntie has earned a little pocket money. And while they're gone, mom can take a break, or do a little business, or entertain a guest for a few hours. And those bank patrons, so moved by the abject scene that they drop a couple of dollars in the woman's hat to ease their guilt, why they're feeling good about themselves now too for having helped this little family of desperate means. It all works out, you see. A beautiful symmetry."

Yousef brandished his plate and rose to join the line again. "Still hungry," he said, offering to fetch his guest a refill.

"I'm good. Thanks."

"You sure? There's cake," he tempted.

Nic waved him off. He pushed his mac and cheese around his plate with his fork. He'd lost his appetite for food and, for the moment, life.

For the first time, he looked closely at the people milling about the church parking lot or shuffling along in the queue to be fed. Men and women of every shape and description comprised the crowd: old, young, tall, short, fat, thin, white, black, brown, tan, pallid, calm, fidgety, clean, dirty, disheveled, tidy, animated, taciturn. Little families with children stood patiently, while pierced, tattooed teens with backpacks and severe haircuts engaged in their animated horseplay like frisky colts. One man wearing a tan Members Only jacket, loose fitting jeans, and shower sandals, was particularly loud, regaling everyone in earshot with the travails of his day. A few shopping carts, bicycles, and rubbish bags were interspersed in the line, held fast by their cautious owners, while others felt secure enough to set their belongings along the cyclone fence, still under their watchful gaze. He saw a young woman with platinum-bleached hair and long-neglected one-inch black roots in a flowered tank top, stretch pants, and flip-flops, busily picking at sores on her arms, carefully examining the flakes of skin she pulled off for bugs. A few paces back stood an old woman, bent forward into a C-shaped curve, pushing an old-fashioned foldable shopping cart that she used as a makeshift walker. The cart was filled with coats and blankets. Finally he saw Charles again, his earlier sunny and engaging countenance now replaced by a stiff, icy expression familiar to Nic from his own time in jail, a hunted look that spoke of hopelessness and fear, but that unmistakably said, "Don't fuck with me."

Nic was suddenly overcome with despair. How had these lost souls, with their vast, immeasurable suffering and pain, all come to be in this place, at this moment? The totality of their lives of abuse and self-abuse hovered like an ominous dark cloud over the church lot. In that instant all the cynical, self-serving, and deceitful conduct of human against human came home to him at once. Was there no spark of goodness to be found? Or was there, after all, but one enduring truth—that people were simply wicked? And if so, hadn't he been right all along to look out only for himself? Were his irresistible pangs of conscience, his longing for a glimmer of redemption, just a naive illusion?

There could have been no stronger affirmation than this tragic street scene for his newly embraced philosophy: stay away from people at all costs. Evil was everywhere, nothing exalted or soaring but far more pedestrian—a lowly, primitive thing that welcomed everyone to its bosom. All evil needed to take hold was for humans to be mean, stupid, and lazy. And he could not deny they certainly were all that.

Returning to their spot, Yousef sat and ate, wordlessly scrutinizing Nic, who, still shrouded in his hoodie, stared straight ahead.

"Not feeling well? I know, the mac and cheese is way filling. You were smart to stop after one helping. I'm starting to feel kinda heavy laden myself," he said, placing both hands on his belly and moaning. He picked at his fruit salad.

"That's not it." Nic decided that, since he would never encounter Yousef again, there was no reason to censor himself. He unloaded his thoughts on the young man. "I've done some bad things, Yousef. Really bad. Somehow I was hoping to run away from all that out here on the street, escape my past and replace it with something pure. But it keeps running right alongside me. I can't seem to dodge it."

Yousef sat pensively awhile, making sure Nic had had his say. "Can't run, man," he said finally. "You should know that by now, Nic. This ain't your first rodeo. Run away? To where? That's what all these folks are trying to do. Outrun the truth and themselves. It's the coward's way out, and it'll never work. I know, believe me. I've been trying to outrun myself for the past four years. Eventually you got to turn and face reality, face yourself, and push through it."

"You paint a pretty depressing picture."

"No, man, it's not depressing. Just the opposite. Everything is as it should be. It's nature's way. Redemption takes time. It ain't easy, and it sure ain't free. There's a cost. But if you're willing to pay the cost, it's right there waiting for us."

"What cost?"

"A piece of you has to die in order to be reborn."

"OK, here we go . . ." Nic set his plate down and moved to get up, away from the coming sermon.

"No, no, man. Sit, sit. I don't mean reborn like that, although a lot of folks go that route, and that's fine. Personally I've never understood how you can just dump all your wrongdoings onto some mythical being and go your merry way. Sooner or later you have to pay the toll. That's how I see it."

"So what's the secret? Give."

"I'm talking about abandoning the part of your brain that tells you to serve only yourself. Our lizard brain has us convinced there's not enough to go around, that life is a battlefield and everyone else is the enemy, so you'd better look out for exactly no one but yourself. But it's not like that at all. There's plenty for everyone, plenty of wealth and power and love. It doesn't have to be a zero-sum game."

Nic considered the young man's words, then mounted his defense. "OK, so if you're so smart, what are you doing out here, wandering around with your dog, living like an animal among the zombies?"

"Hey, first of all, let's not talk down our dear animal friends, especially Rex." He petted his beloved dog, who looked up devotedly at him. "He's smart, loyal, doesn't judge, always looks out for me, and knows I'll always do the same for him."

"Sure. Sorry, Rex. I wish more people were like you."

"Indeed. Second, I won't be out here forever. You won't be either, you'll see. But I've done some bad shit myself. Really bad shit. Things I'm really ashamed of, I won't lie."

Nic thought of his own sketchy past, all the bad deeds from cheating a friend at cards to the murder of Richard. "So why not just get up and leave now? Get away from here, away from these people, back to your old life?"

"I can't, not yet. I've got to do penance before I can earn my way back into the world. We're all suspended out here, we zombies, each of us in our own self-imposed purgatory. Just like you, friend. You know you've done something wrong, you've admitted it, but you're not able to confront your demons yet full face 'cause you're afraid. As long as you give in to fear, they will continue to haunt you. They'll possess your very soul, until you cast them out."

"Like an exorcism, right?" Nic laughed sarcastically. "Is that what I need?"

"If you say so. It'll be about as much fun as an exorcism. It's not going to be pretty. But when you finally get up the nerve, you'll find the strength to do it."

Nic sat glumly with head in hands. "Nice pep talk." He felt worse than ever, but Yousef's words made sense to him. He had struggled with his demons for years, though had never named them as such. They took the form of bad dreams that woke him up trembling, sweating, alone, and afraid. Or the waking flashes of perfect recall of his past that lasted an instant, only to send tingling fear waves down his spine for the rest of the day. Since he'd been on the street, the dreams were coming night after restless night, his days continually assailed by painful memories and intrusive thoughts. He was not sure how much more he could take before going completely mad, though he was certain that this was indeed what drove people insane—not bad chemicals, or short-circuits in the brain. No, it was their failure to reconcile the horrors they had imposed on others, or that others had imposed on them, that drove them over the edge.

The only way to survive, he was convinced, was to encircle yourself with an impenetrable wall and hunker down behind it. But then you became your own jailer, and being held captive behind that wall was as good as being dead.

Yousef tossed out the paper plates, dried Rex's water dish, and jammed it deeply into his backpack. He wrapped two pieces of cake in a napkin for later while he stood waiting for Nic.

"Coming?"

"Naw, you go ahead. I'll be fine."

"Look," Yousef said, squatting next to Rex, "I can understand why you might prefer to be on your own. But Rex and I, well, we feel kind of responsible for you now. We've got a nice campsite staked out, probably nicer than anywhere else you'll find tonight on your own. Besides, now you're part of our roving band of gypsies. Rex will miss you terribly if you go away. Come on back with us. I've still got to show you the ropes. I'm afraid you might perish out here, among all these . . . characters."

Nic looked at him wryly. Evening was racing toward night in downtown Morley, the sidewalks growing dim just before the streetlights flickered themselves awake. To Nic it had become a familiar scene, when the apparitions, possessed by their personal demons or influenced by substances natural and unnatural, emerged from their ghoulish haunts to roam in the darkness. He had managed to dodge them the past three weeks, but was not in the mood to do it again tonight. He could do worse than hang out with Yousef, and Rex provided an additional measure of safety plus was a comfort in his own right.

"Sure" was all Nic said, as he rose to rejoin his posse.

30. FOLDING, PART I

In the ensuing days, Nic happily tagged along with Yousef and Rex on their daily route. Yousef made good on his promise at the Social Services office, scoring a new tarp and a two-man igloo-style tent for Nic, brand-new in the box, donated by a local adventure gear store. They picked up new toothbrushes, soap, underwear, and socks. With some coaxing from Yousef, Nic rummaged through the charity bins and found a thick, near-new winter coat that fit him perfectly.

The next order of business was to gather redeemables for the can and bottle drop. Yousef knew by heart the collection days for every neighborhood in Morley. Competition was fierce, and fights had broken out over turf infringements, forcing the three to trek considerable distances on evenings before pickup days to be the first to sift through the neighbors' curbside recycling bins, usually coming away with bags of valuable swag. After their rummaging, Yousef made certain to leave the site fastidiously clean and neat. "As if we were never here," he instructed Nic.

Yousef, Nic, and Rex enjoyed two hearty meals a day together, first from the breakfast line at the Presbyterian Ministries Kitchen—scrambled eggs and sausages, oatmeal, warmed day-old scones and muffins, coffee and juice, even hot cocoa if you preferred—and later on back at St. Michael's for dinner. Technically Rex, not being human, wasn't allowed to partake, but having grown fond of the beast, Nic secretly split his meals with Rex, with Yousef's silent approval of course.

Nic soon came to recognize the diverse characters and plots manifest in the streets around him, a daily playbill of tragicomedy, kabuki, and physical schtick, at once entertaining and disturbing. In a weeks' time, he could casually report to Yousef, "Oh, look, there goes Old Gray; he isn't dead after all," or warn them, "Watch it. Here comes Mad Molly," to steer them in the opposite direction.

His favorite was One-Legged Sue, who, in her rusty, tattered wheelchair, propelled herself around town in reverse by pushing it backward using her remaining foot. She was completely edentulous but refused to wear her dentures, making her appear years older than her actual age of twenty-nine. She always greeted Nic with a cheerful toothless grin.

"Hey, Yousef, who's your handsome friend?" she'd ask whenever they encountered her on the westbound onramp to Interstate 14, her usual panhandling spot. To Nic, she seemed fragile and helpless, but Yousef assured him she was well looked after by her part-time boyfriend, La'Darius, stationed across the street at the eastbound ramp, where he kept a protective watch.

The street denizens of Morley were keen to recount their unique stories of how they'd come to dwell there. Some, like Charles, had been released from incarceration with no prospects for employment or a permanent place to reside, no sought-after trade skills or advanced education, no social supports, and certainly no belief in themselves to succeed. Others had lost everything to drug or alcohol use and, having fallen to zero, continued using only to plummet even further. Many carried a diagnosis of at least one psych disorder—bipolar, PTSD, schizophrenia, schizoaffective—but were often untreated, undertreated, or had ceased taking their meds or going to clinic, either out of spite or simple forgetfulness. Eviction was a final common pathway for many, placing blame for their hardships squarely on "my fucking landlord!" rather than anything they might have done themselves.

It struck Nic as odd that even the most destitute among them seemed to have a new cell phone, tablet, or other electronic device. He would observe young men in threadbare clothing, splayed across sidewalks blocking the passage of pedestrians, surrounded by garbage and debris yet casually scrolling, swiping, or texting on their phones. This particularly irked him because, since his encounter with

New York Harry, who'd wrecked his device, he'd had to watch helplessly as his cell charge dwindled from yellow to red and finally to black. He had tried charging it without success, ultimately consoling himself that the signal might have given away his whereabouts to the police.

"We'd better get you a new phone, sir," joked Yousef. "You've got to keep your thumbs in shape," he added, making mock texting motions.

"How do we do that?"

"A burner." Yousef explained how he could use the untraceable prepaid device to call or text, then discard it for another. Nic was ecstatic. Why hadn't he heard of this before? Though he still had no one to call, the burner helped him feel a little less isolated, particularly when Yousef would disappear with Rex for a day or two, eventually returning with some prize booty they could either sell or use to enhance their lives, but in the interim leaving Nic on his own.

On one such occasion, Nic awoke to find his two companions off on their rounds. He missed them. He'd grown happily accustomed to their warm tent and hot meals. Life was not so bad after all. He was surer than ever now that the promise he'd made to himself—to never go back to the real world—could be realized.

On that morning he discovered to his surprise that he also missed the fun of foraging for half-consumed fast food. He'd never adjusted to going through the church food lines by himself and, with Yousef and Rex away, thought it would be good sport to provoke the unwary townsfolk with his scary presence.

Nic scanned the perimeter around their site. Thievery was a constant factor in their daily movements. Despite the unspoken rule that, no matter how desperate, one did not go into another man's tent uninvited, there was plenty of larcenous aggression running counter to that ideology. The possibility of getting knifed if one transgressed seemed to strengthen everyone's moral resolve.

Reassured their camp was far enough from stray foot traffic to be secure for a short while, he threw his hoodie over his head and walked slowly toward the whoosh of the highway traffic. Instead of the huge black garbage bag he'd originally used, he now carried a compact rucksack with all his essential gear. Yousef's influence was welcome in this regard; it had restored a bit of order and dignity to his otherwise reprobate life.

The fare at Don Emilio #7 was particularly appetizing, evidenced by the long lines that formed every workday around noon. Warm tortillas, fresh-made salsa, perfectly seasoned asada and carnitas, enchiladas oozing with *queso fresco,* and pozole heavily topped with cotija. Young men on construction crews would wait patiently on their lunch breaks for a home-style meal that felt like a warm hug from Mama.

Arriving at the restaurant, Nic employed his usual methods, first scavenging through the tables and trash cans on the patio, scoring some still-warm tortillas and a bit of refried beans but nothing substantial. Mostly the plates were scraped clean. *These boys are hungry today,* he thought. He decided to go inside, sit among the diners, and wait for them to become uncomfortable with his passive intimidation. This had worked elsewhere, though he doubted it would be as successful with the mostly male clientele at Don Emilio's. On his way through the door, he saw a familiar face.

In a booth, by the window overlooking the highway, sat Anita Gomez. A young man in his early twenties sat across from her. She jotted notes in a spiral binder and typed on her laptop as she asked him a list of questions. She appeared kindhearted and sympathetic, but was otherwise all business. The boyish man, wearing a white T-shirt and jeans, sat with shoulders rolled forward and a face of full of contrition and obedience. Anita was the busiest parole officer in Hensen County, carrying a caseload of two hundred or more men and women recently released from incarceration. She was also Nic's parole officer.

When Nic had requested transfer of his parole supervision from Indiana to California, he needed a sponsor. Richard had gladly vouched for him, housed him, and promised to help him find a job. He'd also encouraged Nic to keep up with his PO check-ins. With Richard gone, Nic had loosed his mooring and drifted out of the system while doing his best to disappear. He'd so far managed to elude detection and capture, but today's chance encounter with Anita convinced him that every law enforcement agency within a hundred miles must be looking for him. He rebuked himself for allowing such a stupid tactical error that could jeopardize everything.

Recognizing Anita instantly, Nic did not slow his pace or make eye contact but proceeded directly out the opposite door in one continuous motion. Had she spotted him as he crossed the highway? Did she catch him in her peripheral vision on his way through the restaurant? At six foot four, with his long thin legs, broad shoulders, and distinctive neck tattoos, his was not a form easily mistaken, even with his hoodie pulled over his head.

Rather than darting back across the highway in Anita's full view, he walked fast as he could in the opposite direction, ducking into the placid neighborhood behind the restaurant. He felt exposed among the neat, grassy landscapes, open garages, and slow-moving SUVs. Children played cheerfully in their driveways. Watchful moms stood close by, eyeing him blankly. The rucksack added slightly to his legitimacy over the plastic garbage sack, but he was still an oddity on these streets. He kept his gaze low, his stride steady. After a mile or so, he turned onto a feeder street headed toward the highway, crossing it at a pedestrian overpass, then slipped into the dense line of brush leading to the river.

He hewed close to the riverbank, bushwhacking his way upstream for another slow and arduous mile until he again found himself in familiar territory. He did not have a plan beyond simply getting under cover and staying out of sight. He spotted their tent and thankfully saw no signs of intruders, but no Yousef or Rex. He slipped inside and zipped up the tent.

Once again Nic found himself at a crossroads. He was certain a net was closing in on him. Even if Anita had not seen him today, he suspected she was already in relentless pursuit since he'd missed a couple of appointments with her. Should he stay in Morley and lie low? No, it was only a matter of time before she got to him. What about turning himself in, throwing himself on their mercy? The parole violation alone could have been enough to land him back in prison. Now with Richard's blood on his hands, he was sure to stand trial and end up on the inside again, this time life without parole. No, his only option, the least of all evils, was to pack up his gear and get out.

He deliberated the decision with deep regret. He enjoyed the companionship of Yousef and Rex, had felt a lively camaraderie in their merry band that was new for him, not to mention protection from the elements and predators, human and otherwise, that roamed the night. The days were already growing shorter, and there was a bite in the air. His hoodie had become more than a disguise; it was essential on cool sylvan mornings. The prospect of lighting out on his own gave him no joy. But wasn't it bound to come to this after all? His dream of living the idyllic life of a primitive vagabond . . . that was a fool's fantasy by any account.

He looked about the tent despondently, finding little to take with him. Every accoutrement of their comfortable survival in the cold world—camp stove, fuel, lanterns, batteries, can opener, extra tarps, blankets, dry and canned provisions, even the tent he now crouched in—had been procured either by or with the aid of Yousef, who had graciously shared it all with Nic. He could not bring himself to steal from his benefactor. He threw his personal items—toothbrush, toothpaste, socks and underwear, extra clothes—into his pack and set it by the tent's zippered entrance. He checked the time on his throwaway phone. His companions had been gone for most of the day. Surely, they would be home soon. He laughed softly to himself. *Helluva home, this little pup tent.* He tarried awhile longer, hoping they would arrive directly. In spite of his agitation, he fell into a restless sleep.

He thought of Rex. The dog's essence permeated the small tent and everything in it. Surely, he thought, the three of them must all smell of dog given their close quarters. He would miss Rex: his loyal devotion, his chipper attitude in the face of adversity. For an instant, Nic thought of staying, then quickly dismissed the notion.

Nic thought too of the dog he'd briefly had as a boy, who, like Rex, was big and goofy, true blue and sweet. He tried but could not remember the dog's name. *Was it Jack?* So long ago since that day his father had taken the dog away to the pound. *Too much trouble*, his father had said. *Can't afford to feed him no more.* He tried again, but the name would not come to him. *Jake? No.* What he did recall vividly, from long decades ago, was sitting alone on his back porch, waiting and waiting past dark for his dog to come home, hoping it had all been a terrible mean joke, looking up the street and then down the street, around the corner, in the backyard, behind the shrubs and trees, in the thicket and in the neighbors' yard, searching, hoping, calling out for *Jinx! That's it. Jinxy! Here, boy! Good dog. Where are you,*

Jinx? Come! But Jinx would not come. No comforts would be enjoyed that night, no loyal hugs, no warm breath, no wet stinky fur. Only the empty place in his gut remained, the gnawing ache, the hollow that would not be filled.

Awake again, on his back, he tried to get serious about planning his escape route but could not concentrate. He turned onto his side, rolled into a ball, his breath heaving, eyes clenched, body shuddering. *You fucked it up again. Loser!* a voice chided him. He tried in vain to quiet the voice, covered his ears, buried his head. *You'd think you'd be used to it by now. Loser!* He wailed in anguish to drown it out. *Loser!* It would not be silenced. *Better get running, loser. Go on, boy, run. Run!*

He wanted only to stay put, just awhile longer, a brief moment of repose to settle the restless trickster inside his head, tame the ugly beast. But no. No, he could not stay. He would run again. Run hard and fast. He unzipped the tent flap, grabbed his pack, and was gone.

31. FOLDING, PART II

Puffy white clouds moved slowly across the blue sky over Fayetteville. The warm morning sun sparked the industry of a family of wrens digging for worms in the flower bed. With help from Little Tommy, Joan pulled their dried and crispy laundry down from the backyard line and loaded it into the blue IKEA basket, hauled it in, and dumped it onto the kitchen table for folding. Tommy ran in behind her as the screen door slammed.

"I can fold clothes too," he said, joyfully holding out his arms. Last week she had taught him how to match up his socks by tucking one into the other, and he'd done really well. Now she showed Tommy how to fold a T-shirt and handed him one of his own little shirts to practice. As she folded and stacked the towels, bedding, shirts, jeans, underwear, and socks for the rest of the family, Tommy stood at her side folding his one shirt to get it just right, then, frustrated, unfolding it and starting all over again.

It had been three months since she'd heard from Nic—no surprise in itself. The longest she'd ever lost contact with her brother, including stints in jail, was four years. But this time was different. Since the brief encounter with her family, right after his release from Plainfield, the image of Nic's face haunted her. She worried about him—out of jail, moving cross-country to a strange place, sponsored by some old man she knew nothing about. *Pen pal! Ugh!* She could hardly believe it. She wished she had stood up to her unsympathetic husband, advocated more strongly for her little brother when Big Tommy had refused him respite. But she had taken the low road and watched Nic dissolve into the mist that cold morning. Her attempt to preserve harmony had worked. Nic's name had not been spoken in their home since, and it tore at her.

At least weekly she'd tried to contact Nic, sent texts, left messages. He never returned her calls. She dared not contact "this Richard person" directly; now she wished she had. Eventually Nic's phone stopped working. Soon after, Anita Gomez alerted her that Nic was AWOL, and his sponsor was dead. From that point on, every day and long into the night, she anxiously fussed with her phone, checking her texts and answering calls from unknown numbers, usually robots offering her health insurance or scammers threatening to notify the local police about some grave tax irregularity. But no word from Nic.

Little Tommy finally folded his shirt to his satisfaction and with outstretched arms presented it proudly to his mom.

"Good work, little man," she said with a hug. "It's perfect. Now go get your book out. It's time for lessons."

"Which one?"

"Let's look at *The Jolly Postman*."

"OK, Mommy" he said gleefully and ran into the front room.

"I'll be right in, sweet pea."

She felt her phone hum in her pocket. She didn't recognize the number; the caller ID showed only "United States." She answered it anyway. For the third time this week, a mechanized voice alerted her that her electricity was about to be turned off in the next hour. She hung up and bundled the clean and folded laundry in both arms, first stopping in Tommy's room, then his sister Cecily's, and finally the hallway linen closet. As she set the last towel in place, her phone buzzed again. *That's enough!* Whether a machine, or some pathetic wretch in a boiler room on the far side of the planet, she wanted to rip the entity a new one, just for fun.

"Take me off your list, you sonofabitch," she screamed into the phone, "or I will hunt you down and rip out your goddamn throat."

"Joanie! Is that you, sis?" Nic laughed. "It sure sounds like you."

"Oh my God, Nic! Is that . . . ? I was just . . . Oh, never mind." Joan laughed along with her brother as she broke into tears. "Where the hell have you been? Why haven't you called me? I've been worried shitless."

"Hey, sis. Yeah, sorry. I've been kinda busy out here."

"I don't care how busy you were, you should've called, dammit. I could strangle you."

"Hey, last time I got the boot from Tom so hard, my ass still hurts, or don't you remember that? I thought it'd be smart to stay out of your hair for a while."

"Oh, who cares about that now?" she said impatiently. "Tell me where you are. We need to talk." She could hear highway traffic in the background.

"I actually don't know where I am right now." He had been on the move for the past forty-eight hours, walking surface streets all night and, when it was safe, bumming rides on the highway during the day. Now he was between towns, sitting behind a dumpster about fifty miles northeast of Morley, using up the last remaining minutes on his throwaway phone. He looked over his shoulder. "I'm outside a Circle-K somewhere. Listen, my phone's dying. I gotta get off. I just wanted to check in, let you know I was OK."

"Wait, how can I reach you? We need to talk, Nicky. There's something I need to tell you."

"I'll be easy to reach soon enough," he said sardonically, "if they ever catch up with me."

"Nic, you've got to turn yourself in. You didn't have anything to do with . . . you know."

"With what, Joanie? What are you talking about? How much do you know?"

She finally let on that his PO had contacted her. From Anita, she knew Nic had vanished and could not be found, either in Morley or nearby Rellman. He also was a person of interest in the investigation of Richard's death. It would be disastrous for his parole if he did not check in with her right away.

"You talked to her? Goddammit!" He shouted obscenities into the air so loudly she had to move the phone away from her ear.

"Of course I talked to her. I'm your sister. And your last sponsor too, remember? You disappeared. I was really worried. What else was I supposed to do?"

"I can't believe you talked to her. What did you say? Go ahead, tell me. I'm so fucked anyway."

"Don't worry, I didn't tell her anything. I had no idea where you were, and I still don't. Nicky, shut up and listen to me. They've been looking all over for you. You can't just break parole."

"I haven't missed a meeting."

"Liar. You missed two, then vaporized into thin air. Please go back and turn yourself in right now, Nic."

"I can't, Joanie."

"But why? You've got to."

"I said I can't!" he yelled into the phone, drawing the attention of a patron walking into the convenience store. "A lotta bad shit has gone down out here that I may have had something to do with it. There was a fight, see—"

"Shhh, someone may be on the line. Now you hush up and listen to me. I told you, you had nothing to do with any of that."

"But I—"

"You've been exonerated, stupid. Did you hear me?"

"What?"

"I mean, practically. Anita told me all about it. They're not trying to hang anything on you; they just want to talk to you."

"Oh hell, that's such cop bullshit. Don't be an idiot, sis. I thought you were too smart to fall for that line of crap."

"No, really. They know all about the big scuffle at that town meeting. They reviewed the tape. They saw your friend get hit in the head by someone else, then watched you swoop in like the fucking Caped Crusader and rescue him. You're a goddamn hero."

Nic listened silently, not wanting to reveal the details of what had ensued at the house later that night. "I still say she's bullshitting you."

"Would you please shut up and listen? Whatever might have happened, you had nothing to do with . . . with his outcome. They did an autopsy. He was drunk, and I mean, like, *way* drunk, like 'in a coma' drunk."

"So what else is new?"

"But besides that—are you listening?—he passed out and stopped breathing, then they figure he had a heart attack and died. Did you hear me? A heart attack. That's what killed him."

"But what about the whack on the head?" he asked, thinking of both the town brawl and their fistfight later that night.

"He had, what did she call it, 'nonlethal injuries.' A broken nose, nothing else."

"But that can't be. Him and me, we had a—"

"I told you, shut up." She checked the front room to make sure little Tommy was not getting into trouble. He sat quietly, reading his picture book. "Now you listen to your big sister. You call Anita as soon as you get off this phone. Get your ass back there and check in with her. She's not looking to send you back to jail, Nic. She wants to help you. I believe her."

Nic believed it too but would not admit it. Anita was a seasoned PO who could tell the truly rotten from the merely misguided. She had always been a straight shooter with him.

The phone in Nic's hand made a mournful series of beeps, then when silent.

"Nic? Nicky! Are you there? Oh shit." Joan threw the phone down, exasperated. She had one last piece of information for her brother, something Anita had told her, before their call went terminal. There was an attorney looking for him. A private attorney, not a public defender or ADA, not this time.

Little Tommy appeared in the doorway. He held his book out to her.

"I read it all the way."

"Good boy. Let's pick another one."

"OK, Mommy. Mommy, you said *shit*."

"Did I, honey?" She took a knee and beckoned him to her side. "Oh, I'm sorry," she said, stroking his head. "I shouldn't have. Do you accept my apology?"

"Yes," he said and hugged her. "I love you, Mommy."

"I love you too, dear one."

"Mommy, was that Uncle Nicky?"

"Yes. But promise you won't tell Daddy. Keep it our little secret?"

"Yes, I promise," he said, nodding. He seemed to understand the feud between the two grown-ups.

She held him close as Tommy buried his head in her bosom.

32. ALMOND BISCOTTI

Nic dropped his rucksack on the white shag carpet, drew back the dining room drapes, and peered into the garden. He'd made it home by cab, stopping at the market for a few provisions, but was too tired to make dinner.

The perennials he'd planted in the early spring had been transformed by neglect and a parching summer into gray carcasses, listing to one side as if praying for a sip of rainwater. The annual color spots were completely obliterated. Only the hearty geraniums and ice plants remained viable, though even they looked beaten down by the afternoon heat.

He walked through the house as if for the first time. Stopping at the wall of framed pictures, he encountered Richard, alive as ever, submerged in a hot tub tippling margaritas with Dale.

The sunlight reflected brightly off the white piano in the den, forcing him to squint. *Where the hell is Birdy?* he thought, looking around, until he remembered the bird was with Leland. Richard's desk drawers were locked. He imagined Leland had taken possession of the cash and gun as well.

Nic returned to the living room and sat in the blue recliner, still troubled by the events of the day.

Nic had been back in Morley for a couple of days. He'd spent the first night sleeping upright at the Greyhound station, preferring to avoid the stifling environment of the shelters. From there he'd gone directly to the Morley Life Resource Center, where he used the facilities to wash himself and the clothes he'd been wearing since he'd split from Yousef and Rex many days ago. After a renewing shower, shave, and change of clothes, he felt prepared to meet his parole officer.

He had checked in with Anita Gomez by collect call the day before, just as Joan had cajoled him to do. Anita did not sound surprised to hear from him and suggested they meet at her favorite coffee bar, It's Bean a While, where she often met her charges. He arrived to find her situated at a table for two, her laptop open and notepad ready. She wore a cream-colored suit and oversize rings and necklace. Her nails, also a pale cream, were impeccable. They clicked as she typed. He sat down across from her.

"I'm so glad I contacted your sister. I've been trying to find you for weeks. I was about to report you as a no-show, had all the paperwork filled out already, see?" She showed him her screen. "All I had to do was hit 'submit.' Truth is, I really didn't want to. I knew you'd be back."

"Thanks."

"I took the liberty of ordering you a coffee. Black with two sugars, as I recall. Biscotti?" She pushed a small plate with two almond biscotti toward him. She had already eaten one herself. Nic wasn't hungry but did want to confirm his status with the police.

"So you're telling me they're not trying to hang something on me?"

"No, no, you're fine. Why? Should they be hanging something on you?"

"Not at all."

"Good, let's keep it that way. No, all they want is to talk to you about the violence at the town hall meeting. You were there, and they want your statement, that's all. Just meet with them, tell the truth, and you'll be done. No, *I'm* the one you should be worried about," she said, tapping her chest. "We've got our own mess to clean up." Her voice was firm but not judging. "So, Nic, where exactly have you been?"

"Sorry, Anita, I didn't mean to blow off our meetings."

"We're supposed to meet every couple of weeks. You missed two meetings, which is definitely not good. You're in better shape now that you've reemerged, but—"

"So we're cool?"

"No, we are not cool. Answer the question. Where were you? You disappeared and did not inform me of your new location."

"What new location? All my stuff's still at the house. It's not like I moved away or something."

"Moved, disappeared, what's the difference? Where the hell were you, on a Sandals vacation?"

"Sorry, I was kind of in shock when Richard died. Everything happened so fast, I—"

"OK, so don't tell me. I'll assume you were hiding out somewhere. That's a red flag for sure." She scowled and was about to move on when her eyes lit up. "I know, let's call it bereavement time!" She searched her screen for the right button, then clicked 'Other,' which opened a free-text box. "I'm sure you must have been grieving after the death of Mr. Kornbluth." She began typing. "How do you spell bereavement?"

Nic pondered the tumultuous months under Richard's roof, the wild days and nights, their altercation after the town hall, and finally his abrupt departure to the streets. He'd harbored every emotion imaginable that night: anger, fear, guilt, shame, alarm, despair, distraction, apprehension, revulsion. Why not throw in a little grief?

"Grief? Sure, grief. I had grief. Definitely grief."

"Good," she said. "Now we're getting somewhere." She clicked through the online form, then referred to her list. "OK, now, about your new sponsor. Who did you have in mind?"

"I hadn't thought much about it."

"You'd better think about it now. Your parole sponsor—who also happened to be your employer; we'll get to that in a second—has just passed away. We'll need to identify a new one as soon as possible. We've got a little breathing room, given the unusual circumstances of his death, but not for long. That disappearing act of yours really put us in a bind. Now the clock's ticking."

"I don't know anyone here." *No one who isn't living in a tent,* he thought.

"How about your sister? She did it last time. It's the safest option, but it would mean moving back to Arkansas."

"No fu— Sorry, no frigging way. I'm not going back to that hellhole. Besides, the brother-in-law won't have it. He doesn't want me within a hundred miles. Thinks I'm gonna be a bad influence on his little family."

"What a surprise. Look, you might want to go see my friend Donna. She's a good egg. Upstanding citizen, lots of connections, that sort of thing. People look up to her, civic-minded people, progressive types with strong opinions about criminal justice reform, know what I mean? She may be able to help you get hooked up with someone." She wrote Donna's name and number on the back of one of her cards. "I'll let her know to expect you."

He took the card and set it on the table without looking at it.

"Now, about a job. Got anything lined up?"

"Nope."

"So I'm afraid you're going to have to check in with the unemployment office."

"Oh, for Christ's sake. Really?" He was beginning to doubt the wisdom of returning to Morley. "That place is a total waste."

"I know, I know. But unless you have a job, starting like today, you're going to have to show the parole board you're at least making a good faith effort to find one." She handed him a glossy full color pamphlet with directions to the county's Employment Development Department. The cover depicted a happy constituent being helped by a caring and knowledgeable office worker.

"Great." He flippantly tossed the pamphlet on the table.

"I am trying to help you, Mr. Troxell. You would do well to lose the attitude, at least while I'm sitting here busting my behind to keep you out of jail."

"Sorry."

"And while we're on the subject of employment, have you ever considered losing the, uh . . ." She tapped her own neck, indicating the location of the swastika that adorned Nic's. "If so, this may be the time."

He pulled up his collar in an attempt to hide it, but it lay just below the jawline; nothing helped. It had been an embarrassment for years, one that served him well in prison but crippled his life on the outside.

"I'll think about it."

"Good. In the meantime, wear a turtleneck. Now, what about a place to live? What about funds?"

"Do I look like I have any funds?"

She ignored his snark. "I am hoping you'll be able to go back to living at your previous abode, temporarily that is, until the estate is settled. At least you'll have a roof over your head. That's a start. But what do you plan to do about basic living expenses?"

"Unemployment, right?" He waved the pamphlet. "Won't that take care of it?"

"Not for a while, friend. Average time for them to cut a check is about four weeks. You'll have to figure something out till then. Which brings me to my final point." She handed him the card of Leland Lam.

"What's this," he asked, examining the card.

Leland L. Lam, Esq.
Attorney at Law
Estate Planning, Wills, Trusts, Probates

"He is—or rather *was* Mr. Kornbluth's attorney."

"What's he want?"

"I have no idea. If I had to guess, he's looking to hire you back as caretaker for the property. Call him. Fingers crossed; that'd kill two birds with one stone. Hopefully there's some pocket money in it for you, at least for the short term. Please be up-front with him about needing some cash. You worked long hours for that guy without much to show for it. Just saying."

"Will do."

"OK, good. Now, I understand there was a bird at the house when Mr. Kornbluth died?"

"Mr. Bird."

"Yes, Mr. Bird. So good news for you; he's also been taking care of the bird."

"The lawyer? Wow, that's dedication."

"I know, right? How much fun could that be?"

Nic did not answer. His thoughts flew back to the first time he'd met Birdy, the day Richard had introduced him to the chore of cleaning his cage. Since then he'd spent long afternoons in one-sided conversations with Birdy; he felt they had developed a close rapport.

"Was there anything else?"

"No, that should do it for now." She rose and offered her hand. "Nic, I am so, so glad you decided to get in touch with me. I know it's been a lot these past few weeks. But I've seen people rise above far worse situations and make new lives for themselves. I believe you can too. Hunker down, stay clean, take one day at a time." She flipped over her business card on the table. "Here you go. My contact info has changed a little. And call Donna. Let me know how things are going. I'm always here if you want to talk. Otherwise I'll see you in two weeks."

"Thanks. I'm going to try." He actually meant it. He nodded to her from the door as he passed into the street.

Anita brought her empty cup to the counter and helped herself to a refill. She had established the little coffee shop as her alternate office. They knew her by name, and she felt at home there. She waved at the barista who was wiping down the espresso machine. The morning crowd had died down, and no new customers were in line.

"Is this a good time?" she asked.

"Yes, perfect. I'll be right there."

Anita sat back at her table in preparation for her next meeting. She poured a splash of milk into her coffee. She did not stir but allowed the brown and white liquids to dance and swirl in her cup naturally. As she munched on a biscotto, Anita flipped her notebook to the next page and opened another online form. The barista came out from behind the counter. She was visibly pregnant, moving slowly and cautiously, ungainly in her late third trimester. Her thick, short-cropped hair stood straight at attention, held up by a red bandanna encircling her head. Her substantial arms, legs, and belly pressed against her tight blouse and leggings. She sat down in the chair opposite Anita, the one that Nic had just previously occupied, and noticed the seat bottom was warm. Anita looked at her sympathetically.

"So, Darla, how are things?"

Nic called Leland Lam, Esq., immediately after meeting with Anita, and the attorney invited him to his office. Nic's intention was to cut a deal that would allow him to stay in the house on Dahlia Lane temporarily. In the meantime he would be willing to care for the house, even provide aid and attendance for old Birdy, for expenses only but otherwise for free while Richard's affairs were settled. He hoped they would take him up on his offer and not throw his ass out. He'd had enough of the street.

Nic spent his last three dollars on two busses, the 78 and the 149, to get to downtown Rellman. He walked from the bus stop along the tree-lined boulevard, through the parking lot replete with Teslas and Lexuses, then toward the entrance of the tall glass-clad building. The powerful air conditioning nearly blew the massive door out of his hand when he pulled it open. A well-spoken security guard in a crisp white uniform shirt with an official-looking patch sat low behind his counter, monitoring screens of the building grounds, stairwells, and parking lot. He greeted Nic, pointed to a sign-in sheet, and asked politely who he was there to see. While Nic wrote on the sheet, the guard eyed him suspiciously but soon concluded he was no threat. He had gotten used to seeing every description of human walk through these doors seeking the services offered therein.

A whisper-quiet elevator catapulted Nic to the eighteenth floor so rapidly his ears popped. The Lam Legal Group occupied the entire floor. He received the same welcome from Lam's receptionist as he had on the first floor—professional, restrained, wary—and took a seat in the waiting area overlooking the city.

Attorney Lam welcomed Nic cordially into his office, a vast space with outsize furnishings that made Lam, himself a slight man in a beautifully tailored, fashionably diminutive suit, appear as a small boy playing dress-up in Daddy's den. He enunciated perfect English in a silky baritone.

"So, Mr. Troxell. How are you holding up? I know you've been through a lot these past few weeks."

"I'm fine," Nic said tersely. *How does he know what I've been through?* he thought. *Lawyers always pretend to know everything.*

"Good. I hope we can get to know each other a little better as time goes on. I'll get right to the point. As you may have figured out by now, I am the executor of Mr. Kornbluth's estate."

"Oh."

"Richard spoke of you often, Mr. Troxell. He contacted me about your arrangement before you arrived in Morley. To be perfectly blunt, I advised strongly against it, thought it was risky, to say the least."

"Risky? For who? I was taking a risk too."

"Yes, but of course you were . . ." He hesitated. "Never mind, water under the bridge. Richard had done his homework and seemed to be very comfortable with things."

"Homework. Like checking up on me?"

"I checked up on you, Mr. Troxell, with the approval of Mr. Kornbluth. Wouldn't you have done the same? I actually advised that we write a contract between the two of you, sort of a prenup, setting out expectations and what have you, but he wouldn't hear of it. Richard always led with his heart, not his head; I don't need to tell you that. He had a penchant for helping people he thought needed help, one lost soul at a time."

Nic sat silently in the overstuffed leather chair. He felt scrutinized, judged, even despised but refused to reveal himself, wearing the deadpan expression he had honed over so many years of navigating a hard and unfair life.

"You seem to have touched his heart in ways that no one had done before, not since the passing of his friend Dale. You know about Dale, of course," said Lam, speaking in the present tense of Richard's paramour. "His passing left a tremendous hole in Richard's heart. The whole town really. Everyone missed him terribly. Richard was of course devastated. It took him weeks to emerge from a very deep melancholy. Honestly, I didn't think he was going to make it, but eventually he pulled himself out.

"Anyway, while Dale was alive, everything was held jointly between them. After his death it all reverted to Richard. To his surprise, and mine, Dale had effectively cut out his entire family. I suspect it was revenge for their having shunned him early on for his lifestyle choices, you know. But it stood up in probate, and Richard was left with a very nice bequest."

"Not sure why you're telling me all this," Nic broke in, leaning forward. "Listen, here's the deal. Bottom line, I need a job and a place to stay. Otherwise it's either back to Plainfield or back to Arkansas, and I'm not having either. I got pretty good at running the show at Richard's house. Maintained the yard, the house, did all the small jobs inside and out. Never needed to call a handyman. The hair salon too. Plumbing, electrical. Even took care of the bird. I'm offering to do it all again, starting now. Expenses only, plus a little spending money if that's doable. I hear you're dealing with the bird yourself; I know how much fun that is. So how about it? I can start today. Tell the family or whoever it'll be a lot cheaper than hiring someone else. Even if they want to sell, it'll take a while, and in the meantime, they'll need to keep the place up."

Leland Lam leaned back with his fingertips together. "It may be best if I share a letter Richard wrote just before his passing." He passed an envelope to Nic, his name written on the front in Richard's recognizable hand. "I think it will explain a lot."

"What's this?" he asked.

"Go ahead, read it. I've got some paperwork to catch up on. I'll be just out there." Lam rose and exited his private office. Nic carefully unsealed the envelope, extracted the letter, and read it silently:

My dear Nicholas,

Well, here we are, come full circle. I don't know how I got here, wherever that may be, but I hope you are well and still above ground. I have a few things to say to you that I never got around to, so here goes.

You remember when we first met online? I didn't know you at all. You were just a handsome face with a sad story, like so many of your fellows sitting in jail waiting for the day you'd be free. But I saw something in you then, something very special. Turns out I was right.

I wanted to see you get the break you deserved, Nicky. That's why I asked you to come and share my life with me. When I think of all you've been through, someone as smart and sensitive as you—well, it just broke my heart. I know you wouldn't have done half the things you've done in life if you'd gotten the love you needed, something we all deserve but so few of us get enough of.

I've been lucky in life, it's true, and I've done well. But I also busted my butt. I've been tough, made some smart deals, and looked the other way when maybe I shouldn't have. I never judged my own actions, when I might have been harder on myself. Mostly, I never thought much of anyone else but me.

It's been a good time all around, and I have no real regrets. I have made so many mistakes I can't count them all; though, funny, as I near the end of this long journey, I remember each one and the hurt it must have caused. I still don't know how to make amends for all those terrible deeds, and I guess I'll go to my grave with an unbalanced account. But I think I might have a chance to do something that could help just a little bit.

As they always say, you can't take it with you. I left behind a pretty big nest egg along with a lot of unfinished business. Maybe I'm feeling a little guilty now that I'm at the end. Maybe I'm just trying to redeem myself from the other side in the eyes of God and Man. Call it a dying man's last grasp at salvation. I sincerely want my good fortune to help others, something I never could bring myself to do while I was still walking around. I know you will be able to figure it out for me.

Nic, my love for you is undying, though I can't say the same for this old corpse of mine. I know I've been a royal pain sometimes. But you were the best thing that ever happened to me. I hope you can find it in your heart to forgive me for all the hurt I must have caused you. Perhaps my little gift will help you do that. Otherwise I may need to come back and ghost you until my soul can rest easy.

Please take what I have given you and do good in the world. Maybe we can both be saved, together.

Your friend always,

Richard

Nic read and reread Richard's letter, as Lam looked on. It didn't make any sense to him at first, but its implications were slowly sinking in.

"Lots to process, I imagine," said Lam, trying to be supportive.

"Mm-hm."

"Let it percolate for a while. To answer your question, I am fine with your resuming your duties as caretaker for the property, if that's what you really want."

Nic was deeply relieved. He momentarily dropped his surly facade. "Oh, that's great, man, thanks. Thanks a lot. I can go back right away? I don't think I'm ready for another night on the . . . I mean, out on my own."

"Yes, you can go back this afternoon if you wish. You know the security code?"

"Yup, zero-two-one-four. Richard's birthday."

"Good, here are the keys."

"Got my own," Nic said, pulling out a keyring from his pocket.

"Yes, of course."

Lam assured Nic he would have a warm, secure, clean, tidy, and fully functioning home to move back into. In addition to arranging the cleanup, the attorney had also assumed responsibility for the electric, water, sewer, gas, internet and trash bills, the car payments, insurance payments, tax payments, and mortgage payments, even the cable bill, though no one was watching cable in the empty house. He had done so out of pocket, knowing once the estate was settled he would be reimbursed.

"But there is more."

"Go on." Nic was hoping the subject had finally turned to finances, expecting to be rewarded a few grand in "keep quiet" money—a tiny percentage of the estate but enough to ward off a claim of disinheritance.

"Nic, I need to discuss the will with you in detail."

"Sure, man, sure. I know the drill. Family swooped in and are eager to sell the place."

"No, not exactly. Here you go." He handed Nic a thick sheaf of bound papers, Lam's own working copy of the will, littered with Post-its and margin notes. He pointed to the pertinent paragraphs circled in yellow marker. "You might as well read it for yourself."

Nic took the document from him and read it.

To Mr. Nicholas Troxell, my friend and companion, I leave the entirety of my estate, including each of the assets listed below, described in detail in Appendices A through L, and commonly known as:

1) the house and lot on Dahlia Lane, my principal residence
2) sole controlling interest in MRK Holdings, LLC, and MRK Management, LLC
3) the commercial shopping center known as Morley Plaza, including all rental properties and adjacent land, and all current and future income resulting from these properties and land
4) the residential lot and apartment complex on Copley Terrace, including all resultant rental income
5) nine residential lots and homes on Forsythe Drive, including all resultant rental income
6) four residential lots and homes on Macalister Street, including all resultant rental income
7) all assets contained in my checking accounts, savings accounts and certificates of deposit held at Morley Community Bank
8) the contents of my safe deposit box, held at the main branch of Morley Community Bank
9) all of my paper assets, stocks, and bonds, including current and future dividend payments
10) all other personal items not specifically named, including all clothing, jewelry, household furnishings, and appliances
11) my beloved Subaru
12) Mr. Bird

Nic looked at the long list in disbelief. "This can't be real" he scoffed, tossing the papers on the desk. "No way."

"Oh, it's real all right. Why, you look upset. I'd think you'd be pleased."

Nic shook his head. "This will never stand up. You know someone is going to challenge this, and they'd win too."

"I cannot guarantee that no one will challenge Richard's will. It happens all the time, but in your case, I don't believe they'd be successful, even if they tried. The best defense in these cases is an airtight document, and I am certain this one is."

"Why so sure?"

"Because I wrote it. Richard and I met about a month ago, right here at this desk. He asked me if it was possible to leave everything to one person. I assured him it was; I had no idea at the time he meant you. But he appeared to be of sound mind and very clear about what he wanted to do. He made his wishes known to me in great detail, and I included them in his will verbatim. He did so, by the way, without any sense of coercion or undue influence and said as much."

"But, Mr. Lam, you know about me, about my record. Anyone gets wind of this, even if they just spent one night with him twenty years ago, they could trump up some kind of palimony suit, say that he made them promises, which would not surprise me if he did, and then come after me. You're sure there's no one waiting in the bushes out there?"

"We did a thorough investigation, even hired a private investigator. We couldn't turn up anyone. What's more, we made a video recording of Richard basically reading an edited version of that letter he wrote to you, plus that list there and some other impromptu comments. He gave quite a compelling speech. Want to see it?"

"Nope, no thanks."

"I'll send you a copy for your records, just in case. He talked about autonomy, self-determination, dreams fulfilled, how he wanted to do good in the world after he was gone. He talked about you a lot, how kind and gentle you were, how principled. Called you his success project. Made a convincing argument too. It's unlikely any reasonable judge would think otherwise. I believe we're good for now, Nic. As good as we can be."

Nic rubbed his brow as he ran the list again. He considered the consequences of Richard's generosity. He knew how to boost a car radio or win a bar fight, how to fix a fence or unclog a toilet, but those grunt skills would no longer cut it. The demands of the straight world, a world he had successfully avoided until now, suddenly lay at his doorstep. *My life is over. It'll never be the same again.*

"So what now?"

"That depends. How much experience have you had in real estate and finance?

"None."

"Asset management."

"Same."

"Have you ever had a bank account? Written checks?"

Nic was silent. He recalled when his mother, before she took off for good, had marched him down to the local bank to open a savings account with him. She held his hand and walked up to the teller saying, "This young man would like to open an account at your institution. Nicholas, give the man your money," and Nic handed up his three dollars and forty cents, the amount left over from the five dollars in birthday money he had received from his aunt. He had already spent a dollar sixty at the corner store for doughnuts and a chocolate milk, but his mom had insisted he save the rest. The account accrued twenty-eight cents interest before his dad caught wind and closed it out.

Since then, he had lived a cash-in-pocket existence, until he had moved in with Richard.

"No, no bank accounts."

"That's fine. We see this not infrequently. We'll work on it together, get you up to speed. Fortunately, I have my CFP as well, so I can advise you formally."

"Your what?"

"Certified Financial Planner." He handed Nic a different business card from the one he already had. "I'll help you sort things out."

"Hmm, wouldn't that be a conflict of interest? I mean, you being the executor of the will and also advising on investments?"

Lam looked impressed and a little chagrined. "Great question. See, you have plenty of savvy in this area already. Simple answer, yes. There are a couple of disclosure forms to fill out to make it all legal. But let's cross that bridge later. No need to delve into that today."

"OK, later then."

"For right now, let's get you back on track. The first of the month is coming fast, and you're about to receive a lot of rent checks all at once. Then there's the monthly expenses. Don't want to get in arrears on those. I can walk you through all that whenever you're ready. We prepared a power of attorney for you, which you will need to transfer all real property deeds to your name at the county office, plus bank accounts, credit cards, and everything else. Also, you might want to consider putting everything into a trust at some point."

"I can't think about all that right now."

"Of course. Why don't you get yourself a good night's sleep and we'll talk tomorrow? Or better yet, take the weekend off, how's that? We'll chat Monday morning. I'll set you up with my assistant, Greta. She's a specialist in these matters. She has a great checklist she can walk you through. Sound good?"

"OK, sounds like a plan." Nic turned to leave then stopped. "I, uh . . . don't actually have any money right now. Could I possibly get a small—"

"Advance? Sure. Will a thousand do for now? That should get you through the weekend." He handed Nic an envelope with ten one-hundred-dollar bills. Nic signed a receipt and left Lam's office relieved, anxious, and confused.

Nic rose stiffly from the blue recliner and walked into the kitchen. He ran his finger along the sideboard and noticed it was polished clean. The kitchen walls and floors were scrubbed, the glassware and dishes neatly arranged, and the entire house swept, vacuumed, and mopped. Even the dent on the refrigerator door had been wiped spotless.

He found a business card on the kitchen table, with "Thanks for choosing us!" and a smiley face handwritten on the back:

New Morning Restoration
Specialists in Trauma Cleanup
and Biohazard Removal

Nic had accrued quite a few pieces of paper in the past twenty-four hours, as is often the case at times of calamity and crisis. He slid the card into his shirt pocket, along with the one from Anita, two from Lam, and a torn scrap with the phone number for Detective Sergeant Crowell, with whom he was to meet tomorrow regarding the investigation of the Town Brawl.

He returned to the living room and collapsed.

33. PURPOSE

A brilliant sun filtered through a lone spider's web outside Pickwick's bay window. A drenching downpour had spilled recklessly over the gutter, causing its proprietor to scurry upward, where she sheltered patiently under the eave. Now she cautiously climbed back down into the sun's warming rays, perching herself at the hub of the tenacious radial spokes she had built to await whatever would next cross her path.

Inside the store, Geoff swooped around the window's frame and sill with the narrow vacuum tip, pulling cobwebs out of the air. Flies seeking the store's cool comfort had found themselves trapped, scaling the glass in all directions or ramming into it repeatedly in search of an exit, eventually falling exhausted to the sill. Geoff's vacuum sucked up their desiccated bodies with a *thwippp*, sending them along the hose—*bbrrttt!*

Donna busily inspected an old vinyl record: Beethoven's Symphony No. 7 by von Karajan. She blew the dust off the disc, checked for gouges, and set it on the turntable. The scratchy version of the masterwork immediately enhanced her joy.

"What a day, right?" she cheerily called out to Geoff over the majestic tune. "So bright."

"Yup, really nice," he called back.

The returning sun had just come to rest on her burgundy floor runner when a tall broad shape filled the doorway, blocking its rays. Silhouetted by the light, it was impossible to see its face or features as it walked into the store, past Geoff, and straight toward Donna.

Sensing an ominous presence, Geoff quickly silenced his machine and came to full alert, nonchalantly circling the store and reemerging on Donna's left flank.

"Hello. Welcome in." She turned down the von Karajan. "Beautiful day, isn't it?"

Nic looked around the store, sussing out the small space and its thousands of titles displayed in a labyrinth of shelves, bookstands, and glass cases that seemed to go on forever.

"I'm looking for Donna. Anita sent me."

"Sure. You must be Nic. Anita called to say you might be stopping by."

Framed by her books and proffering a serene smile, Donna reminded him of Margaret, the head librarian at Plainfield Prison, who could always find a volume to spark his interest among its sadly sparse collection. He hoped Donna would be as resourceful as Margaret.

Geoff hovered over Donna's shoulder, listening to their exchange. He eyed the other man uncomfortably, his gray hoodie, tight-fitting jeans, and panoply of tattoos on his hands, chest, and neck. He thought he recognized him from his weird encounter at the hair salon but couldn't be sure; it had happened so fast.

"New tatt?" Geoff asked in an attempt to break the ice, noticing an area below the man's right jaw line covered with a gauze bandage that seeped orange-pink fluid.

"Nope."

"Removed one then?"

Nic did not respond but looked around uneasily.

"So how can we help today?" Donna asked.

"Like I said, Anita sent me. She spoke to you, right?"

"About needing a parole sponsor? And suggesting I might help, since I sponsor one of her charges already?"

"Yeah, that's right."

"So . . ."

"So . . ."

"So are you asking me to be your sponsor?"

"Yeah, I'm asking."

Geoff winced. *Ooh, you'll need to ask a little nicer than that, friend,* he thought.

"I'll need to know a little more about you first, Nic," Donna replied in a teacherly tone—calm, exacting but sympathetic.

"Such as?"

"Such as your crime," she said cheerily, "how long did you serve, how long you've been out, what are your goals now. So tell me about yourself."

Geoff, never having been this close to a real ex-con before, stood wide-eyed, eager to hear all about Nic's infractions. In thirty seconds Nic related an abridged version of his conviction in Indiana for "manslaughter two," his time served and time remaining, the arrangement with Richard to do his parole here in California, and his benefactor's recent unforeseen death. He made sure to leave out any details that might prove unflattering to himself, also omitting the fact that he had taken over all of Richard's holdings, effectively making him their landlord. He saw no reason to enlighten them on this point.

As Donna concentrated on Nic's story, an excited Geoff shouted, "Oh my God, now I know where I've seen you before. You're that guy."

"What guy?" he asked.

"The Town Brawl Hero. They must have showed that clip of you a hundred times on the news, plus like a hundred thousand reposts, the one where you're saving the old hairdresser at the city hall riot. You're a real internet phenomenon."

"Oh my, yes," said Donna. "Anita didn't warn me we'd be in the presence of a celebrity. The whole town's been looking for you—to thank you."

"He died right after, though," offered Geoff. "Too bad. He seemed all right."

"Yes, tragic," Donna chimed in. "Still, you did a wonderful thing, risking your own life for him."

Nic did not want to be a hero. After weeks of hiding out in the woods, dodging the police, and making himself invisible, exposure to public scrutiny made him jumpy. But he was desperate now and knew it. He pressed his case, assuming his most civilized veneer.

"Sorry, I'm kind of tight for time right now, so I'm asking politely, ma'am, will you please take over as my parole sponsor."

"No."

"No? What do you mean? Why not?"

"Nic, I understand your plight, and my heart goes out to you, but I'm afraid I won't be able help you in this regard."

Geoff jumped in. "See, she's got a lot on her plate right now," he said with a measure of pride. "Like running the Morley Campaign for Equitable Development and figuring out what's going happen to this very shopping mall we're at right now."

"I'm sure Nic doesn't want to hear about all that, but... You're aware of the massive building project planned for this section of town? Well, everything came to a screeching halt after the commotion that night at the town hall. We were all at a loss for what to do next. So once the dust settled, we created a brand-new committee to figure it all out, and they elected me chair."

"That takes up all of her spare time, see?"

"Geoff is correct. And what with keeping the shop open, plus working down at the mayor's office with the planning department, I simply could not take on another project right now. But I'm flattered that Anita thought of me."

"She's running for mayor too!" blurted Geoff.

"Now, that might be a little premature. Call me crazy, but after spending all that time downtown, I seem to have caught the bug. Yes, I'm thinking about dipping my toe. Can you believe it?" Geoff and Donna laughed together.

Nic felt stymied, toyed with, marginalized, and out of options. "I'm outta here," he said, spinning on his heels.

"But I can certainly ask around," she called to him. "Maybe someone on the committee would be willing to—"

He was half way to the door when Geoff shouted eagerly, "Wait! Wait, I'll do it! I'll be your sponsor." The room went silent, save for the ticking clock and the sound of a bird chirping in the hydrangea outside the door. Donna turned squarely in Geoff's direction, a broad quizzical smile across her face betraying her shocked disbelief. "Seriously," he repeated, "I'd like to do it."

"You know," Donna said after a moment, "that's an absolutely terrific idea."

"I know, it's brilliant, right?" agreed Geoff, though he was not sure why he had volunteered. Was it his fascination with criminals and crime, his deep instinct to protect Donna, or his innate impulsiveness? All were at play in that moment.

Nic turned reluctantly and walked back to the desk. He was not impressed with Geoff, his cherubic face, callow ways, and quirky mannerisms. And he was thoroughly annoyed with the overly cheerful Donna. But he faced a yawning gap that needed to be bridged, so for now expediency won out. He figured he could always abandon Geoff later if he got sick of him, and in the meantime, he'd be easy enough to manipulate.

"OK, sure. Let's do this. What's the name again?"

"Geoff," he said, offering his hand in earnest. They locked eyes and shook vigorously, each applying his strongest grip and matching the other squeeze for squeeze. "Good, then," Geoff said gleefully. "Done and done."

Donna, seeing order rescued from chaos, could not have been more pleased.

"Wonderful! Welcome to the family."

Nic suppressed his visceral distaste at having to join this sorry lot. He simply nodded and grinned.

"Come with me," she said triumphantly. "Geoff, can you mind the store for a minute, please?" She had already disappeared around the corner and into the stacks. Nic had no choice but to follow but not before catching a sidelong grin from Geoff that told him, *Yup, that's how it is around here. Get used to it.*

A moment later he found Donna in the Religion/Spirituality section. Her fingers ran along the spines looking for just the right book to consummate their new alliance.

"Ah, here we go." She handed a book to Nic and immediately returned to her search.

Nic read the title silently: *Forgiveness: Releasing Your Past and Getting Your Life Back*. Donna did not allow him time to react before handing him another title.

"There. I think you'll enjoy these."

"*Love's Practical Lessons: A Twelve Step Course in Mercy*. Listen," Nic said, handing the books back to her, "I appreciate what you and Joe—"

"Geoff."

"What you and Geoff are doing for me, but I can't really use these."

She refused to take them back. "Nope, you take these and read them. Just the big ideas if you like, but read them you must. You want a sponsor, right? That's the deal. Besides, you're part of our family now, and this is required reading. Stick them under your pillow. Maybe you'll absorb some of the wisdom that way. We could all use a little more wisdom, don't you agree."

Nic felt his shoulders relax and teeth unclench as his defenses suddenly and inexplicably fell away. "Look," he said in softer tones, "I'm not sure what kind of person you think I am, but there's no book that's gonna cure what I have. I'm not a nice person, ma'am; ask anyone who knows me. I don't deserve this kind of attention. I don't want it. I'm just trying to get from one day to the next without, pardon my French, fucking up again. So please, take your books and let me be on my way. I'll find someone else to sponsor me. Or maybe I should just go back to Arkansas, or back inside where I belong."

"Wait. Nic, it's true, I hardly know you, and I'm not here to judge. But anyone with eyes can see you've lived in pain your whole life, which I'll bet didn't start with jail, am I right? You've been through a lot, a life full of twists and turns, some bad breaks and not always the right choices, maybe not enough love when you needed it the most. This is a turning point for you, friend. You're out on your own now, free and unfettered."

"I don't feel free," he confessed. "I feel hunted. All the time."

"You can never be free as long as you carry around all that baggage with you from years gone by. Wake up! Life is giving you a priceless opportunity to shake off all that negativity and start a whole new chapter. You'd like that, wouldn't you? To be truly free? Free from being angry all the time. Free from all those sad feelings and memories and dreams that haunt you."

"How do you know all this?"

"Not to be hard-hearted, Nic, but you're not exactly unique. There are a million people just like you. We all carry around baggage, plenty of it. Some people are handed a real shit sandwich of a life, and still they do just fine. It's because they make the choice to step out of the darkness and into the light when they're given that chance. Opportunities are like portals in the universe. They open up for us on occasion, and if we have the courage, we can step through into a new life. To be liberated from that darkness is a divine gift, and we must recognize and accept it with grace. Otherwise, *wham*, the portal closes. It doesn't wait around forever. If we're stubborn or afraid or just lazy, it slams shut, and all we can do is hope it will open up again someday, which it may, but for some people it does not." She pulled back her sleeve. "You see this scar? A poor soul attacked me not long ago, just outside my store here. Boy, I was upset about it for a long time. Geoff's still pissed off at whoever it was. But soon I realized that if I didn't forgive that person, I'd have missed one of life's divine opportunities. I dare say the person who did this to me has missed a lot of his."

"I'm not very good at forgiving people."

"You'd better get good at it fast, or else it'll eat you alive. I know it's not easy. It's one of the hardest things we can do. We want to hold on to our anger as tightly as we can or, worse, want to get even, as if revenge will reverse all the wrongs that have been done to us. But forgiveness is like a warm breeze, a gentle rain, a cleansing ray of sun. Take your pick. It renews our spirit, scrubs it sparkling clean. So please, take these. Look at them. I insist. That's the deal."

He wanted to protest but knew the conversation was at an end. He would do as she asked. Her wise words and kind eyes seemed to drill down into his soul. He was desperate to find his way back to stable ground and would need their help to do it, so he would take her silly books. But a strange sensation overwhelmed him as they walked back to the desk, as if a gangrenous limb had finally been severed, replaced with something alive, fresh, unknown.

Geoff had been watching their interaction on the store's security cameras but quickly closed the app as they approached the front desk.

"I see you have homework," he said to Nic without irony, pointing at the books. "Would you like a bag?"

"No, I'm good." He asked Geoff to write down his name and contact information. "I'll get it to Anita. She'll be in touch with you, I guess."

Geoff gave him a double thumbs-up.

Nic was tempted to divulge more about himself, about the will, his relationship with Richard, his new status as landowner, but thought better of it. He lingered while he found his voice, simply stating with downcast eyes, "I, uh . . . appreciate what you're doing for me, both of you. I'll try not to let you down."

"You won't," Donna replied, "I know you won't."

Back home, Nic leafed through the two books Donna had given him and tossed them on the table. He would get to them eventually, his promise to her crowded out by the words in Richard's letter rolling around in his head: *"Something special in you . . . Best thing that ever happened . . . We all deserve love . . . Forgive me."*

Forgiveness had never been Nic's strong suit, no matter how often he heard how liberating it could be. He was not interested in forgiving his father for his abuses and neglect, or his mother for abandoning him and his sister. And despite Richard's generous gift—no, his ostentatious and absurd gesture—he did not much feel like bestowing absolution upon him either. Not now anyway. He considered it a bribe, a payoff, an indulgence purchased at great cost, with the promise of spending less time in Purgatory and squeaking through the Gates of Heaven unnoticed and unscathed. To forgive him would be to endorse fifty years of his heartless acts. *It's not that easy, Richard old boy,* he chided. Children who spill their Cheerios deserved forgiveness. Well-intentioned acts that have woeful consequences might also be forgiven. Everything else, whether by omission or commission, Nic considered equally evil.

He wandered in a fog from living room to kitchen to dining room, then into the bedroom. The space smelled heavily of Richard; the scent of his cologne mixed with tobacco clung to the walls. As Nic entered Richard's capacious walk-in closet, he gazed down rows and rows of the colorful clothing, number ten on Leland Lam's list, now all his.

The mileposts of Richard's long and serpentine life were depicted in the garments on display: the cardigans, sweater vests, bow ties, button-down shirts, pleated woolen trousers, then the flares, dashikis, polyester shirts with long, long collars, leather toreador jackets, bubble-top platforms, wide and narrow lapels, scarves, loose drawstring pants, pastel silk jackets with sleeves still rolled up, spiked belts, and multicolor inlaid boots. In its respective era, each article would have been considered exquisitely smart. Now they seemed exhausted and forlorn, having already enjoyed their inevitable comeback (as fashion will among youth, fascinated by anything that predates them) before descending into their final demise.

What was Nic supposed to do with all these rancid rags? He refused to wear them, long harboring a phobic superstition about dead men's clothes. Besides, despite regaining some of his lean habitus subsisting on the street, his broad shoulders and long legs would never fit into Richard's tiny shirts and pants anyway. He picked out a few representative examples to prove his point—slinky white knit bell bottoms and size seven ankle boots—and threw them down in disgust.

He vowed to rid himself of the whole mess and would have put off the task to another day, when, in a fit of anguished madness, he furiously began gathering armfuls of clothes on hangers and dumping them one after the other into the middle of the closet floor. He returned to the racks, circling the room until every stainless-steel rod and hook lay bare and empty. A four-foot-high mountain of jumbled garments had now formed, all a tangle, hangers jutting out randomly, nearly filling the room. He climbed over the pile, carefully navigating the ever-tightening space, and nearly skated on a slick patent leather jacket, righting himself at the last moment. He moved on to the built-in white melamine drawers and did not stop until every drawer had been pulled out and overturned, its contents emptied onto the pile: socks, underwear, gloves, cuff links, ties, T-shirts, cargo shorts, bike riding shorts, robes, jackets, sweatshirts, sweatpants, gym shorts, trainers, ball caps, more shirts, more ties, more scarves. The mountain of apparel now stood at over five feet, with hangers and drawers dispersed everywhere. He was breathing heavily now, the veins on his forehead popping out. He turned his fury to the built-in vanity and, with arms thrashing, swept away bottles and tubes of moisturizer, bronzer, concealer, skin tightener, tweezers, brushes, combs, scissors, a personal groomer, and two hair driers onto the floor. One gilt-framed mirror remained on the wall above the vanity. He looked up to see the sweating countenance of a man at his rope's end, hunched over, chest heaving, fiery eyes glaring back at him. He pulled at the frame's edges, and when it wouldn't come, he pulled harder. He then remembered hanging this very mirror for Richard some months ago and using heavy mollies to secure it. This time he yanked with all his strength and the mirror came crunching and cracking and snapping off the wall, pulling chunks of drywall and hardware with it, spidering into small shards as he threw it across the room. Now he was spent for good, staggering about, his breathing labored. He kicked at the detritus, stubbing his toe on a drawer, then screamed up at the ceiling, shrieked so loud in that confined space his own ears throbbed. Now he crumpled in a heap onto his knees, falling headlong into the deep solace of the garment pile, his face buried in it, surrounded by the dense unmistakable smells of the man he had come to hate and to love. Tears gathered at his cheeks. They fell and hit the sleeve of a pink polyester shirt but rolled right off.

34. ALONG CAME BETTY

On a warm spring evening, Jeremy patiently studied the menu board overhead. Would two larges be enough? Three too many? He advanced to the counter.

"One Vegan Delight, one Mega Meat Special, and one Caprese. All large."

"Drinks?"

"Two pitchers of your IPA and eight glasses, please."

The counter guy pointed to the stacks of plasticware by the drink dispenser. Jeremy headed back to the table with his pitchers and a number on a little metal stand, then made a second trip for the yellow tumblers, paper plates, and a thick stack of napkins. He sat down across from Celine and Deb.

"Whatcha get us?" asked Celine, squirming in her seat with childlike glee. Jeremy reported his pizza choices, which caused her to clap in anticipation. He watched her antics warmly. When Celine was happiest, her mood was contagious and gave her an endearing charm. She seemed to him more relaxed than she'd been in months.

They had not seen each other since the night of the pivotal town hall. Celine wanted to share some good news with him, and tonight's organizational meeting promised to be the perfect opportunity for them to chat. (Civic engagement gave her a warm feeling too.)

After all these months, Celine still sought Jeremy's attention and approval, even if he was forever off the table as a lover. She'd stopped home after work and changed out of her office garb into a more flattering white T-neck pullover, black jeggings, and maroon Doc Martens. *You look great,* he'd told her on arrival. She beamed.

Celine had been promoted to the position of district manager, which meant more humane hours and better pay but greater responsibility. Despite this, she was more tranquil and joy-filled than ever. She'd been an attentive pupil to Deb, whose teachings gave her insight into the inner workings of both the central office and their local branch. Celine became an expert in the strengths, vulnerabilities, and quirks of her diverse staff. With these tools, combined with her own native smarts, she got the most out of her employees while maintaining a contented and efficient shop. Their online customer ratings soared, surprising Deb and delighting Celine.

Deb was chock full of joy tonight as well. She had finally left the Social Security office, admitting she no longer had the temperament to deal with other people's delinquent behavior. The gig had been a drag on her soul for years, threatening her mental, physical, and spiritual well-being. She'd grown heavy, stooped and slow carrying her cumbersome burden. Then out of nowhere appeared Celine, the perfect foil for her elegant escape. Whereas Deb took every human transgression personally, Celine marched forward cheerily without looking for agreement. She was a natural.

In the interim Deb and Celine had become an item, which Deb announced to her shocked family one Sunday morning after church. Free of her millstone job *and* hooking up with Celine, she now felt liberated to live on her own terms, read her mystery novels, keep in touch with her bridge buddies, and pursue her beloved quilt making. She quit smoking, took water aerobics classes three days a week, walked every day, lost thirty pounds, and even abandoned her cane. Together they had gone on LGBT-friendly cruises to the Mexican Riviera, taken bus tours of Sonoma wine country, and at least once a month visited the Screaming Eagle Indian casino, where, under Deb's tutelage, Celine became proficient at blackjack. Her newest hobby was healthy eating. Around four o'clock each weekday she would set aside her activities, head to the kitchen, study her online recipes, and have a delicious and creative vegan meal ready by the time Celine arrived home. Over dinner they would gossip and giggle about the eccentricities of staff and patrons at the office, as Celine recounted her successes and failures in the messy realm of government service. Deb loved Celine's storytelling, spiked with gentle humor and a good-natured innocence geared toward a happy ending.

"So what's on the agenda tonight?" asked Celine, glancing at her phone. Donna was not late yet, but by Celine's internal calculus, three sizzling hot pies would soon be on the table, and she hoped that event would align precisely with start time.

"We shall see," said Deb. "Did you see her email? Whoo, that girl's just full of ideas."

"Ideas are good," said Celine, "the more the better. But I hope tonight we can pare things down to a more manageable list."

Jeremy chuckled. "Dream on, girlfriend. Donna is a force majeure. Best to climb aboard and hang on tight."

Jeremy had become a frequent visitor to Pickwick's and was well acquainted with Donna's loveable yet overpowering ways. He considered his trips to the bookshop a refreshing breather from his daily routine. He also found Donna intellectually stimulating and physically pleasing, though she had at least a decade on him. Geoff was always at the shop and kept a tight watch over Donna's exchanges with the tall, fair-haired, blue-eyed Jeremy, but he didn't mind. Geoff was an endless source of entertainment for him—dorky and a little peculiar but quick and funny.

From Geoff he learned about the collapse of the development plans for the mall and surrounding acreage, and the burgeoning grassroots effort to reinvigorate the conversation, this time with input from the "real stakeholders," which meant small business owners and their patrons, apartment renters, homeowners, commuters, nonprofits, contractors, union reps, advocates for the homeless, and yes, even the homeless themselves, although none of the last group had yet shown up.

Jeremy poured himself a beer and offered the same to Deb and Celine, who declined. The sports channel played in the background. A group of enthusiasts at the next table was fully engaged, reacting to every completed pass, breakout run, interference call, or sack. Jeremy was drawn into the game, as the casual fan will be, by the colorful, high-definition display of masculine power and skill. He shouted, "Whoa!" with every adroit interception or violent tackle, siding with Denver, the team closest to them geographically, which made no sense really, since no one in the pizzeria owed any special allegiance to Denver over Atlanta that he could see. The two women completely ignored him, except for throwing him a brief glance with each of his loud interjections, then returning to their own private conversation. Jeremy soon realized they were gossiping about Darla.

"What's that about our mutual friend?" he asked.

"Ex-friend," Celine corrected.

"We've got that in common, eh?"

Deb cared little about her two companions' previous relations with Darla but loved to tell a good story. "I was just explaining how my sources tell me your mutual ex-friend got off pretty easy that night. They could have hung a charge of aggravated assault on her, but she pled to disorderly conduct and simple battery."

"Sounds bad enough," he said.

"Suspended sentence? Probation with community service? Please! She should have done some serious jail time, in my humble opinion. But the judge showed mercy, supposedly because she was pregnant.

"So she *was* pregnant!" gasped Celine. "God, I knew it!"

"Mm-hm. And my source also says the mayor might have exercised some influence with the judge to give her a lighter sentence. Now why on earth do you suppose that was?"

A rattled Jeremy was barely able to keep up with the story.

"Wait, Darla's pregnant?" *How did she get pregnant?* he asked himself. (The usual way, he imagined.) *And whose is it?* He remembered their initial encounter, literally *over* the counter, at Videodrome. Had they used protection? He couldn't say but knew they'd at least tried to during their turbulent weeks together.

"*Was* pregnant, friend. Now she's walking around Rellman with a baby on her hip."

Then total recall. Of course they hadn't used anything the first time, and they were pretty slapdash every other time too.

"Rellman? Since when?" asked Celine. She seemed blasé about the pregnancy, knowing Darla was capable of fucking anything on two feet to get by.

"Yep, Rellman. Go figure."

"Girl movin' up!" They both laughed.

Celine and Deb continued to talk casually about Darla, then focused to other matters of more interest to them. Their voices fell away, replaced in Jeremy's head with a low pounding. He poured himself another IPA; his hand shook as he brought it to his lips. *A kid? How could it be? Who's the father?* There was no denying it could be his. He also knew Darla did a lot of couch surfing; that's how they'd gotten together, after all. He tried to map out the past year, divine the timing of their first hookup, shack up, and final breakup. How old was the kid now? When exactly did she move out, and when did they stop doing it before then? He'd forgotten all these details. *Wait, she was showing at the town hall!* That had been the shocker neither he nor Celine dared to acknowledge out loud. *How far along is a woman when she starts showing?* He had no idea, having had no firsthand knowledge of the miracle of gestation.

He'd been down that road only once, a journey that abruptly ended one Saturday afternoon—driving a girl to the clinic, giving her a hundred dollars, all the money he had, waiting for two hours, then dropping her off at her apartment. He could barely remember her name now. Sandy, maybe? He couldn't recall her face either, only her full, well-proportioned hips and straight brown hair she wore in a bun. He'd felt pangs of remorse that day and for many weeks afterward.

Now years later, a more sober, thoughtful Jeremy appreciated the gravity of making babies. He'd even begun to long for a sweet wife and rug rats of his own, a quaint family scene he'd no doubt picked up from one of his vintage films. But if Darla's kid was his, hadn't he become the most despicable character of all—the rogue father who abandons his child to a cruel and unforgiving world? He had to know.

Jeremy's reverie was cut short when a passel of meeting-goers arrived at once, as if all alighting from the same bus. In walked Dr. Sunita Reddy from ReddyCare, followed by Shannon Wise, head of the West Morley Neighborhood Association; Judy Gershon from Urban Gardens Coalition; and finally Donna and Geoff. Accompanying them was a man Jeremy had never seen before. He seemed intimate with Donna and Geoff, tall and broad-shouldered, wearing a blue V-neck sweater over a white button-down shirt, tan slacks, and brown loafers. He projected an air of humility and dependability. He carried in his left hand a thin leather valise, leaving his right open to shake hands and greet folks.

The group distributed itself around the table after brief hellos and hugs. Donna stood to present their newest member.

"Everyone, please . . . let me introduce a special guest to you all and, I'm hoping, a permanent member of our planning group: Mr. Nicholas Troxell. After the unfortunate passing of our neighbor Richard Kornbluth, Nic has taken over as the new owner of Morley Plaza and most of the properties affected by the Morley Pointe Crossing project. My hope is that, with fresh eyes and renewed energy, we'll continue to design a town center that works for all of our citizens. Nic, did you have any words for the group?"

As if on cue, three hot bubbling pizzas arrived at the table. The smell of cheese and Italian sausage suffused the air, and everyone's mouth watered. Nic sensed no one wanted a long speech, nor would abide any barrier between them and the hot pies.

"Thanks, Donna." He stood and shoved his hands in his front pockets. "Folks, I'll be quick. A lot has happened over the past year. Lots of changes for me and for the town too. I never thought in a million years I'd be standing here talking with you all about making things better. For some reason I got lucky, moving out here, meeting Richard. Most of you didn't know him well. He wasn't perfect, but he was a good man and, in the end, wanted to do the right thing. Donna, Geoff, you all have been really good to me as well. I feel like I've found a home here in Morley, and I want to give back. Sometimes people just need to catch a break, and they can turn their lives around. This project might be a way to give a lot of folks that break, whether it's a good job, getting off the street, or just being treated fairly. Morley's been down for a long time, but now I think the town's ready to get its act together and come roaring back. I hope I can help. Thanks."

The members nodded and applauded, full of praise and admiration for their new associate. His heartfelt speech, and of course ownership of key properties, elevated him from stranger to player in an instant, though not quite reaching "first among equals" status. Donna would forever hold that position.

"Let's dig in," she shouted with elation. "We've got lots to do tonight."

The small group was the perfect size to foster a cohesive identity yet large enough to permit intimate side conversations or brief respites from the colloquy without feeling isolated. Nic fell into the last category. He had overcome the distress of standing before the group but now sat second-guessing his own words. Had he revealed too much about himself or been too toadyish in his praise for Richard and the bookstore couple? He still wondered how he'd arrived in this space and time, and what he could contribute. Just a few weeks earlier, he had hung suspended over an abyss. Something had taken hold of him; he'd been yanked up by the nape like a helpless puppy and dropped into a new reality. These were his people now. For the first time, he had purpose. He felt his own life force stirring within him; it felt natural and good.

Nic owed his transformation in large part to Geoff, his newly appointed parole sponsor and best bud. While Geoff took on these roles gleefully, Nic's natural distrust threatened to shatter the whole arrangement. Geoff doggedly refused to yield to Nic's pessimism, despite Nic's showing up late or not at all for their planned get-togethers. He introduced Nic to his varied interests—contract bridge, American history, foreign languages—and slowly Nic was drawn in. As their relationship warmed, Nic developed a sense of duty to the younger man, discovering their structured routine allowed him to think more clearly, make his P.O. appointments, and take better care of himself.

Nic had lost track of the books Donna had given him, mislaying them for weeks under a pile of unrelated papers. Eventually he found them and tiptoed into their gathered wisdom. It would be a stretch to say he studied them and systematically applied their teachings, but the very act of thumbing through them, or just holding them, had a salutary effect.

He'd met again with Attorney Lam to settle Richard's affairs and transfer titles. He began to see his future more clearly. Managing his many properties seemed to be a task for which he was well suited. It felt good to be on his own, busy most of the day then savoring a job well done as evening fell. He spent time with Geoff and Donna too, though they were homebodies and mostly enjoyed each other's company. They would invite him over to spend evenings working on their community organizing campaign, which they thought great fun but which Nic found quite dry.

Meanwhile, across the table Celine, Shannon, and Donna engaged in an animated three-way chat-and-chew about the good and bad aspects of government. Judy and Dr. Reddy got better acquainted. Deb and Geoff, not having much to say to each other, contentedly looked on with interest, occasionally nodding earnestly and of course eating.

Jeremy continued to stew in his own juice about Darla's baby, nibbling unenthusiastically on a slice of meaty pie. It tasted like cardboard in his mouth.

Donna surveyed the table and, confirming everyone was well into their first slice, called the meeting to order. She tapped her yellow plastic tumbler with her plastic fork, producing a *thunking* sound that made everyone laugh. Conversations quickly died down, all attention fixed on her. Donna's manner was, as always, calm, benevolent, and matter-of-fact. A natural charisma simply poured off her, creating an intimate space within the noisy pizzeria. She was everyone's perfect friend, sister, mother, daughter, lover.

"Again, thank you all for coming. Let's get to it. Our first order of business is to discuss our potential projects, decide what we want to tackle first, then divvy up the work. You'll see a rough list in the handouts."

The group sat deadpan with the lists in front of them. Some reached for more pie. Celine and Deb, the only two authentic bureaucrats in the group, obediently scanned the list. Both came to the same conclusion independently. Celine raised her hand.

"Um, shouldn't we set some ground rules first?" she asked.

All eyes turned to Celine, then back to Donna. Celine's query appeared to take Donna completely by surprise.

"Ground rules?"

"Yes, like meeting etiquette, procedures for raising questions, settling disagreements," replied Celine.

"And rules of respect and inclusion," offered Deb. "And pronouns."

"Pronouns?" asked a confused Geoff.

"Yes, of course. Also, we'll need a SWOT analysis, scope of work statement, timelines, deliverables, a list of stakeholders and potential allies, and a membership policy."

Donna was dumbfounded. She knew she'd be reliant on the knowledge and experience of her allies in the government trenches. But she did not want her feet mired in needless process. Nor, frankly, did she want to share leadership with anyone, not at this juncture.

As the group awaited her response, Geoff in one swift, uncalculated motion resolved the issue and rescued his beloved Donna from Procedure's murky quagmire.

"Just do it," he said abruptly, looking at Deb and Celine not with animosity but a fierce determination to simply have done with it and move on.

"Geoff, that is a wonderful idea," said Donna. "Ladies, I think this would be a terrific project for you to take on. Write those rules, timelines, all that other stuff you mentioned."

"Also, formal mission, vision and value statements. Plus, a Gantt chart," chimed Celine, tickled at having scored points with the group plus landing a critical project for her and Deb to work on together.

"Gantt chart. Sure, why not. Go for it. And bring them back to the group for discussion next time."

"Done," said Celine and Deb simultaneously. They high fived.

"Good. We'll wing it till we get something in writing. Now please take a look at the rough list you have in your handout. It's just a draft; we can add or modify things as we go." They slowly turned their attention to Donna's far-reaching and grandiose list. Shannon suggested that, to make it more manageable, the list be divided into a few big ideas—Building and Construction, Support Services, and Culture Change.

"So under Building and Construction," she read aloud, "I have number one: a three-story mixed-use building with affordable and midlevel housing above, locally based retail shops and businesses on the ground level, plus an attached community center offering classes, meeting spaces, and daycare."

"Nice!" "I love it!" "Sounds like Morley Pointe Crossing, only better!" declared the crowd simultaneously.

"Number two: reconfigure the intersection of Morley and Pine with a traffic circle surrounding a central fountain and brick piazza, food carts, and places to sit and recreate." The group nodded their approval. "Number three: convert at least one five-thousand-square-foot brown field into a tiny-home village with centralized restrooms, shower and laundry facilities, a little library, and a community kitchen."

Shannon turned to the group for feedback, as they sipped their beers and munched on pizza. Jeremy broke the silence, stating out loud what everyone else was thinking.

"A little ambitious, no?" he said, silently noting that few of them had the means to foot tonight's dinner, let alone sufficient capital for a building project.

"Ambitious? Why, yes!" exclaimed Donna, redirecting Jeremy's contrary view. "Bold, improbable, impossible! That is precisely what we want tonight. I know this may be a lot for some of you. I'd simply ask you to have faith in the process. We're in a crisis here. We need to use our collective imagination to create a new reality.

"Imagination is what separates true innovators from everyone else. Just think where we'd be if, ten thousand years ago, someone said, 'Hey, why don't we build a village here,' or 'Let's get out of this dusty old valley.' And the practical response was, 'Ooh, sounds pretty ambitious. No, we're good. We'll just stay here scratching in the dirt, eating ants, starving to death.'" The group laughed at the imagery. "Every successful idea starts with a tiny seed. Nurture it, water it, give it sunlight, and it'll grow into something magnificent. But you've got to have faith."

"The substance of things hoped for," said Nic as all eyes turned to him. "What? Just saying."

"Why, that's beautiful, Nic, thank you," said Donna, heartened that someone, perhaps the most important member of their group, was starting to get it.

"I read it in a book." He winked at her.

"So what you're saying," Dr. Reddy recapped in her charmingly dense accent, "is that we've got to dream big now, so that someday we may get everything we're asking for?" Donna and the group nodded their agreement.

"OK, then," said Shannon, "after that kumbaya moment, I will continue." She went on to catalog the remainder of their to-do list. The vision to end homelessness included an organic farm to train, employ, and empower the homeless; a voucher system to incentivize camp cleanups; an enhanced recycling program to turn plastics into usable materials; peer-to-peer mentorship for repatriation into society; fast-track access to on-site mental health and addiction services; and an overall philosophy promoting the dignity of work, self-esteem, and personal responsibility.

"Thanks, Shannon. Nicely summarized. Now, who wants to take on what?" Silence again ensued as they looked at the daunting list before them. "Listen, we may be a tiny band of warriors now. But as our numbers grow, so will our influence. But for now, on this beautiful spring night, among friends, pizza, and beer, just take a look, see what fires your passion. Like this one," she read aloud, "'rerouting traffic through a roundabout, with an Italian-style piazza and fountain.' Wow! What? Millions of dollars and years of planning away, right? Here's how I would approach it. Start with a simple phone call to the Department of Transportation. See if there are already plans for improving that intersection. Take a friendly sit-down with a councilperson or a city planner. Put in some face time, drink some coffee, plant an idea, build a relationship, make it personal. Then if the idea starts to take hold, find allies, link up with the business community, recruit their support. Baby steps, see?"

Dr. Reddy cautiously raised her hand. She offered to look into wraparound counseling and addiction services for the local homeless population.

"I'd love to help with that," said Judy. "Count me in. But of course, urban gardens are my thing. I could really use a strong young man to help get that project off the ground." She looked around the table. Her eyes landed on Jeremy, who finally raised his hand.

"Wonderful, thank you. Who's next?"

"Guess it makes sense for me to take on the building projects," said Nic laconically, thinking of his construction skills and, of course, his vast land holdings.

"Need a partner?" Shannon, who had been watching Nic out of the corner of her eye, smiled imperceptibly.

Nic took a long look at Shannon for the first time since their arrival. An undefined element was missing from Nic's life, but not until he'd taken full notice of the charming Shannon did this elusive void made itself clear. She seemed to share the same revelation. There was something comfortably familiar about her—of a certain age but with an open smile and long wavy hair tastefully lightened. She'd retained every bit of her youthful charm. She wore a bulky, loose-fitting sweater that failed to conceal her pleasantly curvy figure, skinny jeans turned up at the cuff revealing a butterfly tattoo on her left ankle, and white sneakers that looked as though she'd lost her shoelaces but were really slip-ons.

"You got it!" he replied.

Donna was elated. "Geoff, can we take on the tiny homes idea together? I think that's logical."

"Not sure how you mean, but absolutely."

"I mean, with your special interest in getting the homeless off the street."

"Oh," Geoff said, suppressing his surprise. "That's right." Everyone at the table laughed, Geoff the loudest.

A buoyant optimism floated over the group, as the empowered team members coalesced into a unit. Side conversations bubbled up around the table about their chosen projects, and folks made the first overtures toward a deeper bonding. Donna let the chatter continue, genuinely feeling the love in the room and recognizing its strategic benefit. She sensed everything was going to be all right.

Donna was about to suggest taking a ten-minute bathroom break when she watched the final participant arrive in the parking lot and alight from his white Escalade, driven by a young dark-haired woman. After saying their goodbyes, the woman pulled out onto the highway as the man walked toward the pizza shop. A lumpy bumpy shape was attached to his front side, with little arms and legs that wriggled wildly.

Donna saw a narrow window for one final consolidation of her role as leader before the unexpected guests walked in and stole the show.

"People, we're going to take a short break. Bathrooms are just there on the right. Before we do, I wanted to take a moment to thank you sincerely for your engagement and unselfish dedication to our community. The stakes are high and go beyond the problems besieging our dear little town.

"There are dark forces lurking in the world, friends, forces that seek to corrupt, tear down, or take from the many to benefit the few. Relentlessly they wait for good people to let their guard down. But I believe ultimately in the power of good over evil"—the team murmured their agreement—"and in people like you, who don't merely grumble or look away, but cast a bright light into the dark places. We are doing God's work here, work that demands we remain happy warriors. So let's keep our eyes on the horizon. Thank you all. You make me very proud."

The group applauded and cheered, showering their cherished leader with cries of "Yay Donna!" She waved off their praise while basking in it.

The last attendee had walked in unnoticed during Donna's speech and stood in the shadows against the wall. He was impressed with Donna's authenticity, convinced he had made the right decision. He waved to her.

"And look who's here," she said with exaggerated surprise. "It's Mayor Purnell. My goodness, come in, Mr. Mayor. Please join us. Have some pizza. And who is your adorable friend?"

Mayor Rusty Purnell wended a path between long tables and benches toward the congregation, looking fresh and relaxed. Strapped over his shoulders in a Baby Björn lay a beautiful, wiggly, drooling, clapping, wide-eyed baby boy, who showed his glee with kicks and squirms.

"Everyone, this is Randy. Randall Alexander to be precise."

"Oh my gosh, he is so-o-o beautiful," said every woman at the table in near unison, rushing over to pet him and get a closer look. "Is he—?"

"No, I'm just minding him for a friend who had to go to work," he explained, dodging the obvious question. "He just turned eight months today."

"Must be a pretty good friend," Deb whispered to Celine with a skeptical look. She studied the baby carefully, its tangle of dark curls, green eyes, olive skin, and straight features, comparing them with Rusty's florid complexion, red hair, and full face. *Nope,* she confirmed to herself, *there is no way on God's earth this child belongs to that man.* She thought then of tonight's earlier conversation about the notorious Darla. Over the past months Celine had bared her soul to her about everything that had happened between them—their first encounter, moving in, then breaking up, her rebound crush on Jeremy, the capricious Darla making her own move on him that ultimately ended with Darla throwing them both over. *I wonder,* she thought and turned her eyes slowly to the opposite side of the table. There sat Jeremy, alone and sullen, hunched over his beer in a brown study.

"Well, he is simply adorable, Mayor," said Donna. "Can we hold him?"

"Gee, I don't know. He's kind of my precious cargo for the night."

"Nonsense," said Shannon, grabbing for the child. "You're surrounded by a bunch of experienced mothers here."

"He was getting a little heavy," said Rusty. He hoisted little Randy out of his carrier and placed him carefully in the arms of Shannon, who cradled him with confidence and cooed to him in baby talk: *Who's so precious? Who's a handsome boy?*

The infant was getting fussy and Shannon picked up on the cue. "Is that—?" she said, pointing to the bottle caddy Rusty had set on the table.

"Oh. Yes, I guess it's that time again." He brought out a small glass feeding bottle and handed it to Shannon.

"Ooh, still warm. This isn't—?"

"It sure is."

"Now, that is what I call concierge service," she said to little Randy, popping the nipple into his greedy mouth.

Donna snuck up behind Rusty and stood at his elbow. "Thank you so much for coming, Mr. Mayor."

"My pleasure. You seem to have all your ducks in a row. Very impressive."

"They're a very dedicated group. I think we can make a real difference."

"I hope so. Truly I do."

"You arrived at a good time. We were just about to take a break."

"Wait, did I miss your big reveal?"

"Um, no, I was waiting till a little later."

"Oh, then allow me, with your permission," he said, "since I may need to leave a little early."

"No, don't, I . . . Well, OK," she acquiesced.

"Everybody, everybody," said the mayor in a commanding voice. "Your attention please. I have an important announcement." All eyes, including those of patrons at nearby tables, turned toward the mayor, fascinated by the spectacle of local political celebrity. "Two announcements, actually. First, as you know, we've been through stormy times here in Morley, and I feel I've done all I can do as mayor to sort things out. While the important work must continue, I have decided I will not be seeking reelection in the fall."

The crowd let out a collective and full-throated "Aww!" While most meant it sincerely, others were being either polite or ironic, though Rusty cared not at all which.

"Thanks, folks. I'll definitely be sticking around and staying involved as a civilian, probably poking my nose into things that aren't any of my business. I really believe we can turn things around here in Morley, which brings me to the second announcement. It seems your fearless leader's been holding out on you. Donna, why don't I turn the floor over to you."

"Thank you, Mr. Mayor. As you've heard, Mayor Purnell has decided to serve out his term, then continue his engagement in Morley's future as a private citizen. We know how effective community activism can be in creating a prosperous and livable city, and we wish him well. But Rusty's decision has opened up an opportunity I could not in good faith disregard. So come this fall, I will be your candidate for mayor of the City of Morley."

Donna's team, along with the whole pizzeria, went crazy, enthusiastically endorsing her candidacy, or at least her moxie, by applauding, cheering, pounding the table. They had little choice. Her charisma was absolutely magnetic.

Above the tumult, Rusty made one final proclamation.

"And . . ." He waited for the crowd to quiet. "And Ms. Hart has my ardent endorsement and unqualified support going forward." Another wave of cheers ensued.

"Now, enough speeches," Donna broke in. "We've got work to do. Take a ten-minute break, and we'll reconvene at exactly seven twenty-five."

The team slowly dispersed. Judy cornered the mayor to talk his ear off about urban gardens. Celine and Deb hastened to the restroom, discussing the approach they would take to construct their supporting documents. Shannon shuttled little Randy over to Dr. Reddy, who continued to happily feed, bounce, and converse with him, and made a fast beeline to Nic to discuss their mutual interests.

Jeremy for his part made no eye contact with his teammates but slid past them straight to the parking lot, where he paced and vaped nervously.

Donna retreated to the warm comfort of Geoff's company.

"Well, my friend, congratulations," he said, their heads tilted together to be heard over the noisy room. "So far I'd say this has been quite a success."

"Oh, good, you think so? Thanks. Was the announcement a little premature?"

"Not a bit. It had to come out sometime. Besides, you can't plan everything. These things have a rhythm of their own. It's a smart politician who can read a crowd and embrace the moment. I'd say you handled it . . . adroitly."

"Why thank you," Donna said with an earnest smile. "I'm not sure I'm ready to think of myself as a politician."

"Mmm, OK, how about Queen of the Universe?"

"Better."

"So it shall be." He poured them two glasses of IPA. "A toast to my queen." Their tumblers clunked. "Now may I finally call you Elizabeth? I've been wanting to, you know. It befits you so well."

"Uh, no, you may not. You know I hate that name."

"But, Your Majesty, Elizabeth is, after all, your name. And before you perjure yourself about preferring to use your middle name, let me remind you, your middle name is not Donna, but Donatella, which I also love. You don't want to be one of those politicians who give themselves phony stage names just to win votes? I mean, it's not as bad as calling yourself Bobby when your name is really Piyush, but—"

"But Elizabeth! Ugh! Too many gross nicknames."

"What?"

She listed them with visible disgust, enumerating each on her fingers. "There's Betty, Betsy, Bitty, Beth, Bess, Bessie—"

He caught her rhythm and joined in. "And don't forget Liz, Liza, Eliza, Leeza, Lizbeth, Lizzie, Lissie, Libby, Liddy, Ellie, Elsie."

"And her cultivated cousin Elspeth."

"OK, I get it, though it would be perfect for someone with multiple personalities."

"But I don't have multiple personalities." Donna smiled sweetly. "I have exactly one personality, which I'm perfectly happy with."

"Me too." Geoff leaned over and kissed her on the cheek. "Wait—Izzy! We forgot Izzy."

"Ew, now that's going too far."

Outside in the parking lot, the blinding white floods above cast an unnatural glow over the cars and asphalt, splashing ghostly shadows in all directions. Jeremy's head was shrouded in the impenetrable fog emanating from his vape device. He sucked in again, long and hard, and exhaled another milky white cloud that lingered long about his face and shoulders. Through the dissipating haze, he could just discern the tender scene inside, the warmth, camaraderie, and good feelings shared by the ebullient ensemble. His gaze followed the baby boy as the group lovingly passed him around, tickled him, played peekaboo, and fondled his little feet and hands.

What was he to do? He held no claim, enjoyed no standing, no legitimate place among these wholesome people. He was nothing more than a sad punk, retreating at will to his comfortably distant, made-up world. Now, this blob of protoplasm called Randy inexplicably beckoned him to join the human race, to sacrifice every fragment of his being for the wriggling mass. The feeling was raw, foreign, and unshakable.

He watched as Shannon was about to pass the boy back to Rusty. She nodded toward the rear of his diaper, holding him up at nose height. Rusty leaned forward, sniffed, and recoiled. He juggled the diaper tote in one hand with the kid in the other. Donna, watching the interplay, snatched up little Randy and volunteered to take him to the changing station, if Rusty would please hand her the tote.

Jeremy unconsciously jammed the vape machine into his pocket and moved in the direction of the boy, first slowly, then at a quick trot across the lot. He burst through the restaurant door and in an instant was at Donna's side.

"I can do that." She looked at him in cheerful disbelief.

"Do you know how to do this?" Her supportive but skeptical tone made him feel like an adolescent.

"Sure, how hard could it be?"

"Have you ever done it before?"

"I'll learn."

"Come with me," she said, keeping the child and handing Jeremy the tote. They walked to the unisex bathroom in back of the pizza shop and entered.

"Pull that thing down," she instructed, indicating the changing table. She set little Randy onto the curved surface and safety-strapped him in, then from the tote extracted a box of wipes and handed them to Jeremy. "OK, ready? I'll talk you through it."

She guided his hand as he unsnapped the blue onesie and peaked into the diaper to check for poo. He could already smell it but now had visual confirmation. He then opened the soiled diaper and, under her direction, turned down the adhesive tabs to protect Randy's skin.

"Now pull out a couple of wipes. Clean front to back." He precisely followed her instructions, awkwardly at first, then with confidence. He pulled Randy up gently by the legs to elevate his bum, finished wiping, then rolled up the diaper carefully with the soiled wipes and poo inside and removed it neatly. "Good. You're a natural." He smiled goofily. "Did you check for any rash?" He hadn't. "That's OK, next time. I didn't see any. Someone's taking good care of him, that's obvious."

"Not the mayor. That's also obvious."

"Enough of that; we're not done. Get out one of the clean diapers." He reached into the tote and came out with a diaper, plus some white ointment, which she refused. "Let's keep things simple. Now lay this out flat. Good." He did so and proceeded from there on his own, instinctively sensing the next steps. *Like wrapping a package,* he thought. Position the corners, fold in gently on each side, snug but not too tight, remove the tab covers, secure the sticky tabs and voilà! He snapped the onesie closed and lifted Randy to his chest without asking.

Jeremy and Donna walked back to the dining area together, with Randy clinging to Jeremy like a baby koala. The folks at the table went nuts again, taking a break from their break as they gushed over his cute self.

"Now doesn't he look happy?" said Deb. "In fact, you both do."

"Full stomach and a clean diaper," declared Jeremy. "Who wouldn't be happy."

Rusty reached for the tote from Donna and slung it over his shoulder, then put his two hands out to Jeremy to retrieve the baby.

"Thanks for changing him. That was above and beyond. I can take him back now. He must be getting heavy, and we're going to reconvene in a minute."

Jeremy made no effort to remove Randy from his chest. "No, he's fine," he said, bouncing the baby gently. "I really don't mind. I'm good."

Rusty was mildly put off for an instant, then acceded. "Well, as long as you don't mind."

"Nope. All good."

Donna stood silently by, watching the dynamic between the two men. The wheels were just starting to turn when she noticed her cadre slowly taking their seats, on time and ready to return to work, just as she had asked them to do. She strode back to her place at the head of the table.

"OK, folks! Let's get started."

ABOUT THE AUTHOR

Patrick Howard lives and works in the Pacific Northwest.

ACKNOWLEDGMENTS

There are so many people to whom I am grateful for helping make this work a reality:
First, Carrie Brunett, my beautiful wife and partner here on Planet Earth, who has always looked out for me.
Tom Carleton, my brother from another mother, for his technical wizardry and honest advice.
Tara Candoli, for her good humor and wisdom.
Kathleen McFall of Pumpjack Press, who cheered me on and generously taught me how to publish a book.
Ian Koviak and Alan Dino Hebel at *the*BookDesigners, who worked patiently and diligently to create some gorgeous cover art.
Sally Glover, Ashley Little, and Marinna Castilleja at Kirkus for their precise yet gentle hand in editing the text. It was revelatory.
The Portland Write Club: Lainie Yarris, Laurel Berge, Nicole Deiorio, and Rachel Bengtzen. Thanks for your candid feedback, chapter by chapter.
And all the teachers who challenged me over the years to write better: Miss V, Mrs. Stevens, Ms. Looney, and others.
Thank you all.

Made in the USA
Las Vegas, NV
12 August 2022